Q

A NOVEL

Paul A. Nigro

RIVER
OAK
PUBLISHING

Q

ISBN 1-58919-000-9

Copyright © 2002 by Paul A. Nigro

Published by RiverOak Publishing,
A Division of Cook Communications Ministries
P.O. Box 55388
Tulsa, OK 74155

To the Reader

Though not universally accepted, the idea of a hypothetical source document (or documents) used by both Matthew and Luke is held by scholars of all traditions, and a wide spectrum of research on the subject, both popular and academic, is available.

Southwestern Seminary is a real institution, but the classroom scenes are completely invented; they owe more to the author's own teaching experiences in church settings over the years than to actual seminary lectures. This should comfort the theologically squeamish.

The churches in Fort Worth and Charleston are fictional and depict the extremes of our religious culture. Sometimes it is in exaggeration that we see ourselves most clearly.

Paul A. Nigro

for Cindy

Book I

Part 1

The Way of
the Teacher

Thou hast [appointed] all these things
in the mysteries of Thy wisdom
to make known Thy glory [to all].

—The Thanksgiving Hymns, *Hymn 3*

Galilee, A.D. 27

EZRA STAGGERED TOWARD THE TAX BOOTH, PANTING. HE BENT OVER with his hands on his knees, catching his breath. "It is amazing how the people *listen,*" he said between gasps. "They actually sit there quietly, hanging on every word."

"It is because he mesmerizes them with his eyes," Matthew scoffed.

"Stop, now, you greedy pagan! I suppose if he charged admission, you'd be right there selling tickets!"

Matthew laughed. "Probably, but at least then you could get a decent seat."

Matthew's joke provoked an amused grin. "Not even you could make it so. There must be thousands surrounding him. You know, it is said he cannot even come through the main gates of a town anymore without all its residents rushing out to greet him. It is like John all over again."

"And the message?"

Ezra thought for a moment before answering. "Stories. John could never have told stories—he lacked the patience. But Jesus is different. He is just as direct but not so confrontational. He tickles your ears before boxing them."

"And you find this appealing?"

"It is like a fresh wind is blowing through his teaching. He is true to the prophets, yet he seems to have his own authority. Even you might benefit from a few hours on the hillside with him."

Matthew cringed. "Really, Ezra! Have you not yet given up on me? You've been preaching to me since we were children."

"No one knows the Law better than you, cousin. You owe it to yourself to give Jesus a chance."

"I know enough about the Law to know that it is an impossible burden, and your brothers only make it heavier."

"You evade the issue," Ezra said, wagging a finger in Matthew's face. "You are an incurable cynic."

"Do not be so convinced of that," Matthew answered. "I am not without hope for Israel." He paused, not sure he should continue. "I have made certain . . . inquiries."

"Oh?" Ezra's eyes brightened. "Of what sort?"

Matthew shrugged. "Do you think anything that happens in Galilee escapes my notice? What do you think people speak of as they pass by here?"

"I see. And you have inquired about Jesus, then?"

"Oh, yes. Quite a few of our fine citizens have him chasing the Romans out of Jerusalem with an army of angels and peasants!"

Ezra winced. "The rabble is clueless, as you know. Give them their daily bread, and they make you a king."

"You speak truly." Matthew paused to fiddle with his scales. "But they are wrong about this king."

Ezra watched him intently. There was something more to this story, and he knew it. "You are leading me along for your own pleasure, I see. Please speak plainly."

"Alright." Matthew leaned over his table. "The kingdom of Heaven he speaks of. Where does it reside?"

Q

Ezra blinked, surprised at the simplicity of the question. "Why, it is dawning now!" He made dramatic circles with his arms. "It is soon to be here."

"And how does it arrive? On camels from Egypt?"

"You mock that which you know nothing of," Ezra said spitefully.

"I do know that there is no such kingdom coming. What you wait for is already here. The kingdom of Heaven reigns in men's hearts when they follow God. This is nothing new; Jeremiah taught it, as did the rest of the prophets. But you and your fellow teachers are slow to heed the truth, Ezra. You see in it only what you want to see. And now you see Jesus the same way. I tell you, if you expect him to purify Israel for you, you will be disappointed. He speaks of the ideal, not the real."

"Are you always to be so pessimistic?"

Matthew shrugged. "I am a Jew."

Ezra stared at him. Slowly, they both broke into grins.

"If you could meet him, you would think differently."

Matthew's grin widened. "But I have. The little band of fisher followers is not exempt from taxes, you know."

Ezra closed his eyes, praying for patience. "You could have told me sooner."

"But your passion makes for such good sport!" Matthew exclaimed, slapping Ezra on the shoulder. "You are caught in the net every time."

The scribe's eyes narrowed. "It would be a wide and well-woven net that catches us both," he said.

Matthew regarded him respectfully. "I am not so easily persuaded as you."

"But you do see it, don't you, in his eyes?" Ezra goaded.

"See what?"

It was Ezra's turn to smile. "The kingdom of Heaven, of course."

Matthew said nothing and returned to his ledgers, a sure sign that the conversation was over.

Ezra meandered to the outskirts of town, having already picked up the scent of rumor in the wind. He approached a group of women who scurried back and forth in front of a large house, talking excitedly. Drawing closer, he saw that some were laughing through tears.

"What has happened here?" he asked.

They stopped immediately and looked at him with disdain. "Are you Jews always so bold?" said one.

"Is there a law that says I cannot ask a question of a Roman?"

There were four women in all, of varying ages. The youngest of them answered Ezra. "You tell us!" They looked him up and down, smirking at his luxurious blue and white robe. "You are one who knows all things!"

Ezra became embarrassed. "I know the Law of God," he said. "It is my inheritance, and this is my country; I will not be addressed this way by the likes of you!"

"Move along, then, Jew! Or my father will bend your back with such a load as to make your tassels drag in the dust!"

"Hush, daughter!"

The older woman scuttled the teenager toward the house. "Forgive us, sir. We are not often so brazen with strangers. But today we are beside ourselves with joy and not mindful of convention."

"And not used to being questioned by Jews," he added.

"Few are willing to stoop so low," she said. "We know we are despised and would return home instantly at the emperor's call. But I will gladly speak to you today, because the gods have looked favorably upon our household."

"There is but one God, madam, and he cares for all of us."

She was stunned. "Do you really believe that?"

Ezra consulted his book and read from it. "'If God cares for the flowers that are here today and gone tomorrow, will he not care that much more for you?'"

"That is in your Law?"

"No, not exactly. But it is a true saying. So tell me how God has blessed your household."

She looked back at the house anxiously. "It is my husband's servant. He . . . "

Just then a loud voice interrupted them, followed by the heavy footsteps of troops. A Roman officer led them; he was coming fast, and Ezra regretted having approached these women, mindful of what the youngest had said.

"I am come from Capernaum!" he shouted. He stopped abruptly, carefully examining the scribe. He turned to his wife. "He is well now, is he not?"

She was astonished. "Yes! How did you know? He sat up on his pallet just an hour ago. He has taken drink. He is sitting at the table now, strong as he ever was!"

The officer, overcome with emotion, fell to his knees and clutched the hem of Ezra's robe. "The God of Israel has healed my servant, as I knew he would."

Astonished, Ezra reached down to pull the man away. "Give praise to God, then, not me!" he said.

The officer stood, recovering his emotions. "You are right. I must return to Capernaum to thank him, after I have seen with my own eyes his mighty works." He turned and headed toward the house.

"Capernaum?" Ezra called out, amazed. "Does God now abide in Galilee?"

Standing in the doorway, the Roman shouted back. "Indeed he does! Go and see for yourself. The people follow him everywhere he goes. He is Jesus, the Nazarene."

It was late afternoon the next day when Ezra met Matthew at the tax booth. "The kingdom of Heaven is indeed upon us, cousin! I have seen it with my own eyes."

Matthew was preoccupied with his accounts and looked up briefly before going back to work. "Your head is in the clouds again, I see. Tell me, have you any interest in practical matters?"

"Is it so otherworldly to apply the healing arts? I have seen a sick man made well by faith alone."

Matthew's head bobbed up suddenly. "What say you?"

"Ah, apparently you are not so practical that you have no interest in miracles! You heard me clearly: I know a man who was sick unto death and was healed at the word of a certain Rabbi we both know. By his *word,* Matthew—he spoke it to the man's master, there, in Capernaum, miles away. And the young man was healed at that very hour."

Matthew seemed unnerved at the news. "You know this for a fact?"

Q

"I saw the man, and I spoke to his master, a Roman . . . "

"Centurion," Matthew said.

Ezra stepped back. "How do you come to know of this?"

"It is the talk of the town. And not only this, there have been other healings as well."

"Would not a man such as yourself attribute such things to idle gossip?"

"I would have," Matthew said gravely, "if I had not known some of these people personally and heard their testimonies and seen the results. Look around—do you see any travelers about? They are all gone to see him, carrying their lame and ill."

"Do you know where they are?"

"At the home of Simon's mother-in-law."

Ezra grabbed Matthew by the shoulders. "Come, cousin! Let's go there and see the mighty works of God!"

Matthew stiffened. "You go. I cannot."

Ezra beheld his cousin with a look of concern. "Why?"

"I have no malady that I should need healing."

Ezra frowned. "Nor have I, but we need not be healed ourselves to offer praise for what God grants to others."

Matthew slammed his fist down on the table. "Must you stand and argue? Go!" He motioned with his hands, urging Ezra to take his leave.

The scribe's disbelief at this reaction soon gave way to anger. "You make excuses now, as you have always done! You are afraid of God, that is all. You know him better than those cursed money books, and yet you stay away. You are as proud and stubborn as a Pharisee!"

"Don't lecture me, you hypocrite!" Matthew shouted. "At least I chose a profession I could live with, free of your insufferable rules!"

"*My* rules? You yourself know that I have sought a better way." Ezra was clearly hurt by the accusation, and Matthew relented. The tax collector reached into his robe and pulled out a leather bag, tugged at its mouth, and emptied its contents onto the table. The coins fell in a loud cascade, bouncing and rolling until all was silent.

"You go," said Matthew softly. "My master calls. I will remain here."

"This is foolishness. Come now, and join me," Ezra pleaded.

Matthew looked him straight in the eyes. "He will not have me, and you know it. No man can serve God and riches."

Ezra shook his head in wonder at the man whose mind he had always admired. If only he would use it for a greater glory than his own.

The scribe stood outside the modest home, watching the masses coming and going. The lame were being carried, and the blind were led by the hand. A small band of lepers kept their distance, hoping Jesus would come to them; every so often they would call out to someone to bring the Rabbi word that they were there. Those who were being healed ignored the lepers as they returned from the house, euphoric and absorbed in their sudden freedom from whatever chains they had shed. Ezra listened to them closely, trying to share in their joy, and his heart was encouraged.

The night passed quickly, and daylight revealed a new stream of seekers, those who had heard of the healings in the night and had come a great distance to find the Rabbi. They limped and staggered in, some howling in anticipation or pain, only to be ushered back outside. Ezra's ears could not discern what was being said, despite the raised voices. There was confusion, and some scuffling broke

Q

out in front of the house. Ezra recognized James and John, the sons of Zebedee, trying their best to keep the peace. Ezra came closer to find the reason for the disturbance; somehow, inexplicably, Jesus had left the premises.

Ezra quickly scanned the horizon, but there were no indications of the route the Rabbi might have taken. To travel far on foot would have eventually invited a following, which Ezra assumed his departure meant he desired to avoid, so Ezra reasoned he might have made for the sea. Or perhaps he had retreated to the hills, to a solitary place, as he had on previous occasions. If so, he would not take kindly to being interrupted. Ezra chose the sea.

He walked along the shore, checking carefully for evidence that Jesus had come that way. Had he stopped in any one place, there would have been talk of some kind or empty houses and boats, abandoned at the prospect of catching up with the Teacher. Ezra considered again his having hidden himself away; surely this had been his intent, for even the disciples had been left behind.

Ezra sat down by a cove where several small vessels were anchored or pushed up on the shore. He looked out at the calm sea and pondered how his life would soon change. He thought of Jerusalem at Passover, of the Temple filling with people. He saw himself assigned to the Pharisees and Sadducees, to interpret the new teaching for them in light of the old Law. A new order was being introduced, and with his education Ezra was sure to be an important part of it. There was no question that Jesus was already approaching the heights of the famous rabbis Shammai and Hillel; Ezra was perfectly suited to write the teachings. Had he not already recorded those utterances which, had he not been there to report, might have been lost?

He was eager to follow. He had waited all his life for a teacher worthy of his considerable gifts. He had given his criticisms of the Tradition, but none had taken him seriously. They only laughed at him and scorned his ideas. They would soon swallow that laughter!

Ezra was so preoccupied with his visions that he almost missed them—a small group of men, tired and grumpy, led by one who separated himself from the rest. Ezra saw them as he daydreamed; and just as they were getting the boat ready, he realized what was happening. He jumped up and cried out, the words nearly catching in his throat.

"Jesus—wait!"

The Teacher turned, expressionless, to face him. Jesus spoke not a word as Ezra ran to confront him.

"Rabbi, forgive me, but I have sought you for days." He was breathless and flushed, overexcited. "I am Ezra the scribe; see, I have been recording your sayings." Jesus examined the book as Ezra held it in front of him. "You are a fascinating teacher, and I believe you are sent from God. I wish to be your student."

Ezra bowed his head and waited.

"Have you shown that book to anyone?" Jesus said at last.

Ezra looked up at him, startled. Three of the disciples were standing knee deep in water by the boat. "No, I . . . I have kept it to myself."

"That is good," Jesus said and turned to walk toward the water.

Ezra ran after him. "Wait, please . . . you don't understand—"

Jesus stopped and turned to him, smiling. "I am honored that you consider my teaching worthy of your study," he said. "But where I am going you cannot come."

Q

Ezra was devastated. Confused and desperate, he reached for the sleeve of Jesus' robe. "It is no hardship for me. I am willing to do whatever you ask. I will follow you wherever you go."

Jesus looked at him with compassion and said, "It is not with me that you belong. The foxes have dens, the birds of the air have nests, but the Son of Man has no place to lay his head." With that, he removed himself from Ezra's grip and got into the boat. Stunned, Ezra could only watch him go.

"You will see me again, Rabbi," he cried weakly.

"Of that I have no doubt," Jesus said as the disciples pushed the boat out into the water. "May God watch over you, devoted scribe."

They watched each other as the distance between them grew until the boat was out of sight.

The storm that arose that day was as violent as had ever been seen in Galilee. Ezra took shelter in the synagogue, where the mission of Jesus was being debated among the leading men of the town.

"If he is not stopped, he will provoke the Romans to destroy us all for fear of revolt," one said.

"He is harmless, a wise teacher who thrills those needy souls who have nothing better to do," said another. "His time will pass."

"His healings cannot be explained or denied. Many believe he has been sent by God," said a third man.

"He casts out demons by the ruler of demons!" replied a fourth.

"He has no respect for Moses."

"He violates the Sabbath Law."

"His sayings are hard; who can understand them?"

"I knew his father, a good and simple man, though he did not live long enough to give his son proper instruction."

"Can any good thing come from Nazareth?"

Ezra remained a silent observer, still perplexed by the encounter with Jesus. When asked repeatedly, he finally admitted there was veiled truth in much of his teaching. The men regarded him cautiously. Ezra longed to pull out his book and teach them from it but dared not.

The discussion continued until the winds and rain suddenly ceased, causing the men to look around in wonder. They walked outside to find the sun breaking through rapidly scattering clouds.

"How strange," one of them remarked, saying aloud what all of them were thinking. "The storm was, then almost instantly was not. I do not think I have ever seen such an unusual occurrence." After another moment's glance skyward, he shrugged and went back inside.

But Ezra continued to gaze out over the lake, out where he knew Jesus and his chosen followers were. He was embarrassed to find himself crying, with large tears pouring over his cheeks, through his beard, and onto his tunic.

It was nearing evening when a certain scribe struggled to the abandoned tax booth, the dingy white and blue raveling of his oversized robe trailing behind him in the dusty street. The sea stretched out before him, peaceful now after the storm. The shore was busy with people bartering and trading goods. A small group of men who were waiting there called out to him as he approached.

"So, it is a new line of work for you, eh, Ezra?," one of them said, kicking the dust impatiently.

"One racket's as good as another," a second man muttered. They all snickered softly, as if they lacked the energy for hearty laughter.

Ezra, accustomed to such derision but in no mood to argue, ignored the remark. "Why is my cousin not here?" he snapped.

The man who had spoken first answered. "Good question," he said curtly. "If it weren't for that guard over there, we wouldn't be waiting." He stared at the scribe with contempt. "You want to try your hand at the tax game, so we can get on our way?"

Ezra looked over at the soldier. It was unlike Matthew to leave his station unattended. He approached the Roman, who, like everyone else these days, seemed to want nothing to do with him.

"Sir, please tell me, is my cousin, Matthew the publican, off about some business that you know of?"

The words that the soldier uttered were offered in choppy Greek, but the tone was clear enough. It was often hard to understand these people, but their resentment of all things Jewish was reflected in their voices, as in every gesture or glance. It obscured the meaning of the message momentarily. Ezra stepped back subconsciously, causing the guard to pause briefly, wondering if something had been misspoken in translation. Ezra was mystified; was this soldier speaking the truth? That Matthew had done this was almost unthinkable. *Impossible.*

The scribe turned, red-faced, back toward the road. He clutched the sheaf of papers inside his robe tightly to his chest as he stumbled down, descending to the shore, his steps determined now, his ears deaf to the shouts of the men as they defamed his family name.

"Your cousin is at the door," said a slender woman with dark eyes. She was speaking to her host but looking intently at the man who sat beside him. "He insists that he must speak with you."

Matthew had been dreading this. He excused himself from the table and made his way through the crowd. He opened the door and stepped outside, closing the door quickly behind him.

Ezra had been craning his neck, peering behind Matthew to get a glimpse of what was happening inside. His face was dark. "What in God's name! . . . "

"It is a party, that's all—a few of my friends are here."

"A few! You have a small village in there! I don't remember receiving an invitation."

Matthew blushed. "You could not abide these people for five minutes."

"And you have no shame in this, Matthew—harlots prancing about your home like it is the neighborhood brothel?"

"It is a dinner party, Ezra." His voice vibrated with irritation. "Now, state your business please."

"You left your station early today," he said bitterly.

"Yes. Arrangements had to be made . . . "

"You left the emperor's money uncollected. There was a line all the way to Bethsaida."

"It is of no consequence. I am no longer in that line of work."

Ezra's mouth turned down at the corners. "And yet you play host to the tax collectors' convention?"

"You can stop it now, cousin. We both know why you have come."

Ezra saw sadness in his eyes. "Matthew, you could have told me."

Q

"When? There was no time! He appeared and summoned me—so I left. I could do no other! Do you know what it is like to be hated all your life and then to be invited . . . to be *wanted* . . ." He stopped in mid sentence. "Ezra. I am sorry."

The scribe's voice cracked with emotion. "Have you spoken to him of me?" he asked.

"I have."

That was all. Ezra understood what the answer meant.

Once back inside, Matthew looked around the room. He marveled at the mood of the party. The normally raucous crowd was reserved, even serene. Jesus reclined at the table, engaging a handful of them in debate. It was the closest most of them had ever been to a Rabbi.

Jesus saw Matthew across the room. He said some parting words and gestured as if to promise his quick return before walking to where Matthew stood with his back against the closed door.

"His place is not with us," Jesus said, placing a hand on Matthew's shoulder. "He has accepted the will of God."

Matthew looked away, not wanting his annoyance to show. "He may have accepted it, but he doesn't understand it, nor do I." He sighed. "Does Ezra merit less in the eyes of God than any one of our guests here this evening? Instead of sitting under your teaching, he is cast out into the darkness alone."

Jesus smiled. "Do not grieve for your cousin, Matthew. There are many who slumber in the light, while others who labor in darkness light the way."

The young tax collector grunted at the enigmatic statement, shook his head, and returned to his guests.

Galilee, A.D. 28

"THIS TALK OF WEDDINGS AND WINESKINS IS NAUGHT BUT FOOLISHNESS," Ezra was saying to Matthew. "John never would have spoken in such riddles."

"He is simply trying to communicate a new teaching in ways that all can understand," Matthew replied.

"No. I do not accept that. The question we asked was worthy of a substantive answer. The Pharisees fast with good reason, and none of John's disciples were ever asked by him to neglect such an important spiritual discipline. So why does Jesus not require it of you?" Ezra's face reddened as he jabbered on, waving his arms in protest.

"Do you rant like a madman because you—a learned scribe and teacher of Israel—cannot grasp the simple meaning in the parables?" Matthew said, laughing.

Ezra huffed and paced around Matthew anxiously. "Who can understand such gibberish?" he cried, raising his hands to Heaven.

"Stop, now!" Matthew said, still laughing. "You go on like an old woman! You are jealous that you were not chosen—this is at the heart of your anger. Do not forget how well I know you, dear cousin."

Ezra fumed. "How is it, then, *dear cousin*"—he spoke the words contemptuously—"that you, a tax collector, are deemed worthy and I am not?" He stood defiantly, his hands on his hips.

"Well, for one thing, I am not forever pestering him with accusations thinly disguised as questions, like some know-it-all!"

Q

Ezra took this counsel to heart. He sat down upon the ancient stone wall that meandered along the hilly seascape. "It is not that I am a know-it-all but that I desire to know so much that I linger in Galilee."

Matthew sat down beside him. The vista was beautiful, as the sea dotted with boats glimmered in the distance before them. "You should return to Jerusalem and resume your studies there," Matthew concluded. "Perhaps by Passover we will find you at peace with your faith."

The scribe said nothing, but Matthew knew he was not considering his proposal. "I'm sorry," he said at last, "but I cannot do that either, for I am no better respected there than here." He folded his arms across his chest and sulked. After a few moments, he stood and walked down the little hill toward the shore. "When I return," he called back, "I will have the answers I seek."

Two hours later, Ezra's sandled feet were brittle and hot. He paused several times to refresh himself and to await the hospitality of strangers, though none was offered. At length he resigned himself to a journey of several days, driven by an insatiable quest to satisfy himself about the perplexing Nazarene rabbi. He finally did admit to some consternation and shock due to the rebuff, but he should have had no reason to react thus; his personality was known to be abrasive, and perhaps he would have caused more than a little interference with the mission. And yet, what sort of mission was this? Wisdom could be found whenever this teacher gave instruction, but to what end did it lead? No doubt the hand of the Lord had been with him, for Ezra had seen it with his own eyes. But there was something more here, and it was very disconcerting.

He took the traditional route around Samaria, lest he become defiled in some way by its uncleanness. Advancing south by way of Scythopolis, he crossed the Jordan and camped by the hot springs outside Pella. Onward he traveled, southbound through Perea, skirting west around the arid waste places of the Dead Sea, until he came at last to the mountain ranges high above. There, between two deep wadis, more than two-thirds of a mile above the Dead Sea, he found the black fortress where John was imprisoned.

The fortress was attained by a bridge from the east, some fifteen meters high. Four spectacularly stark towers rose above him and to either side as he walked into the paved courtyard. He inquired of one of the Roman soldiers where he might find the Baptizer and was led down a long corridor, along which were several rooms. The soldier left Ezra in front of one of the doors made from heavy timber and braced with iron. The scribe thanked him, and as the soldier walked away, Ezra knelt somewhat self-consciously at the small aperture at the base of the door and called to the man inside.

There was a rattling and dragging of chains inside the room, and then suddenly the face appeared, drawn and pale but ever strong in visage. "They chain me so I will not reach out to trip them as they pass," he said, "and of course I will if ever I am able! For hours, days even, I think upon this and am amazed at how I can study this only to conclude sadly that it can never be done and that I am forever lost."

"John! Do not speak so! It is Ezra of Jerusalem. I will be your companion here."

John beheld his face. "What news is there from Jerusalem?" John asked anxiously.

"I cannot say, since I have been following Jesus in Galilee these past months. His support is strong, and yet he proceeds slowly, in an unrecognizable pattern. He has an inner circle . . . "

Q

"Andrew. And Peter . . . ," John said.

"Yes and several others, including my kinsman Matthew."

"I do not recognize the name. Is he one of us?"

"No. He has left his tax station to sit under the Rabbi's teaching."

"A publican!" John erupted. "It cannot be!"

"It is odd, yes. But Matthew is a good man, although not all who follow Jesus are. There are harlots and sinners of diverse natures. I wish to ask you, John—are you sure that he is the coming one, or shall we look for someone else?"

John closed his eyes. Ezra's neck began to pain him as he peered into the chamber, watching the man who at one time had set all Israel afire with his prophecy. "Has he spoken against Herod?" John asked softly.

"I know not of one occasion."

John's jaw tightened. "Has he confronted the Pharisees and priests and those such as you, the keepers of the Law?"

"He has addressed the vanity of their ways, though without causing offense, certainly not as you did." Ezra paused. "As for his opinion of the scribes, I cannot say he is much enamored of me."

The prophet opened his reddened eyes. "And my people . . . "

"His disciples are baptizing, and many are following him."

John reached out suddenly through the opening and clutched Ezra's cloak with his bony fingers. The heavy shackles struck the door with such force that Ezra instinctively backed away, but John did not let go. "You must return to Galilee and ask him your question. Tell him John desires to know."

"With all respect," Ezra said, "I am not the one to . . . "

"Go!" the Baptizer shouted with the fire of old in his voice. "Tell him John must know."

Capernaum, A.D. 28

THE ANSWER HAD SO IMPRESSED EZRA THAT HE HURRIED BACK TO THE fortress, only to find John wasting away in his cell. The report seemed to bring some comfort to the prisoner, but the dramatic change in his countenance and demeanor in the space of a few weeks troubled Ezra greatly. He returned to Jerusalem to plead for the prophet's release but found little support among his brethren who feared Herod's wrath as much as they had despised John's sharp criticism. His petitioning only further alienated the scribe from them, and he made the lonely trek back to Machaerus with a heavy heart. When John's execution finally came, it was almost too much for Ezra to bear. What would he do now? There was but one place left to go.

"I can't talk now," Matthew insisted, trying to turn away.

Ezra grabbed his outer garment. "Wait. You can talk to him, I know you can."

Matthew turned, irritated. "Release me, cousin!" Ezra complied. In softer tones, Matthew tried to console him. "It's not like that. You don't just go up and give him advice, just like that. He always comes back with something. I just can't."

"He'll listen to you, I know he will," the scribe pleaded. "You're not like the others. Peter is a loudmouth, and those rogues James and John . . . "

Q

"You have said well," Matthew agreed. "And I want to keep it that way. He has already rejected you once. How can I ask him again? Especially today, with all this bickering going on."

"You wish to remain in his good favor then," Ezra said, looking down at his sandals. "And as my advocate, you would endanger your position, is that it?"

Matthew looked Heavenward for help. Just then, James came walking up to join them.

"Is this scribe never to learn his place?" he thundered.

Ezra glared at him with scorn. "It is extraordinary that you would speak to me about one's place, since it is so important to you to have the Teacher's blessing that you dominate your brothers so."

James raised his voice even louder. "You arrogant dog! I have left everything, and as such I will inherit much! As for you, go scribble your notes and return to the comfort of Jerusalem, to your pious friends, those hypocrites! We have no need of your services here!"

"James," Matthew cautioned, "he meant no harm . . . "

"No? And I suppose he meant no harm in bringing news of the Baptizer's death, either! You are a scab on the face of Israel, Ezra, and if you linger, I shall pick at you until you bleed!"

"James!" Matthew shouted, gripping the disciple's shoulders in both hands.

"You misunderstand me, James," Ezra retorted, his voice shaking, trying to control the rage. "I only meant to show my concern. I wanted him to know."

"Oh yes," James quipped, now calmer under Matthew's physical control. "You tell him that, right after the scribes of Nazareth try to kill him in his home synagogue?"

"He could not have known about that, and you know it," Matthew growled. "Listen, both of you," he counseled. "These are stressful days. Ezra, I suggest you go home."

"It is because you are ashamed of me," he said.

"No, Ezra . . . "

"It is because you do not wish to jeopardize your position in the Teacher's eyes."

James spoke up, surprised. "What's this now, Matthew?"

"Nothing, it's really not . . . "

"Are you concerned that as a tax collector your dishonor follows you? I had wondered why Judas was given the cash box instead of you."

Matthew closed his eyes, the anger rising.

"No surprise, really," James continued. "I suppose there are few in Galilee who wouldn't curse you still."

With that, Matthew pushed James, and he fell to the ground. In seconds, the crowd that Jesus had been teaching some distance away seemed to move closer, and at the fringes came other disciples, as Ezra slipped away. There was sharp arguing and pushing and shoving followed by an abrupt silence as Ezra watched from a distance. The disciples stood humbly, some disheveled and dirty, as Jesus approached. He watched them for a time, then summoned a small boy to his side. The crowd had parted just enough for Ezra to look clearly into Jesus' face, and their eyes locked. The boy was looking at Ezra, too, and he wondered if the boy had seen the tussle and knew that he had started the fight with his petty whining and provocation. How foolish—grown men acting like children! How then could children, seeing this, know how to act?

Q

The scribe was convicted and reminded of the awful truth yet again: he was not worthy to follow.

Later that night, he meditated over and over on the words he had heard and written down, "Whoever then humbles himself as this child, he is the greatest in the kingdom of Heaven."

Jerusalem, Passover, A.D. 30

EZRA SAT DOWN AT HIS WRITING DESK AND DRAGGED THE STYLUS slowly over the paper, completing the last of his journal entries. He was saddened, and angered, that it would be the last entry, for the life that he had been documenting was about to be cruelly and prematurely snuffed out. Why should he care? The Rabbi had flatly rejected him, would not admit him to his gatherings, hardly acknowledged his presence in the crowd, never answered his direct questions. Why should he care, then, that Jesus was innocent of the charges? Was he not guilty of other crimes? Surely—something. No. Ezra had looked, and there was nothing, certainly nothing to deserve this.

He blew upon the words softly to dry them. Should he blow too hard, they might smear; and they would have to be written again. Would he change the words then, change the story, so that someone might someday wish to read it? He blew harder, but they had dried already; the work was done.

The scribe lost himself for some minutes in the pages of his composition. He paused to marvel at the depth of the Rabbi's sayings, so clear and simple, and yet so incomprehensible, stunning in that they hadn't been spoken before, so profound were they in truth. And yet much of it—perhaps all of it—*had* been said before—even written in the Law, the other writings, and the prophets. It was all in the way one looked at it, the Rabbi said; but to find the truth there, one must strip away one's own desire to make it say what one wants it to say. Yet only the Rabbi himself, it seemed, could do that;

for Ezra had looked all his life, knowing something more than the leaven of the Pharisees existed—but where?

If truth could be known, this man Jesus surely knew it. For this reason Ezra had continued to follow, drawn inexplicably to one who seemingly wanted nothing to do with him. He could have protested, to be sure, but sensed it of no good purpose. He was used to being brushed off, disregarded, disrespected. Today the Rabbi knew something of rejection as well.

He looked out the window into the glare of the sun. The shouts of the people crammed into Jerusalem's winding streets were like the din from a distant stadium, rising and falling on the wind. Out there, not far away, they would be leading the Rabbi to the hill. And for what was he dying? "Truth," he had said. "All those who know the truth hear my voice." Ezra listened for it, closed his eyes, and thought hard. When he opened them, they were wet with the dew of grief.

Truth, indeed. "What is truth?" Pilate had demanded. It was more a statement than a question, naturally.

Truth is whatever is needed to serve my interests. It is the mockery I make of the Roman law. It is the disfigurement Caiaphas and his brethren perform upon the Jewish Law. But it is no longer the Law of God or Caesar we are following. It is our law, our truth.

Ezra wrapped the pages in cloth. He wasn't satisfied with the ending. He would write it all again, someday, after he had time to think, to understand. He would add more of his own thoughts, his conclusions on the matter. But this was done now. He could write no more.

He arose and went to the window. The shouting seemed to be moving now, traveling like some beast roaming through the corridors of the city. He knew where it was leading.

"And I, if lifted up from the earth, will draw all men to myself." It was a strange saying, suddenly becoming clear. "He who loves his life shall lose it, and he who hates his life in this world shall keep it to life eternal." There was no question that the Rabbi had intended to die a martyr's death; he had been provoking the authorities all week. And what—did he expect his disciples to rush to his aid? No, for he said just today they would not, when Pilate asked him. Perhaps he was resigned to the fact that they had already fled. Or did he expect the masses who had hailed him "Son of David" in the city gates to rescue him? No, they had tried to make him king once, in better days, and he had refused. What then?

Ezra's defense of the Rabbi had left him friendless, though it should be said that his friendships were always tenuous at best. What a fool he had been to think this man Jesus was God's anointed one! Were the hosts of Heaven at this very moment racing toward the holy city to declare him so? The absurdity of it all melted into indignation and disgust for the puppet procurator who quivered at the end of Caiaphas' leash and hatred of him who held it. This was a criminal act, a disgraceful episode in the history of a disgraced people. Whatever they thought of him, had they listened to the Rabbi, perhaps Israel could have been redeemed. She was crucifying, it seemed to Ezra, her last and best hope.

He flew to the door, and out into the city he ran, following the snake of voices as it slithered over the stones of the narrow road which led to the hill, grumbling of his nation's shame and his own.

The Sabbath day brought no rest for Ezra. He walked haphazardly through the crowded streets, the masses preventing him from breaking into full stride. His heart throbbed in his chest as if he were in a dead run, but his mind was clear, knowing his pursuers were likewise impeded. They knew where he lived; but there was only one way to get there, and he should arrive first. He would have precious little time to explain to his mother what was happening, though he hoped events would explain themselves. She had not understood in all this time, so she could not be won over now. He realized he could not ever return to Jerusalem, and as he caught glimpses of the familiar shops and homes of boyhood friends, he allowed himself brief pangs of private grief. His name would surely be defamed, as was that of the Rabbi himself, but so be it. Had the Rabbi not said, "I came to bring truth to the world, and all who love the truth know what I say is true"? One could not deny what one knew to be right, no matter what the cost. All his friends and family had abandoned him—all but his sister Mara, who tried to believe, and Matthew, who was hidden somewhere in the city. So what had he left to lose? Just his life, and even that seemed meaningless now, after what he had seen the day before—on that wretched hill.

Gradually he had been convinced that the Rabbi was indeed the Coming One, though now the fragments of his messiahship could not be fused together in Ezra's mind. Ezra possessed from his earliest days a fascination for the Law, and he studied it with reverence and intensity. Deep within him there seemed to be the ability to see in the Law what others failed to see, and yet his giftedness did not lead to higher esteem among his peers but to ridicule. Never a popular boy, he was even less popular as a young scribe; his presence brought an awkwardness to social gatherings, and his opinions were seldom solicited. Strangely, his radical views led to a perverse notoriety among the teachers of the Law, and his name was used in some circles as a byword for shame. Despite this ridicule he did not feel like an outcast, because he had found a deep and abiding joy in the study of God's Word. He was content.

And then the Baptizer appeared. With a blazing curiosity, Ezra had watched him work. His preaching rejuvenated Ezra's study of obscure prophesies. And then, the growing excitement of their apparent fulfillment led him to the Rabbi, whom he had followed in these last years, though from a distance.

The Rabbi's trial had been a sideshow. Ezra watched the proceedings in stunned silence. The travesty of it all welled up within him, along with the dreadful pain of his dashed hopes—the stunning realization that he had been so wrong about the Rabbi. The ache grew in Ezra's heart as he sat in his house, having retreated there in the midst of the trial, only to return again to follow the condemned man through the narrow streets, as the jeering and abuse filled his ears. The outrage of their treatment of the innocent Jesus, mixed with his own lifetime of mockery at their hands and the pain of his shattered faith, fused into fury. There, in view of the three crosses in the unnatural gloom, he confronted the smug Caiaphas himself. "You are a murderer and a dog!" he shouted, pointing an accusing finger at the high priest, and ran away, the earth rumbling strangely beneath his feet.

The high priest winced at the words. He had heard such blas-phemy before. He turned to whisper in the ear of his attendant and disappeared into the sea of men. The attendant glared at Ezra. All those standing in the crowd knew what that look meant.

An hour later, Ezra burst through the door of his mother's house, frightening his sister Mara, who was home alone. He raced past her into the next room and emerged with a scroll and several loose pages. "Hide these—now! I must go away," he said, breathless. The stunned Mara accepted the papers. Retreating to the door, he called out, "When they have gone, read the sayings and hide them in your heart. Then burn them, for if you are caught with them . . . "

He could not finish. She nodded, tearfully, knowing even then that she would not obey him. In an instant he was gone, and she slipped the scroll into the folds of her robe, cradling it tenderly, like a baby.

The Dead Sea, A.D. 30

A HALF-DOZEN SLENDER MEN ROBED ENTIRELY IN WHITE SCRAMBLED over the rocky sand like crabs from the cluster of buildings to greet Ezra as he stumbled into the Community. He turned his dry lips into a tired smile in anticipation of their welcome; but as they reached him, they began to unwind the colored outer garment from his body, saying nothing as they led him forth. He was instructed to sit on a stone ledge outside the main structure of the compound, a long assembly building with a tower. At length a tall man with narrow shoulders and a prominent hooked nose approached.

"My name is Ezra, and I have come recently from Jerusalem. Is this the settlement of the people known as the Chasajja?"

The tall man grimaced. "It is said of us that we are pious, yes. We have given no name to ourselves." His voice was chirpy.

Ezra released a long breath. "I am a scribe. I seek the community of John. Is this it?"

The man frowned but said nothing.

"John the prophet. Surely you know him. The Baptizer."

The man looked down over the long slope of his nose. "I know him. He was here for a very short time. He was not initiated," he said.

"What then is your opinion of him?" Ezra asked.

"We regard him as a man of God," he answered in his nasal tone. "He chose another way. We wished him to stay, but . . . "

"You know what happened to him, then," Ezra interjected.

35

"Of course. He was . . . impatient." There was an awkward silence before the man spoke again. "This is all I will say about John. He still has followers, but you would know that. Why then have you come here?"

He knew Ezra would not answer the question. The tall man extended his hand, and Ezra stood to take it. "The desert calls men for many reasons," he said warmly, "as does God. The first calling opens our ear to the second."

They walked slowly into the building, where the men could be seen silently cleaning after the midday meal. The tall man said, "Our founder came into the desert because he could not abide the corruption his fellow priests had made of the Law. He believed that our souls are imprisoned in these physical bodies, that we must subject ourselves to discipline that we may be pure and acceptable to God. We do not own property, for it only encourages pride and incites conflict. We are servants of one another."

"The Son of Man came not to be served, but to serve, and to give his life as a ransom for many," Ezra said softly.

The tall man stopped and stared. "What?"

Ezra smiled at the curious look on the man's face. "I understand what you believe. I have seen it demonstrated."

The man frowned. "It cannot be demonstrated outside the Community. We are the pure ones," he said rather haughtily.

The scribe ignored the remark, smiling to himself that for all his purity, this aged one was still a mite immodest. "I meant to say that I agree that men should aspire to such things; I have seen the best in men—and the worst."

This seemed to satisfy the older man. He led Ezra into a large room where stacks of scrolls lay neatly on long tables. "This is our scriptorium," he said proudly. "We are not solely engaged in denying the flesh but also in feeding the mind and spirit."

Ezra's eyes widened as he scanned the room. "May I work here?" he asked excitedly.

"After your time of probation, which lasts one year," he answered. "You will work in the fields during the day, taking care not to defile yourself by touching anyone or speaking when silence is required or violating any of the rules. Your rations will be reduced if you do. When you have learned our ways and have submitted to the washings, you will be admitted. Then, you may labor here—but your other responsibilities to the brothers must not be found lacking."

Ezra heard the words, but his mind was elsewhere. The tall man noticed this, looked over the Pharisee's dirty robe, and wondered aloud, "It is unusual for a scribe to travel without his books."

Ezra blinked himself back into the conversation. "My work was left behind, for the edification of my sister. It amounted to the sayings of a Rabbi I followed for many months." His voice cracked; the fatigue from the hard journey and the emotional strain of the past week seemed to fall heavily upon him all at once.

"This Rabbi," the tall man asked, "do I know him?"

"I think not," said Ezra, regaining strength to his voice. "He himself found some notoriety, especially of late, but his teachings are difficult and obscure. He largely will be forgotten, I fear."

"Then why write of him?" the man said, his head cocked like a perched bird.

"Because his life was lived magnificently," Ezra declared. "Magnificently. And his words were powerful and prophetic."

"Then why do you say he will be forgotten?"

"Because," the scribe said, stiffening to say the words without showing the emotion behind them. "He ended badly."

The older man said nothing as they walked into the bright desert sun. They stopped as a man approached them carrying a white robe and a hoe. He extended these to Ezra.

"What is the hoe for?" Ezra asked.

"To bury your excrement," said the tall man.

It would be a hard life, Ezra knew, a life of contemplation. There would be time to think, to write again what he had seen. By now Mara would have destroyed his work, realizing the danger it represented if found. Hopefully she had hidden the sayings in her heart. Maybe others, someday, would understand.

That night, in the darkness of the cave, he knelt by the fire and scratched out the first words of his new work, the words by which some two millennia later he would be introduced to the world.

Part 2

A Promise Kept

Jerusalem, A.D. 31

"I CAME AS QUICKLY AS WORD REACHED ME," SAID A BREATHLESS Matthew as he pushed open the door of his aunt's modest home. It was the first day of the week, and the streets were busy with commerce. A gaggle of children had announced his approach, having sent word to him that he was needed. After waiting patiently for him outside the Temple, they now led him stumbling along by the hand nearly all the way. "Is there an emergency?"

The women were seated at a roughly hewn table, hands in their laps. "Not an emergency, but . . . " The older one grimaced in the direction of the younger. "We thought it best not to wait, times being as they are."

Matthew gathered his outer garment about his knees and sat with them. "Tell me, then, what is it that has you so troubled?"

The woman spoke again with a cracked voice. "My son . . . ," she began, then collapsed into sobs.

Matthew went over to his aunt and placed his hands gently on her heaving shoulders. The corners of his mouth were turned down in a stern grimace. "It concerns my cousin, then?"

The younger woman nodded. "It concerns something that belonged to my brother," she said.

"We don't want it in the house!" cried the other woman suddenly. Matthew recoiled his hands and stepped back.

"He has brought shame to this household!" She stared at Matthew, the implication being that he would certainly understand. "You take it now. I do not wish to be reminded of him," she said through tears. She turned her body, indicating she had nothing else to say.

Matthew's cousin Mara slipped quietly from the table and led the bewildered disciple into the back room where her brother Ezra once slept. In a soft voice, she began to explain the events of that morning.

"It has been months since she could even speak of him. The memories of the high priest, standing here in our own house . . . " Her voice trailed off.

"That devil Caiaphas," murmured Matthew. "Ezra was no threat to him. Of all people, why him?"

"Because he spoke out, cousin, when all of you fled for your lives," she answered, still calmly, though her words sizzled with feeling. "He was the only disciple with the courage to condemn them for their evil."

"Ezra was not a disciple, Mara," Matthew counseled. "He was a scribe, like one of them. You know that."

"Like one of *them?*" She laughed without smiling. "You know yourself he was never taken seriously. He was a miserable failure by their standards and a defector as well."

"As I said, he was no threat," he repeated. "To hunt him down like a dog was cruel. Why persecute him for saying what the rest of us have long thought?"

"Blasphemy, they said," she interrupted.

"What? Caiaphas is not God, is he?"

"It was not that but his devotion to the crucified one that angered the high priest."

"No! He simply reported the facts. He was not one of us, I tell you."

She shrugged and remained silent for a moment. "Then explain this," she said quietly. Walking to the corner, she lifted several pages from the table and handed them to Matthew. "These are what remain of his writings. He left them with me before he left, minutes before they came. I surrendered some of the papers to the guard, to slow him while Ezra made his escape. He read them and burned them in the other room. And that was the end of the matter . . . "

"Until today. What happened here this morning?" Matthew petitioned.

Mara drew in a deep breath. "Last week, my mother was approached by one of your people with some food. She politely refused their kindness; my other brothers, as you know, tend to her needs. But these men came again today very early, inviting us to the Temple." She looked down humbly. "I wanted to go with them."

"But you didn't, obviously."

"Of course not. Mother was angry. After the men left, I asked to go alone, but she would not permit it. That is when I showed her the writings. There has been much talk in the street of late, of healings and such, and many are following the Way."

Matthew warmed to her gentle spirit. "You must pray for your mother, as I will. As for you, nothing keeps you from believing, Mara, except your own fear."

"We have all known fear at one time or another, have we not, cousin?"

He looked at her bright eyes rimmed with moisture, her plain face somehow beautiful now in its honesty and hope.

"You want me to ask your forgiveness for running away?" he wondered aloud. "I do ask it, for I see now how poor Ezra might have gotten himself in such trouble without protection. I'm sorry." He held the papers close to his body. "Know this, good cousin. Your brother will not be forgotten. He will be heard." He swept away a tear from her cheek with his finger. "I promise, his voice will be heard."

Jerusalem, A.D. 50

"IT'S YOUR FAULT AND YOURS ALONE, MY GOOD FRIEND. NO AMOUNT OF counsel from me will change the fact that you alienated this man and caused irreparable damage to his pride." The speaker was an animated man with light brown, thoughtful eyes which jumped and glimmered under bushy gray brows as he spoke. "The fact that you come to me now for guidance only confirms your desperation."

The larger man stood with feet set apart, his large right hand rubbing his sunburned, bald scalp. "You don't know him like I do, Matthew. I fear the worst from this meeting."

Matthew folded his arms across his chest and smirked. "You can't bear to face him now that you know that he is right."

Peter frowned. "There are those among us who will not accept his views. And his manner of speech is contemptuous. He is not from us, and he cannot dictate how affairs should be handled in Jerusalem."

"And where is it decreed that you and the brothers should dictate matters in Antioch?" Matthew replied.

Peter's eyes narrowed. "There will be a division; it is unavoidable. This man Paul knows only one way—his own."

"Ha!" Matthew's exclamation startled Peter, for he heard in it more sharp disagreement than honest amusement. "You can't be serious, man! Who is more headstrong than you? Shall I begin to document your exploits when the Master walked among us? Shall we go for a stroll on the waves this afternoon, or shall we slice off some poor fellow's ear . . . "

43

"Matthew, you insolent publican!" the big man shouted back. "I have no time for your mockery! I tell you, you don't know this man. He will destroy the fellowship with his insistence in this business with the Gentiles."

"I am told that Barnabas is coming along," Matthew said. "He will temper Paul's fire, will he not?"

"Perhaps. But will he have a chance to speak, with that insufferable blowhard holding forth . . . "

"Now, listen, my brother," Matthew said calmly, "you must rid yourself of these prejudices. As I have said, you gave this Paul no worthy welcome all those years ago when he first presented himself a changed man."

"Changed man?" Peter was incredulous. "Ask John Mark, whom your changed man only recently sent packing!"

"That was by mutual agreement, I understand," Matthew said.

"We shall inquire of Barnabas when he comes. But I have no need for hearsay regarding Paul. His conduct to me in Antioch was unforgivable."

"And what of yours? They tell me that all was well until the brothers from Jerusalem arrived, and then you disassociated yourself from the Gentile believers. You did that Peter, and he justly condemned you for it." Matthew jabbed an accusing finger.

Peter's broad forehead wrinkled with concern over downcast eyes.

"Listen to me," Matthew advised, using the outstretched finger to tap Peter's stalwart chest. "This Paul knows what it is like to be an outcast. He was preeminent among the Pharisees once, was humbled by the Lord himself, and returned to Jerusalem to the cold shoulders of those he persecuted. He has fallen far in his place in this world. He is sympathetic to the Gentiles. Can he be faulted

Q

for that? They belong in the kingdom of Heaven. Who better than Paul to invite them in?"

Peter sighed. "This is not about Gentile salvation. No one argues against that. It is about Judaism itself. Should they or should they not be required to keep the Law of Moses? There are many who think they should."

"Come now, Peter, the case is made plain. The Lord intended the Law to lead us to him, and now that the kingdom has dawned, what use have we for these rules? All they are good for now is to divide men. Why impose them on men for whom the Lord died to bring near? Is his sacrifice somehow insufficient that these observances must be added? Was not the veil of the Temple rent on the day he brought salvation to us all? And did not God teach you this lesson only recently yourself, through the witness of Cornelius and his household? What God has made clean . . . "

"let us no longer consider unclean," Peter acknowledged. "You are so articulate, Matthew. Perhaps you are just the one to mediate this affair before the conference."

"Nonsense. We both agree that Paul is right in this matter, just as he was in Antioch. It is only that you cannot bear to share the stage with one as forceful as yourself. You must humble yourself, Peter, and speak out to the council. They still look to you for leadership. Your voice can avert this division you claim must occur. Your vote will sway the brothers. You must join Paul in his argument."

The big man took a hard look at his fellow apostle. Matthew chose not to participate in matters of Church leadership, active as he was in spreading the faith. Despite his brilliance, he was forever in the shadows, if only by his own choosing.

"It is hard," Peter said at last, "to forget past humiliations."

Matthew looked up at him, puzzled. Peter's smirk revealed the remark aimed more at Matthew than at his own humbling experience with Paul. "I sense you are trying to shift the focus of our conversation, Peter, and I'm wise to your game. I say truly, I have no bitterness toward those who once despised me. Have I not called you brother these past twenty years?"

"You have yet to refund my tax money, dear brother, you Roman pawn!" Peter goaded.

Matthew rolled his eyes and laughed. "I am clean of this, I say. But you will have to prove to yourself that you are clean as well. There is no need for me to attend the conference. I know you will do the right thing and speak in support of Paul."

The two men embraced and went their ways, each with renewed convictions and deep in thought. Matthew loved Peter, knew him intimately well; Peter was transparent, childlike in temperament, and full of contradictions. Yet no man living could match him for his strength of character and unyielding devotion. He had been a giant among them from the first day.

Matthew pondered this other man, Paul. He shivered at the memory of the early days when Saul, as he was then called, brought the heavy hand of the Sanhedrin to bear against the Way. He was indomitable, a tower of fortitude and guts. That such a man could be capable of compassion to those outside Judaism must be an act of God's grace indeed. And yet he had given himself over to terrible hardships—as much as did any of the Twelve—for the sake of those he once hated, the Gentiles. He was a man without a country, hated now (ironically) by the Jews, accepted only at arm's length by the established believers in Jerusalem, always on the move, forever pushing forward, testing boundaries. Was he a tortured soul seeking sanctuary in his lonely mission or a trustworthy servant risking everything for the truth? Or both? Time would tell.

It was a cynical city, Jerusalem. Loved, hated, proud, conquered, fickle, loyal unto death. Matthew longed for the hills of Galilee, where things were simpler, clear as the sky but where the people could be just as unforgiving. He remembered those lonely days in his tax booth, when his only friends were fellow outcasts like himself— soldiers, sinners, wine bibbers—and one forsaken scribe.

This last thought preoccupied him as he descended the narrow, winding street to the rooms where he lodged. His mind struggled against the painful memory of that solitary figure, similar in some ways to Paul, a man rejected by sinners and saints alike. Only God knew what lay deep in the hearts of men like these. They were inscrutable, disconnected from the world, so completely refined by their singular tragedies that they, unlike so many who are tied to place and position, could be urged onward by the call of God alone. Did they understand these things? Could they see past the frame of their own circumstances to grasp the greater purpose behind their lives? Or were they simply driven toward their destinies by some unseen force too powerful to comprehend? Would their anxieties and burdens and regrets and obsessions burn their works into cinders to be blown away with the ages? Or would the legacy of their disfranchisement brand them into history's pages to inspire the generations following?

Matthew walked to the small desk where his writing materials were kept. From his tax-collecting days, he was much skilled in the taking of precise notes, and from his priestly lineage, he inherited the respect for the pure Word he had seen his own generation defame by their prideful actions. For some time, he had been searching the ancient texts, looking for the proofs of what he himself had seen, prophesied in days of old. He removed the well-worn scroll—the same which he had copied from his cousin Ezra's papers so long ago—and placed it in his cloak; he had long since culled its contents for his own use and maintained it as a keepsake, a memory of an old friend.

He would be leaving Israel soon. As he walked from the house into the sunshine, he began to regret not staying to meet Paul. They had at least this in common: they loved the heritage of their people but could not abide their hypocrisy. Matthew patted his outer garment and felt the scroll underneath. He would leave this treasure for Paul as a gift, to remind him that no matter how isolated he might feel in this city of confusion and bad memories, he would not have been the first to walk alone.

Antioch, the Spring of A.D. 52

"MUST YOU ALWAYS ARGUE ABOUT EVERYTHING?" THE THIN, DARK-haired man pleaded with his shorter, burly companion.

"You have missed the point entirely," he responded. "I have no qualms with your plans; it's just that the work can't wait." The two men walked purposefully through the heart of the city along the wide colonnaded street, Mount Silpus rising sharply to the south before them. "You've seen what happened in Galatia. I'm not willing to risk more of the same."

"You are impossible. Impossible!" the taller man quipped. He stopped dead in the center of the thoroughfare, unconcerned that the crowd might hear. "You can't ever stick with anything. Always moving on to the next place, stirring up controversy . . . "

"Hold on, now!" the stocky man shouted. "Could you have made the sacrifices asked of me? It is not by my will that I must travel these lonesome roads." His single eyebrow scrunched itself up and down like a bird of prey in flight.

His lanky companion sighed. "You are a tortured soul, Paul, I must give you that," he replied. "And I agree, only time will tell if I can keep pace with you, step for step. But it is not from fear that I must ask you to wait. Just a few months, that's all. I need time to get the facts down, to organize my thoughts . . . "

Paul fumed. "Then I will go without you." He began walking on ahead, his bowed legs pounding the paved stone with determination.

Luke stood in the street, laughing. "You go on ahead, then," he called out. "While you're gone, after the biography is finished, I'll send for John Mark—surely he can provide the necessary details of the journey, instead of you."

Paul whirled, his eyes ablaze. Seeing the broad smile in the narrow face of his friend and fellow believer, his spirit softened. Luke walked up to join him.

"Please try to understand, my brother," Paul began, his emotions now under control. "It's not that I am impatient, it's just that . . . "

"You are always impatient," Luke interrupted.

Paul ignored the remark. "Its just that the council in Jerusalem has ruled on the matter of the Gentiles. Now we must go forth with the Gospel. God has ordained it." He was politely insistent.

"I do beg your pardon, but do you know with whom you are speaking?" Luke answered. Paul hesitated, realizing that Luke spoke of his own Gentile birth. "Of course you do. So do not question my concern for my own," he scolded. "Now, consider my point. Theophilus has prevailed upon me to write this narrative of our Lord's life for our people here in Antioch and to give an account of how so many have come to embrace the Way. Can't you see how this helps our cause?"

Paul blinked in the sunlight, his heavy brow hanging ominously low.

"Don't you?" Luke pleaded. "I have already begun to gather sources, and no one has yet told the story from the Gentile point of view. There are several various scrolls floating about that reflect assorted traditions and sayings; someone needs to sort out the truth. By the way, did you know that there is word that John Mark is also preparing to document our Lord's life?"

Q

Paul grunted.

"It would be a much-needed work, should he write it, destined to be well known. Theophilus, however, has wisely asked me to delve into those matters of peculiar interest to the Gentiles here, such as our Lord's concern for the outcasts, his perspective on earthly riches. Are you demanding I should refuse the opportunity and follow you to points unknown? To do so would leave the writing of our sacred history solely to John Mark. And should he also be the one to plot the record of your journey? No doubt the name of Paul will figure prominently there, though in what light I cannot say." Luke patted Paul's hunched shoulder.

"You grind with a heavy boot, Doctor," Paul said sharply.

"Yes, but you are being unreasonable now, as you were then. Had you been a little easier on him during the first journey, he might never have sought out Peter, as he has apparently done, to gain his perspective on things. Surely he would have remained devoted to you, an able member of the team."

Paul muttered something inaudible and picked up speed as he marched along. "Let him write, then. He's not coming with us on the second journey," he snapped, painfully aware—as was all the Christian community—of his dispute with Barnabas over Mark but not yet ready to mend fences with either man.

"That's your decision," Luke said. "But I tell you, his book will stand forever. Now, you can go on if you want. I will stay here and tend to what has been asked of me. Think, mind you, before your stubborn spirit forces yet another ruined partnership, that it will not be you who provides me with the details of the first journey for my chronicle. And you will have no physician to tend to your ailments while you are away."

Paul thought to himself for some moments. "Let's compromise," he said, more in the tone of command than petition. "We journey now with the Gospel, and when we get back, you write. Or we pause, some days at a time, to allow you the opportunity to research. Perhaps we could choose an extended stay in Rome, and you can be about your work there. You make time for my calling, and I'll make time for yours."

Luke smiled, weary of the verbal swordplay but pleased with the result. Arguments were necessary in dealing with the strong-minded Paul. Difficult as he was, few, Luke knew, were the men courageous enough to assume the mantle of apostle to the Gentiles. But, for his own part, few aside from Luke could sway the great man's mind once he set himself to a course of action.

When they had reached the house with the low ceiling where they headquartered, Paul excused himself briefly and returned with a large satchel.

"I am not completely opposed to your ambitions," he said. He presented the satchel to Luke. "The books and the parchments," he announced proudly. "You will find much of interest here for your writing."

Luke carefully unrolled the scrolls one by one, recognizing many of the ancient teachings immediately. A singular papyrus gave him pause. Holding it reverently, he extended it in his hands as far as he could and stepped to the window to scan the text. "What's this?" he asked, excitedly.

Paul walked to his side. "That one . . . is something I picked up in Jerusalem on my last visit. It is well told, they claim, and was introduced to the brethren by Matthew, who has since departed for Ethiopia. The author is unknown. The apostles know the stories, of course, and had no real use for it, especially given its . . .

Q

irregularities; so they gave it to me. Suitable, don't you think? If there are other copies, they are unknown to the church."

Paul looked over Luke's shoulder, watching his lips move slowly as he read. Suddenly conscious of Paul's hot breath on his neck, Luke rolled up the scroll and faced him. He was visibly moved.

"This is a treasure indeed," he whispered, "a window on the soul of God."

The statement surprised Paul. "Absolutely not!" he retorted. "This is not by the hand of Moses, is it? Nor the work of a prophet, is it?"

Luke's thin fingers cradled the scroll gently. "No. But it is the work of a witness."

The two of them sat silently together in the warm room, the one already shaping in his mind the vast work he would present to Theophilus, the other looking out the window toward the future, dreaming past Syria, to Cilicia and beyond.

Part 3

The *Way*

The Dead Sea, August 31, A.D. 70

THE SOLDIER LAY BACK AGAINST THE WALL HEWN FROM STONE. IT
was cool inside the scriptorium, the first time he could
remember being cool in months. He carefully removed the guards
from his shins, then removed the breastplate. He sipped from the
cup and closed his eyes.

He was much too old now for war. As a young man, he had been
stationed in Jerusalem and had not understood the passions of her
people. Theirs was a zeal that bordered on obsession. In the beginning he abhorred them. Now, he envied them. They had a reason
to live, a higher purpose that fueled them to fight against impossible odds. His purpose had been to command, to control, to kill—all
these years. It had ruined him, emptied him of self-respect. He had
seen too much.

The water was almost gone, and he asked for more. The scribe, a
man as old as himself dressed in a white robe, was not averse to
serving him, a bizarre contrast from the defiant behavior of the
Zealots and the teachers of the Law he had known, who fought
with one another with almost the same fury as they hurled against
the Romans. He took the cup again and offered his thanks in Latin,
and the scribe nodded his understanding.

"The Temple is no more," the soldier said weakly. Not that it
meant anything to him, particularly. It meant little, it seemed,
even to the scribe. Here, among the scrolls of his scriptorium, he
had spent his days, happily carrying out the humble duties

required of him by the Community. "They will be coming back here again, and soon."

He spoke of the legions under the command of Titus, son of the great Vespasian, who had begun this terrible campaign some four years earlier before being summoned to Rome to be made emperor. The soldier had been in Jerusalem when the procurator Gessius Florus plundered the Temple treasury, when the Jews complained loudly at this despicable act (as they had so often, about so many things), and when Florus responded by sending guards rampaging through the city to loot and vandalize. The soldier had himself taken part, though unwillingly, performing his duty as would an actor in a play, harming no one. He was there when more troops arrived from Caesarea, when they humiliated the Jews by not so much as acknowledging the welcome they had been commanded to offer, and the riot ensued.

The soldier smiled at the memory of it. He had not seen Jerusalem in such a stir since the Passover many years ago, when the Rabbi had come. He knew better than to think that his countrymen would act in any way other than they had always acted. Though the Jews had surprised them and taken back the city, the Romans would act swiftly in response. So unlike the ways of the Rabbi, so long ago.

The emperor Nero commissioned Vespasian, his finest general, to put down the rebellion. Word spread that he soon succeeded in sweeping through Galilee. By this time the Zealots were fighting among themselves for control of Jerusalem as Vespasian advanced. The followers of the Rabbi refused to take part and fled the city.

"You know, I cannot help thinking it could have all been avoided," the soldier said. "A great teacher once warned them, saying, 'A day is coming when your enemies shall surround you on every side and will destroy you, and will not leave one stone upon another because you did not recognize the time of your visitation.'" The scribe looked at him, enraptured. He apparently did not know the saying.

The soldier's mind turned to the horrific images of the last few days. Titus had first swept into Jerusalem in late May, breaching first the outer, then the inner wall, laying siege to the city from within. His eighty thousand troops surrounded the Jews, cutting off any supply of food. In July, he resumed the attack, taking the fortress of Antonia and burning it. On August 6, the daily sacrifices in the Temple ceased; in a week, the Roman legions had burned the glorious porticoes, and soon they were dismantling the precincts. As the fires were set, the decree went forth from Titus that all the people were to be taken captive and the city utterly destroyed. It was then, tortured by the smell of rot and smoke and the pitiful cries of the once-defiant Jews, that the soldier slipped away and began the long solitary march to the Dead Sea.

He had been here before, when Vespasian had finished with Galilee and was stomping through Samaria. His regiment had joined the army at Jericho, which succumbed easily. In a few days, the giant army had plodded on to the regions of the Dead Sea in pursuit of the Zealot leader Simon, son of Gorias, where the peaceful settlement of the Essenes was sacked. It had saddened the soldier to see it, for these were holy people—"the pure ones," as he had heard them called—who had no argument with Rome. He had determined to return and warn those few who remained, should they ever be threatened again.

The soldier could not know that the fighting was far from over, that upon his return to the wreckage of Jerusalem, he would soon be sent to the nearly impregnable fortress of Masada. He was not yet preparing himself for the long three-year siege; for the building of the ramp against the western wall, some 260 cubits high; for the construction of the tower that would look down over the wall. He would himself peer over the wall and be one of the first to see the bodies and know that the invasion would not be necessary. Shocked that the 960 Jews inside the fortress had taken their lives rather than be captured by their hated enemy, he would look upon the corpses with respect whereas the others would hold only contempt. In that moment he would remember the words of the old scribe dressed in white on a hot afternoon three years earlier, in the cool of the scriptorium at Qumran.

"The Teacher you speak of, he is the Nazarene?" the scribe asked.

"Yes."

"And you knew him?"

"I saw him, many times. I heard him speak. I know of his followers. Many have been killed over the years."

The scribe watched him carefully, studied his long, dirty face. "And yet you take up the sword," he said. The scribe's eyes were like pebbles, dark and round, hard and unblinking, as he beheld the soldier.

"It accomplishes nothing, I know."

The scribe grunted his assent. "It is as you say," he muttered. "Your people and mine, they do not understand the Way."

At first the soldier thought he might be speaking of a destination but then realized he meant something more. "The Way," he repeated. "You are a follower, then."

The man in the white robe smiled. "I tried to be." He stood up with some effort. "And I try to be," he added. "Please come." He waved a frail hand.

Q

They walked to a table, where a box lay open, its lid on the floor. Beside it lay a leather book wrapped in a thin white cloth. The scribe explained to him what he wanted him to do. "It has been there several days," the scribe said. "I have had no heart to place it among the others. It has been my companion for a long time."

The soldier listened as the man explained how he had followed the Rabbi from a distance, writing down his sayings and sharing them with his fellow Jews. "They had no tolerance for his teaching," he said bitterly. "They were corrupted by their own desire for control. It is that which is killing them now. It is God's judgment."

The soldier listened with compassion as Ezra continued. "It was evil what they did to him." His face twisted with anguish. "I could do nothing to stop it."

"And this?" the soldier asked, lifting the book in both hands.

The scribe smiled. "My former writings—did not survive. This is my recollection of the teaching." The soldier looked down at the leather volume reverently. "Come. It is time."

The sunshine seared the soldier's already burned neck as he scaled the cliff with the box under one arm. He was strong but still weary and stiff from the journey. He placed the box down inside the aperture of the cave and hoisted himself up. Before him were many large earthen jars; they were filled with scrolls. Turning back toward the entrance, he looked down at the old scribe.

"The Word of our God stands forever," the man in white called out, his voice drifting upward like a straw in the wind.

The soldier blinked into the sun. Below lay the vast and terrible wilderness, where men had perennially gone to hide, or to find themselves, or to prepare to fight another day. The sand and rock stretched itself to the horizon, far beyond the limits of his sight.

Part 4

The Codex

Jerusalem, February 12, 1949

FLAKES OF DRIED SKIN DRIFTED ONTO DR. TERENCE KNOTTY'S SHOULDERS as he rubbed the back of his sunburned neck with his bandanna, itself wet with sweat. After nearly a week, he was coming to the conclusion that his sojourn into the new independent nation of Israel would be for naught. He was dressed in khaki pants, dusty boots, and what was once a clean, white oxford-cloth shirt with tab collars. A leather satchel was slung over his shoulder and, though all it contained was a folded newspaper, a journal, herbs of questionable origin, and some cigarette paper, the strap seemed to cut into the soft, tender skin of his shoulder like a saber.

He sat down amid the noisy foot traffic of the Jerusalem street and relieved himself of the heavy burden. He reached inside and removed the *Times,* glancing again at the page-four article which was exposed by careful folding. For the last time, he read the announcement on April 11 of the previous year that a manuscript of Isaiah dating from the first century had been found at the monastery of Saint Mark in Jerusalem, along with others. Then, he tossed it to the ground where it was soon trampled by barefoot boys, chatty women, and busy merchants, all too preoccupied with their own affairs to notice it.

He laughed. From where he sat on the Nablus Road, he could walk from Israel into Jordan and back again, as if the separate worlds of Arab and Jew were comingled into a horrific knot in a giant ball of yarn. Troops still wandered about, keeping the peace. He took out a bent, homemade smoke and stuck it in his mouth.

With so much political and military activity here in recent months, little attention was given to what Knotty was beginning to believe was the greatest archaeological find in recent history, perhaps one of the most significant ever in biblical studies. He had assumed as much when he first read the reference to the Essenes while wasting away in his London flat. This group had been the focus of a good portion of his scholarly pursuits, even at the expense of his devotion to Matthew, before his personal habits became known to the administration. He admired the Essenes—they fascinated him. Looking out at the chaos of life in modern Jerusalem, he seemed to connect with their desire to remove themselves to the desert, to the waste places on the northwest shore of the Dead Sea.

Less than two years earlier, a goatherd went searching for a stray in that arid desert. Scrambling around in the jagged hills near Qumran, he picked up a stone and chucked it into the dark recesses of a cave. Hearing a clink, like the sound of breaking pottery, he entered to find several ancient jars with lids; some of these contained leather scrolls wrapped in tattered fabric, preserved for centuries in the dry, stagnant air, untouched since their deposit long ago. Since that time, more scrolls had been discovered, and Knotty knew only too well that untold treasures were sure to be circulated in the region. With no job and no aspirations to secure one, he had set out in hopes of obtaining a document or two himself, as soon as the cease-fire was announced.

He had located a handful of rather naïve patrons through his association with a wealthy antiques dealer in London named John Ravenswood, a young man of means with an ego to match. He explained that certain influential families in Israel routinely discovered relics by means of a highly organized network of snitches and

Q

spies, who kept their ear to the ground for interesting finds. It would not be at all surprising if these caves at Qumran had been scoured and plundered dozens of times, their contents sold and sold again, before the proper authorities were consulted. Knowing Ravenswood to be a religious man, Knotty explained that manuscripts and fragments such as these might include original autographs of New Testament books or historical data which confirmed their truth. Indeed, such documents might even reveal the Essenes to be early followers of Christ himself, thus validating the claims of the Gospel. It was important, therefore, that this material be brought forth by responsible Christian scholars, or it might become corrupted or lost forever.

He took a long drag and squinted into the hazy sun, exhaling slowly. He had been so proud of his success that day. But now, having been turned away at Saint Mark's and with no responses to his inquiries, he faced the prospect of returning home empty-handed.

Knotty flicked away the cigarette and scratched his blonde beard. He lifted the satchel and stumbled forward with a heavy gait for several steps, until his legs remembered what to do. Several people bumped into him with no apology, and he made his way haltingly up the road. In the midst of this convergence of sight, sound, and humanity, he felt a tugging of the satchel. Instinctively, he grabbed the strap with both hands and darted forward to escape the pickpocket, colliding with a corpulent woman so forcefully that he glanced off her broadside and fell into the street. Turning and spitting dirt, he looked up into the searing light to see a small man in spectacles standing over him.

"You are Mister Knotty?" the man asked, showing blackened teeth and a rather large mole under the left eye.

Knotty sat upright, slightly dizzy from the heat and the tumble. He had seen the man before.

"You are?" the man repeated. In the din of the crowd his shrill voice was hardly audible.

Knotty raised himself to his feet and found he towered some ten inches over his inquisitor. He nodded yes.

"Good. Follow now." With that, he wrapped his bony fingers around the strap just above the satchel and led Knotty through the crowd, looking back periodically and smiling like a Halloween pumpkin.

In minutes, they arrived at a black car parked illegally in the street. A door opened in the back, and Knotty was invited in.

The driver stared straight ahead as if Knotty were not there at all. In the back seat, a well-groomed man in a European suit smiled. He was very dark, with short, curly hair and a sharp nose.

"You like books?" the gentleman asked.

"Well, of course," Knotty answered, clearing his throat. "I'm a professor of biblical studies."

The man nodded approval and replied, "You have come to the right place, then!" At this, the driver snickered, still looking ahead. The thin man, who had jumped in the front passenger seat, was laughing too.

When this subsided, Knotty spoke up. "I have an interest in your books," he said gravely. "Particularly anything related to the Christian New Testament. I'm a Matthew scholar."

The well-dressed man said nothing further. For a few seconds, he examined his manicure, then spoke some words Knotty did not understand to the driver, who started the engine. The short man who had led Knotty to the car suddenly turned around and held up a white cloth in front of Knotty's face. His intent was clear.

Throughout the trip, Knotty mused that if they had wanted to rob him, they would have done so already. He had already put the word out that he represented wealthy Englishmen, and they no doubt assumed he had little cash with him. Any transactions would be handled by wire. As the car bumped along, these thoughts comforted him, and he grew excited at the possibilities that awaited.

When the car stopped and the blindfold was removed, the madness of the Nablus Road seemed a distant memory. The only similarity to this place was the sun, which streamed into the narrow alley where the car had been parked. The small man exited and opened the door for Knotty, who unfolded himself from the vehicle on aching legs.

Without speaking, they entered through a heavy, arched door, to a room arrayed in fine rugs and heavy furniture. It was cool, though Knotty knew not how this could be possible, since windows cut high in the walls were open to the air. He was directed to a table where two men stood and with a wave of a hand departed into a nether room.

Knotty sat and waited. At once he became aware of a strong, suffocating odor and the presence of flies. The small man blinked these away, unconsciously.

The two men emerged with a heavy clay box, about two feet long, and set it on the table in front of Knotty. He recognized it immediately as an ossuary—an ancient coffin.

"Books," he said to the well-dressed man, pushing the box away with both hands. "Books, not bones."

The gentleman smiled and said nothing.

Knotty sighed, then huffed in frustration. "This . . . this is very nice, but I'm not an archaeologist. What do we have in here, the bones of Jesus? Come now! Do I look so foolish? Jews didn't cremate people, unless they were very, very bad. And they never used coffins for bones, corpses, or what have you. Please. This is very fine, probably from the Greek period, possibly quite important, actually." He paused, considering his own remark. "Nevertheless," he resumed, "I wish to see parchment, papyri. Scrolls, you see. Books."

The dark-skinned gentleman's smile grew wide. "Yes," he said cheerfully and waved a finger in swirls at the two men who had borne the ancient box. Without a word, they carefully lifted the lid.

Knotty looked quizzically inside. What he saw stopped his heart; he would say later, the very muscles of his windpipe constricted at the sight of it. He looked at his host; the eyes implied a request to touch, which was granted with a nod.

He was holding in his hands a codex, a predecessor to the modern book. It had a thick leather cover and backing and several loose-leaf parchment pages in between. The script was unusually large, penned by a careful hand. There were blank spaces in spots, again, quite unusual, given the value of the writing materials. A leather thong, obviously not original to the codex, had been used to bind the sheets together.

"There are pages missing," Knotty said, caught up in the excitement of the moment, unconcerned as to how his words might be construed. There was no response.

"What in heaven's name am I looking at?" he said to no one in particular. As he lifted the sheets, he began to catch familiar words and phrases expressed in common first-century Greek, as it was spoken in Palestine. There were also words written in the wide margins, apparently in Aramaic. Slowly, he began to translate in his head easily the trains of words he had seen so often in his study of Matthew's text, anticipating from memory what the next line should be, until he was forced to stop abruptly when encountering unexpected commentary. Confused, he carefully removed a few pages with twittering fingers and laid them side by side, gently, on the table. He looked back and forth from one to another, his head tilting this way and that, his lips moving silently. Flies buzzed, unheeded, around his sun-reddened ears. *There is a pattern here,* he thought to himself. And then he knew.

Terence Knotty, formerly esteemed professor of holy writ and current dabbler in recreational medications, wiped his sweaty palms on his stained khakis and wondered for a moment if the whole experience might be drug-induced, until the silken voice of the dark man in the expensive suit leaned forward and whispered.

"You like books?" he hissed. He placed a well-manicured hand firmly on Knotty's sore shoulder and crouched closer. "We have books."

Book II

Part 1

Acts of the Prophetess, Ignored

I (thank Thee, O Lord,
    For) Thou has placed me beside a fountain of streams
    In an arid land,
And close to a spring of waters
    In a dry land,
And beside a watered garden
    (in a wilderness).

—From the *Hymns Scroll*, Hymn 18
Discovered at Khirbet Qumran, 1948
Author Unknown

1.1

THE KITCHEN WAS A FORTRESS OF CINDER-BLOCK WALLS PAINTED BABY blue with only one window above the front door facing the street. On one side was a gravel lot bordered by a high chain-link fence. A bare, bent rim was mounted flat against the block wall eleven feet above the ground—the extra twelve inches added to discourage dunking and prevent injury. The men often clung to the fence in the hot afternoons like human kudzu, waiting for the door to open for the evening meal. Now, they were streaming outside into the blinding morning sun, having finished breakfast. The day, with all of its opportunity, blazed ominously ahead, like a welcome mat before their shuffling feet.

On the other side was an alley extending from the street to the back of the building, where there were four parking spaces. Delivery vehicles entered by the gravel lot and parked there, leaving the deliverymen to walk down the alley with their hand trucks toward the pantry. A two-story plumbing supply store formed the other wall; six large plastic garbage pails were lined against it.

Gigi blasted through the heavy door into the alley, dragging a green trash bag filled with scraps from the day's first meal. She was slight of build but surprisingly strong, and she lifted the bag high enough to drop it squarely into the first barrel. A pungent odor arose as the bag settled down toward the bottom. She snatched a short breath and held it, tipped her head back, and stared into the glaring sky, blinking until the air cleared. Pausing for a moment, she leaned back against the building and looked down the alley, exhaling. A few of the men were straggling by, on their way to wherever they spent their days. She was tired, and it was barely past breakfast.

Inside, Tinky was wiping down the counter and issuing the remaining few volunteers some final instructions. She was big and imposing but with small, cherubic features in her round face, and had little hands and feet. It was she who had earlier announced the end of breakfast as she meticulously reviewed the inventory from the hollow of the cavernous pantry. Her voice could boom like a foghorn or drift like a gentle mist, depending on the urgency of the moment.

Gigi wiped her hands on her jeans. The faded yellow counter reflected a bright sheen from Tinky's spritzing under the bare florescent light. "Anything else before I go?" she asked, assuming she already knew the answer. She glanced back at the corner where the mops leaned lazily to make sure her book bag was where she had left it.

Tinky paused and then stood, hands on hips. She was flushed and breathing heavily. "Get me some help, sweetie." She smiled and blinked, her eyes tiny brown pebbles in the sea of her pink face.

Gigi nodded and sighed. The Kitchen was desperate for volunteers. Food was not a problem; the local markets saw to that. Workers, however, were another matter. Tinky was the full-time director, with Gigi her part-time assistant. They were limited to a few dozen retirees from the nearby Baptist church, some adult Sunday-school classes and missions groups from the surrounding Christian community, and a few seminarians. This was not nearly enough to handle serving three meals a day to the homeless men, running the clothes closet and food pantry, providing vocational

71

counseling, coordinating medical services, teaching the Bible studies, staffing the day care . . .

It had been this way for about six months, since the opening of the glamorous Restoration Outreach Center, newly sprung from the fertile loins of Restoration Fellowship, the largest congregation in the metroplex. "The ROC," as it was affectionately known, attracted not only many potential volunteers but legions of poor people as well. They wandered toward the suburbs from downtown to the ROC's spacious and well-appointed rooms, where they could be fed, clothed, and given medical attention by efficient, well-trained personnel. Television cameras hanging in the corner of each room attracted a great deal of attention from the men, who often jockeyed for position in front of the lenses.

"Oh, and one more trash bag," added Tinky. "Then you can scoot."

Gigi sighed and wandered across the dining hall to the front door to retrieve the last bag, which was still open and not quite half full in its barrel. Tinky was obsessive about trash and demanded that it all be taken out after each meal, no matter how sparse its contents. Gigi tied a knot in the top and heaved it up and free of the barrel. Dragging it across the room like a weary Santa with his bag of toys, she made her final trip to the alley, shoving the heavy door open with her backside.

On her previous visit, she had secured all the lids, which now required removing until a can empty enough for this last offering could be found. She set the bag down and tugged at the first lid; too heavy. The next one might work. She tipped it off and saw that it held only one bag. Turning again, she reached for the trash bag she had dropped and lifted it, her 112-pound frame straining not so much from the bag's weight as from the morning's work. It was then that she saw the hunched figure thirty feet away, just inside the back entrance to the narrow passage.

She dropped the bag into the barrel, then paused to watch. The stranger turned his head slowly in her direction. At first he looked like a teen, but his manner reflected an older man, perhaps in his twenties, certainly no older than she. He had closely cropped hair and wore a denim jacket, with heavy black work boots protruding from his jeans. He stood up fully when he saw her. She could see that he was holding his elbow with the opposite hand in an awkward position.

"Are you—OK?" she asked, too softly for the distance between them, but he nodded that he understood. In that moment it seemed as if they both wondered what to do. Gigi mentally measured the distance to the door, where just inside, Tinky stood scrubbing. She looked toward the front of the building and the street to find the sidewalk empty. It was just the two of them.

He took a step forward and stopped. She called out, a bit louder this time. "Are you hurt?" He looked down at his elbow and then up at her. "A nick is all. Be all right," he said. The accent was decidedly British.

Gigi walked toward him, past the door and any idea of retreat. As she approached she noticed a glint of steel in the man's left ear lobe. "Let's have a look," she said.

"It's alright, not to worry," he assured, sliding back down the wall into a crouch. "Just a nick here is all." She slowed and took a few more steps before stopping her advance.

"Is there something we can do for you?" She sensed something very strange about this man but felt no danger. He was tentative, halting in his movements, as if he wanted to talk but wasn't quite sure. "Breakfast is over, but I'm sure we could . . . "

"I just want to rest is all," he said abruptly and quietly.

It was clear to Gigi that this person needed help, and it was not in her nature to turn away from such an opportunity. She stepped quickly to the man and knelt next to him. She could see that he was unwell, pale and perspiring, though the sun was bright this morning and the spring air still quite cool. "I'm Gigi," she said.

He laughed.

"What?" His laughter totally disarmed her.

"You don't look like a Gigi," he said. "Sounds like a French poodle."

She beheld his grin with wonderment. He wasn't looking at her—intentionally, she thought—inviting her to study his features. His eyes were small and green, his cheekbones high, and his nose rather large. He was not handsome, just interesting.

"It's Chinese, actually," she quipped. "Or at least, it's short for something Chinese. My mother could say it. Dad just never could say the whole thing right."

"An American, your father?" He turned to her. Her Asian features were softened into something quite remarkable. She had a broad face with sparkling black eyes and straight black hair, which fell in thick, wavy sheets to her shoulders. She had a tiny nose and mouth and a very appealing petite figure of which he had immediately taken notice.

"Yes, and since we're naming nationalities, you don't seem to be from around here yourself."

He laughed again. "No, no, I'm not. Far away from here is where I'm from. Can you guess?"

Q

"England."

"Very good!" He seemed to wince as he spoke and understood that she noticed. She reached for his arm.

"It's really quite well, just a nick now," he said curtly. It was clear he had no intention of showing her his injury.

"You've been cut. You need to get that looked at." She spoke with the authority of a seasoned caregiver.

"I'll not have any looks from you or anyone else just now," he pouted. "If you could, though, I might like a bit of toast." She didn't believe him. He had said earlier that he wasn't hungry. He was looking away again. Did he want her to go?

"I'm sure we can scrounge up something. Would you like to come inside?"

He rolled his eyes.

"OK, then. You can sit here and bleed, and I'll go toast a little bread for you, and you can eat it out here with the cats and the garbage." She smiled a cutesy smile.

"I don't see any cats," he growled.

"Look, I need to get to class," she huffed, frustrated. "If you want me to . . . "

"You're a student, then?" He suddenly seemed cooperative.

She stared at him blankly, surprised. She was intrigued by this quirky Brit and his earring. "I'm a seminarian," she said.

"Really," he said, puzzling. "What kind of seminary?"

"Baptist."

This evoked another burst of laughter that caught her quite by surprise.

"Something wrong with that?" She shot back.

"Oh, I'm sorry. It's just . . . interesting, that's all." He smiled and looked off, apparently happy for the moment with his own joke.

"OK. I suppose one doesn't meet too many Chinese-American Baptist seminarians in some back alley in Texas. So. What is it exactly that you do, hmm?" she demanded.

He paused and looked her squarely in the eye. "I'm a criminal, just out of prison. A thief by profession," he said coldly, the mirth drained out of him.

Gigi saw that he was serious. She stepped back. Her body tensed.

"Don't be alarmed. I'm not very good at it." He made no move to rise.

She continued to back away slowly. "I'll get you that toast," she said. He smiled and closed his eyes, leaning his head against the wall as she scampered to the door.

"Took you long enough to take out the trash," Tinky scolded. She was looking at her watch. "You'll miss class if you don't get going."

The big lady watched Gigi fumble with the bread. She blew on her coffee to cool it as Gigi chattered about her schedule and how she barely took time to eat and ought to be more concerned about such things like her dad said and how she needed more sleep, too, "But right now I'm late, so I'll see you tonight"—and then she left, book bag slung over one shoulder, toast in hand.

The alley was empty, as she expected it to be.

It was a short walk through the alley to her white Chevy Nova parked in back. The car held some fascination for the men who frequented the Kitchen because the word *nova* in Spanish means "it doesn't go." There were times when, in fact, it didn't, but Gigi's

Q

limited budget wouldn't allow for a new car. Her father had rebuilt the engine prior to her leaving California, and she had found a local mechanic who, unlike so many others, went out of his way to help nearly impoverished seminary students. As a result he had a steady stream of business.

Texas was not unlike her native state, big and welcoming to other cultures. It was a place to dream, a place for dreamers, where no one would tell you something couldn't be done. Except one thing.

She deliberately looked straight ahead as she approached the car, quickly jumped in, and tossed the book bag onto the passenger seat. Stuffing what remained of the toast into her mouth, she sped from the lot somewhat recklessly. She would be late for Dr. Dunbarton's class again, which was becoming an unintentional habit of hers. Dr. Ashley Dunbarton—or "A.D." as he was affectionately known to his students—was young, single, and particularly shy. A post-class discussion concerning the lecture was always welcomed. She liked him. He was the only one she knew who really believed in her dream, in spite of the doctrinal debate it often raised.

It was this singular theological point that had begun to warp her attitude toward the Church as a whole. She knew she sometimes went too far in her criticisms, yet she clung to them anyway, so tenacious was her desire to pastor a congregation. She had applied for internships and staff positions in local churches to no avail. She had placed her name on the pulpit supply list but was never called. After almost two years of graduate school, she was still relegated to that same ministry list prescribed for females: children's worker, youth leader, maybe music, maybe education, possibly missions—if she could just find a husband. But not preacher. Not that.

Gigi drove south through the heart of the Hispanic section of town. She felt strangely at home here with the outcasts of glamorous

Fort Worth. This was where her ministry was, far from the gleaming spires of Christendom, where distinguished older men in expensive suits and lapel flowers proclaimed the Word in lofty language or where young fireballs challenged the style but not the substance of the faith. There was something terribly wrong with it all, she felt. For all its flash and power, it seemed hollow, soulless. But what she experienced at the Kitchen—that was real.

Southwestern Seminary was situated appropriately on a hill, like a lamp that could not be hidden. The largest seminary of the largest Protestant denomination in the country, it sent hundreds of its sons and daughters all over the world each year to spread the Gospel. Gigi parked the car and walked hurriedly across the tree-lined campus to Scarborough Hall, glancing up at the massive stone frieze portraying the great Baptist leaders of the past that graced the entrance to the rotunda. She would have liked the chance to meet each one—Furman, Broadus, Gambrell, Tichenor, and the rest, notable chauvinist theologians all.

The class was well underway. Dr. Dunbarton seemed pleased at her appearance in the back of the room as she quietly took her seat. A.D. never took attendance; in fact, he knew few of the students' names—his "grader" scored the exams and completed the grade reports. But he did know Gigi, who often hung around to make her presence known when the lecture was over. No classes were scheduled in the following hour, when Chapel was held in the auditorium.

"Now read the verses in your *New American Standard Bible*, please," the professor was saying to a student on the front row.

The student read in a monotone voice: "As it is written in Isaiah the prophet: 'Behold, I send My messenger ahead of You, who will prepare Your way; the voice of one crying in the wilderness, "Make ready the way of the Lord, make His paths straight."'"

"Thank you. Now, you will find that Mark is not only quoting Isaiah but also Exodus 23:20a and Malachi 3:1. Does that make Mark a liar or just someone with a poor knowledge of Scripture?" Dr. Dunbarton was wearing a tan sweater vest over his long-sleeved, light blue plaid oxford shirt with an open collar. His long neck swayed above his narrow shoulders like a submarine periscope in choppy water. The student who had read the passage stared down at his Bible in desperation, fearing the wrath of his peers should he choose either answer. Gigi smiled; A.D. was always pulling things like this.

"You may hold on to your answer for a moment," the professor advised. He looked about the room and pointed to a beefy man in the back stuffed into a navy blazer a few sizes too small. "And you, sir—what translation have you?"

"King James," was the answer.

"Ah, good!" He sat on the corner of his desk and folded his arms across his chest. "Go ahead, then. Same verses." He closed his eyes to listen.

The big student read as if shouting over hurricane force winds. "As it is written in the prophets . . . "

"Stop!" A.D. slid from his perch and held out his hands like some kind of bizarre Bible cop. "Did you say, 'prophets?'"

"Yessir." The student looked around for support, finding none.

"Well, please help me understand this. Where is the reference to Isaiah?"

"I—I don't see it here, sir," the student said softly, turning red.

"And what did you do with him, then? Just toss him out on his ear? *'The prophets?'* Which prophets?" The teacher was smiling now, but the student was still troubled.

"I—I don't . . . "

"Of course you don't! It isn't there, is it? That's because, as we have seen, the quotations are not from Isaiah only. So, therefore, the *King James,* although the reference is nonspecific, would be technically more correct than the *New American Standard,* right?" A.D. was still smiling, his long arms outstretched in the fashion of an exasperated, guilty child. He paused and looked out over the classroom, then sat down on the desk again, shoulders slumped. "Are you buying this?"

Gigi could not tell exactly what he was trying to do. She knew he preferred the newer translations. Was he now touting the superiority of the *King James?*

"Think, people. Think!" he charged. "Any novice with a parallel translation will see Isaiah disappear. He may ask you about it. The whole doctrine of inerrancy may rest upon your answer, as well as the petitioner's fragile new faith. What are you going to say to him? Think! If the *King James* is older by some 350 years than the *New American Standard,* why is it correct and the newer translation is not?" He leaned forward and frowned. It was clear that no one had an answer.

"What would you say, Miss Vaughn?" The question startled Gigi. Her smile faded to instant embarrassment as heads turned on swivels toward her.

"Uh, scribal error, maybe?" she said, grasping at the first idea that came to mind.

Q

Dr. Dunbarton clung to his frown. "Scribal *error*. Hmmm. That will probably get you in trouble with the deacons."

Gigi sat back, relieved that it wasn't a terribly painful rebuke, secretly pleased that he assumed that she might actually have some deacons to deal with someday.

"But not far from the mark—no pun intended," he continued. "The recent translation is based on older Greek texts which have been more recently discovered, long after the *King James* was translated in 1611. The *New American Standard* may be incorrect, but it is closer to what Mark may have actually written. Some scribe in antiquity, while copying the manuscript, noticed the error, removed the only partially proper reference to Isaiah and made 'prophet' plural, thus correcting the intent of the verse. He was not—in his mind, at least—correcting Mark but some earlier, lazy scribe before him who copied it incorrectly. He believed he was making things right by making them clearer. He loved the Word too much to let this kind of inaccuracy get by him. He was a good scribe."

A.D. stood and placed his hands in his pockets. "Not bad, Miss Vaughn. But you're still in trouble with the deacons." Several students laughed at this attempt at humor, while others glared at Gigi, the ones who saw her as a "teacher's pet."

The bell rang precisely at this climactic moment, as it often does when sacred truths are imparted, as if to hammer them home for good. Gigi casually approached her professor as the others filed out on their way to the chapel or to an early lunch.

"That was a dirty trick," she said wryly.

"You got lucky," he counseled. "But I'm serious about what I said. Never—and I mean *never*—use the word 'error' in relation to the Scripture when you're talking with a layman."

"You act like they're totally ignorant. You can't be right," she argued.

"Listen, Gigi. We have over five thousand papyri manuscripts dating from A.D. 125 to A.D. 200. There are lots of little differences in them, but they bear a striking similarity to one another. That's enough to convince me but not the average layman. He wants everything to line up perfectly. And whether you'll admit it or not, you know why." He paused, not really expecting she would answer, but she did.

"Because they love their little Christian world where everything is clean and nice and black and white. They're not prepared for any challenges to it. As long as they can maintain their fantasy, they can keep on enjoying it." Her words were pushed forth by her passion. "Their faith isn't tested. It's not real. It's culture-driven. It's comfortable. Any challenge to the tradition threatens to burst the bubble. That's why they crucify people."

Ashley Dunbarton was rather shocked to hear the words put forth so powerfully. Even he rarely let his mind entertain such notions. But here was this diminutive young woman with the bright, beautiful eyes insisting that it was so. She spoke with no hesitation, no fear of reprisal. There was a term to describe it . . .

Ah, yes. Prophetic.

Truett Auditorium was not particularly full for such a well-known speaker. Bobby T. Raeburn of Restoration Fellowship was down in front a few minutes before the service was to begin, nodding and chatting up a few members of the faculty who were doing their best to be gracious. Raeburn was in his early forties with a distinguished look to his tanned and rugged features; he wore an expensive camel jacket over black boot-cut jeans, and a

crisp white shirt with a banded collar. His boots were richly tex-
tured in red leather. He was one of a kind.

As Dr. Dunbarton came loping down the aisle past her seat, Gigi
regretted her pointed words. They had surprised even her; apparently she had subconsciously deep convictions on the subject. But
she had to be careful to whom she expressed them. It was easy to
be branded these days.

The opening hymn was old and bold; Bobby Raeburn looked up
at the worship leader with the open hymnal lying unread in his
hands. He made it obvious that he did not need to look at the
words to sing this song.

The introduction was brief, since everyone knew his story. Young
Bobby was a carpenter by trade who grew up in a singing family,
performing solos in church by the age of five. He had built houses
during the week and provided special music in country churches
on the weekends when one day he felt led to speak in the midst of
a concert. Several people made commitments to God, coming
forward to express repentance even while he was speaking. That
afternoon, the church, which lacked a preacher to serve its eighty
members, asked him to be pastor, and Restoration Fellowship was
born. Raeburn eventually became known for his homespun style,
his straight talk from the pulpit, and his carpenter's parables,
which many said evoked the very spirit of Jesus' teaching. He was
truly charismatic—in the best sense of the word—and his church
grew wildly as the population swelled around it. In nearly twenty
years, the country congregation had become the biggest religious
show in Cowtown.

Raeburn was in the middle of a book tour. *This Old Church: A
Blueprint for Remodeling the House of God* was already a big seller, and
today's chapel message seemed little more than another shameless

promotion of the thin, large-print volume. Gigi cringed as Raeburn pointed and shook and waved his arms like a windmill. Preachers often exaggerated their gestures in a gigantic sanctuary; but the seminary chapel, large as it was, seemed way too intimate for this.

"When you go house hunting," he bellowed in a high-pitched drawl, "what're you hunting for? I'll tell you what. You want a house with four things. These four things are very important. You gotta have these four. Not just two or three. You need all four." Raeburn strutted around behind the pulpit like one of those wacky cat toys on rotating wheels that change direction only after they hit something. Arthur Doer, a professor of homiletics, was visibly agitated during the introduction, as if the speaker had dragged his fingernails against a blackboard.

"First, it has to be *inviting*. You want to walk in and just go, 'Whoa!'" The whoop would have triggered a reaction back at Restoration. Here, the congregation sat unmoved. "Look at your church. How do you *feel* about it? Is it inviting? Will people want to come visit? Is it warm? Down at Restoration, we say the church can't get on fire until it gets warm—do you hear me?" Gigi rolled her big eyes. *How can we not hear you—you're screaming,* thought Gigi.

The homiletical style that was so effective at Restoration virtually bombed in the seminary chapel. In a stunning display of indifference to the weighty point that Raeburn was making, A.D. was on the front row, thumbing through the pages of his Greek New Testament, apparently preparing for his next lecture.

"Now, just because a house is warm and inviting doesn't mean it's strong," the preacher continued. "What's holding it up? Good, solid studs, that's what—eighteen inches on center."

Gigi momentarily pictured a row of hunks in tank tops and swim trunks kneeling around the pulpit in prayer.

Q

"And what is it that's holdin' the church up? Is it the programs? Is it the money we give? Is it our works?"

Why didn't I just go to the library? thought Gigi.

"No! It's God and only God—he's the great big stud of the church!"

This point, which also would have elicited howls at Restoration, was certainly valid, and Gigi thought she noticed a few of the professors actually show some interest. Or perhaps it was shock. Even so, the faculty was generally quite spiritual and appreciated the truth in whatever manner it might be presented. But this was short-lived.

"The strength of the Church is God, and so his people must be strong for him," Raeburn exhorted. "We don't question him. We don't try to figure him out like he's some mystery. We take the Word at face value and obey it." The professors were still squinting up at the preacher, unsure if they should applaud this or take offense at it. "Strength doesn't come from speculation," he said. "Strength comes from certainty."

Gigi pulled out her pad and scribbled this down quickly, hoping no one saw her do it.

"You also got to have a house that's weatherproof. When I was a boy, we had one with a leaky roof. Whenever it rained . . . " (this illustration was long, tediously related, and hardly believable, especially the part about using the bucket to continually collect drinking water for the family dog). "What I mean is, you got to keep the outside—outside! And the inside stays warm and dry. See, we don't want what we call 'culture' to get in and weaken the timbers. Intellectualism, materialism, political correctness, all this gender equality and gay pride and worldliness—it's all just bad weather! Preacher, keep it out of your house!"

Gigi figured this chapter must have been written by a ghost writer and Raeburn was struggling to call the lofty words to mind.

"Like that attempted robbery by some unknown thief we read about in the paper this morning," he continued. At the word "thief," Gigi was suddenly alert. She turned to the seat behind her where another bored student happened to be covertly reading the *Stockyard Dispatch*. He flipped it around to show her the small headline: *Suspect Sought in Dispatch Break-In*.

"Some burglar broke into the newspaper offices. Now, what was he trying to steal? The news?" Gigi turned again to face the front. Her brain clouded for a moment. Raeburn was waiting for a laugh and in fact laughed himself. "Why, you can't steal the news! And you know what? You can't steal the truth of God either! All that stuff from the world can break into the house, but the truth can't be taken. Now, they can take some offering plates or bust out a stained-glass window . . . "

The analogy was being stretched even beyond its original limited scope, but Gigi was hearing little of it. She was thinking again of the alley and the young Englishman with the injured arm.

The fourth point (and it was once more emphasized that you need all four) had something to do with the responsible home-owner adding value to the neighborhood by keeping the house in good condition. This somehow became a justification for the ROC, which had, according to Raeburn, elevated the living conditions of the surrounding area by helping its needy citizens, when actually it had simply imported them. Ordinarily, Gigi would have been upset at this, but she was preoccupied.

Too preoccupied, in fact, to notice the young man with the bristly haircut in the denim jacket, favoring one arm, sitting behind her and to the left, not more than twenty seats away.

Q

Later that afternoon, in the quiet space of a library reading chair when the majority of students had gone, Gigi's mind strayed from her textbook to the incomprehensible world of modern religion. Here, ensconced in a fabulously endowed institution for the study of God, sat one of the brightest students that would never have the chance to do what Bobby T. Raeburn had done that morning. She shut the book on her thumb, knowing that she was too far removed from its subject to revisit the pages anyway but wanting to leave the option open. Options—that's what her advisor had offered her in the first year—for a career in ministry, opportunities that satisfied most of the women who enrolled here. But none appealed to Gigi; she wanted to preach.

She tossed the book thoughtlessly on the floor. She closed her eyes and smiled at the mental picture of Raeburn flailing wildly in the chapel service, inaudible. Turning the sound off was easy in her mind, but it was far more difficult to separate the caricature of the man from the reality he represented. He was untrained, uninhibited, standing up there in his red boots with a message he could preach but could not explain, performing in the pattern of his boyhood idols. And despite this he had been extended the hand of fellowship by the seminary because of his big church and his book and his radio show and his outreach center and because every other school was doing it, jumping on Bobby's bandwagon. While Gigi Vaughn—she of the perceptive mind and true servant's heart— was forced to tolerate it like the rest of them, because people were coming to Bobby T's church in big numbers; and that meant God must be with him, that he must know something they didn't know, that he must be doing something right.

Gigi left the library burning with resentment that such a thing could be tolerated here, where everyone knew better. In reality she realized the injustice she felt was not for this at all but for the barriers to the fulfillment of her own calling established by this same religious community. It was all in the way you looked at Scripture, they said. But what about Bobby T. Raeburn's weekly dismemberment of homiletic principles?

As she walked across campus to her car, Gigi's heart softened. She loved it here. The wide lawn shaded with trees calmed her spirit. The pleasant sounds of the birds that flocked to the hill in the late afternoons reminded her of God's providential care. Surely he still had the world in the palm of his hand. The thought humbled her. Perhaps her righteous anger was really something else—a sinful desire for the attention, the unqualified acceptance, the glory that Bobby T. Raeburn enjoyed. Perhaps she was not so different from him after all.

Gigi spent the rest of the afternoon studying for an upcoming exam. She missed supper and the sunset, hiding in the library. As she drove back to her apartment, the stars had become visible. She thought of stopping to pick up a half-gallon of Blue Bell Caramel Turtle Fudge ice cream, but her body ached from the long day, and it didn't seem worth the effort. She envisioned a bath, a bag of chips and a root beer, and falling asleep with Grantham's *Systematic Theology.*

The apartments were brightly illuminated and showed the evidence of activity within: desk lamps shining through windows where students labored over keyboards; colorful shadows dancing on the walls from TV sets; music playing, the melodies diffused by the walls, leaving audible only the steady beats; girls with cell phones chatting on balconies.

Gigi entered her apartment and tossed her keys onto the adjacent table, kicked off her loafers, and dropped her heavy book bag, immediately heading for the bedroom, flipping on the hall light as

Q

she went. Her Los Angeles Raiders jersey was still in a heap on the bathroom floor where she had left it that morning. She undressed rapidly and threw it on. It hung down to just above her knees and made for a comfy nightshirt.

Junk food on the brain, she walked briskly toward the kitchen, stopping to heft Grantham's weighty tome from her book bag. Cradling it between her knees, she snatched the bag of stale tortilla chips from the cupboard and held it in her teeth while rustling through the refrigerator for a bottled drink, the cold air from the open door chilling her bare legs and feet. Thus prepared, she let the door swing shut and walked out into the still-darkened den.

The lamp from the end table clicked on. A pale, grubby Englishman pulled back his hand and smiled.

Gigi would have likely screamed if not for the bag in her mouth, but she instinctively chucked Grantham in the intruder's general direction. He deflected it easily and set it respectfully on the table.

"What are you . . . I can't believe you . . . " Gigi subconsciously rubbed her knees together. "You can't just . . . how did you get in here?"

"Picked the lock," he said calmly. "Look, I need your help . . . "

"You didn't need it this morning." She was indignant. "You could have waited at the shelter for me to come back; I was there all night."

He nodded. "Of course. But you see, that's not the kind of help I need."

The mystery of it all was tantalizing. "Fine," she said. "But I want to know how you found out where I live." Her eyes glowed with intensity.

"Good guess," he said with a wave of his hand.

"Right, of all the places in town, you just happened . . . " She was rocking on her toes awkwardly, embarrassed and unsure of herself.

"No, no, no. The car. I guessed it was yours. You know, you really should lock your doors. And your glove compartment. Oh, and your back seat needs a good cleaning."

Gigi turned her head, disbelieving. "You were in my car when I . . . "

"And in the chapel meeting," he quipped. "That Rector, he's quite a tart, yes?"

She looked straight at him, still in shock. "But you . . . "

"Well, of course I didn't want to trouble you for a ride back, but I managed to get one. Thank you, by the way, for the map. It was most helpful."

"The map?"

"In the glove compartment. Along with your registration, insurance card, blue book from last semester's ethics exam . . . " He paused. "Shoddy work on that, hmm?" He looked smug.

"I was going to protest that grade . . . " Gigi shook her head as if to clear it of the conversation. "OK. I'm talking to a criminal, a wounded one . . . "

"It's quite better, actually. Just a nick, I told you," he interrupted.

"Who broke into my apartment . . . "

"Well, yes, but it's quite vital that I . . . "

"To discuss my grade in ethics?"

They both fell silent. A smile curled around the corner of Gigi's mouth, giving him permission to do the same. "Now, I'm going to put some clothes on, and when I come back, you're going to tell me the whole story, beginning with your name."

Q

"It's Jeremy," he said pleasantly. "Jeremy Croft. On his majesty's secret service, if you please." He stood and bowed elegantly.

"I thought England only had a queen at the moment," she said as she backed out of the room.

Jeremy folded his arms across his chest and struck a formal pose. "That's not the sovereign I was speaking of," he muttered to himself.

The sun had slipped below the horizon, but the ocean still glowed with its light. Carter Rutledge never tired of looking at the sea. In the late afternoon, he would often work at the home his family had owned in Charleston for three generations, watching the receding tide from his veranda while mulling over his notes. He counted the waves as they swelled, plunged forward into froth, and receded, inspired by their gentle cadence—a comforting reminder of God's presence in a constantly changing world.

Carter Rutledge knew about change. He had lived the last six years of his life alone, having lost his wife, Henrietta, to cancer shortly after their youngest child married. They were looking forward to getting to know each other once again after raising their four children. Carter had even hired a new assistant pastor at Seventh Baptist to allow him more free time to spend with Henrietta on their veranda, enjoying the view together. A familiar pang of loneliness distracted him from his notes. He considered calling his friend Mildred Dunbarton, just to talk. Instead, he contented himself to stay and watch the water.

Henrietta once observed that the waves seemed to come in sevens, with the seventh the strongest, the most violent in its break. He fixed his gaze on the glimmering sea, thinking. Suddenly he was troubled, sensing a warning of some kind that he could not put into words. This was the seventh year since his life was redirected; was he about to endure another, unexpected misfortune? Looking out over the expanse of ocean and sky, he slowly dismissed the fear of impending personal disaster, but the apprehension remained. *Something* was about to happen, he felt sure of it—something of far greater consequence than his list of personal concerns—approaching with a strength and violence he had not seen before.

God is the catalyst for such things, Carter knew. And when he acts, there is nothing one can do to stop the wave from breaking.

1.2

JEREMY TURNED OUT TO BE QUITE CHARMING FOR A BURGLAR. A PICK-pocket from childhood, he had gained a reputation for himself in the more fashionable suburbs of London, where he learned the art of breaking and entering. A series of robberies performed too closely together landed him in jail; he was caught in the street with goods in hand, the victim of a stakeout by a local constable. In prison he had been taken in by a group of Christian inmates and regularly engaged in Bible study with them, which was more appealing than his other options for entertainment behind bars. He found he enjoyed debating against the idea of God with the Christians. Then, when two more skeptics joined their study, Jeremy found himself arguing *for* God. To his great surprise, he soon found himself believing what he was saying. His faith grew, even if his personal life did not. Upon his release he floundered for a while, taking a job as a driver for a well-known art and antiqui-ties dealer, which proved too great a temptation. He was caught moving some of the merchandise in the middle of the night and was sent back to prison, this time for what appeared to be a lengthy stay.

Gigi found his story somewhat tragic. She listened sympatheti-cally to his tale through the first bag of Doritos and into a second, touched by his sensitive retelling of the facts studded with peculiar phrases. Fascinated, she seemed in no hurry to bring the story into the present circumstances; it was Jeremy who came eventually to the heart of the matter without having to be asked.

"Mr. Ravenswood, my former employer, came to visit me one day," he recalled, sitting cross-legged on the floor across from Gigi, passing back the bag of chips. "He said he could arrange for my walking papers if I would agree to do a job for him across the pond. It was odd coming from a respectable man like him, and I must say I was tempted. But I had determined this time to live right, by the book—the Holy Bible, you know—and I wasn't interested. So I'm in my cell a few days later, and the guard comes up and says, 'You're free'—just like that. Well, there's Mr. Ravenswood waiting for me outside the wall."

"Still begging you to steal for him?" said Gigi through a mouthful of chips.

"Ah, that's just it. He wanted me to do the job all right. Even more so now, after I had refused him the first time."

She stopped crunching and swallowed. "That doesn't make sense."

"Hang on," he urged. "See, this is no ordinary job. He told me of this ancient document he was trying to acquire. Very mysterious, this bit of what he told me. He said some call it a lost book of the Bible. But it's not that, he said. It can't be that."

Gigi was transfixed. "So, he thought it must be very valuable," she observed.

"You know, that's what I thought," he answered. "Quite wrong about that, I was. I'm sure I won't get this right, but I'll try." He drew in a quick breath and released it. "It's not that he wanted this item for his collection. He wanted it, it turns out, to keep others from knowing it exists."

"That's weird," said Gigi, after a moment.

"Quite."

Q

"So, did you get the details? I mean, just what is this missing book?" she asked.

He stretched his legs out and leaned back against the sofa. "I don't know, exactly. There was, it appears, a group of scholars called the Society of Saint Matthew, who went looking for this document, found it, and hid it. They felt that the world was not ready for it. A wealthy man of a very old family, a Benton Cole, who, with or without someone's help, passed away recently, kept it in secret for decades. Naturally, steps were immediately taken to recover the document and deposit it in a secure location, but, rather shockingly, it has turned up missing. Ellis Cole, heir to his father's estate, says he has no idea of this book. But the Society thinks otherwise."

"They think he has it and won't give it up?" she queried.

"On the contrary," Jeremy corrected, "they think he sold it. It is clear that he has no real interest in spiritual matters."

"And this Mr. Ravenswood . . . "

"A most interesting gentleman. He has a theory concerning the whereabouts of the document. He sent me to fetch it." He placed his hand to his chest proudly as he said this. "Devoted Christian thief that I am."

"And he thinks it's here . . . in Fort Worth?" she asked, incredulously.

"Yes, and I think he's right. I went after it last night as instructed. Not a clue as to what I'm doing, of course. But someone's on to me. Of that I am certain."

They sat for a time, pondering the matter. It was Gigi who spoke first, as if suddenly remembering something. "What happens now?"

"That," he said emphatically, "is what I was hoping you would tell me." He flashed a devilish smile that hid an unquestionably devious plan.

Gigi left the next morning with Jeremy, who spent an uncomfortable and nearly sleepless night curled up in Gigi's car. They drove north toward the heart of the city to the Kitchen, where Jeremy's introduction to the art of preparing breakfast for the homeless was about to begin.

The plan was that Jeremy would stay at the Kitchen and help Tinky in whatever way he could, while Gigi considered how she would approach the matter at hand. When he told her who the man was that the Society of Saint Matthew suspected of having the document, she concocted many imagined schemes—none of them particularly reasonable—to prove the theory. Once she had performed this vital task, she reasoned, Jeremy could ply his particular craft, for the betterment of all mankind, or so it seemed. The whole thing was farcical—but intriguing all the same.

Jeremy laughed and joked with the men in his peculiar foreign manner, which helped them to deal with the tragedy of the previous evening. Emilio, who was never seen without his shoebox stuffed with letters addressed to him, had left unnoticed in the middle of the night. He was not well known to the group, having come to them so recently. It was said that on those nights when he failed to show up, he was either intoxicated or seeking to enter such a state; perhaps this is why he had ventured forth undetected, since alcohol was not allowed anywhere on the property. This last foray was to be his last. His body was found by one of the men early that morning in a bus stop, dead from what seemed to be natural causes.

The men were saddened, though not profoundly affected by the loss of their fellow stranger, for such things were commonplace in their world. But for Gigi, a deep regret settled in her spirit, and she wept at the thought of poor Emilio's last hours.

Q

She was still somewhat weepy when the last bag of garbage was removed to the alley bins and she headed off to class. Tinky was delighted with her new helper and was reviewing a list of projects for Jeremy as Gigi walked out. She could hear him inside laughing at the first item on his list: new locks.

A.D. was not particularly inspiring on this morning, perhaps the victim of spring fever like everyone else. Gigi, too, was preoccupied with Jeremy and Emilio and the mysterious lost book. Could it be that such a thing was actually true? And how might she find out? There was a way, as Jeremy urged—simply apply for a job and ask questions—but it was a long shot. Somehow, she would have to get deep into the heart of the empire and close to its sinister emperor.

She was dressed in blue jeans and a white, tight-fitting sleeveless shirt, and drew more than her normal share of glances from the male students. There was only one other girl in the room, a thin, sickly-looking redhead named Mary who rarely uttered a peep. Sitting together, they were an odd pair, elected to such pairing by default, as in a few other classes. Mary was at the seminary because of her interest in religion and lack of other opportunities; she did not share Gigi's desire to pastor a church, but each of them offered mutual encouragement to the other.

"It is clear to most conservative scholars that Mark was the first Gospel written for a variety of reasons," Dr. Dunbarton droned on. "For one, it is the shortest of the three synoptics. Matthew and Luke are significantly longer. This suggests that . . . ,"—he changed his tone and craned his neck, peering into the heart of the class— "What *does* it suggest, hmm?"

He was looking at a husky student who, after a moment, gave an answer, though he had not been asked. "That the others copied him?" he tried.

A.D. grinned. "So you've been told. Now give me one good reason why."

Gigi raised her hand. "Because if Mark had access to the other two, he wouldn't have left so much out," she said.

"I suppose not," agreed the professor. "But who is to say that Mark didn't *purposefully* leave out certain things, devising a short work full of action, lacking long narratives, to better impact his Roman readers?"

There was quiet in the room after this. The teacher's eyes twinkled, and he lunged rather awkwardly for the chalk. He drew three vertical lines on the board, the one in the center longer than the others.

"Let's say Matthew was written first and Mark used him as a source. Now, when you go to the actual passages in both Gospels, you would naturally expect to find Mark's account shorter than Matthew's. I mean to say, you certainly wouldn't expect Mark to have added anything to it, right? Especially since he would be preparing a condensed version of Matthew's work." His eyes darted back and forth as he read the students' faces. "But that," he said emphatically, "is not what we find.

"Assume each one of these lines represents the length of a passage as it is found in Matthew, Mark, and Luke. What we find is that, despite his gospel's overall brevity, the accounts of the same stories in Mark are actually *longer* than in Matthew and Luke. And, since almost every verse of Mark appears in the other two, the conclusion is that . . . well, what are we to conclude?" He was petitioning the student with whom the discussion began.

"That Mark must have been written first and was known to the others, who edited his work for their own purposes," he said proudly.

Q

"Right," affirmed Dunbarton. "But we can't just leave it there and say, 'Oh, well, that's it, then.' We have to look deeper into the texts themselves for more clues." He glanced at the clock. "Next time."

The class deflated from its attention and gathered itself for the march out of Scarborough. Gigi wandered up to the front, as she almost always did.

"I'm curious about something, sir," she said. The respectful address and innocent look on her face struck the teacher as odd, but he remained composed. "Where did all the stuff in Matthew and Luke come from that they didn't get from Mark?"

He sat on the corner of the desk. Mary had crept up behind Gigi as if she were afraid they might be separated, spoiling the intimacy of the conversation somewhat for A.D. "You're referring to what is called the Q material, but that's practically half the course on textual criticism. I'll teach one of the sections next semester, if you're interested." Gigi frowned. He realized that she wanted an answer now, so he continued.

"OK, well, Matthew was a disciple of Jesus, remember. He would have had first-hand information. And Luke used other sources—he basically admits to that in the first four verses of his Gospel. And then there was the oral tradition. That's it in a nutshell."

"I see." She pondered this for a moment. "What are the other sources that Luke used?"

The teacher frowned. "Look. You need to take the class on textual criticism. Let's head to chapel. The dean will be taking names." He gathered up his lecture notes, returned them to their place in a three-ring binder, and stowed that in a worn leather briefcase.

"Wait a minute. You can't just leave it hanging like that until sometime next semester," said Gigi rather forcefully. Mary had stepped up and stood looking over Gigi's shoulder. "I would—we would," she insisted, acknowledging her shadow, "like to know about these sources."

She had not moved, though Dunbarton was nearly to the door. "What is it about this that seems to be so important?" he quizzed, sincerely curious.

Gigi relaxed a bit. Her shoulder twitched, as if to shake off Mary's clinging presence. "This is going to sound stupid," she admitted. "I met this person who thinks a lost book of the Bible has been discovered, and . . . "

The professor's snickering made her stop. Even Mary made a few gurgly, mirthful noises. "OK, I know," she said, resignedly. "It's nuts. Forget I mentioned it." She tugged on her book bag and started for the exit quickly.

"No, wait, I don't mean to make sport of you, really," he assured as she waltzed by him. He sighed. "Let's go to my office."

She turned and flashed a mischievous look that suggested she had been expecting the invitation all along.

Jeremy lingered in the food preparation area, talking to Tinky about crullers, tarts, and other English pastries that he thought might go over well, enjoying her interest, knowing it was directed toward him more than the subject of his banter. Americans were delightfully curious about the English, and he was enjoying the minor celebrity status. It was certainly better than scrubbing floors, fixing toilets, and changing locks.

When Tinky returned to her preparations for the next meal, Jeremy strolled down the hallway, its flaking yellow painted walls reviving a childhood memory of a shabby London hospital. There was a tiny closet with handmade wooden shelving, which housed various tools, hardware, and fixtures. In the center of the closet was a bucket and mop, covering a drain in the cement floor.

Jeremy kicked the bucket aside and wedged himself inside to poke around. The new deadbolt locks had been purchased some months ago as part of a fund drive by some local churches but, like many of the items, had been resting in the closet since then, with no one to perform the actual labor. He carried one of them to the front door with the tools for the installation.

There was a keyed lock on the doorknob that had been the only security afforded by the front door for about six months when another key had broken off inside the old deadbolt just above it. Jeremy carefully removed it with a screwdriver and tossed it aside. The new one fit perfectly.

The sun was warming nicely as Jeremy worked. A pleasant breeze blew against his neck. He opened the heavy door wide against the inner wall and removed the old strike plate in the door frame to install the new one. Instinctively he lifted his head toward a sound, not really audible but sensed—a warning sound, not uncommon but unfriendly.

He turned. There were voices around the corner—soft, not street voices, not volunteers. Questioning. Subdued speech; there was no need for it out here in the bright midmorning. Jeremy gripped the screwdriver tightly and waited.

There was a shadow approaching. Stopped now. Angular, broad shouldered. Hesitant.

Jeremy's options were few. To slip inside would put Tinky in unnecessary danger. To run would invite pursuit, or worse. He chose to hide and wait.

Another shadow encroached, and they both moved forward. Jeremy backed into the room, looking for an opening to run but not wanting to give away his position just yet. Two men appeared. One was wearing a blue suit and looked more like an executive than an assassin, and in fact he might have been. His companion was similarly dressed, though less polished in appearance. They were startled to see Jeremy in front of them in the doorway, with one hand behind his back.

No one spoke. The first man paused, then raised his hand as if he thought he could just snatch Jeremy by the collar like a misbehaving child. Jeremy stepped further back into the room and crouched. The second man jumped ahead and stumbled over the doorstep. Jeremy ran toward the back of the building.

Tinky was in the pantry, organizing starches. She heard the scuffle and stepped out to see. Jeremy vaulted over the counter and charged toward the back door. Tinky quickly fell back into the pantry, clutching a bag of rice. She saw the two men giving chase into the alley. In a moment, she could hear the sound of her own breathing.

Fearing the men were armed, Jeremy knew the foolishness of running down the alley in either direction. He would make an easy target, and with no possibility of witnesses, there would be no reason for the men to hold their fire. He darted behind the bins.

The first man emerged in the alley followed immediately by the second. They were thinking: *Could he have gotten away so fast? Surely he . . .*

Jeremy pushed over the barrel and leapt at the first man. The screwdriver found its mark deep in the man's thigh. The man screamed and kicked wildly, throwing Jeremy off, against the wall. The other man closed in. Jeremy looked up the alley into the sunshine. It blinded him momentarily, its distant soft light peaceful and inviting, finding him there in the cool alley like the welcoming approach of a dear friend.

"This lost book of the Bible business is hardly taken seriously nowadays, simply because the canon has been closed for so long now," Ashley Dunbarton was saying. He was sitting in an overstuffed red chair with tassels, something old and supposedly historically important, like many of the furnishings and knickknacks in his small office. Every cranny in the wall-length bookcase was crammed with papers and assorted objects. A poster of an aerial view of Charleston, his hometown, graced the cream-colored walls.

Gigi had related only part of the story. She had said nothing of Jeremy Croft and his cross-continental quest for the secret document supposedly owned by one of the most powerful men in the Southwest. She said only that she had heard about the Society of Saint Matthew and their discovery of a biblical document. At the mention of the Society, Dunbarton's eyes narrowed. His next statement came out with an edginess in his voice that had not been there before now.

"Let's say this Society does exist—some group of scholars or archivists, possibly dealers in ancient books—and they have this scroll or something. Why don't they produce it?" he speculated.

"Well," Gigi began cautiously, "what my friend said is that it was kind of controversial."

"Oh. Then all the more reason to produce it. There have been many extrabiblical manuscripts that have been quite informative to our understanding of . . . "

"No," Gigi interrupted. "I mean, they think this really could carry the authority of a New Testament book." Mary was sitting next to Gigi, her head cocked to read the spines on the volumes in the bookcase.

"Wait a minute, Gigi," Dunbarton said. "That's not for some obscure 'Society' to decide. The canon was closed in the fourth century. The New Testament, I mean. At the Third Council of Carthage. All twenty-seven books."

"But I don't see how you can just say something is or isn't authentic without even seeing it," she protested.

"You are going down a wrong path," he counseled. "Authenticity is not the question. Canonicity was determined after centuries of debate. Some books were accepted quickly. Others came slowly but had broad followings. Still others were used as authoritative in select places but not everywhere. It was a complicated issue."

"But how can we just say nothing new could be discovered in the last sixteen centuries?" Gigi asked. "That sounds like some kind of cover-up to me."

"Yes, I guess it does. But honestly, in all these centuries, nothing has been found that meets the requirements for canonicity," he said.

"And what are those?" intoned Mary, surprising them both by actually using her voice.

"There were several—*are* several. The books had to have enjoyed a wide acceptance, and their teachings would have been consistent with the faith as it was universally established. This is the problem with opening the canon. Some churches in the second century and later were using texts that were instructive but had certain elements that made other churches hesitate to embrace them. Some

Q

of these are well-known today, like the Shepherd of Hermas, the Gospel of Peter, the Didache . . . "

"So they got left out," concluded Gigi.

"Right. By the fourth century, the Church fathers were fairly familiar with all the books in common use, so the odds of finding something new today that would have been unknown to them are infinitesimally small. Even if we did come upon something, it would simply fall into that large category of early documents that round out our understanding of the time. It could not seriously be considered scriptural unless . . . " His voice trailed off.

Gigi moved up to the edge of her seat. Her wide eyes begged an answer.

"Well, unless it were proven to be apostolic," Dunbarton added.

"You mean written by an apostle." Gigi assumed.

"Preferably. For instance, in Second Corinthians, Paul refers to what we have come to call the 'severe letter' which most scholars believe cannot be First Corinthians. In fact, in chapter five of what we call First Corinthians, Paul directly appeals to a previous letter he had written to them about associating with immoral people. This can't be referring to the so-called Severe Letter. The Severe Letter was connected to a visit that took place in between the writing of the two letters we have. No such visit is alluded to in First Corinthians." He paused, waiting to see if they were following this. It had come to sound something like a lecture, and he was aware of the intense natural inclination for his students' minds to completely shut down when thus confronted.

"So you're saying that Paul may have written a letter before First Corinthians . . . ," Gigi said. "And then after First Corinthians there was a visit, which prompted this 'severe letter' thing. And then he wrote Second Corinthians?" She cocked her head to the side in a rare Asian gesture.

"Which implies four letters, not two," he summarized. "Now, granted, there are those who break Second Corinthians into two distinct letters, so this 'severe letter' would have actually been incorporated therein originally, but this is unlikely. I think there were probably four."

There was a prickly silence for a moment. "OK, Dr. Dunbarton. So how can you say that the canon is closed? If we found one of these letters, wouldn't it have to be considered?" Gigi demanded, hopeful.

The teacher leaned back, relaxed, totally in his element. "You've got two schools of thought here. One says that there are things in the Bible that don't come over with a great deal of authority, things we don't fully understand or that we disagree upon as to their interpretation. They believe other documents would, if discovered and included, clarify these issues. The other bunch says no, the early church knew what was needed, and that's it. Just because an apostle wrote something, that doesn't mean it has to be in the Bible."

"Like if we found Paul's grocery list or something?" Gigi said, laughing.

"Yes, that's a good example," he chuckled. Back to the lecture. "They may have known about these other letters and decided, despite their authorship, that they really didn't need to be preserved. We should trust their judgment under the providence of God."

"That's what the scholars say," Gigi commented.

"The conservative ones, yes," he said. "That's us."

"But," she went on, "if we did happen to find something that claimed to be apostolic, and let's say it contradicted something in the Bible . . . "

Q

"Hold on there, Miss Vaughn," he cautioned. "There are already plenty of those—on the *surface* of the literature. That's why proper exegetical methods are used. That's why we have seminaries . . . "

"So it probably wouldn't amount to much, you're saying."

"Probably not. I mean, we've discovered all kinds of things even in this century, at Nag Hamadi and Qumran, for instance, which people are saying cast doubts on traditional Christianity. But it hasn't made much of an impact, not a dent, really. It would take something really incredible to shake things up significantly."

"Like a big, fat letter from Paul," Gigi said, "that commands all women everywhere to preach the Gospel." He thought he saw her wink at him as she said this.

"Well, don't hold your breath," he said. "But yes, a big, fat letter from Paul would cause a stir, if such a thing still exists, which I seriously doubt. Or something else, possibly . . . "

"Something else?" Mary questioned, again startling them both.

"Yes. Something very early," he speculated. "Something close to Jesus himself."

The two women looked at him. He stared, thinking, at his poster of Charleston with its celebrated historic steeples, musing about how, when placed under careful examination, the relics of our past fail to justify our respect for them. But we continue to venerate them, all the same.

Professor Grantham was handing out weighty theological postulates the way a kindly grandmother might offer you some snickerdoodle cookies, so lovingly and yet so persuasively that his students could do naught but swallow them whole and yearn for still more until the session was ended. Dr. Grantham's rapid-fire lecture style earned him his nickname and a healthy respect. His Systematic Theology class frightened away all but the most serious of students, and any others who ended up there were often either unaware of what awaited them or were left without other options to fill the degree requirement. But the more serious among them soon learned that they were sitting under one of the finest Baptist scholars of the century.

Gigi had for some minutes stopped taking notes, having had great difficulty keeping up with the profound thoughts that were invading her mind, choosing instead to simply listen and ponder what was being said. She was thus engaged when she noticed the secretary motioning at the door.

"Me?" she mouthed silently. The secretary nodded in the affirmative and smiled at Dr. Grantham as Gigi gathered her books and prepared to leave.

"Good session today?" the lady whispered as they exited, leaving the anxious Gigi with the distinct impression that she was trying not to alarm her.

"Humpty Dumpty," quipped Gigi, wanting to get to the reason why she had been called from class.

The woman looked blankly at her. "Dr. Grantham's analogy of the Augustinian pattern of Adam's fall," Gigi explained. She stopped walking and faced the secretary. "What's this about?"

The older woman's forehead wrinkled with concern. "We've had a call from a Tinky Weatherby at a place called . . . "

"The Kitchen?" Gigi felt her heart pulsating suddenly. "What happened?" She put a small hand to her dry throat.

Q

"Well, we're not sure. Some men apparently broke in. She said to tell you they were after your friend Jeremy. She wants you to . . . "

But before she could finish, Gigi was already running out of the quiet building, the heavy door swinging in her wake as she burst into the sunshine. The woman watched as it closed softly, once again sealing off the safety of theological study from the danger of the world outside.

Traffic seemed unusually heavy for midafternoon as Gigi gunned the Nova's rebuilt engine in short bursts, weaving back and forth along the four lane to pick up time where possible. More than ever before, the story seemed implausible: a British crook in Fort Worth to steal an ancient manuscript to preserve Christianity—and the crook knows nothing, really, about it. A gray Buick kept pace with the Nova as she shook her head in disbelief for no one to see.

Why had she been so quick to believe this? Surely Jeremy had taken advantage of her, a handy cover for whatever illegalities in which he may have been engaged. It seemed to have caught up with him at last, and Gigi silently chided herself for allowing him to get so close, possibly endangering herself and, more importantly, those who frequented the Kitchen. And yet, somewhere in the back of her mind, there remained a slight hope that the preposterous story were true.

Berry Street was fairly wide open, and Gigi took full advantage, roaring ahead at a speed well above the limit, careening through the yellow light onto Hemphill around the majestic Travis Avenue Baptist Church, where she had attended during her first year in town. Behind her, the gray Buick ran the light, nearly colliding with a baker's delivery truck, forcing it to swerve off the road. After this, the Buick slowed down considerably, having determined the Nova's destination by now, which left further risks inadvisable.

Gigi pulled into the small lot next to a patrol car and ran down the alley. Ducking under the yellow tape and yanking open the door, she found Tinky leaning against the counter talking to the officer, who was finishing up a bowl of chowder.

"Oh, sweetie, you got my message!" the big woman exclaimed, as if the sight of Gigi threw her back into the emotional trauma that had marred the earlier part of the day. Her round face grew solemn. "Jeremy's gone."

She said this with temerity, expecting some kind of dramatic reaction no doubt, not knowing the nature of Gigi's relationship to the young man.

"Where?" was the only response.

Tinky looked at the officer, who for the moment had stopped slurping. "I don't know, honey. There were these men—I was in the pantry and couldn't see much, but they chased him through here, and . . . "

"We have reason to believe that the young man was involved in an attempted robbery at the Withers Tower a few nights ago," the policeman said, wiping the corner of his mouth with a napkin. "We believe the suspect is British. According to INS, he arrived in this country less than a week ago. Did some time over in England, small-time stuff, probably in more trouble than we know. I suggest you stay away from these kinds of people, miss."

"When did this happen?" Gigi said, blinking.

"Right after breakfast," Tinky answered. "It happened real fast." She looked down and wrung her hands nervously.

"You don't seem overly concerned about this," Gigi said to the policeman. She was breathing even harder now and sensed the imminent loss of her composure.

Q

"We've been here for over three hours, miss. We can't do anything more. The crime scene people finished up an hour ago."

Gigi was startled. "Crime scene?"

"There were traces of blood out in the alley there."

Gigi looked at Tinky, who it appeared was about to cry. That she feared the worst was evident.

"And what did your crime scene people find out?" Gigi interrogated.

"Inconclusive. Not much blood out there. We haven't tested it yet, could be anyone's. But by the look of things, there's been no murder. They usually leave a body, when they've been crossed by one of these hoods, you know, to send a message. So my guess is he's not dead . . . yet." The policeman had his thumbs tucked in his belt.

"What do you mean, 'crossed?'" Gigi insisted.

He looked at Tinky. "Our witness described two guys in suits running through here after this Mr. Croft. I assure you they weren't detectives, miss." His condescension was offensive.

Gigi walked around them and sat down in one of the plastic chairs. The officer muttered a few words to Tinky and left. She came over to Gigi and sat beside her.

"He said he might want to talk with you again," she said as gently as she could. Gigi nodded. Changing the subject, she offered Gigi some time off. "Why don't you just forget work the rest of the week. We've got Emilio's funeral tomorrow afternoon, and that will be hard enough on you. Get some rest and come back on Sunday. What do you say?"

It was good advice, and Gigi accepted it in the spirit in which it was given. "We'll see," she said, a faint smile appearing. This relieved Tinky, and she petted Gigi's small shoulder, not sure of what to say next. Gigi took a deep breath and closed her eyes. Nothing else needed to be said.

The gray Buick was parked some fifty yards from the entrance to the lot when the white Nova appeared. The two men watched as the girl headed inside, hauling a book bag that seemed to slow her down.

The apartment was as she and Jeremy had left it. She sat down on the sofa and looked around. He had not left any evidence that he had been there; only a glass half filled with root beer and an afghan in a pile on the floor remained. She sat there, very still, for several minutes, looking at every little thing, as if to reclaim some small piece of the mystery, to keep it alive. There was the crumpled remains of the first bag of chips, a stack of magazines that had not been touched for days, the TV covered with a dusty film . . . her eyes scanned the room, inexplicably, for clues to Jeremy's life. This would stay with her, she knew, unresolved, for a very long time.

Her vision became fixed on the table where her computer rested. There were several books toppled over on the shelf above the monitor; someone had rustled through them.

She stood and walked to the table. One of her pens lay there, having been taken from the blue and white Dodgers mug where she kept them. She pulled out the chair and sat down. She clicked on the machine.

The whirs and internal tapping of the computer's brain soon yielded a familiar screen—then the flash of a message. A floppy had been in use and was removed from the computer when it had been shut down. Gigi followed the proper steps and rebooted. There was nothing unusual about the desktop display. She moved the mouse around and opened a few programs. Nothing here that was not her own.

Q

She clicked the button to check her e-mail, enduring the high-pitched dial-up sounds for what seemed an eternity. She immediately looked for sent items but found nothing. She went to the recycle bin and found that it had been emptied. *Interesting.*

Moving quickly to her inbox, she found one unread message. She scrolled the lines as quickly as she could, scarcely believing what she was reading.

My dear Jeremy!

We have been long awaiting your first contact. I have just received it, arriving at the shop this morning. So pleased that you have found a safe haven, but I caution you not to reveal too much of your purpose to your newfound friend. We are about a serious business here, quite fraught with danger, and there are spiritual forces at work as well. You would do well to guard your steps; you are in a foreign country with no support but prayer, which, I might add, has been most fervently offered on your behalf since your leaving England.

Do not be discouraged at the fruitlessness of your initial effort. It is no small task to which you have been called, and formidable is the stronghold you assault. No matter, in time God will prove you victorious in your endeavor. Keep to the faith!

I will forward your report to the other members of the Society. Our scholars are renewing the task at hand, to find the irrefutable evidence we know must exist. Our agents in the Middle East are vigorously pursuing every lead as well. We will uncover something soon, I pray. Do not grow weary, as we shall not, for the twenty-seven years of our labor is but a blink in the eye of our Lord, who waits patiently for all to be revealed. Should you succeed, all will be well. Should we succeed before you, all the more shall we rejoice to terminate your mission and receive you at home!

Given this new association in which you have such confidence, we have arranged for your next envelope to be deposited in Timnah in a few days time. I warn you again not to engage the girl too deeply in this affair, for obvious reasons. God bless and God's speed.

John Ravenswood

Gigi read the message three times, pausing at the unmistakable references to her own involvement in Jeremy's enigmatic assignment. Now that he was missing, she felt almost obliged to take up where he had left off. If his life were endangered, she might want to contact the police and reveal everything. Perhaps he had escaped, slippery character that he was, and would soon reappear. Or perhaps he was dead. If either of these last two options were true, she would have to remain silent, at least for now. If not, she would be violating Jeremy's trust, betraying the Society, and effectively exposing the whole episode for public scrutiny.

It was a bizarre situation, almost too incredible to accept. She wanted to be done with it, to forget it. But there was something powerful here, something far more important, it seemed, than she knew. She decided to bet on Jeremy.

All this time, the pointer had been hovering over the delete icon. Now, as if her hand was guided by some unseen force, she moved the mouse and closed the file.

1.3

A GREEN TENT STOOD OUT AGAINST THE BROWN GRASS OF THE LAWN. Gigi could see Tinky's distinctive figure standing beside the tent, talking with one of the diggers. She parked along the roadside and walked slowly toward them; no one else had arrived yet, and she seemed almost embarrassed to approach them. They each turned their heads and smiled, silently.

"Hello," Gigi said softly to the digger. He was dressed in a tan jumpsuit stained with dirt and leaned on the handle of his shovel. He nodded respectfully, and she turned her attention to Tinky. "Are the men coming?"

"Tom's bringing them in the van," she answered. Tom was a retired volunteer who shuttled the men to work odd jobs and to services. She looked at her watch, its small face and dainty gold braided band stretched tightly around her wrist.

It was a clear day. The three of them looked around, avoiding eye contact, unsure of what to say. Gigi noticed now that the tent was faded and ragged; it apparently remained standing outside through the seasons. There were no chairs, only the dark hole in the earth.

A black car suitable for such occasions rolled up quietly behind them. A thin man in a cheap, steel blue suit exited from behind the wheel. His passenger followed: an athletic looking young man of about twenty-five years, broad shouldered, in a blue jacket and grey slacks. His pale yellow tie featured a wide knot, and his collar reached out over his jacket lapel, as if the shirt were brand new—right out of the bag. He carried what Gigi immediately recognized as a leather-bound study Bible.

She watched him intently. He stayed close to the other man, perhaps afraid to miss some point of etiquette, as if it mattered here. Funerals for the indigent were rarely conducted with anything but simple words and a sad resignation.

The young man finally noticed Gigi, making her uncomfortably aware of her appearance. She had one black dress, and although it was more suited to a night on the town than for a funeral, it was the best available option in her closet. As they casually looked at each other, she realized where she had seen him before.

The dingy white van came rumbling in, right ahead of the hearse. Tom pulled up to the curb, got a step stool from between the seats, and placed it next to the side door before he opened it. The men tumbled out slowly, and two chose to stay in the van and smoke.

The man in the cheap suit directed several of the men to carry the coffin over next to the hole, where they placed it carefully on the dormant grass. Gigi noticed that the digger had retreated to an old pickup truck, where he sat in the cab smoking with another man of Hispanic origin. She knew the routine; after the service, they would begin to perform the interment, whether everyone had gone or not.

The young man began to speak. One hand held the big Bible at his side, while the other was kept in his trouser pocket.

"My name is Cody Campbell," he said in a voice higher than one might expect. "I knew Emilio for only a short time. I visited him in the nursing home, before . . . "

He was talking honestly and ran aground on the harsh reality of what had befallen Emilio. He swallowed. "He didn't get many visitors in the nursing home, so he seemed to enjoy my visits." He looked down into the hole and spoke into it. "He couldn't read. Not English, anyway. Probably not Spanish either," he said, his voice lowering so that it seemed to Gigi that he might have been talking to himself. "I used to read to him." He laughed, surprisingly.

At that, he opened the Bible and entered the preaching mode, that land where voices and posture are caricatured into the unmistakable pattern of clergymen everywhere. At that, the men lost interest and began to slump and shuffle.

Gigi's eyes narrowed as she listened. He was good, and this was a performance, no doubt about it. But she reasoned he was doing it to insulate himself from the emotions that were lurking there. Cody Campbell was not one of them yet; he was still a real person, struggling to remain genuine, afraid of his feelings—as so many ministers are—hiding today behind that universal plastic persona they had both seen so many times in chapel.

Everyone was relieved when it was over. Gigi glanced at Tinky's watch; it had been about twelve minutes. Tom was helping the men into the van when Gigi made straight for the preacher, cutting him off before he made it to the safe confines of the black car.

"We've been in some classes together," she announced.

He smiled, "Yeah." It was a nice smile, relaxed. "You knew Emilio?"

"I work at the Kitchen, mornings and evenings. And Sundays." She added this last comment with enthusiasm, hoping he might ask about it, but he didn't. "Emilio used to straggle in some nights. He used to read us all those letters he had with him from the church." Her tone was not quite accusatory but clearly suggestive of something she sensed was not quite right. "What's up with that?"

Cody put his hands behind his back and puffed out a little. "He couldn't read," he said.

"I know. He just pretended," she agreed. "But what were those letters—do you know?"

He seemed to deflate somewhat, realizing there was no escaping this encounter. "They were from the church, just as he said. He would get them in the mail, couldn't read them. When I would go over, I would read them to him." He stopped abruptly.

"Why do I think there's more to the story?" Gigi asked brightly. Her curiosity was peaked.

"You never looked at the letters," he stated. She shook her head.

He sighed. "Can you ride me back?" The question came with a total shift in demeanor on his part. "Sure," she answered. He waved to the man in the black car, who, being already tired of waiting, immediately started the engine.

"Those letters were about our building program. They asked for people to give whatever they had—money, property, putting the church in their wills—whatever. I'm a pastoral intern. I got assigned some visits . . . " He looked out, over Gigi's head. The tiny muscles in his jaw tightened.

"It's a very large church, you know. They—I'm sorry, we—have thousands of members. It's one of those fundraising campaigns, you do it by the book. A total blitz of cards, letters, visits . . . "

"So he really was a member there," Gigi affirmed, trying to follow.

Cody laughed. "Oh, yeah. About three years ago, some other intern went over there, told him about the death of Jesus, made the guy cry, hauled him back over to the church, and baptized him with a bunch of homeless guys that same night."

"Sounds like a mighty evangelistic thrust," she quipped.

"More like padding the baptism numbers." His voice betrayed his disgust.

"Anyway," he continued, "I got assigned all the nursing homes. I went to one place, the lady was already dead. No one at the church knew." *Or cared,* Gigi sensed he wanted to add.

Gigi could almost feel his anger returning.

"So I find Emilio there with his crocheted tissue box cover, a chipped coffee cup, and a pile of letters from the church. He was so thrilled—he had saved them all. I was supposed to make the pitch for the building fund, but . . . "

"No way could you do that!"

He grinned. "No, I couldn't do that. So I read them as if they were from the pastor written personally to Emilio. I used these letters as a way to, well, I guess disciple Emilio."

They looked at each other silently for a moment, he in his resentment, her in tender compassion for poor Emilio.

"He had those letters with him, still?" he asked.

"Are you serious?" she said, laughing. "We listened to them over, and over, and over . . ."

They both laughed. "I kept going to see him, until he moved out, you might say. He had a nephew somewhere, I think. I left my name, in case he came back. They called me for this."

He looked back at the diggers, who were nearly halfway through.

"C'mon," said Gigi. "Let's head back."

Gigi stretched in a peculiarly feline way before opening her eyes. She had been sleeping the better part of two hours. Sunlight streamed into the apartment. It was nearly four.

She looked at the sprayed plaster finish of the ceiling, following its peaks and whorls with her eyes. Her body felt heavy, resistant to the impulses in her brain to move. Blood rushed to her extremities and made them feel that much heavier.

She turned her head, swung out her legs, and sat upright on the sofa a bit too quickly. She felt oddly short of breath. Her temples pounded.

A friend once told her that the dreams were born in guilt of never having known her mother, as if she could somehow be responsible for her death. It was like losing a limb, the friend said; you still felt it, though it was no longer there. Such things were beyond Gigi, who saw in the dreams something far simpler and yet more profound—the reminder that she existed for a reason, that God had preserved her, given her a future that must be found, a redemptive purpose.

One afternoon with nothing scheduled—no classes, no volunteer duties—seemed like an eternity, almost too much unscheduled time, burdensome in its slow, measured pace. The apartment was quiet, rather untidy too, preserved as a typical student habitat, replete with strewn books, clothing, plastic cups half-filled with Coke, and thick dust. She felt safe.

As her head cleared itself of old thoughts and embraced the present, she blinked herself into the acute awareness of the unresolved crises she faced. There was the appearance and disappearance of Jeremy Croft, who by now, she had convinced herself, must be safe, though she assumed this without any evidence. It was undoubtedly an exercise in denial, and she knew it. Since nothing could be done about him, she would focus on his divine commission which must still be carried out. The enigmatic e-mail from John Ravenswood now drifted to the front of her mind; it was coming together, slowly, not nearly fast enough to prevent some unspoken, unpredictable disaster, which was to be associated with a most powerful name. A mysterious document—a parchment? A scroll? What were his words . . . *they felt that the world was not ready for it.* She smiled for no one to see. She understood this, without having to know why. The world wasn't quite ready for Gigi Vaughn, either.

According to the standard progression of thought patterns, Gigi suddenly regarded the most pressing situation of all, and bolted toward the bedroom closet.

It was a breezy evening and cloudy, the wind gusting around in short bursts, swirling about Gigi's legs as she attempted to hold down the long skirt. It was pastel-colored with a floral print; worn with her sandals and peach-colored fitted sweater, it gave off a weird glow against the darkening sky. Cody, gentleman that he was learning to be, opened the door for her, and she ducked into the restaurant just ahead of a strong blast of air that might have tested her modesty and turned more than a few heads in the vestibule. As it was, it shoved her inside; with her hair askew and clutching handfuls of fabric below her hips with both hands, she stumbled forward as if she were stepping off an escalator too quickly. Cody didn't seem to notice this goofy entrance as he followed, stepped around her, and petitioned the hostess for a table.

So far he was doing everything right, mixing the right amounts of cute with swagger. He showed up at Gigi's door with what at first looked like champagne but turned out to be sparkling white grape juice. They had a few laughs over the risk he had taken being seen in seminary country with the brown bag, where alcohol was strictly taboo and its possession might lead to expulsion. He described his approach the way a screenwriter might pitch the opening act of a spy thriller—sprinting from car to car, dashing across the open lot into the courtyard, hiding in the bushes by the swimming pool, leaping three stairs at a time to her door, the bag hidden in his coat with the shiny foil-covered cork sticking out.

His cologne was not too strong, and his clothes were clean—jeans with an ivory, western-style shirt (complete with fake pearl snap buttons), and a chocolate-colored suede jacket. The boots were too worn for her tastes, though she knew how hard it was to part with a pair of boots once they had been broken in. He had nicked himself shaving just below the left ear, which indicated that he took his grooming seriously. His short hair sported a light gel. Her only real complaint was the wide belt with a huge silver-plated buckle with some farm animal engraved on it and the name "CODY" carved into the leather strap around back, which she noticed later and confirmed her dislike for this particular accessory. Overall, however, he was an impressive specimen.

From his clothes—both this evening and at the funeral—and his haircut and his vehicle (Ford truck, very clean, no bumper stickers), Gigi figured her date to be a fairly conservative guy. He had chosen the Lotus for dinner, a popular, moderately expensive Chinese place with a killer buffet, figuring, she supposed, that she would have a preference for this type of cuisine. He wasn't trying to show off; he wanted to please her. *Not bad.*

They settled into a booth, facing each other. Gigi's wavy hair kept falling into her eyes, an effect of the ill wind which threatened to be a chronic problem all evening. He smiled as she repeatedly flipped it back but said nothing. A few minutes later, she noticed him primping

Q

his own tiny curls and caught on to his complimentary mockery. She flipped wildly in response, giggling stupidly.

The waitress, whose approach was stealthy and sudden, interrupted with a frontal assault of two menus, though in hanging on to them, she gave away her expectation that they would both go for the buffet, which they did. "Less work for her," observed Cody.

"I thought about waitressing when I first got here," she answered, "when I first realized . . ." *Whups. Way too soon for this, Gigi.*

His high forehead crinkled. "What?"

"Well, that there were limited opportunities in ministry."

"Oh, I know," he agreed. "What've we got . . . five thousand students? Not that many positions to go around. I've got friends driving five hours to preach and not getting paid for it, just to get some experience. It's the old thing, can't get a job without experience, can't get experience if you don't have a job."

She watched him twirl his napkin. Maybe this big guy was a bit nervous too. "But you got the internship," she said.

"Yeah. But only because I whined about it to my Sunday-school teacher, who happens to be the associate pastor's next door neighbor."

Gigi liked the honesty. "But you've proven to be deserving of it," she said, not really knowing if it were true. "At least the way you ministered to Emilio proves you are."

Cody looked down at his hands, still visibly moved by the experience. "When I first came here," he began cautiously, not looking at her, "I had this place figured for some kind of heaven on earth, but I'm finding out that it's not much different from anywhere else. I mean, the people are good, it's just . . . " His voice trailed off. He looked at her in appeal.

" . . . that they're human. They're subject to pride, competitiveness, lack of compassion, hypocrisy . . . "

"You talk like you've run into it yourself," he said, his eyes squinting as he smiled.

"Yes," she said, snapping her head back to flip her hair. "But, see, I think we all go through it here. Then we realize God's in control of things, and it's OK."

"That's a bit simplistic, don't you think?"

"Of course," she answered. "Think about it. The Bible is complicated, but faith is simple. Preaching is a lot of words, poses, gestures, mental pictures, inflections, analogies—complicated, but you might get one line, one simple point out of it when it's all said and done. Running a church takes years of training, but it boils down to loving and leading. To God, things are simple. We make them hard.

"In this environment," she continued, "you have to think that way, or the Bible becomes a textbook, people become projects, and the Church becomes an institution. But it's a body, and God is its head. What is the head thinking? That's what we're to focus on. Nine times out of ten, we're preoccupied with the kneecap, the fingernail . . . "

"The hair," he said, catching her flipping.

As they slid out to head for the buffet—a startling display of fried, broiled, and stir-fried items—Cody nearly ran over a man who was slipping into an adjacent booth. Everything about this man was gray: his suit, his complexion, his hair, his attitude. Cody apologized, but the man said nothing, knowing it was he who had caused the collision in the attempt to get into that particular booth. He nodded, not wanting to draw further attention to himself.

Q

The place was noisy and alive with motion. Gigi saw a married couple she knew and a few other guys. She decided, in deference to her date, just to wave a greeting and not to converse. They looked at him as if they knew him, too, but no acknowledgement was made by Cody.

Gigi looked with wonder at the alarming pile of food Cody was creating. It arose atop his plate, Tower-of-Babel-like, seemingly into the infrared warmers above the counter. The sight of this led her to drop a chicken wing back into the steel tray, as if the two of them together were allowed only so much.

Cody glanced at the gray man again as he went back to the table. Odd that he would choose such a place to dine alone. He was drinking coffee.

"So, you never said how you liked the internship," Gigi said, wishing she had perhaps waited until he had reduced his rations a bit before embarking on so potentially lengthy a subject.

"I'm basically a glorified gopher," he said, surprising her. "I was going to ask you if you need some help at the Kitchen, actually."

She turned her head, thinking. "Sure," she said warily. "But it's volunteer. And let's remember, *I'm* the preacher."

He slurped up a noodle and nodded eagerly. "Can't wait to hear you," he said, still chewing.

"I think you've already heard me," she joked, referring to their earlier discussion.

It would be nice having him around. Real nice, in fact. But it might have an adverse effect on the men who were used to seeing her there alone. And she needed to keep her mind on her work. If she were going to plunge in that deep, he would have to be worthy of it.

125

"Let me ask you a question," she said. "Are you interested in the work at the Kitchen or just in me."

"You, mainly," he said, swallowing first.

She tried not to show the effects of the flattery. "Well, I take my work very seriously. Most people have no idea of the needs that are out there. It's only when you get involved that you can really understand."

He had stopped eating and was listening closely. She was obviously speaking of something dear to her heart.

"Incarnational," he said.

"Hmm?"

"Incarnational ministry," he repeated. "Jesus came into the world, lived as a man, all that. You can't be effective unless you can identify, relate. Believe me, I understand. Here I am, the intern, reading imaginary letters to the forgotten souls in the nursing homes week after week, while the big church sleeps. They don't even know those people exist. And I wouldn't have noticed them either, wouldn't have thought to care, if I hadn't been sent there."

"It ought to be part of the curriculum," she advised.

"Right. Make the students do it for credit. Then maybe they won't get sucked into that Restoration Church mentality, where ministry is so blissful and pathetically shallow at the same time."

"Love those red boots," she said, winking.

"Yeah." He scooped up a forkful of pepper steak. "We ought to drag ol' Bobby Raeburn down to the Kitchen one night, so he can proclaim the truth to the masses when he emerges from the darkness."

"Kidnap him," Gigi urged.

"Park him over a big tub of greens and hand him a serving spoon," he added.

"Make him clean up the drool," she shrieked, a little too loud.

"Oh, that's good," he paused. "Really, though," he said thoughtfully, pointing the drippy fork in her direction, "you ought to get the word out. I mean, a girl preacher in a homeless shelter. It has quite an appeal."

"Chinese-American girl," she said wistfully, "banned from the pulpit, cast out of the church, takes to the mean streets"—she waved her hand dramatically like a painter poised before his portrait—"sharing with the outcasts, the dregs of society."

"Great story," he said, munching.

It is a great story, she mused. The thought struck her like a thunderbolt. A great story. Simple.

The young man in front of her shot glances her way as he continued the excavation. The white of the porcelain plate was peeking through in spots. She liked him, though he seemed all too common for her thoughts right now. She tried to relax, a girl in a peachy sweater in a Chinese restaurant on a windy, spring Friday night in Texas, sitting across from a hunky guy with his name etched into his belt, worrying about saving the world. She slowly pushed her black hair back and smiled as he moved the food around on his plate, preparing to plunge in again. *Go with it,* she thought. The world had survived this long without any help from Gigi Vaughn. Surely it could hang on just one more day.

The gray man paid his bill early, so he would be ready when the couple finally decided to leave the restaurant. They were not mindful of him, and he relaxed with his coffee. The girl's voice was strong but high-pitched, and while he knew when she was talking, he couldn't make out all of the words. He was curious but not sure what he should listen for anyway, since the details of his assignment were not explained to him. Mr. Withers simply wanted to know where she was and whom she was with at all times. The job was easy enough.

He managed to slip out behind them at a safe distance and emerged in the parking lot just as the young man's truck was pulling away. He assumed they were heading to a movie or the mall—certainly not a nightclub, which would have been fine with him. But they drove straight to the girl's apartment building instead; the gray man watched for her darkened windows to become illumined. He phoned in from the sedan and reported.

"She's upstairs with the cowboy right now," he barked into the cell phone.

"Has that cop shown up yet?"

"Nope. Don't expect him to. How's the leg?"

"Hurts."

There was silence for a moment.

"This is going nowhere. These are nice kids."

"You tell *him* that. Guys like him are paranoid."

"No. Learned a long time ago, he's not interested in my opinions."

"Can you get some pictures?"

"What?" The gray man shouted, confused.

"Pictures. Of the girl—you know. We could use them later, if there's a problem."

The gray man laughed his edgy laugh. "Two preachers caught in the act, is that it? I told you, these are nice kids."

"Well, you better have something in case this thing blows up."

"Me?" The gray man was indignant. "You're the one who screwed this thing up, not me."

"C'mon! I was ten yards ahead of your sorry butt!"

"Yeah? So what's your excuse then? If you could've held him down for ten more seconds, I wouldn't have . . . " The gray man's argument stopped abruptly. "Hey. Just a second . . . the cowboy's coming back out."

"Serious?"

"Yeah. See what I mean?"

He saw Cody walk out into the early evening, jacket slung over his shoulder, whistling. He walked straight to his truck, turned over the motor, and pulled out onto the street, momentarily looking right at the gray man, although there was no sign of recognition. Then Cody was in traffic, his tail lights fading quickly.

The gray man shook his head. "I would figure she's in for the night. Should I follow the cowboy now?"

"No, no. Stay put. You were told to watch the girl. That's what you do."

As soon as Gigi shut the door, the exhaustion that had been somehow dormant during her date with Cody suddenly and power-fully returned. She was pleased with herself for making it an early evening, though it would've been nice to let him stay awhile, as he clearly hoped she would invite him to do. But she needed sleep, had gobs of homework to get done, faced the imminent approach of Sunday morning with no sermon prepared, and now had a new fixation, which had struck her somewhere between the egg drop soup and the *moo goo gai pan*. She would have to prioritize and hold rigidly to her agenda to accomplish it all.

She clicked on the computer. The last thing she remembered from class, Grantham's analogy of Humpty Dumpty, whizzed around in her brain. She imagined a beautiful Eve standing in the center of the lush garden, handing the forbidden fruit up to an egg-shaped Adam, sitting high upon a stone wall. His cartoonish eyes danced at the exquisite taste of it, then, carried away in the sensation, he toppled, bobbing for a moment—Eve's delicate hand now placed fearfully over her mouth—and plummeted down, his tiny, thin arms flapping to no avail, all his mighty works failing to rescue him, Eve watching, breathless and in horror, birds chirping, unaware of the impending catastrophe, Adam shattering the innocence of the garden with his fall. There it was—Sunday morning's sermon.

She reread John Ravenswood's e-mail once again. There was no record in her computer of what Jeremy had sent, but he obviously had told Ravenswood where he was and how he had hoped Gigi might assist him by some more legitimate means in confirming the whereabouts of the ancient document. Even so, given Jeremy's lack of confidence, how did the Society plan to obtain it? Perhaps there were bigger guns than Jeremy waiting to be fired. Perhaps not.

She stared at the last paragraph. "We have arranged for your next envelope to be deposited in Timnah in a few days time." This could only mean one thing. Somehow Ravenswood knew about Timnah, but how could Jeremy? He would have had to ask her. Interesting. And there were clearly other recruits involved in the mission. Maybe the boys in Britain had this thing worked out after all. Tomorrow was Saturday—as good a time as any to find out.

Unlike many campuses, Southwestern's Roberts Library was alive with activity on Saturday mornings. This was so, because in addition to the rigors of graduate education, many of the students held ministry positions, which involved Sunday sermons, meetings, studies, and other events requiring thorough preparation. Having settled on a topic—which Gigi found often the most difficult aspect of her work—she found a quiet spot and, over the course of an hour or so, had assembled a variety of resources to help her get the message down on paper. When she first began preaching, she assumed the congregation of a few bedraggled men and desperate single mothers had little insight into matters of theology, and as a result, her messages were shallow and often poorly received. They never said so, but she knew that they felt they had been short-changed somehow, that they were being given platitudes in place of hard biblical truth. Gigi learned that many of them were no strangers to preaching; in fact, several had grown up in religious environments. They were often uneducated but not necessarily ignorant—they knew full well what their poor choices had wrought. They had grown weary of preachers who treated them like victims, who feared confronting them or offending their values. On the other extreme, they didn't need to be reminded again of the wages of sin. What they needed was a way out of the pit.

The Kitchen provided the right mix of benevolent care, encouragement, and practical skill-building. Gigi's task with the men was primarily serving, cleaning, counseling, and directing them to others for help with specific problems. But her focus was what she called the "Main Event," the service of worship which underscored all the efforts of the previous week. It was God's point of view on their lives, putting it all into perspective, to the end that they might find motivation to build on what they had received and become contributing members of society.

Saint Augustine was a fellow who sowed plenty of wild oats. He confessed a misspent youth quite willingly after the fact, which Gigi thought somewhat amusing—she was familiar with the testimony of many a preacher whose attitudes in confession seemed more like boasting than remorse. But who could doubt Augustine's motives? He stood as a giant on the pages of theological history, refuting this and that, creating an integrated view of things, which fortified the

Church against the heresies that swirled about it. It was not Gigi's purpose to reveal any of this to her hearers but simply to paint a broad picture and then break it down into the simplest of scenes—unlike Bobby T. Raeburn, who seemed to do just the opposite.

In her reading she found that Augustine's view of the fall of man was so severe that it effectively enjoined all people into Adam's rebellion so that his sin was passed on—quite literally through the sexual act—to future generations. Original sin was like a stain that could be washed away only by baptism, which of course needed to be performed as early in the child's life as possible—a teaching which was compounded during the Middle Ages when the black plague ravaged the European population and newborns had no guarantee of seeing many days of life. It was this idea that Gigi wanted to make clear, that while there are no simple solutions to complex problems, God provides a way back from even the most devastating personal catastrophe.

She closed the books and stacked them neatly on the corner of the table, stuffed her papers into her book bag, and began the descent to the first floor. The sermon was only now simmering in her mind; it would take shape early Sunday morning and be delivered fresh and hot. But now it was time to satisfy the other curiosity that had kept her only half focused on Augustine's deep thoughts, the one that had possessed her utterly since her strange encounter in the alley. Gigi descended the stairs slowly, as if afraid some menace might come jumping out at her, somehow aware of her intent.

She scanned the first floor—nothing out of the ordinary. Walking briskly into the open, she finally came to a closed door. No one was watching her. She stepped inside.

For years, the seminary had been taking part in digs at a tell in Israel, the site of the ancient city of Timnah, a military outpost in

Judah best known as the setting for some of the exploits of Samson. Here, in this little room, were the spoils of those digs—pottery and ostraca, mostly, representing different eras as the excavations unearthed treasures from deeper inside the tell. Few students actually took the time to tour this little room, and on this day, as usual, it was empty.

Gigi's heart pounded as she snooped around the displays. What was she looking for? An envelope, according to Ravenswood, must be hidden here by now. Perhaps she was too early. Her heart throbbed in her throat, and she feared knocking over some of the fragile clay vessels that were standing on the floor and on tables all around her. She began to peer into them, one by one, taking care not to touch them. At length she came to a tall earthen jar standing against the wall on the far side of the room. She felt the skin on the back of her neck tingle as she looked inside and saw not an envelope but a kind of file, dark brown, folded over and secured with an elastic band. She reached in and removed it, scraping the sides of the jar and tottering it a bit.

As she was steadying the pot, she heard the almost imperceptible swivel of the door behind her. She turned slowly to see a man she vaguely recalled seeing before. The man was dressed all in gray, looked older than he was, and did not appear particularly interested in the artifacts. He was staring directly at Gigi.

Though the stare was not necessarily unfriendly, Gigi feared the worst. Thoughts of Zechariah the prophet—chased into the Temple precincts to where he presumed he had sanctuary, only to be put to death as he clung to the horns of the altar—flooded her mind. Was it possible that this man would attack her here, in the bowels of this sacred institution? Why not? She reasoned. It wouldn't be the first act of hostility performed on God's property.

She had quickly hidden the file behind her and was tucking it into the waist of her jeans as the man stepped forward. He held his hands out to demonstrate no threatening intent, but Gigi slid along the wall, sidestepping a few exhibits. In front of her was a table upon which rested a small clay bottle; she grabbed it and threw it in the gray man's general direction, and he ducked. The bottle crashed against the wall, exploding into powder and shards, shattering the muffled silence of the carpeted room—making more noise, in fact, than the room had probably ever heard. Running around the table, Gigi managed to clobber the man in the back of the head with her book bag as he attempted to rise. The book bag proved to be an effective weapon in that it contained, among other objects, Grantham's weighty Volume One. The man fell to one knee. Gigi slung open the door and escaped into the amber light of the library.

She ran from the building and out over the lawn, around Fleming Hall and in front of the Rotunda, the old chauvinists of the frieze looking typically disinterested. She didn't look back, not once. Only when she had reached her car and spun dizzily out of the lot, over the train tracks, spilling out onto McCart, directionless, did she feel the odd pressure against her tailbone and remember the folded file. Turning onto Alta Mesa, she finally sought refuge in the parking lot of a Catholic church, where she pulled it out.

It was, indeed, an envelope, though not the mailing kind. It was made of thick, brown cardboard, with a flap to seal the opening and a thick, cloth-covered elastic band attached to keep it from opening accidentally. She turned it over carefully in her hands. On the outside, someone had taken a black marker and had written a large letter Q. Inside, there were fifteen crisp one-hundred-dollar bills.

1.4

U NTIL NOW, GIGI HAD NOT ENTERED INTO THIS HERSELF—WHAT was *this?* Adventure? Misunderstanding? Crime? It was as if she were watching a movie starring Jeremy Croft as the dashing good thief, two as-yet unidentified bad guys, and a mysterious document that may or may not have any relevance for today. She had merely been the audience. Or, at best, an extra.

After this morning's attack, however, Gigi now was a full-fledged cast member. If this frightened her, she did not realize her fear. The rushing adrenaline gave her a heightened sense of excitement, overwhelming what her common sense was trying to say.

She tried to calm herself to sort things out. Only two possibilities existed: either someone had seen that e-mail from Ravenswood, or Gigi was being followed. The latter was the more probable explanation since her apartment did not appear disturbed in any way, and even if someone had gotten into her computer, it was unlikely that he or she might know the significance of the reference to Timnah. An intense, nervous fear gripped her. She could not go home.

It was a foregone conclusion that she would stay at the Kitchen this evening, despite the men-only rule, and the availability of the other option—the women's shelter. She wanted the protection of the men, especially the male volunteers. But the more she thought about it, the less secure she felt. It would be an obvious refuge, and once they found she was there, how could she leave unmolested? She would have to find another hideaway.

A stray thought hit her that she should just head straight for California and the waiting arms of her dad. She would have to call him today anyway, because he always called her on Saturday nights unless she had advised him otherwise, and tonight she wouldn't be there. He might not understand the whole affair, but at least he would believe her—especially when she showed him the cash.

Gigi stuffed the envelope into her glove compartment and locked it, remembering Jeremy's advice. She wished he would suddenly reappear and save the day somehow, but wherever he was—if, in fact, he was OK—he could not have known of her predicament.

She drove a few blocks to a convenience store, where she asked for a telephone directory. There was only one Ashley Dunbarton listed, in the Wedgewood subdivision, less than a mile away. She snatched a road map from a display beside the counter and spread it out, to the clerk's visible irritation. Finding the street, she folded up the map and returned it, walking quickly out to her car, muttering directions. A right, a left, two rights, and she'd be there.

The house was small and set close to homes on either side, with a tiny square of grass in front. A.D. was outside, making the identification easy. He was pushing a mower, likely the first cutting of the year, and did not notice her approach. She was out of the car and halfway up the driveway before he stopped.

"Gigi?" he spurted, wiping sweat from his face with the back of his hand as he cut the throttle to the mower. The question was more a statement of surprise to himself than directed at her, but she translated it more like, "What are you doing here, at my house, on a Saturday afternoon?" It was not advisable for male professors to be alone with female students, especially not single professors, especially not at home.

Q

"I know this is weird," she said, "but I need to tell somebody what's going on." She looked unnerved, unusual for her.

A.D. was wearing a plain white T-shirt and plaid shorts, with black socks and old loafers. Sweat pasted the cotton shirt to his narrow shoulders and chest. He waved her to follow him inside, somewhat unsettled himself at both her epiphany on his front lawn and his own rather grungy appearance. Too late now to do anything about it.

She was talking before they got inside the house. It was tidy (thank goodness) and sparsely furnished. He directed her to a seat in the small living room. She stopped for a moment, noticing that the walls were covered with prints of various Charleston scenes.

"You were saying something about Q?" he asked, just now catching up with her conversation. "Oh, just a minute. Where are my manners? Would you like some sweet tea?" Seeing Gigi sitting in his living room suddenly flushed him with excitement.

"That's fine," she said, smiling weakly. She was beginning to relax, feeling safe for the moment.

Gigi tried not to notice her professor's pale, skinny legs as he walked in with two glasses of tea. "They always serve unsweetened in Texas, but I boil the sugar right into mine," he said proudly. Gigi saw a green plant floating in her glass; after one sip, she recognized it as a mint leaf.

"Now, what's this about Q?" he asked again.

After taking several slugs of the tea, she pulled out the envelope and handed it to him. He looked at her suspiciously, opened it, and looked back at her again.

"See that, on the side there, the letter Q," she said, pointing. "There's a significance to that, isn't there?"

He looked at the envelope and shook his head, perplexed. "Miss Vaughn, I'm afraid I have no idea . . . "

"Q!" she shouted. He still was not getting it. She drew in a deep breath. "OK. Remember what we talked about the other day, the lost book of the Bible?" Her eyes were wide and full of color.

The pensive look returned to his face. "I see. You're saying this reference to Q may have something to do with the source document used by Matthew and Luke. Alright." He was talking softly, like one might to an excited child, or a mental patient.

"You think I'm out of my mind," Gigi said flatly.

"Of course not," he said, eyeing her warily, not sure what else to say.

"Please listen. I know you'll understand," she said, appealing to his sensitive nature with her most feminine tone. "My friend—the one I told you about—was sent here by these people in England called the Society of Saint Matthew, to steal this important ancient document. He's since disappeared."

Gigi watched A.D.'s face for an indication of how he was receiving this information, but he just looked blankly ahead. "Go on," he said calmly.

"Sure. Now this Society had the document for a long time, and this guy died who had it, and then it kind of fell into the wrong hands. So it's here in Fort Worth, and they want it back because it has some pretty explosive stuff in there." She was trying to stay focused, her emotions now catching up with her, making her flustered and nervous.

"How did you come to have this?" he said, holding up the envelope.

"I'm getting to that. One of these guys at this Society sent an e-mail to my friend, which I got instead, because he was chased by some thugs and has since vanished. It said this drop-off would be at the exhibit in the library. I went and got it, and some man in a gray suit is after me now."

He pondered this for a moment. "Gigi," he said at last, "how did you get mixed up in such a thing?" It was an expression of genuine concern.

"Well, I don't know, it just happened," she answered. "Jeremy— my friend—thought I could be of some help. He tried to break into the *Dispatch* offices to get the document, but really he has no clue where it is . . . "

"The *Stockyard Dispatch?*" he asked incredulously.

"Yeah. It's Daniel Withers who has the document."

A.D. stood up and began to pace back and forth, Sherlock-esque. "You realize this whole thing is completely preposterous," he said.

"Of course!" she exclaimed. "But do you see that there's something to it now? I mean, look at that money."

They both stopped and stared down at the envelope on the coffee table.

"Gigi, what do you know about Q?"

She looked up, innocently. "Only what you said—some kind of source document for the Gospels. I was hoping you could . . . "

"*Hypothetical* source document," he interrupted. "There is no book of Q, exactly. It's a theory put forth by scholars who believe Matthew and Luke must have had a common source for the passages unique to them but not found in Mark."

She was puzzled. "There's no book of Q?"

He looked down at her, intensely. "There's no book of Q."

With the white Nova safely ensconced in A.D.'s garage, they headed back to campus to review some of the professor's resources about Q. "I'm only just now getting into it," he said. "For the class on textual criticism . . . the one you'll be taking."

Gigi smirked. "Who needs the class with this kind of on-the-job training?" she said. She sat slumped down in the front seat of his compact car, just in case.

They rode on in silence for a while, both of them mulling over the situation in their minds. Dunbarton had reservations about plunging Gigi deeper into the affair, realizing that a little education might do more harm than good. "Have you considered calling the police?" he said finally, turning into the faculty lot.

"Not really," she replied. "I doubt they'd believe me."

"They'd believe you when you showed them the money," he said.

"I suppose. But what about the rest of it? Like Daniel Withers is in the habit of sending secret agents after seminary students?" she scoffed. "Besides, if we make this thing public, something unpleasant might happen to Jeremy."

They walked into the building and up to the office without encountering a single soul. "You're in the middle of some serious business here, Gigi," he said. "I think we should consider involving the authorities. Has it occurred to you that these Society people might not be what they seem? Really, if they want the document back, why don't they just make Withers an offer?"

"Its not about money, sir," Gigi said, falling back on the term of respect instinctively as she fell heavily onto the red sofa. "There's something about that document that they don't want to become known—for the sake of Christianity itself." She regretted this rather pious outburst almost immediately.

Q

"Right," he said, nodding his head up and down. "Then the document in question can't be the supposed Q at all. There's nothing the least bit controversial about it. In fact, all we're talking about here is a collection of sayings, undoubtedly compiled by more than one person over the decades following Jesus' death. It was probably well-known among those early believers, since both Matthew and Luke had independent access to it."

She frowned. "You seem to know an awful lot about it . . . considering it doesn't exist."

He sat down behind the desk. "Well yes, people have different theories about this thing. Back in the 1800s, some German scholars came up with the idea of the two-source hypothesis. They reasoned that Mark was written first and was a source for the other two synoptists. The second source, which they concluded must have existed, they called simply *quelle,* which is German for "source." In time, it came to be known as Q.

"Since then, of course, attempts have been made to reassemble this collection of sayings, which isn't particularly difficult to do. You just pick out the passages common to Matthew and Luke, and there it is." He was leafing through a folder he had culled from a metal filing cabinet while he was speaking. "The problem is, most of these scholars take a decidedly liberal position about this material."

"You're losing me," Gigi complained.

"Yes, well, I'm sorry. Let's slow down somewhat." He sat down again and assumed the posture of a counselor. "These passages, you see, are all similar in style; that is, they are nearly all sayings of Jesus or teachings he gave. So there are some very conspicuous omissions. You'll not find any miracles among these texts, no birth narratives, and most problematic of all, no death and resurrection."

He studied her face for a moment, looking for a reaction, but she sat still, thoughtful.

"So, what we are left with is something like a book of quotes, which has led some to conclude that . . . " He was perusing papers as he lectured and struck upon precisely what he was looking for. "Ah, here it is. The esteemed Lester Bothwell has summarized it plainly." He handed a typed letter to Gigi. It was addressed to Dunbarton and signed by the learned professor from the University of South Carolina. "Believe it or not, I know this guy," he said.

Gigi scanned the brief note:

July 15, 2002

Dear Ash:

Forgive my late response to your inquiry about The Jesus Seminar, *but I have only just returned from sabbatical leave in Munich and have had little time to catch up with my correspondence. Of course, the seminar was illuminating beyond words, and without doubt we are closer to the Jesus of history than ever before. I shall hastily prepare a complete set of papers for your file and continuing research.*

The highlight of this year's event was a thorough investigation into the nature of the so-called lost gospel Q, *with which I am sure you are familiar. It is clear now that much of what we have come to call "Gospel" is fraught with difficulties relating to unfounded spectacle, similar to modern tabloid journalism. One should say that* Q, *being the earliest documentation of the sayings of Jesus (along with* Thomas, *naturally), places our true Christian heritage in focus, leaving the superstitions of our ancestors in tatters on the cutting-room floor. This is not to say that you should take your scissors to Luke, for his contribution is important to our understanding of the developing religion. But I do believe we have discovered the Teacher at long last and are no longer required to offer explanations for those traditions which are, quite frankly, indefensible.*

I look forward to the fruit of your labor in due time. Until then, I remain,

Yours truly,
Lester B. Bothwell, Ph.D., Th.D.

Gigi handed back the letter. "Fruit of your labor?" she asked.

"Yes." He snatched back the paper and returned it to the file. "My book on textual criticism. Can you just feel the arrogance sliding off the page of that thing? Bothwell was an undergraduate professor of mine years back—specializing in comparative religions, if you will. Religion to him is an intellectual exercise, nothing more. He makes my blood boil—always has. My interest in textual criticism is based in part on a desire to prove him wrong."

"So, what's the point?" she wondered aloud.

"Only to show you what this Q hypothesis really is. There's nothing to hide here that hasn't already been unveiled. Even if there is a document called Q, and even if Daniel Withers does have this document, so what? The cat's already out of the bag, Gigi. And it hasn't dented Christianity one bit."

She looked at him, blinking. "Are you saying . . . "

"I'm saying that liberal scholars have already made their findings known. Since the discovery of the *Gospel of Thomas* at Nag

Hammadi in 1945, which was simply a collection of sayings, the search for Q has become an obsession with people who are out to prove that Jesus was just a man who had some profound, witty sayings to his credit and that later he was mythologized by followers who sought their own agendas, not his. Well, that's been done. So I disagree with you about this society's motives. I think you should go to the police, tell them you met this friend who was mixed up in some trouble, that he's missing now, and that you came upon this cash by mistake and want out."

"What's the deal with this *Gospel of Thomas?*" she asked.

He cocked his head in amazement at his inability to sway her. "Sign up for the class on textual criticism," he sighed.

It was a short walk from Ashley Dunbarton's office across campus to Barnard Hall, the girls' dormitory. Mary was in her room reading when Gigi surprised her with the rather lame but believable story that a water line had been broken at a construction site near her apartment and the water would be shut off at least until the next day. Mary bobbed her carrot-top to the story and without any hesitation welcomed Gigi to spend the night.

"Didn't you bring a suitcase or something?" the pale-skinned girl asked.

"Actually, no, I thought I would just stop in at home before church in the morning. Maybe the water will be on by then."

This seemed to satisfy Mary, who had no roommate and was delighted to have the company. In the space of a few minutes, the anemic-looking mouse of a girl transformed herself into a veritable chatterbox, taking Gigi on a tour of the room and commenting on nearly every possession along the way.

Q

"Want to get some pizza?" Mary suddenly exclaimed like a preadolescent at a slumber party.

"Sure," Gigi answered. "Listen, could I send an e-mail to my dad before you call? He might want to know where I am."

Mary agreed, of course, but before she let Gigi near her laptop, she had to get settled on exactly which toppings should be ordered.

Gigi sat down and did exactly as she said, firing off a short message to her father that she was staying with a friend and gave him the phone number if he wanted it but explained that she would try to catch up with him sometime Sunday. Then, she clicked the mouse and typed in a second message to an address she had memorized:

Mr. Ravenswood:
Subject: Q

You sent Jeremy Croft an e-mail at my e-mail address, but he never saw it. He was chased by some men, and now he's gone. I went to Timnah per your instructions, and I have the envelope. I am being followed now but have not contacted the police. I don't know what Jeremy told you about me, but I am prepared to do whatever I can to help the Society, because I have a feeling that it is the right thing to do. I have an idea of how I can help, about which I have told no one. But I need some details about why this is so important. You obviously have at least one agent (?) nearby, and I need to know how to contact him. I can get you information, but I'll need someone to do the actual work. You can e-mail me at my e-mail account

145

(not this address!) with your response. Please do so ASAP. If I don't hear from you tomorrow, I will have to tell the authorities everything I know. They have already questioned me about Jeremy and said they might come back.

GV

Gigi glanced at her watch; assuming a six-hour difference, it would be about ten o'clock at night in London. If she stopped by her apartment after church, it would be late in the day over there, and Ravenswood would have had plenty of time to respond. All she would have to do would be to get in and get out unseen.

After deleting the e-mails and clearing them from the hard disk, she turned to Mary, who was frantically searching her desk for coupons. "Forget it, Mary—my treat for having me over," she said cheerfully. "But if you don't mind, when you're done, I need to make one more call."

It was a sunny Sunday and still warming to typical Texas levels when Gigi walked outside Barnard Hall to wait for Cody. He appeared right on time, smiling from behind the leather-wrapped steering wheel through the sparkling clean windshield. How cute; he had washed the truck.

Gigi hopped in and patted him on the arm playfully, an odd greeting but one that almost made him blush. "A little under-dressed for preaching, think?" he commented. He was making an excuse to look her over, she thought.

"I don't usually like to gussy up at the Kitchen. I see you're wearing your best boots, though."

He nodded at his understanding of her little joke. "Got my hat down behind the seat too. Do you guys have a pew for hats? In my home church, all the men tossed their hats onto the back pew as they walked in—kept the youth from sitting back there passing notes," he drawled.

"Youth like you?"

"Yeah."

"Well, we don't have one. We've got a shelf and a coat rack, though."

"That'll do fine," he said, desperately searching his mind for something to keep the dying conversation going. "So, what's the sermon on?"

Gigi looked straight ahead and said, "The Augustinian pattern of the Fall of man."

He turned his head to eye her profile and found nothing to suggest she was anything but serious. He glanced back at the road, then at her again. "Serious?"

Gigi's chin crinkled as she suppressed a smile. "Sure. It's a sophisticated crowd, you know."

It was good that they were approaching their destination, because Cody was rapidly running out of wit to match hers. He parked the truck in the lot as she directed, and as he came around to join her, he reached out for her hand.

Gigi looked at the hand and took it. "Scared?" She winked, and they walked into the cool alley toward the side door.

In a lot of ways, Cody reminded Gigi of her dad: strong, plain-spoken, confident, and easy-going. Her father, however, was also impatient, impulsive, and reckless—qualities she could not yet discern in Cody—and that was good. She couldn't see Cody wandering about in China, falling in love with a teenage girl who spoke a different language, then having a child with her—

without the benefit of marriage. But she could see him charming a girl into a relationship against her better judgment, just as her father had done.

Gigi instructed Cody to set out the chairs, which he did dutifully, finally sitting down in the last row with his hat on the chair beside him. Carl, who had seen them enter but who had not yet approached, watched him warily from the shadows of the adjacent hallway. It appeared to Gigi that Carl, who of all the regulars was most attached to her, was in his infantile state today, and she prepared herself for a potential conflict. She opened the refrigerator and took out a carton half-filled with eggs and carried it into the improvised auditorium. The Methodist lady was already seated at the piano, having entered quietly on tiny feet. Gigi walked over and handed her a folded sheet of notebook paper with numbers identifying the hymns for the service, and turned over an empty trash bin for the pulpit. She spied Cody watching her and felt strangely embarrassed.

The relative calm of the setting was broken by the entrance of the women and children, the latter storming the room and fanning out, tipping chairs and pushing each other rudely. Tinky, who had driven them over from the women's shelter in the old van, lingered outside to speak to a man parked under the basketball goal. She invited him in for worship, but he declined, saying he was simply there to meet someone. The majority of the men who had spent the night were now out there, too, milling around. Tinky made a valiant attempt to herd them inside, to no avail.

Gigi handed out hymnbooks during the prelude, coming at length to the back row where Cody was trying to keep an impertinent black boy away from his hat. Gigi spoke to the boy gently, and he slunked away, his narrowed eyes prophesying another try.

Q

She took the hat from Cody and placed it gently on the shelf at the back of the room. "No passing notes," she whispered as she walked back by him. She noticed that a few of the women were looking unashamedly in Cody's direction as she headed up the aisle.

A husky dark man stepped to the front to lead the music. Several buttons were missing from Manny's shirt, revealing a hairless chest. He swayed as he directed the cacophony of singing, humming the tune over the hard notes of the piano. He had been doing this for several weeks now, and the congregation seemed to like him. Fortunately, Tinky's booming voice cut through the din like a foghorn, and some convergence of message and tune could be followed by those who cared to learn.

Gigi began her sermon by carefully removing an egg from the carton she had set on the overturned bin. The people watched, curiously, as she turned it in her fingers. "Humpty Dumpty sat on a wall," she said, tossing the egg from hand to hand. Even the children's voices fell silent. "Humpty Dumpty had a great fall," she continued and suddenly hurled the egg at the wall behind her, where it splattered yellow goo over the painted blocks.

The children squealed with pleasure at this, standing up—some on their chairs—to see what she would do next. She continued in a rhythmic cadence, "All the king's horses . . . ," she heaved another egg at the wall—"and all the king's men . . ."—then another— "couldn't put Humpty together again." Finally, the carton now tucked under her arm to keep it from the circling children, she fired one more, leaving the back wall a mess of runny yolk and eggshell shrapnel.

She lifted the plastic barrel and pushed the carton under it, then grabbed one of the kids. "See that wall?" she shouted, turning him around and holding him firmly by the shoulders. "Some people say that's you!"

After a few seconds of chairs scuffling and throats clearing, quiet filled the room. Gigi waited for all eyes to return to her before continuing. "That's what they say—about you," she said softly.

A few tears of recognition were shed. Manny looked down at his shoes. The children had found their way back to their mothers and were either seated or reaching for laps. Only Carl disconnected from the emotions filling the room; he was still watching Cody, who sat fixated on Gigi's every word.

"You've had a great fall. You can't be fixed. You're hopeless. You're not worth the time or effort to try to repair. You've been in jail, and you'll just be back there again. You can't keep away from alcohol. You have an anger problem, can't get along with anybody. You have babies irresponsibly, expecting someone else to pay for them. You steal. You won't pull your weight. You're not willing to work. You have no skills and can't contribute. You don't want to learn. You're a bad influence. You spread disease. You're selfish to the core. That's what they say about you."

She looked at the somber gathering of homeless men and women. "And you've been victims too. You haven't gotten any breaks. You're a bad risk. You started with little and ended up with less. You've been used. You've been fooled. You've grown tired of trying to climb back to the top of the wall. But you haven't given up; that's why you're here. You haven't given up, because you know there's one person who hasn't given up on you." Slowly, heads lifted.

"A long time ago, a man named Adam disobeyed God. This was the beginning of human sin. He and his wife were cast out of God's beautiful garden, kicked into the street, where they had to fight for themselves—the man working to exhaustion to build a home where there was no comfort, the woman bearing children in pain.

"Given the same set of circumstances, the Bible says each of us would make the same choices they did. But the Bible also says, 'While we were yet sinners, Christ died for us.'

"You've seen the beaten, near-naked figure on the cross. You've seen the crown of thorns. That's what sin does. That's what forgiveness cost. Jesus entered into our world and endured the pain of our separation from God so that we could be fixed. So that we could climb back to the top of the wall.

"As long as we're here, we have to live with the consequences of our poor choices. We must also live with the consequences of others' poor choices. A father who beat us. A mother hooked on crack who abandoned us. A friend who sold us out. A crafty serpent who tempted us. On the outside, we're broken. But on the inside, if we trust in Christ, we can be made whole."

Gigi paused to scan the faces of her hearers. There was hope in some of their eyes. Others feigned indifference. But the Word was hitting home.

"Without Christ, you can forget all the vocational training, all the free medical care, all the nights with a roof over your head, all the hot meals and clothes, all the counseling services, all the sunshine God offers you every day, because you'll still be broken," here she pointed to the egg-covered wall, "always wanting more, never having enough, consumed by bitterness and hatred and jealousy . . . "

Her voice cracked. She thought of her mother, of what she had been told of her mother—a Christian who made a mistake, who had nothing but her faith and a man she loved and a heart full of peace, as her father often said—a heart full of peace.

"Or you can find strength for the soul and the resolve to make your life better, make this world better—starting today."

Gigi was humbled by the power of her own words. Here was life, simply explained—not to do and have everything but to do what you can and have *something*.

"If we have broken hearts, God can fix them. He wants to fix them. But he wants us to do some fixing too. Starting today, we decide to clean up our messes. In his strength, we must learn to make the best of what we've been given. We must go, and sin no more."

They watched her as she walked back behind the counter, opened a cabinet and took out a bucket, filled it with soapy water, and reached down for a bag of sponges. Without saying a word, she walked past the seated worshipers to the back wall, tore open the bag, dipped a sponge into the warm liquid, and began to scrub. Almost immediately, a young woman followed suit, then one child, and then another. Tinky jogged to the pantry and fetched more sponges, until nearly everyone—some singing, some sniffling—was washing the wall.

1.5

"THERE'S YOLK ON HERE!" CODY COMPLAINED, TURNING THE Stetson over carefully in his hands and flicking eggshell from the brim. "You slimed my hat!" He was only half-smiling as he said it.

It was difficult for him to explain that he liked the sermon, was moved by it, and understood its impact upon the hearers. "But you did good," he drawled, still examining the hat.

They were busy rearranging the room to its original condition, and Gigi acted as if she were too busy to process the remark. She realized that he was in an awkward position, not wanting to be viewed by Gigi as offering praise to win her favor. Nor would he have any interest in evaluating her performance in light of the current disdain of women preachers among their peers. To gush over her ability might be perceived as fake or might imply surprise. Either way, he would be inadvertently categorizing her, and she might take offense. Knowing all this, she accepted his casual, understated comment as sincere. It warmed her, and in mulling over these things, she realized how rarely anyone who really understood such matters had ever heard her preach. His assessment was important.

When they finished with the labor, they departed in the truck for Gigi's apartment. She had explained the encounter with the gray man in Timnah when she called him on the previous evening from Mary's room, and from her description he said it sounded like the man who sat in the next booth at Lotus on Friday night. Cody was concerned and nearly demanded she phone the police, but she talked him down. He was too interested in her to cross her too severely this early, but he made himself clear that further incidents would make it hard for him to stay quiet.

The deal they made on this morning was that Cody would watch for any trouble while Gigi went inside to fetch some things, then head over to A.D.'s to pick up her car. From there, she had no real plan, but she had an open invitation to bunk with Mary if necessary.

Gigi turned the key in the lock and stepped back while Cody entered first. He was wearing the cowboy hat and looked a bit like a wild-West sheriff as he quietly slipped inside. He saw no signs of disturbance and checked all the rooms quickly before stepping back outside to guard the door.

She packed quickly, stuffing socks, shirts, makeup, her Raiders jersey, and various other items into a duffel bag, then made for the computer. The wait to access her inbox seemed eternal, but she was rewarded right away with a new message from Ravenswood. It was fairly lengthy, and her eyes eagerly moved over the screen. She only had a few lines read when she heard a sudden sound from her bedroom—like a movement of furniture across the rug—and she yelled.

"Cody!"

He was inside in a second, and he followed her pointing finger down the hall. She turned back to the computer, quickly moved the pointer to the print icon, and clicked.

A sound like heavy footsteps could be heard, followed by a crash she knew to be a floor lamp she had set beside her bed. Cody was threatening someone, and then something thumped against the dividing wall, almost knocking a mirror down that was hanging on the den side. She inched toward the hall, curious but terrified, worried for Cody.

Q

Suddenly, a familiar figure came bouncing off the hall wall, running towards her. Before she could move, Jeremy knocked her down and landed on top of her, their eyes meeting only inches apart, both reflecting fear and surprise. He looked pale, unshaven, and desperate. Just then, his eyes backed strangely away from hers, and she realized that Cody was standing above them, lifting Jeremy by the heavy cloth of the soiled jacket. He slung him hard into the wall, and Jeremy cried out in pain.

"Wait!"

Cody looked curiously down at Gigi, who was now rising to her knees and holding out her hands to plead for mercy. "Stop! Cody, just wait."

She pulled herself to her feet. Cody's fist was pulled back for a punch, his other hand pinning Jeremy against the wall. Gigi intervened; Cody's cologne clashed with the rather rank aroma surrounding Jeremy. "This is the guy who was missing," she said calmly to Cody, pressing her palms against his chest. "It's OK."

Cody held his clenched fist, as if it took extra long for what he had heard to translate through his nervous system down his arm. He was breathing hard, his eyes sharp and cold, and he didn't seem to like the explanation. "This is the thief?" he said at last. She nodded, and Jeremy answered weakly, "Yes—I'm the one."

Cody released his grip, and Jeremy adjusted his clothes, still leaning against the wall. "Who are you then?" He was squinting, possibly due to pain or exhaustion or both.

"I'll explain that. Look," Gigi said forcefully to both men, "I think we should get out of here." Then to Jeremy, "These guys who chased you are after me."

"Oh yeah?" he replied, pleasantly. "That's rich, don't you think? Trying to get to me, no doubt," he observed.

"No doubt," mimicked Cody, who, despite the mistaken identification, still seemed to exude a dislike for Jeremy.

"He's a good hider," she said, smiling. The two guys glared at each other. "C'mon."

She led them back into the den, snatched up the paper from the printer, folded it, and slid it into the back pocket of her jeans. Then she picked up the duffel and ushered them out the door.

They hurried down the stairs and into the sunshine, heading for the truck. Gigi slung the bag into the bed of the pickup and reached into the cab for her book bag. Before throwing it in back beside the duffel to make room for the two of them on the bench seat, she unzipped the bag and yanked out the brown envelope and handed it to Jeremy. "Check this out," she said, lifting herself into the truck beside Cody, who was already inside and gripping the wheel in anger.

"Left my hat in there," he snarled.

"Oh, sorry," she said, not too sympathetically, as she slid up against him. "It had egg on it anyway."

His frown softened at this, and he turned to acknowledge it, when they were startled by a loud *pop* and the simultaneous shattering of the window of the open passenger door. Cody banged his forehead on the steering wheel as Gigi sunk her face into his arm, clutching it with both hands. Recovering, she looked back at Jeremy, who had been in the process of getting in when the shot rang out; he was on the ground.

She slid back across the seat and looked down to him on the pavement. "I'm OK!" he shouted, though not with a full voice. "Stay cool 'til I'm clear—then go!" He said this loud enough to direct Cody, who was frantically looking around for the shooter.

Q

Jeremy, apparently unhurt, crawled under the truck and emerged on the driver's side, then scampered across the sidewalk in a crouch. Gigi noticed he was carrying the envelope as he vanished around the corner.

Almost as if on cue, Cody floored the truck in reverse, stopped, shifted, spun the wheel with both hands, and stomped on the gas, causing the open door to slam shut, nearly smacking Gigi's head as she lay in a fetal position sideways on the seat. Shards of glass from the smashed window fell on the back of her neck.

As she sat up and reached again for Cody's arm, he whipped the wheel in the opposite direction, causing Gigi's head to land heavily on his thigh, as the truck careened out of the lot and turned up the street. His elbow came down hard on her head and she shouted, her nails digging into his leg in response, until he lifted his arm. She looked up.

"Hang on," he said, then made another hard turn, and she clung to him for safety. The truck hit the raised entrance to the complex with such speed that it felt like a front-end collision, and Gigi sat bolt upright. She saw now what he was doing; he had driven around the building in hopes that they could locate Jeremy on the other side and snatch him up before the sniper could get to him. He slammed on the brake and stopped the truck; the metal tingled with heat and speed as it idled. The thief was hiding again.

Cody grunted something undecipherable and threw the truck into reverse once more, then spun the wheel like before, and headed out the way they came. In the excitement they hadn't heard the sirens. In front of them was a patrol car, blue lights flashing, blocking the way.

When it was all done, the officer had given a repeat performance, and Gigi had offered not one particle of helpful information. On the other side of the parking lot, Cody was doing the same.

Jeremy Croft had approached them as they attempted to leave in the truck; a gunshot took out the window, and Jeremy instinctively raced away. His explanation for pulling back into the apartment complex was simple—when clear thinking returned, he had to check and make sure Gigi was OK. That was it.

For Gigi's part, she insisted that she had not seen Jeremy since the day he disappeared, which was true, and she was therefore fairly convincing. She discovered him hiding in her apartment, she said, and he followed her outside.

No trace of Jeremy was found that day, nor any evidence of the shooting, aside from the word of those who heard it and the bullet that was extracted from the wall of the building. At length, Cody and Gigi were reunited, while the police shared their respective stories, and finally released.

"I'm posting a guard out here," the officer said as he approached Gigi to wrap up the report. She wasn't sure if it was for her safety or to keep an eye out for Jeremy's eventual return; this petty criminal was becoming a nuisance to the law.

Once safely driving away, Gigi asked urgently, "Why didn't you tell?" Cody rolled his eyes and laughed, saying nothing.

She didn't insist on an answer. Amazingly, she wasn't afraid for her safety, didn't even feel personally threatened. She possessed a strange sense of security in the midst of the chaos around her.

"Where are we going?" Cody asked, bewildered.

"I don't know. I didn't think to ask you."

"What do you think happened?"

"He got away. I'm sure of it." And she was.

She directed Cody to drive in circles through the south part of town, to try and see if they were being followed. Satisfied that they weren't, she told him the way to Professor Dunbarton's house to get her car, and he meekly complied.

Cody had never taken a class with A.D. and didn't really know him. He had heard Gigi talking about him and was a bit uncomfortable being the odd man out.

"Do you want me to just drop you off?" he asked in a level voice.

She looked at him quizzically. "You don't want to come in?" She was surprised at the reservation she sensed coming from him.

"Well, I've got some things to do," he said.

"What's your problem?" she demanded.

He took in a deep breath. "No problem. I just think you ought to relax a bit, that's all."

"I'm not sure I know what you mean," she answered.

"C'mon, Gigi. We just got shot at, and you're going to go over it all with this professor right now. You're obsessed with this Q thing."

He was right, of course. "I am not," she said softly.

"Oh really?" His voice was increasing in volume. "Why won't you forget it, then—just tell the cops, and go back to your life?"

"Why didn't you, when you had the chance?" She knew this was unfair, and for the first time, she saw his face redden.

"I think you know why." He paused to regroup. "Tell you what. You get your car and have your talk with the prof. I'll pick you up later, and we'll grab some Tex Mex, OK?"

"Excellent idea." She could feel herself calming down.

Cody started to grin. "Your treat this time. If we're going to get nearly killed over this thing, at least we ought to enjoy the spoils of war!"

She didn't laugh with him, for good reason.

"Gigi?"

"I gave the envelope to Jeremy."

Cody's neck flushed with color, as if a heat rash was just below the surface, waiting to appear. "You *gave* it to *him?* What were you thinking?"

"I—just wanted to show him . . . I didn't know that . . . "

"Gigi! What are you getting out of this deal, huh? What?" He pounded the wheel like a spoiled child.

"It was his anyway," she said, disgusted with Cody.

He steamed silently. The cab of the truck sizzled with tension. She saw his jealousy of Jeremy. Their minds were on different things.

Cody dropped her off at the professor's house and waited for the front door to open. She waved back at him as she stepped inside, and he slowly drove away.

A.D. couldn't help but notice that Gigi was dressed exactly as she had been the day before. He was fairly spruced up himself, having only recently returned from church. They sat in the den, where Gigi held a folded sheet of paper; after reading it, she handed it to him.

> *My Dear Miss GV,*
>
> *I was quite alarmed at your message but pleased that you gave such kind consideration to me in reporting this troubling news about Jeremy. He is a resourceful lad, and no doubt he has escaped harm, though I must admit to more than a slight bit of concern over his disappearance. I expect that you will keep me posted as to the young man's welfare, as I will you, should I hear from him.*

Q

I am truly honored that you deem this affair worthy of your interest but must caution you as to the potential dangers that await. I cannot in good conscience author- ize your further involvement in this matter and do instruct you to desist in your activities on our behalf. It is indeed a mighty God we serve, and no matter what meager resources we present for his use, he will magnify our efforts for good. Now that we have been found out, we must trust him to provide another way.

You are, nevertheless, entitled to an explanation. As a young man, I was much engaged in religious causes, and, blessed with earthly means, endeavored to put such means to use. Along with a friend named Benton Cole, I gave financial support to a mercurial scholar named Terence Knotty, who convinced us that impor- tant religious documents had been recently discovered and were being secretly traded about the Holy Land. He went there in earnest and returned with the most remarkable book, which we did then properly identify as, despite its rapidly deteriorating condition, the very Q of the two-source hypothesis! Knotty fancied himself as an expert in Matthew studies and to our surprise and fascination soon concluded that this could not be the version of Q employed by Matthew and Luke in the writing of their respective Gospels; furthermore, he contrived that this particular Q did in fact pre-date each of those Gospels, that Matthew eventually served as its editor, and, most shocking of all, that Matthew had a personal association with its author! Given the radical forms of some of the traditional texts therein, he quickly proposed that a written tradition must endure to sustain this connection and prevailed upon us to invest further in the enterprise.

Terence, it turns out, was correct about one thing: there were more treasures left to be revealed from the caves near Qumran, and in the years following their first appearance, speculations associated with these "Dead Sea Scrolls" were legion. Even as I write, there is no telling how many manuscripts have yet to see the light of day. We formed a group of scholars (and I have continued, without great success, to recruit more) for the purpose of unlocking the "clues to Q," if you will, and to diligently pursue the possibility that some written tradition exists to explain why this book appears as it does. For without this explanation, those of weak faith may surely be misled by its contents. So far, despite a quarter century of labor, the efforts of the Society have not borne fruit.

Doctor Knotty, I regret to say, succumbed to the instincts of our baser nature and eventually found himself so addicted to certain hallucinatory substances that he was unable to continue in his research. In such a state, we feared that even if he were successful, his credibility, and ours, would be seriously questioned. So we put the book away, and the Society dwindled in both interest and number to the present day.

You may keep the money, of course, as payment for exposing yourself to injury, and we will spare no expense or exertion to search for Jeremy. We will find him lurking under some tumbleweed, I trust, in good health. Until we do, I covet your prayers for our

Q

cause and wish you the blessings of our Lord, in whom I remain,

Yours faithfully,
John Ravenswood

"So. That's it then," A.D. said, folding the paper and returning it to Gigi.

"That's what?"

"That's the end of it, at least; we've come to a brick wall. Interesting stuff here, though." He mused professorially, stroking his chin.

"I'm sorry?" she protested. "That's the end of what?"

Sensing an argument coming, Dunbarton assumed the posture of her academic superior. "This quest of yours. There's nothing more for you to do. Besides, they are asking you to stop." His face melted into an expression of fatherly counsel. "Good advice."

She felt an electric pulse in her blood but held back the words that were forming in her brain, trying to break through the thick anger brewing there into the open air. She huffed, closed her eyes for a long moment, then flashed them intensely at her teacher. "I can't," she insisted.

A.D. sat back in his chair and observed her. She was like a hummingbird, charged with an energy that was part of her being, relentless, insatiable for something he could not identify. The quest, as he had called it, had consumed her, had eroded all reason.

"Let's think about this then, OK?" he suggested. "You don't know this Ravenswood person. You have trusted an ex-convict. You have been watched, followed, and nearly killed. You are obviously exhausted. And for what? Some kooky theory about a document that no scholar except this drug-addicted Englishman thinks exists?"

She listened.

"Seriously, Gigi," he continued. "This is probably about fame and fortune, and that's all. Daniel Withers has plenty of both and obviously wants more. So he has a nice little collectable—who cares? Only those men over in England who think it rightfully belongs to them. Is this really any of your concern?"

She opened her mouth to object, but no sound came forth.

"And let's say the whole thing is exactly as you've been told. We've got an old manuscript that contains some surprises. OK, then why hasn't it appeared yet? And if it does appear, what's going to happen? I'll tell you what—nothing! The conservatives will have explanations for the variants. The liberals will attack their positions. Same old story. Nothing will change. There will be an article in a few erudite journals, and it'll be over. Christianity goes on without needing Gigi Vaughn to save it. God can take care of himself."

As he said these last words, he saw something let go inside her, not a surrender exactly but an acknowledgment. She was a strong person, and only strong, direct words could reach her. He wanted to sit next to her and embrace her—like an older brother consoling his sister who just broke up with a boyfriend, but he sat there motionless, waiting. She was at a turning point emotionally, a crossroads of mind and heart.

"This—'quest' thing. It's all about me, really. I suppose that's obvious," she admitted quietly.

"It doesn't mean we can't talk about it," he said. He was trying to soften the effect of his admonition. "This theory about Matthew knowing the author of Q is fascinating. Some clue in the text of that document—a direct statement, you think like, 'My buddy Matthew was in his tax booth when Jesus called him?' Or maybe

Q

some common phraseology. Maybe even the party, the one at Matthew's house—perhaps some new dialogue from the dinner! Wow. Or it could be this guy is another publican, a secret follower?" His eyes were bright with speculation.

"Could be," she said. It was clear she was distracted. Overtired. Numb. "Listen, Dr. Dunbarton, can I use your phone to make a couple of calls? Then I've got to run."

"In the kitchen," he said, forcing a smile.

The kitchen was small, uncluttered, with tan Formica countertops and oak cabinets. It was so clean she wondered if A.D. ever used it. The ice maker rumbled as she placed the first call, using a prepaid phone card fished from her purse.

"Dad?"

She knew he had been waiting all day for her call. He asked right away if something was wrong—he had a father's intuition about that. She insisted she was OK and recovered well enough to get through the conversation. For a few moments, she wished she were back home in California, far away from the stresses of seminary life, from the questions she had to answer about herself. Her father approved of her unconditionally. She was his only child; she could always run home to him and be comforted. But she knew this would never happen. She had to move on, be on her own. But she missed her father so very, very much.

"Cody?"

The second call was harder to make. But this time, she faced the regret and refused to let it linger. Like her father, Cody was willing to hear whatever she was prepared to say. But unlike her father, there was not yet enough between them to make him stay if she remained an enigma. It was time to open up.

165

"I feel like I'm in this tunnel, and I'm running through, trying to get out, and it breaks into two tunnels, and I don't know which one to follow. Then I'm frustrated more, so I pick one and run harder, but that leads to more tunnels . . . "

He was listening intently to this lovely girl, continually reminding himself to listen and not just to admire her looks, despite the fact that she was saying nothing yet of any real substance. His fajitas had been sizzling a few moments ago, but as he sat attentively there, a third thought intruded—they were getting cold. Was it OK to eat? Was she so fragile that reaching for a tortilla might imply disinterest? She had a taco salad—taco salads can sit there all night and not be affected. Her words were not enough to hold him, so he contemplated the oval shape of her face, the ivory smoothness of her skin, the high, soft cheekbones, the wavy black hair, those eyes . . .

"Aren't you going to eat that?"

This wasn't the transition he intended, but something had to give.

"You haven't been listening," she said, predictably.

"No, wait, I heard all that stuff about the tunnels," he answered. "You don't know which way to go and all that." He brought his hands up above the table and began to prepare his first fajita, his eyes on hers to be less overt about it.

She smiled. "I guess I'm not making a whole lot of sense." She cracked off the edge of the huge taco shell and bit into it. She stopped chewing to think, resumed and swallowed, and pronounced, "I know what it is. I'm angry."

"Oh," he said, rolling and folding. "At me?"

She picked up her fork and thrust it deep into her salad. "You haven't been listening," she said.

Q

He dropped the food and said, startlingly loud. "OK. What are you so angry about?"

Gigi waited, watching him, making sure he was going to pay attention. "I'm angry at myself because I have to keep pushing all the time and never stop to enjoy my life. I don't know how to enjoy my life. I think I know what life means, but I can't accept what my head is telling me. I have to win; I won't be happy until I win. I can't be satisfied. I always have something to prove. I don't know if I do it for God or for myself."

This, Cody was getting. "Go on," he said.

"Sure. I'm angry at you because you're not like me. I'm attracted to you because I wish I could be like you—so cavalier about every-thing—and I can't stand you because you don't relate to me. I'm angry at you because you'll get to do what I can only dream of. I hate that. I have to do something to prove I'm good enough, but nobody's paying attention."

"That's not entirely true. Anyone who's been in class with you knows how sharp you are. And I said you preached a good sermon, didn't I?"

"Yes, you did. But I'm still mad at you."

He resumed eating.

"I'm really mad at the Church. The American Church. Because of what it tolerates. Because of its self-centeredness. It cares about itself more than anything. All over the world people are suffering for their faith. People are dying for it. Here, we have oppression, injustice, bigotry. And the Church gets fatter, more comfortable. Bigger, richer. The streets are full of hurting people. The Church either ignores them or uses them to advance its own agenda."

"The ROC," he observed through a full mouth.

"Yeah. I'm sick of it. We're arguing about who's qualified to preach. Well, Jesus said preach the Gospel to the poor, and I'm the only one doing it, yet I'm not good enough for the Church. And I'm angry at God for letting them get away with it."

"Man," Cody said, still chewing.

"And I'm angry that my mother died when I was three, that who knows how many thousands of others did, too, during the cultural revolution, and that nobody gives a wet slap about it."

Cody stopped eating, looked at Gigi solemnly, then at the diners at several tables nearby, as if embarrassed at what she had said, then back at her. Not embarrassed; alarmed. More properly, awakened. He didn't know what to say.

"I'm—sorry," he said rather formally.

Gigi, eyes puffed and red, clenched her jaw against the tenderness she felt coming from him. She didn't want this, hadn't planned it, wasn't ready for it. She was angry, frustrated, talking without thinking. It happened sometimes. The problem was that she knew few people well enough to open up this way, and they rarely knew how to handle these explosions. They seemed odd coming from such a petite young woman, almost inappropriate. They came from a fire that always burned, that she couldn't always control.

She began to talk more casually, though her voice still rang with emotion. "My father was—is, I should say—a freelance photojournalist. At the time, he was in Taiwan to chronicle the daily lives of the troops there, thought it might be interesting to tell their stories, the guys who were largely forgotten while all the attention was being paid to the war in Vietnam. Safer too. But somehow, through some illegal means, no doubt, he managed to get into China. Met my mother there. She worked in a large factory on a sewing machine. He took some pictures; she was flattered, he said."

She smiled, lost in the memory as her father had gifted it to her. Cody leaned forward, pushing the plates away and crossing his arms to listen.

"They never married. I know because he never talks about a wedding. Surely he'd have pictures of that!" She laughed, and he followed suit. She needed to do this.

"Anyway, her parents got involved with this movement . . . have you ever heard of Wei Jingsheng?"

"Uh—no."

"Oh. Well, he was this famous political prisoner in China for fifteen years. But back in 1978, about the time I was born, he was stirring up people who were dissatisfied with communism—you know, Chairman Mao and that stuff."

"Sure," he said, though the whole business was rather cloudy in his mind.

"He said there should be free elections. He didn't like how communism suppressed the individual. You couldn't be independent. Religion, of course, was discouraged, though some of the churches were quietly organizing and preparing to reopen. After I was born, my mother's family was embraced by some of these people, and it gave my mother the courage to speak out. She was young—just nineteen."

Cody swallowed and felt his throat becoming dry. He was tense, though Gigi was strangely comfortable with the conversation. He took a long drink of tea.

"My grandparents thought it best for my dad to take me to Taiwan when he had the chance. I know he regrets it. He can't talk about it." She paused. "He never got back into China."

They looked at each other silently.

"There were demonstrations—thousands of people, mostly young like my mother, were taken away and sent into the rural areas for what they called reeducation. They lost track of her then."

"How do you know . . . "

"That she died? There were others who came back. Things were changing. The United States was establishing relations with China and breaking ties with Taiwan. Mao died. It got a little better. But for over a decade, it was hell over there."

"You don't remember your mother?" he said softly.

"No, but I have a picture."

"What was her name?" he said, smiling.

Gigi flashed her eyes and squinted a tiny tear. "Her name was Yen Yuan. It has an interesting meaning: 'searching for the cause.'"

They parted casually, Cody being sensitive not to diminish the significance of what Gigi had disclosed by any inappropriate word or act. He let her set the tone for the rest of the evening, which was low-key, even distant. He took no offense at her mood. She was a complicated girl.

Gigi drove home just as the sun was setting: a big, dramatic Texas dusk, full of color and shafts of light peeking out here and there, an amber tint that mellowed everything. As she entered the complex, she immediately spied the unmarked car and its inattentive driver parked there for her protection. She chuckled to herself at the obvious nature of the surveillance and pulled up into her usual space. She tromped up the stairs, tired and happy to be home.

There is something about one's home that maintains its own sense of normalcy; when disturbed, it affords no comfort. The apartment had not been ransacked but had definitely been searched. She knew that much right away. Creeping deeper into the main room, she saw open drawers, lampshades askew, pillows placed in the wrong positions on the sofa. Looking over at her desk, she walked directly to the computer and touched the mouse. The desktop blinked into view, just as she had left it. She could not remember if she had deleted the e-mail from Ravenswood in all the ruckus between Jeremy and Cody. The first one was there, still in her inbox. There was no sign of the second.

As she scrolled around, she suddenly became aware of the urge to flee. Someone had been in her apartment; perhaps she was so spent that it took several moments for her to realize that the intruder might still be there. No point in going further—she snatched up her book bag and duffel and walked quickly out the front door.

The patrolman appeared to be dozing in the front seat of his car as Gigi drove away.

In the hazy light of the fading day, she arrived on campus, hoping Mary was back from evening church activities by now. As she rolled the car quietly into the small parking area in front of the dorm, she caught sight of a gray car parallel parked in the street. The driver was reading the paper and not paying attention; she couldn't see his face, but she knew who he must be. Her skin prickled as she spun the wheel and quietly returned the way she had come.

She pulled the knob on for the headlights and weighed her options. Perhaps her apartment was safe, now that he (they?) had already been inside. Possibly they had avoided the sentry, or maybe they had come and gone prior to his arrival. Even so, she didn't feel safe there. No way could she stay with Professor Dunbarton. Fort Worth Hall was off limits to women; Barnard was being watched. She knew some students in married housing, but how would she explain herself? There was the Kitchen, but they would look for her there in due time, and the women's shelter would be an obvious second choice.

As she drove north toward the interior of the city, she considered again heading straight to California. She had practically no cash with her, but there was a gas card in her wallet. But this would be running away. She was in too deep now; she wanted to pick up where Jeremy had left off. She had an idea that Cody had given her, unwittingly, when they first had dinner together. It could accomplish some good and possibly even lead her to Q. At the very least, it might allow her the opportunity to purge these awful emotions that weighed her down. She knew they were taking their toll on her studies, her relationships, and her general health. She resolved that she would follow through.

She would not involve the police. She would not let herself be found. In the back of her mind, she thought that it was Jeremy whom they wanted; he was the only threat to them. Perhaps they had seen Ravenswood's second e-mail and they would know what she knew. So why were they still after her? There was only one explanation—they did not want her to tell. They were planning something. But what?

Gigi smiled in the dark, both tiny hands gripping the wheel. Let them chase her. Let them follow her into the night. The headlights shot wide beams ahead of her as she drove. She would be found when she was ready. Her time had not yet come.

1.6

TRAVEL DAY CAME FULL OF RENEWED MEANING FOR GIGI. THE SEMINARY suspended day classes on Mondays to allow ministering students time to return to Fort Worth from their places of service. Some students typically drove several hours one way to preach or participate in staff activities on Sundays, often for little or no pay. The seminary had thousands of students, and suitable positions were limited; therefore, one accepted what one could without complaint. The experience might make a significant difference once a degree was earned, since few churches would call a person full-time who had never once preached, presided at a wedding or funeral, or directed a ministry in some way.

Gigi, of course, had doubts that her particular experience would do her much good. Despite having delivered more sermons than the average male among her peers by graduation time, she was doomed to be forever female and therefore subject to those peculiar texts, which had been used for centuries to deflate the ambition of women seeking leadership in the Church. She marveled at the way some preachers lifted these verses out of their contexts and floated them about like timeless truths, whereas other texts which were unpalatable to them had to be understood in the larger scope of the writer's contemporary situation. She could preach but not pastor, teach but not in authority over men, minister but not as an ordained member of the clergy. No measure of skill, no spiritual gift, no amount of brains, no sparkling creativity, no pastoral experience, no demonstration of discipleship, and no sum of the varied tasks associated with care for the castoffs of society would make her good enough. Ever.

She would take matters into her own hands. Her friends encouraged her to wait on God, but it wasn't God who was slamming the door in her face. She wasn't the type to wait forever for something to happen. She would make things happen herself—step out in faith, as it was said—and force the doors open. She had been called to make a difference in the world, and she would seize any and every opportunity to do so, no matter how remote the possibility of her actions amounting to anything. She would trust God to take her efforts and use them however he saw fit.

On this day Gigi drove all through the impoverished areas of Fort Worth, and also to the posh neighborhoods, marking the contrasts. She looked at the church buildings, tried to ascertain the message they sent to those who lived nearby. She followed the homeless men to see where they went after leaving the Kitchen. She considered where to leave the car and where to spend the night. She stopped several times to pray. Was she near the heart of God or far off? She wasn't sure.

So many of her peers were sure they were in the direct center of God's will. They smiled a lot, spoke in that spiritual lingo that sounded so loopy to the uninitiated. Gigi could be sure of God's will only when she looked back at it. Her motives were always suspect to herself. But she believed that God made her a certain way and led her to follow her instincts, sometimes obediently and sometimes not, but in the end she could understand how the divine hand guided her. With such an understanding, she had to be bold.

There was no doubt in her mind that God would use this week of nights on the streets. When she first thought of the plan, it was preposterous to think that anyone would care about the stories she wanted to tell. And then, as circumstances created for her a unique type of homelessness, she began to believe that God, through Cody's unwitting remark, had planted a seed in her heart. She had something to say and knew that God wanted it said. And if she were successful, it might lead her to something else that was just as important—maybe more.

By late afternoon she had found a public lot, one of those with numbered spaces and a big metal cabinet with numbered slots to pay for the parking. People were leaving work and were pulling out in a long train. Gigi found a space and determined to spend this first night in the car, taking advantage of the last few hours of daylight to organize some thoughts on paper and to catch up on Grantham. There was always Grantham—the big gray volume packed with the great ideas of the ages—demanding to be read, its pages going on seemingly forever, its thoughts inexhaustible, like those of God himself.

Gigi found a fast-food burger place a block away and took the food back to her car. The burger was disappointingly thin, and the bread of the bun stuck to it above and below. Onions and ketchup were gobbed on one side with pickles and cheese on the other. Rearranging it only created a bigger mess. Gigi stuffed it back into the paper sack, slurped diet Pepsi through the striped straw, and pulled a notebook from her book bag. She rolled down the window; there was a slight breeze, and the heat of the day was past, not yet suffocating as it would be in the summer months. Sounds of the traffic seemed distant; the tall buildings were emptying fast, and people were hustling to whatever home awaited them. But not all.

Gigi had written for her high-school paper and was considered very good by her peers. Through her undergraduate work, and now in seminary, she had always received high marks and positive comments on her essays and papers. But now the writing was for a different purpose and a different audience.

She made circles with her pen until ink appeared on the page. Then she wrote, deliberately in large letters,

I used to lie in bed at night and listen to the chirping, buzzing sounds of the insects surrounding my house in summer. Once, as if hypnotized by the rhythms of these intricate melodies, I left my room and walked outside on the patio. The noises trailed off to a quiet hum and stopped. They watched me, though I couldn't see them. They came alive in the night, ventured out from their hiding places, flying and crawling, as they were meant to do. And then I intruded, a day creature. They retreated. They would not be seen. I might crush them. I would not understand.

I used to know a man named Emilio. He was powerless as a bug in the bustle of this city. Ignored and rendered insignificant by day creatures, he came alive only at night. He couldn't read. Couldn't work. Couldn't pay for the care he needed. You wouldn't have noticed him as you went about your business. He was hidden from you. He was afraid of you. You were so much bigger than he. All he really wanted was a crumb from your table. Just a tiny little crumb.

The tapping on the window stirred Gigi into wakefulness, into that hazy dimension in which few things are certain. She heard the taps with her sleeping ear, saw only the darkness as she opened her

Q

eyes. The notebook slid off her lap. She sat upright, conscious of a presence outside the car in the dark. She blinked herself awake.

Instinctively she reached for the keys dangling in the ignition. Numbness fled from her extremities. There was a distant light on a pole, which she thought at first was a star. Then she saw more lights on the horizon, the edge of what was once known as Hell's Half Acre.

She tightened her thumb and forefinger on the key. Raising her left arm to the top of the steering wheel, she glanced at her watch—it was just after four. Her eyes adjusted to the dimness. The muscles in her neck tensed; she had heard something. She turned quickly to look out the side window. Nothing.

Gigi released an audible breath. Something was wrong. She wrapped both hands tightly around the wheel.

A sudden avalanche of sound and weight was heaved upon the back of the Nova as the man leaped upon it and walked up to the roof. His shoes were like blocks of stone dropped from above. Gigi shrieked, turned the key and hammered the gas pedal with both feet, but the car was still in park! The man fell upon the roof and dropped his eyes below the windshield line, staring wildly at Gigi, upside down. She cried out something she regretted, then grappled with the shifter, dropping it into neutral. She could hear the drunken man laughing, his greasy hair and forehead bobbing lightly on the glass. She released the pedal and hit the brake, knocked the shifter into drive, and peeled out, nearly scraping an abandoned car parked across the lane and one space to the right. She drove for the light atop the pole.

Seconds later, she realized the man was gone from the roof, and she stopped hard, turning the wheel as she did so, leaving rubber on the cracked asphalt and sending a sharp squeal into the night.

She looked back and saw him struggling to his feet about forty yards away, swaying like a ship's mate on deck in a storm, until he reached the parked car. From below the street light, Gigi could see his fuzzy shape just inside the arc of its glow, saw him retrieve the bottle and slump against the car. He seemed to have no interest in her any longer.

He was typical of the homeless men she knew from the Kitchen: scary, though not really dangerous. They wanted to get close to you if they could, as if they might borrow something of another's blessings by rubbing shoulders. They were curious: what was it, exactly, that made someone else so prosperous and them so wretchedly destitute? What combination of bad luck and bad choices created such human misery? Their days and nights were intermingled, an endless string of unfulfilling moments with nothing to do, but at night they found an energy, freed perhaps from the knowledge that the masters of the world had all gone to sleep. They laughed in the night, played like children, climbed on the roofs of parked cars. This man, now that the excitement was over, simply returned to his bottle, the one unchanging icon of his life.

Gigi was still spooked, her car bathed in the artificial light, like some space cruiser was hovering above her. She took advantage of the illumination to retrieve her notebook and reviewed what she had written before falling asleep. She was convinced more than ever that the story was a long shot at getting published, but she had to get the words out and onto paper, if not for society's instruction, for her own benefit—to chase away the anger, and the dreams.

Hours later, parked in the seminary lot, Gigi pulled her shirt over her head, wincing at the faint odor emanating from it as she did so. She would have to stop at a Laundromat for a quick wash soon—her jeans hadn't been cleaned in almost a week, not to

178

mention the other items she hadn't changed in two days. Except for the jeans, she had two days worth of garments in the duffel, and she extracted from the bottom of it a wrinkled sleeveless pullover with thin horizontal stripes in alternating shades of yellow. Cars were starting to roll into the lot, and she noticed a few of the male students looking casually in at her as they walked on to class. No doubt she'd be summoned to the dean of students in an hour for violating some code of conduct. At times she thought the seminary maintained such a thin veneer of superficial morality that the sight of a girl's bare midsection might rent its very foundation. She donned the yellow shirt, tugging on it, trying to stretch out the wrinkles; the bottom came to about an inch above the top of her jeans. She grabbed her book bag and jumped out of the car, trudging self-consciously to class, stiff and aching from the rough night. She winked at the stony ancients frozen in the frieze, whom she imagined were staring disapprovingly at her navel as she approached the main building.

A.D. was continuing his lectures on the special problems associated with the Gospel of Mark. The focus of this day's study was the aptly-termed "longer ending" of the work.

"We are as certain as one can ever be in such matters that the longer ending was not composed by Mark," he explained. He was dressed extremely well today, Gigi thought, with a light blue sweater-vest and gray tie over his standard white oxford shirt, with gray slacks made of some fuzzy fabric. He was halfway seated on the corner of the desk with his arms crossed. It was a strange posture for a lecture; it exuded discomfort. Wasn't he sure about what he was saying? The more Gigi watched him, the stronger the impression became that it wasn't his subject that was making him so nervous—it was she.

She tugged at the hem of her shirt, a subconscious reaction. But it didn't seem to be her unkempt appearance that bothered him, just her presence. He looked in her direction far less often than usual, and whenever he did, he seemed to lose track of his thoughts.

"There is, of course, gobs of evidence for this opinion," he continued. "What kind of evidence should we look for, hmm?"

A student sitting up close said, "the snake-handling thing."

"How thoughtful!" came the professor's dry response. "Perhaps we should be a bit more scholarly than that and consider the internal evidence. Verses 9 through 20 of chapter 16 contain many words not found in the rest of the Gospel. And there are obvious stylistic variations," Dunbarton said. "And, we have external evidence as well; that being the longer ending is not found in the oldest manuscripts, and it was unknown to prominent figures in the patristic era. So we can safely assume that Mark's original work ended with verse 8 and did not contain the longer ending." He looked at them sitting there satisfied.

"OK. So." A.D. began to take on a disgusted tone. "Anything else?" It was clear to Gigi that there should be something else.

Dunbarton hoisted himself onto the desk and hunched over, supported by his hands, looking like a large, hungry vulture. "You are content with my explanations? You have no further questions regarding this?" he queried. There was no answer.

The professor cleared his throat. "How about, why the heck is it there, then?" The cynicism with which he spoke stung.

"You can't learn if you don't ask questions!" he thundered. "This semester is almost over, and you still haven't figured that out. What, are you here just to absorb whatever we say, suck it up like some kind of bottom-feeder only to vomit it out again, unchewed,

Q

at your congregations? Over and over I have told you that someone, someday, will have an important question about these issues. If you haven't asked it yourself, you will not have an answer. Sometimes there isn't a very good one to be found, but you must at least be able to sort out the various arguments. You can't get away with 'God said it, I believe it, that settles it' anymore!"

The students hung their heads.

"So. Why, Pastor," Dunbarton mimicked, "is this footnote here in my Bible, see?" He pointed to the last page of Mark.

Hearing no responses, he resumed the lecture as if nothing had happened. "Some scholars believe that it would have been unlikely for Mark to end his Gospel with verse 8; therefore, there must have been more, which at some point in history was lost. Scribes picked up the story later and completed it; thus the longer ending." Gigi wrinkled her brow as she stared down at the verses in question while he spoke.

"I tend to agree," he added. "There are short, summarized accounts of information found in other Gospels here in the longer ending. Based on the other evidence and the awkward phrasing of verse 8, clearly, some of Mark's original text did not survive."

"Are you saying that some piece of holy, God-inspired, canonical Scripture is missing? That God wanted to preserve part of Mark but not all of it? That scribes tampered with his work and didn't leave their signatures?" It was Gigi.

A.D. knew immediately where this was going. "You know for a fact, Miss Vaughn, that there is evidence in the Corinthian Epistles that Paul wrote additional letters, which are no longer extant. God, in his providence, did not see fit for us to have them."

"So, God just decided to whack off the end of Mark, so we wouldn't get to see it?" she argued.

"I suppose you could put it that way, but . . . "

"Fine. I can accept that. No problem there," she stated. "It's OK with me, really. So I guess it was God's idea that this scribe sneaked this stupid thing about the snakes in there?"

Dunbarton stammered his answer. "No, it's our job to find and identify the error, what should be included and what shouldn't."

"But some people were wrong about it once before, right? Some scholars must have thought it OK at some point in time, right?"

"That would be correct." He hated it when a student had him on the ropes, and in all his classes, he only had one to deal with.

"So let's say we find this original ending of Mark in a cave somewhere," she conjectured. "Who decides if it gets tacked on?"

"The community of scholars, of course." With Gigi, short answers were best.

"Including you, Dr. Dunbarton?" He was unwilling to answer further.

"Wouldn't you love to check out the original ending of Mark, and those extra letters to the Corinthians, maybe a lost Gospel even?"

He showed a sickly smile but said nothing.

"Think about it, sir! If you had the chance to study such a thing, wouldn't you take it?"

The other students were enjoying the interrogation, and Gigi felt a rare attitude of support in the room. But all her hopes of joining the fraternity were short-lived.

A.D. crossed his arms again. "I think, Miss Vaughn, that I probably would. Now, can we close this discussion?"

She smiled. "In the sense that the canon is closed, I suppose we can," she said.

Q

A chortle bubbled up from some students in the back row. Dunbarton, somewhat flustered, finally said, "You seem to have a lot to say this morning, Gigi, so why don't you teach the class?"

Was he serious? Probably not. But he asked for it. To his amazement, Gigi slid out from her seat and walked straight toward him and faced the class. A few of the guys in the front row were startled by the unexpected appearance of Gigi's bellybutton right out in the open in front of them, and their eyelids flickered mightily in the struggle between spirit and flesh.

"This is really great, sir, your letting me speak to the class." She turned back to A.D. and smiled over her shoulder; the blood was draining from his face. "I have a few things to say to you fellas, and I'm not speaking for Mary back there or any other of the women in the seminary, but let's think about this logically. Here we sit, openly admitting that some uninspired scribe tampered with Mark's Gospel. Did that scribe think he was annotating inspired Scripture, or just an early account of the life of Jesus? For him, Scripture was really the collection we call the Old Testament, which, by the way, there were questions about all during Jesus' lifetime and a generation afterwards. It was only after the Temple was destroyed in A.D. 70 and Christianity arose that the Jews got serious about nailing down the canon, so they'd have some security for their own faith. There were debates about Esther, which doesn't mention God; Ecclesiastes, which is cynical in tone; and Ezekiel, which some said actually contradicted the Law. Proverbs had some inconsistencies, and do I even need to mention the serious issues they had with the Song of Solomon?" As she asked this last question, she looked directly at the first-row students, whose heads snapped up to meet her gaze. They seemed to fade back in their seats as if straining against a stiff breeze.

"You obviously are aware that there was an Old Testament apocrypha—important books from the intertestamental period that a lot of people held in high esteem and followed in spiritual practice. And there were pseudepigrapha—books written under a famous person's name to gain a readership. Some of these, like the Assumption of Moses, were very widely accepted. Did you know that our New Testament Book of Jude—who by the way was one of Jesus' brothers—actually quotes from this Moses book in verse 9 and from another, 1 Enoch, in verse 14?" She looked back at A.D. to confirm her facts, which he did with a nod.

"Did you also know that the New Testament canon wasn't closed until—337?" Again she looked back to Dunbarton.

"Correct. The Council of Carthage," he said.

"Yeah," Gigi continued. "And up until then, there were books we don't now have in the New Testament that a lot of big shots in the Church thought should be in there. So, how come we're so sure now?"

The students sat very still. It intimidated Gigi a bit; she didn't know what they were thinking.

"Now that the wheels are turning, here's another question. Did Paul know he was writing inspired Scripture? Dr. Dunbarton alluded to some Corinthian letters he indicates were written but aren't in the Bible. Maybe they aren't important, or maybe God is waiting to reveal them at some time when they would make the most sense. I don't know. But I can't help but wonder what those letters might say. Perhaps they might clarify some of Paul's other teachings, especially to the church in Corinth.

"I don't have a problem with the authority of Scripture, but it does appear that God expects us to sort out the good stuff and apply it, and he's given us a lot of freedom in doing so. Dr. Dunbarton said a few minutes ago that it's our job to tell what should be in there and what shouldn't. Who knows whether or not we're right in our choices? I see Scripture as a guide that leads us to God, not a rule book or a legal code. Moses put all that down in Leviticus—now *that's* a legal code! You just follow it to the letter. But now we understand we're supposed to have a relationship with God. That's too hard for some of you guys, so you have this love affair going on with the sacred Scripture. You want it to be perfect in every way, just like your obedient little wives and girlfriends. Just like the Pharisees, you make rules, put them in God's mouth, then worship them, all the while violating the truth of God. And some of us are getting tired of it!"

The class was enraptured, listening, concentrating. Mary was gripping the desktop, her red head bobbing to affirm everything Gigi said.

The lecture had grown beyond the scope of Gigi's intent. She wanted to open their eyes, but instead her emotions were taking over, and she feared she would ruin her opportunity with stupid, selfish aggression.

"Listen, guys, I'm sorry," she said. "But I'm called to preach, just like you. You know how you feel about your callings. It's a very personal thing. Now imagine somebody telling you that you can't preach because you've got the wrong plumbing."

Smiles began to break out like spring flowers across the class-room. Relieved, A.D. took the opportunity to regain control of the class. "Thank you, Miss Vaughn. Very enlightening," he said.

Gigi nodded, suddenly assaulted by fear, aware of the scrutiny upon her, realizing none of it could be taken back. Then, as she walked shyly back to her seat, her gentle curves weaving gracefully between the desks, someone in the back began to clap. Then there were others, and soon the room was treated to a controlled wave of applause.

"By the way, before I was interrupted," the professor said, "I wanted to explain why verse 8 is considered an awkward way to end Mark's Gospel. Mary, would you read the verse, please?"

This would be a first. But Mary, emboldened by Gigi's courage, spoke the words right out. "'Trembling and bewildered, the women went out and fled from the tomb. They said nothing to anyone, because they were afraid.'"

The whole class joined in a healthy, refreshing laugh.

In the days that followed, Gigi balanced the duties of work, school, and freelance journalist quite well. She crafted her story around the men and women she knew, but she wanted it to be their story, not hers. That meant asking questions of them, extensive interviews which gave the subjects the feeling that they were important, that their lives had meaning in some way. It was this she noticed more than anything else, that the attention she gave each person in this project was appreciated, perhaps more than all her ministry efforts over the past several months.

By the end of the week, she had stopped worrying about her own safety. Quite often she thought of Jeremy, half expecting that he might pop out from around a corner at any given time. Mostly, though, she immersed herself in the project, reaffirming her own ministry in the effort. There were times, she realized, that she felt as forgotten as the people she served.

After another evening of difficult sleep in the car, she decided to bunk with Mary again. She met Mary at her church for the Wednesday night program, left her car there, and hitched a ride

Q

back to the dorm in Mary's car, an inexpensive American model with a foreign name that looked something like a cloud or a bubble going down the road. She saw nothing suspicious as she walked with Mary into the building, but, just to be safe, she exited a side door the next morning. She told Mary she just got lonely every now and then, and Mary was delighted to have her anytime.

Cody met her for lunch at Wild Bill's and took her to her car. He had taped some kind of plastic sheet to his blown-out window, and he had a new Stetson. She talked most of the time they were together, about her story and the people she had come to know better because of it. She told him about the episode in A.D.'s class, and he seemed to be proud of her. The anxiety was melting away. She was taking control of her life, not allowing herself to be the victim anymore. She was sure of herself and where she was going.

The one plaguing irritant that remained was her increasingly ambivalent feelings toward the Church as a whole. She was outside its walls and saw it as alienating to those whom she was learning to care for. She felt somewhat exiled herself, but she knew this was not the case. If some church ever were to call her to a pastorate, she would probably gain the respect of her male colleagues. Nothing stood in her way but rhetoric, really. And yet she continued to feel that the Church was a boy's club, and an exclusive one at that. Fed a steady diet of party-line theology, it was full of people who failed to think for themselves, who followed their preachers blindly, the same who were deluded by their own high-profile positions into arrogant egomaniacs. She saw a religion of convenience, not discipleship. And this gnawed at her all the time, but she didn't know what to do about it.

Thursday night she found a welcome at the women's shelter. As she listened to their stories, she was overcome with feelings of

187

helplessness, something most of these women now took for granted. Poverty, she found, often led them to grasp at any opportunity for a more comfortable life. And because they were so ignorant, they believed everything and were willing to do anything. Each poor choice brought them farther away from the goal, which led them to even more desperate acts. Their lives needed to be rebuilt from the soul up, and it would take a long time.

And where was the Church in all of this? Handing out rice and canned goods now and then, distributing some used clothes once in a while. Christmas was different, she found; all the churches were compassionate and generous, even kind, for that week. But then, these struggling souls were largely forgotten by the larger religious community, aside from the token handouts. They did care but not enough to get personally involved. Not enough to do what was needed.

Gigi had enough notes for a series of stories by Friday afternoon, when she began to organize her work. She wanted one more interview—a confrontation with a homeless person outside the range of benevolent ministries. She wanted to paint a portrait in words—a picture of life at the very bottom. But cruising sidewalks after dark was far too dangerous for a young woman all alone. There was, however, something that might work.

Around seven o'clock she parked in the same downtown lot where she began the week and walked over to Throckmorton and an old bookstore where friends of hers had worked part-time while in school. It was a truly delicious smorgasbord for booklovers: three floors with everything from rare first editions to best-sellers to trade paperbacks. A little bell clanged on the glass door as she entered the musty shop, which appeared to be empty except for the clerk, a young man in an oversized sweater with a bad haircut to match his attitude. He was cataloging books and paid no mind to Gigi as she ascended the stairs right in front of him to the second floor. The creaks were spooky but appropriate in the otherwise quiet room. Once upstairs, she looked down over the rail and saw the clerk was still busy, obviously rushing to finish his work and close the shop on time at seven thirty. There were a few other browsers up here, which was good; the clerk might not remember Gigi if she kept quiet.

At the back of the second floor, a doorway led to another flight of stairs. The store did a heavy volume in used books; people dropped them off every day in boxes from their garages or attics and sold them to the owner. His habit was to inspect them carefully, taking out what had promise for profit, and relegating the rest to the third floor, where everything was a dollar. Here, one could sift through piles of old books for hours, seeking a real treasure. Gigi's friends had told her that the shop attracted all kinds of vagrants at times, especially in bad weather, because it was the only place downtown still open this late where one might try to spend the night, if one was well hidden. The third floor afforded the perfect opportunity. Gigi's friends had told her that part of their job involved chasing these derelicts out of the store each evening, but she had a hunch the clerk downstairs wouldn't do that tonight. He was in too big of a hurry. She mounted the next flight of stairs.

The third floor was dimly lit. Books were piled everywhere, even on the stairs. These were narrow rooms lined with shelves; it was hard to see the titles on the faded jackets and spines. Gigi walked as lightly as she could, peering into every corner. There was a sound; a shoestring trailed out from behind a box, and the shuffling of clothes behind it gave the man away.

"You know you have to go," she said quietly to the man. His bearded face slowly arose from his hiding place. He did not seem surprised.

"I'm not saying now—maybe tomorrow morning," she said, putting a finger in front of her lips. The man's face broke into a devilish grin.

Gigi moved over to him. "I don't have a place to stay tonight myself," she said, sitting down beside him. He looked at her warily, not inclined to believe the statement, but he accepted it. He was very pleased to keep her company.

She took out her notebook. They could hear the bells ringing as the last shoppers exited. Each time, they paused to listen for approaching feet on the stairs. None came.

The man's name was Ronald. He had served in the Gulf War and had a drug problem, which got him out of the army; he conquered this, he said, but soon became dependent on alcohol, and now he had trouble staying free of both. He had a girlfriend he hadn't seen in over a year, possibly a child by her. He couldn't keep a job, but he had had several good ones briefly, he said. He had lived with his widowed mother, who died while he was in Saudi and left the small two-bedroom house to him and his older sister. She had somehow wrested his share away from him through legal means, and he never sought to defend himself. That was his problem he said; he couldn't stick with anything, got fed up, and took the easy way out.

"This doesn't look like the easy road to me," Gigi commented.

"I've adjusted," he said. "There are places you can stay and jobs you can get to work a day at a time if you need money. This time of year, I like it on the street."

Q

There was a loud snap, then another, and the lights were extinguished.

"We're in!" the man whispered. His foul breath seemed more powerful in the darkness.

Gigi was suddenly accosted by a deep dread. She was alone in the dark with a drug-addicted veteran, dishonorably discharged. What led her to do such a thing?

She stood up. "What places are there, I mean, where do you go when its cold?"

He coughed something up that Gigi was glad she couldn't see. "Well, last winter was my first real time on the street, and this new place opened up south of town that was pretty cool, but I got sick of it," he said, talking more loudly now. "You want to sit and stay awhile?" he beckoned.

"I know that place—they call it the ROC, right?" she said knowingly. She remained standing.

"Yeah! Hey, you been there? They got these cameras, and the food's great. Really, that place was cool."

"But you left," Gigi said.

"Huh?"

"You said you got sick of it."

"Oh, that, well. That place is run by a bunch of religious wackos. They said if I got saved, I could stay another week. I said, "No way, man!" They had these little booklets, and all I had to do was say what was in there. Bunch of Jesus freaks, you know? I don't go for that crap," he said bluntly.

Gigi wrote carefully, not sure that the letters she was forming would be legible in the light. This was something she wished she could explore further, if Ronald turned out to be a gentleman, which she was beginning to doubt.

"Why don't we head downstairs now and stretch out a little?" she said in a bubbly voice. The urgent need to get out of this cramped room was making itself known in the form of nausea and sweaty palms. "There's some light down there, anyway."

"Yeah, and a cash register," Ronald said slyly. He stood up with so much movement that it sounded as if he was falling down. Then he spit on the floor and stretched. Gigi was already on the stairs.

There was only one light on, directly over the checkout area, in front of the painted plate glass window. If she got into trouble, she might be able to break out that way. She descended the stairs to the ground level, well ahead of Ronald. As she landed, she halted, a cry of surprise and fear muffled in her throat.

Over by the door, sitting on a stack of unpriced hardbacks from an estate sale, was a middle-aged man smoking a cigarette, dressed in gray.

1.7

GIGI STOOD FROZEN BETWEEN THE GAZE OF TWO VASTLY DIFFERENT pursuers. Ronald's steps were slowing as he descended the stairs, at first because of Gigi's abrupt stop at the bottom and then upon the discovery that they were not alone in the store. The gray man appeared to Ronald like something out of an old black-and-white detective movie in the way he moved—a colorless agent of some formidable bureaucracy sent there to impose the will of an unseen power. He was not far from wrong.

The man flicked the cigarette butt onto the wood floor and crushed it, an ominous creak rising from his grinding shoe. He thrust his hands into his pockets, perhaps to show he meant no harm.

"Miss Vaughn," he announced, nodding.

Gigi trembled at the sound of her name on the lips of this stranger. "You get your kicks following girls around town? Don't you have a life?"

He looked down at the floor and laughed to himself, shrugging his shoulders. "Look, this hasn't been what you might call a joyride, kid. All I wanted was to ask you a few questions . . . "

"Who gives you the right to question me?" she demanded, her confidence directly proportional to Ronald's presence behind her. "I don't know you—and I'm sure I don't want to know you."

The gray man smiled. "I'm nobody important. I've been sent by Mr. Daniel Withers, a fairly respected man in this city. Ever hear of him?" There was a snappy tone in his voice that Gigi didn't like.

193

"Sure," she answered. "And what would he want with me?"

"Well, for one thing, you seem to have gotten involved with some people who present a threat to Mr. Withers—a certain character named Croft in particular."

"A threat to *him?*" Gigi was incredulous. "It wasn't Jeremy who went around shooting up the neighborhoods."

"No, but he did break into Mr. Withers' building. And there's no denying his intent to steal Mr. Withers' property."

"Right," Gigi said sarcastically. "But you don't involve the police?"

"Actually, there *was* an investigation of the break-in. You will remember that it made the papers. The police considered it a random act. But, as I think you yourself have discovered, they don't follow through—limited resources and all that. So Mr. Withers has decided to handle things personally."

Ronald had crept down beside Gigi and was sliding along the wall. It was unclear if he was planning an escape or an assault. Suddenly, he lunged at the gray man, who smoothly pulled a pistol from inside his jacket and extended his arm, causing Ronald to stop short, the barrel only inches from his forehead. "Back off, you dope," he growled.

As Ronald backed away, Gigi approached. "You're nothing but a thug. I won't talk to you. If Mr. Withers has questions, he'll have to ask them of me himself."

The man put away the gun and smiled. He liked this girl, and it was a shame the circumstances had left her with such a strong distaste for him. But, business was business.

"Your car is waiting," he said pleasantly and reached for the door.

Q

The lights of the city were now familiar to Gigi. The world which they illuminated was no longer threatening. Gigi slunked down in the seat, fixing her eyes on the beams of the streetlamps as the car passed below them, the pulses of light inducing a kind of welcome hypnosis. In the distance the Withers Tower seemed to be pulling them in, straight ahead. She relaxed as the sedan rocked along; she was just one person, nearly invisible against the vast dominions of time, stars, truth. She had only wanted to know more, to be heard more. She had done what so few are ever willing to do—ask tough questions, which lead to still tougher questions, and not to fear the answers. She had reached out for destiny, made the effort, taken the risks. Now, she calmly waited for destiny to reward her, like the first look down into the canyon after the hard climb.

Homeless men and women stood like statues, emotionless, as the car drove past. Gigi took snapshots with her eyes and wrote instant histories for each of them in her head. They were lost to the world but not to God. He knew them intimately and loved them. Suddenly, as the tall buildings of downtown appeared before her, Gigi sensed an inscrutable connection to everything—the poor beggars crawling into their cardboard beds, the heart of the city which arose, Babel-like, as a monument to men's ambitions, the comforting weight of Heaven hanging in the dark night, all around—and a responsibility for it, to make sense of it, to tie it together. The car bumped its way into the lighted parking garage under the Withers Tower, and Gigi felt as if all of that which she had seen outside, though it could not follow, somehow depended on her.

The man in gray said nothing as they walked to the elevator, he clutching her upper arm. She had her book bag with her and thought a hard shot with it might knock him off his feet, giving her a chance to escape. The fingers of her free hand tightened on the strap, preparing to sling the heavy bag toward its target. But then, her brain thought past the immediate danger to the next few moments: she was alone, without a car, downtown after dark, and exhausted from a week on the streets. He had a gun. She loosed her grip on the strap.

The elevator ride seemed interminably long. They exited on the top floor and stepped out into a quiet, deserted hallway. At the other end, Gigi saw what looked like another elevator, and she wondered if they were heading for it or if maybe it was some kind of high-tech titanium doorway into the inner sanctum. Her speculation proved irrelevant; they stopped at an unmarked door along the hall. The thug opened it and pushed Gigi inside, then quietly shut the door behind her.

The man who could only be Daniel Withers sat at the end of a very long table in a richly decorated conference room. He motioned for her to take a seat in one of the plush gold chairs.

"I can stand," she said defiantly.

"Oh, that's very good, Miss Vaughn. You've been watching too many old movies."

"I'm here against my will; and I refuse to do anything you say, not even sit."

"I get the message. But I don't buy it."

Withers was tall and wore a finely-tailored black suit; his angular physique was imposing, and his crisp, clean look made him appear almost too well-groomed. Gigi loathed him immediately.

"How difficult can it be? I don't like you," she said.

"That I can understand," he replied, waving his hand in feigned boredom. "You would be in the extreme minority if you did. But

Q

this bit about not wanting to be here, well, we both know better, don't we." He didn't mean for it to be taken as a question, so she didn't answer it.

He stood and loped around the conference table toward her. "Sit," he repeated, his long body standing over her.

"Are you going to hover over me like a vulture? If not, then I'll sit."

He smiled and pulled out one of the gold chairs, gesturing that he intended it for her. Then he pulled a chair out for himself and dropped his lanky frame into it gracefully. "Please," he said.

Gigi took her seat carefully, as if she expected him to lash out at her with a sharp, sticky tongue like some creepy desert lizard.

"I should think you would be pleased to see me," he said. "After all, I've got something you want. What I want to know is . . . ," he leaned toward her, "why?"

Gigi was nervous and didn't think about her answer. "I'm inquisitive," she blurted out.

"I see that. And quite uptight at the moment."

"I haven't had much sleep lately. I'm a little on edge."

He nodded. "You impress me, Miss Vaughn. You are the kind of person I genuinely admire. Determined. *Passionate.*" The oozy way he pronounced this last word gave her a shiver.

"I'm passionate about God's work," she said forcefully.

"Oh yes, the God thing," he said disdainfully. "It's a shame you can't put your considerable gifts to some productive purpose."

Gigi sneered at him. "Why am I here?"

He sat back in his chair. "Isn't it obvious? There are a rather limited number of people in the world who have information about a certain book, and two of them are sitting in this room. The issue is why you are so interested in such things to behave so irrationally. You must admit, it's quite bizarre: harboring criminals, snatching up cash in brown envelopes, international e-mails, hiding in the slums—strange behavior for such a good little girl." He could have continued but stopped when he got the reaction he wanted.

"I'm not the one shooting at people!" she shouted.

He put up his hands in defense. "I don't know what you mean. Do I look like a violent person?"

"What about your goon outside?"

"Who, Rizzo? Oh, Miss Vaughn, please! He wouldn't harm a fly! In fact, he's one of your biggest fans." His smile broadened, then disappeared, revealing that it had been faked. "Listen closely. I get what I want, and no one takes away what is mine," he threatened.

They beheld each other like prize fighters before the opening bell. At last he broke the silence. "You don't have any need to be afraid of me."

He seemed peculiarly sincere, and she relaxed slightly. "Let's settle something," she said. "We both obviously have a keen interest in Q. Mine is purely theological. What's yours?"

Withers clasped his big hands behind his head, relishing the question. "Well, for one, I'm a publisher. I want to know the truth about everything. How's that?"

"An excellent answer. That would mean we aren't as far apart as it would seem. Except that we hold to different truths."

"How could you possibly know what I believe?" he pleaded, smiling that fake smile again.

Q

"God's people approach life a certain way. They value people; you value things. They trust a higher power; you grab as much power here and now as you can. They live as people bound for Heaven, where these things are meaningful. You have obviously missed the bus."

Withers laughed for an inordinately long time, so long in fact that Gigi almost started laughing with him. "I don't know, Miss Vaughn. Perhaps I am a bit egocentric. But how am I different from your beloved clerics who strut about behind their pulpits with roses pinned to their lapels, silks dangling from their breast pockets, cufflinks glinting in the bright floodlights required for the cameras . . . ." He started laughing again, imagining the buffoonery. "Sometimes I turn off the sound and watch them—it's hilarious! And you know something, for all their pomposity, I could buy and sell any of their churches in a single day."

"Not all of us are like that," she said quietly.

"Oh, I know. That's why you are so endearing! You are truly virtuous, caring for the poor and downtrodden in that fleabag mission like you do. We may not have the same faith, but are we that different in the way we feel about some things? What will you do when you get out of school?"

"I've thought about writing," she said.

"Not preaching?"

"Preachers are a dime a dozen. Their sermons are forgotten by lunchtime. The spoken word motivates, but its power is short-lived. The written word changes lives."

"Yes, yes, I do agree," he quipped. "But you would preach if they'd let you."

"Some will let me, if I were called to it."

"Yes, but most would be critical, wouldn't they? You would never get your due, and you know it."

Gigi could offer nothing more on the subject. She was feeling the anger rising up within her throat, and she dared not lose control and make a bad mistake.

"Admit it," he said, "you're afraid to try. You might not be good enough. You couldn't handle the pressure. So you're chasing after this old book, to see if it will help you put them to shame . . . "

"What would you know about my motives!" she cried, nearly rocketing out of the chair to leap at his throat.

Withers looked at her with such certainty behind his eyes, Gigi had the feeling he did see her motives. She took a deep breath and waited to see what would happen next.

"OK," he said, placing his hands flat on the table as if to indicate the meeting was wrapping up. "Where is the young man, Jeremy Croft?"

"I have no idea."

"What about the other members of the Society?"

"I don't know. Just John Ravenswood, an Englishman. That's it."

She was being honest, and all the evidence he had gathered suggested she was telling the truth. Even so, she was connected to them, and he needed to keep her under control.

"Do you mean to tell me, Miss Vaughn, that you have risked life and limb simply because you want to know what's in this book of mine and for no other reason?"

She looked at him with pity. "There's so much more to it than that. You couldn't understand. I am deeply committed to my faith, and there's a lot that's wrong with organized religion. It's like I'm the only one out there who seems to have it right. Or maybe I'm the one who's wrong. It's confusing." She put her head in her hands.

"No, Gigi, if my opinion means anything, I don't think you are wrong," he said sympathetically. "In fact, there are many people who see the hypocrisy in the Church just as vividly, perhaps more so. Saints such as yourself who make sacrifices for others are very inspiring. You should be encouraged, not dismissed, by your brethren." He reached into his coat pocket.

"What are you doing?" she asked, shocked.

"I'm making a small donation." He tore the check out and handed it to her. It was made out to the Kitchen for twenty-five thousand dollars.

"There is no way I'm taking this from you!"

"Why not?"

"Because I don't trust you, for one thing. You want me to back off, and I won't. This is nothing more than a bribe to keep my mouth shut about this book, which you stole . . . "

"I never did any such thing! Do you have any idea what I paid for it?" He was clearly insulted.

"Blood money!"

He rolled his eyes. "Oh, come on! You really have been watching too many late-night movies! What can I do to show you I'm sincere?"

She eyed him the way a spider watches the bug buzz around just above the newly hung web. She reached down into her book bag and pulled out a spiral notebook. "Read this," she said, handing it to him.

She watched Withers' eyes move over the words; he nodded, frowned, wrinkled his brow in concern.

"This is brilliant," he said.

"Will you publish it?" Her heart was pounding.

He read through her story once again, and a smile found its way to his lips.

"I'll do even better," he said. "The *Dispatch* is one of my smaller papers, but it is important as a place where young writers can develop. You have talent, Miss Vaughn, to go along with your passion. That is a good combination. I would like to make you a regular contributor to this paper. I would like you to write about the religion in this town as you see it. You can have a free hand, with—of course—a little direction from my editors and myself. And," here Withers looked full into Gigi's eyes, "I promise you will help to unveil to the world the greatest literary discovery in the last two millenia."

Without giving her time to respond, Withers reached across the table to shake her hand. She took it, and he squeezed quickly, before she could offer a firm grip. It was a message of how he expected this partnership to go. She prayed silently and tried to calm her dizzying fear. At least she would get out of there alive, but this realization afforded no relief. Feeling the cold hand around her own, it crossed her mind that she might be making a deal with the devil himself, here alone in this exalted tower, with the vagabond army she loved so much huddling for shelter in the shadows below.

Part 2

Steeples on Sandcastles

I am despised by them
  And they have no esteem for me
  That Thou mayest manifest Thy might through me.
They have banished me from my land like a bird from
    its nest;
All my friends and brethren are driven far from me
  And hold me for a broken vessel.

And they, teachers of lies and seers of falsehood,
  Have schemed against me a devilish scheme,
To exchange the Law engraved on my heart by Thee
  For the smooth things (which they speak) to Thy
people.

—From the *Hymns Scroll*, Hymn 12

2.1

THE PROPOSAL HAD BEEN SITTING ON HIS DESK FOR TWO WEEKS. THE Properties Committee was meeting tonight, and they would want an answer. Carter Rutledge sighed; the bank didn't care if Seventh Baptist Church ever withdrew the money that had accumulated in the memorials fund, but pressure from the congregation had been mounting. Why leave all that cash sitting there, doing nothing, when there were needs to be met? Carter had avoided the issue up to now, because the denomination had asked him to lead the church in sponsoring a new mission enterprise for the poor, but he was still ten thousand dollars short of what was required. He had hoped to guide his flock to see the wisdom of investing in those outside the church who were truly needy, rather than on themselves, but this was getting harder to do. Like so many of Charleston's churches, Seventh was developing a fortress mentality. His members were good folks, and they loved their church—perhaps even more than God. Now they wanted an elevator. How could he lead his people to walk downtown to the housing projects when they weren't even willing to walk up the stairs?

He dictated a memo into his handheld recorder, which essentially rejected the proposal because the available funds would not come close to covering the total costs, based on his own discussions with a local contractor. The cost of renovations to the existing building to accommodate the elevator would be astronomical. "You can't just buy an elevator and install it," he explained. "You need to tear things down before you can put things up." He laughed to himself, remembering the prophet Jeremiah's call to "pluck up and break down, to destroy and to overthrow, to build and to plant."

That was the challenge, really: to break down the fortress walls and loose the people to go out into the world and serve. In other parts of Charleston, the Gospel was gaining momentum. Gil Tucker's new church on Daniel Island was one example; Rusty Rowe's innovative mission downtown was another. These men, though much younger than Carter, knew what it took to get things done. He knew he should teach his own people to go and do likewise.

Carter stood up and looked out the window of his study. The neighborhood had changed over the years and not for the better, though the church had done little ministry in its own backyard. The work was so much harder now than it used to be, as were the people's hearts. He was no stranger to difficulty, but he refused to be swallowed up in it. The grave foreboding he had sensed a few weeks ago returned, but it only strengthened his resolve. Let the wave come—somehow, he would lead his church to stem the rising tide.

The pine boards that lent a homey warmth to the coffee shop creaked with the shuffling traffic of the late morning. The overall decor of the little house—now refurbished for commerce and humbly dubbed Yesterday's Muffins—was a kind of eclectic drab, which attracted academics, retired men, stockbrokers and their prey, students, housewives, and the occasional transient. The proprietor—a tall, ungainly, steel-eyed woman with chalky gray hair too long for her age and a preference for sale-rack western wear—remembered each patron's name after his or her first visit; her raspy yet strangely pleasing voice could be heard above the low din of the collective conversations, announcing each customer's approach to the counter. She did not believe in rising with the sun, so the baked goods were never fresh; prepared instead on the previous day, they were warmed over and sold cheap, along with the strongest coffee in town. The regulars boasted that a distinction between a Yesterday's muffin and those made fresh at the overpriced, overmarketed franchised place down the road could not be made by an honest man, and thus the legend grew.

"It never ceases to amaze me how some people's lives get so fouled up," said an attractive, thirty-something jogger just in from her morning run to her friend across the table, a wiry blonde in navy spandex.

"Pitiful!" agreed the blonde with a soft flip of the wrist. "Can you *believe?*" She leaned in to whisper but spoke without a reduction in volume. "One child I can understand. But *three?* And not even to know the fathers!" She threw herself back in the wooden seat, as if hit in the chest with a medicine ball.

The two women picked at the edges of their low-fat blueberry muffins, the blonde swinging her foot over her other leg with an innate hyperactivity. "And you know," she continued, still chewing, "she'll just have more."

The remark struck a chord with her companion. "Naturally," she quipped. "That's the way those people are. Frankly, if it weren't for us, I just don't know what they'd do."

"Live off the taxes of other hard-working people, that's what," she answered.

An indistinct mumbling, disparaging in tone, arose from the next table. The blonde glanced over at the young Asian-looking girl behind the notebook computer. "I'm sorry, were you speaking to me?" she hissed.

Q

"I couldn't help overhearing your discussion. Please forgive me; I found it amusing, that's all. I didn't mean to offend." Gigi's attitude was such that it only intensified the insult.

The blonde stood up. A vein bulged prominently in her neck. Her eyelashes batted rapidly. "Excuse me, but I don't think what we were discussing is any of your business."

Gigi resisted the urge to laugh. "You're absolutely right, it isn't. But it doesn't strike me that you're particularly ashamed of your opinions."

The blonde reached for a chair at Gigi's table and sat down heavily. "OK, then, what's *your* opinion?" Her thin face was reddening.

Gigi folded down the screen, and the notebook slipped into sleep mode. "About what?" she asked innocently.

"About the human garbage that lines the streets of Fort Worth! About the blacks who expect us to pay for their illegitimate children because they can't control their urges, and the Mexicans who crawl over the border and take jobs from our own people, that's about what!" The confrontation was taking on a small audience in the center of the shop.

"Well, for one thing, you don't look like they've hurt you too much. The cost of those tights of yours could feed a migrant worker's family for a month."

"Oh, is that so?" The woman leaned over the table, her face inches from Gigi's. Her friend was standing behind her, waiting to see where this conversation was headed.

Gigi sat with her arms outstretched toward the blonde. "I'm really sorry," she said, this time with a twinge of sincerity. "You obviously work with needy people, and you should be thanked, not criticized." She stood and extended her hand to the suddenly surprised women.

They looked cautiously at each other. "We volunteer at the ROC. Have you heard of it?" the jogger said, still somewhat suspicious.

Gigi nodded. "You go to Restoration?"

The women's features softened immediately. They looked at each other again and sat down at Gigi's table. "I'm Robin," the blonde said. "And I'm Gwendolyn," said the other. "And you are?"

"Gigi Vaughn. I write for the *Dispatch.*"

The new feature story was intended to capture the work being done by the churches in helping the poor, not necessarily to promote any individual congregation but to show Christian compassion in action and inspire more involvement. The two women were typical of the socialites who helped out from time to time, doing so because it was praiseworthy or rewarding for them in some way. It eased the conscience and looked good to others. But Gigi was searching for something deeper. Where were the true servants, the ones who saw the needy as more than objects for their attention to relieve their own guilt—but as real people whom God loved? Where was the true empathy that resulted in sacrifice, not just a ministry of convenience?

After a lengthy exchange, which described the women's experiences at the ROC, Gigi got to the heart of the matter. "Where does the anger come from?"

The blonde jumped in quickly, eager to postulate. "Oh, well, don't you see, it comes from having nothing. Really, Gigi, can you believe they could be anything but resentful?" She snorted somewhat as if to mock the question.

Gigi smiled briefly. "I was asking about *your* anger, Robin."

There was no answer. The anger could have come from anywhere, of course, from an unresponsive husband or a lack of self-respect or a variety of other nuisances that plagued those who crowd their lives with things. But Gigi was fairly sure that she knew the source of the contempt this woman felt for the needy; their poverty made her feel good about herself, but somewhere deep down Robin knew these feelings were wrong. She had too much and gave too little—it was obvious. The message she heard from Bobby T. Raeburn each week was sinking in, if only subconsciously. No one really took the message seriously, not to the extremes Jesus intended, but there were reminders—the poor being the most visible—that those who are most fortunate are undeserving of such blessings. They stood before her in their glorious rags to innocently and wordlessly insist that there was yet one thing the righteous lacked.

Gwendolyn made assorted moves indicating it was time to leave, collecting her cup and napkin and brushing crumbs from her glimmering running jacket. Robin could only stare at Gigi in disbelief, and though the anger was once more rising up in her, she could not allow herself to set it free and thus expose herself again.

By late morning Gigi had arrived at the Kitchen, where she found Tinky running over some of the endless details with Cody, who had replaced Gigi for the summer. He was the cook, custodian, caretaker, and counselor—all in an assistant role—and shared preaching duties with Gigi, who was now spending a larger percentage of her volunteer time at the women's shelter. They were both taking the textual criticism summer class with A.D., and the balance of Gigi's time was given to her new freelance work at the *Dispatch*. Tinky was gracious to allow them to share evening shifts whenever possible so that they also could share free time together.

"Hey!" shouted Cody. "Look what I picked up today."

Gigi's eyes followed him across the big room until he vanished down the corridor to appear again with a package wrapped in brown paper under his arm. He was tearing at the paper as he came, revealing Gigi's first published story, matted and framed. "Nifty, huh?" he said proudly.

"Your idea?" wondered Gigi.

"Mine, actually," answered Tinky. "We're proud of you. Where should we hang it?"

"Somewhere where it won't get egg on it," Cody drawled.

Gigi laughed at this but realized there really wasn't any suitable place to keep it in good condition. As a general rule, glass didn't survive long at the Kitchen. "I'll have to think about it," she said. "I doubt too many of the guests will be reading it."

Tinky and Cody exchanged an awkward glance. "You'd be surprised at how many of them do read," Tinky said gravely. Cody looked down at his feet. Gigi was immediately alerted to some ominous information she expected would soon be revealed.

Cody pulled open a drawer and retrieved a handful of tracts, which he tossed on the counter. "Somehow these got distributed last night. Everybody seemed to have one. The literate ones were reading them aloud in little groups. Once we got a look at them, we decided to take them up."

Gigi examined one of the tracts. It appeared to be typewritten and reproduced on a copy machine. The words "SATAN'S BIG LIE" were written in bold across the front. Gigi frowned. "A serious guilt trip," she muttered.

"Can't argue with the theology," Cody said, "but we thought the tone was a bit manipulative. Check out the back."

"Oh, wow," Gigi said, her eyes widening. "'Exchange this tract for items in our benevolence closet,'" she read. "I've heard of this place. Chisolm Trail Believer's Outreach Center." She looked up. "Wonder if they've got anything in my size?"

Q

The dark paneling of Dr. Crawford LaRue's outer office overpowered the bright shaft of light which streamed in through the one four-paned window, throwing the shadow of a cross onto the beige carpet in black silhouette. The cross motif was appropriately spotlighted everywhere Gigi looked in the small room, where what could only be described as modern religious art served as ample decoration. There was a painting of the crucifixion on the back wall, and near where Gigi sat in one of two dark green, winged-back chairs, there was hung a large monochrome photograph of the church taken from below so that the cross atop the steeple stretched frighteningly Heavenward. Smaller prints, such as one artist's fantastic vision of the rapture, commanded the greater attention. There was even a photo of the founding pastor, awash in pale gloom and the subject's apparent suspicion of the lens. The room was dark and masculine, with its heavy drapes and furniture; and when the tiny secretary entered to announce that Dr. LaRue was now available, she struck Gigi as a mouse scurrying forth to where she wasn't welcome, to snatch a fallen morsel and skitter away.

Crawford LaRue was a large man with gigantic hands and a brown mustache sprinkled with gray. He appeared to be in his mid-fifties, perhaps older, with a distinctly Texan quality about him in his manner and clothing, right down to the pearl buttons on his western shirt, its long collar points reminding Gigi of a 1970s fashion staple she was glad she had missed.

"So you're with the *Dispatch*, I'm told," he bellowed, inviting Gigi to sit. The office was the stylistic extension of the other room, except for the massive desk in the center and bookshelves on each side of the window. When the pastor sat down, the sun shining through the blinds behind his head gave him a kind of halo.

"I am," she said politely. "I'm working on a story about how churches in town are helping the needy. It's a freelance arrangement; I'm a full-time student at Southwestern."

His eyes widened and then narrowed at this, and she couldn't interpret from the expression whether he approved or not. "But the reason I came to see you particularly—is this." She pulled out the tract and held it out in front of him.

The sudden manner in which Gigi presented herself and her mission seemed to make LaRue uneasy. He gripped both armrests of his high-backed leather chair and began to rock. "And what is it that you want to know about it," he said warily.

"Well, just that there's a catch, isn't there? I mean, giving out free tickets for stuff from the benevolence closet, after dangling the reader over the pit of hell with this 'Satan's Big Lie' business—surely there's something going on here that I'm missing."

"That tract," he said, pointing, "is God's truth. These men ruin themselves on alcohol and drugs; they commit crimes and are in and out of jail. They need to be redeemed; that's all we're saying. Do you disagree?"

"Actually, no. In fact I find the teaching quite sound. But you're using it to recruit people for your benevolence work. Why don't you just put the food and clothes in the van and drive up and down Hemphill passing it out?"

"My dear girl, you miss the point," he lectured. "They need to be *redeemed*. They come here and we help them spiritually, not just physically."

"And how exactly do you do that?"

"Why, we witness to them."

"But you don't need to bring them here to do that," Gigi protested.

"No, we don't have to, but we want them to be serious about their decisions. We don't want to just let them wander off into their old habits," he said.

Q

"I see." Gigi felt like he was saying just enough to answer her but not giving the full story. "So, you disciple these men? Where do you house them?"

He paused. "Let's go back to the tract for a moment," he said. "Satan's big lie is doing whatever eases the pain the quickest, whatever satisfies the hunger inside. There is a deeper need—the need for God—and a more satisfying solution—salvation. There are no quick fixes here. We want to absorb these men into our fellowship."

"I'm not sure I'm following your logic, sir," she said honestly.

He exhaled and folded his hands in front of him on the desk. He stopped rocking. "We present the Gospel. We baptize those who receive it. Then we enroll them, and we expect them to attend. We have a special class. We want to keep them in the fold. Now, what is objectionable about that?" He glared.

"Nothing, I suppose." Gigi crinkled her forehead. "But I am a bit offended by your ministry," she commented.

"For heaven's sakes, why?" he asked, incredulous.

"Well, I keep wondering why you would go across town and use this tract to lure people from another ministry where they are being taught the Gospel, fed, clothed, and sheltered," she said quizzically. "Is your program that much more superior that you can justify stealing homeless sheep?"

He stared blankly at her. "We know what we give them is gospel truth. We can't know what the others do. That's your answer."

Gigi nodded. She had heard this reasoning before. "Fine. But from now on, stay out of my Kitchen." She stood to go, leaving a confused Crawford LaRue to wonder if he would get his name in the paper at all.

Outside, the sunshine swaddled Gigi like a sympathetic friend. Almost immediately upon exiting the office, she sensed a commotion around the corner and heard a faint siren growing steadily louder. She trotted down the concrete stairs and hustled along the side of the building. A crowd came quickly into view; several scraggly men knelt around a prone body on the ground. Suddenly the squad cars arrived in rapid succession, blue lights pulsating, shattering the tranquility of the brilliant afternoon. They rushed to the prostrate man, then two of them jumped up and jogged to the storefront building across the street, where a crowd had gathered. Gigi became aware that the distinctive wail of the ambulance had stopped. At length it appeared, rolling slowly into the lot, signifying there was no longer an emergency.

Gigi walked up to the man on the ground. She glanced at his face and was relieved that she didn't recognize him. But two of the men who had been kneeling over him saw Gigi and ran to her; they were regulars at the Kitchen, and they were distraught and stuttering.

"Calm down, now," Gigi said, embracing them both awkwardly. She craned her neck and caught a glimpse of the body being placed on a stretcher and removed to the waiting ambulance. But there was no urgency. The man was dead.

"Who was that?" she asked, extricating herself from the men's arms.

"David!" one of them shouted. "They shot him!" The man was delirious with panic.

"Listen, I need to find out what happened, OK?" With that, Gigi ran toward the crowd across the street, leaving the men to comfort each other. She kept her distance until the police had finished questioning, then raced to confront the officer.

Q

"Excuse me, I'm Gigi Vaughn, with the *Dispatch*. What happened here?" she asked, walking swiftly beside the policeman.

"Read the report," he said bluntly.

"Listen here, this is news, and the people have a right to know what's going on. Are there any suspects?" The officer's mouth turned up in a quirky smile, and she realized how stupid she must have sounded. But this was her first real scoop, and she was totally out of her depth. The officer walked on, ignoring her.

Gigi jumped in front of him and threw back her hair. "Just two minutes," she said, making a peace sign. He paused, looked at her with what appeared to be a positive appraisal, and stopped. "Two minutes," he said.

"Great!" Gigi flipped open her spiral notepad and waited.

"OK. Well, this building is part of that church over there." He pointed to the stony backside of Chisolm Trail Believer's Outreach Center. "They give out food and clothes to the street people. The victim became aggressive inside, apparently trying to make off with quite a haul, and he roughed up one of the girls, they say. One of the young men in there shot him. He dropped the stash, stumbled across the street, and fell down dead. We have no I.D."

"His name was David," she said.

He looked puzzled. Hesitating, he said, "You knew him?"

"Can I speak with those folks?" she said, looking past him. He nodded, and Gigi walked past him toward a growing crowd standing next to the church.

The interview was brief and emotionally charged. Gigi tried to remind herself that if she expected to get any information out of these people, she needed to remain objective. Her questions were short and direct. They seemed highly motivated to explain every-thing in detail, to exonerate themselves of guilt.

"So the man actually grabbed you by the throat?" Gigi asked a young woman in a multicolored top. She was trembling and still clutching at her neck with agitation. "He tried to choke me," she said.

"She was in the doorway," interjected a young man who wanted to do all the talking. He had been the one who had fired the gun. "She was trying to calm him down, to see if we could get him to stay."

"But you got away," Gigi said to the girl. "Is that right?"

"Well, yes. He got scared when he saw the gun. He let me go and started screaming! He started grabbing cans and throwing them at Jody. He was going crazy! That's when . . . ," she paused.

"I fired the pistol," said Jody.

There was a somber silence before Gigi spoke again. "Why was he so upset?"

Jody walked over to where Gigi was standing. He was a thin fellow, frail looking, with red hair and glasses. "He came in with the other men. They all had their tracts with them. We invited them into the back room for a short presentation."

"You witnessed to them," Gigi said.

"Yes, that's what we do," he answered pleasantly.

"I'm a seminary student," Gigi explained.

"Oh, then you would understand," Jody said smiling. He seemed much more at ease with this information. "I plan to go there myself after college."

"OK, you shared the Gospel. Then what?" Gigi inquired.

The young man explained the process in detail. They would give the men cards to complete. Those who indicated a desire to be baptized were enrolled in Sunday school. They were told that if they attended every week, they could receive food on a regular basis and clothing as well. Those who were already Christians were given food this one time only. Those who were not Christians and who refused baptism were given a Bible. This is apparently what sent the man into a rage.

"Most people get baptized, I suppose," Gigi remarked.

"Well, we've only been doing this for a week, but most do, yes," he answered.

"Can I see the man's card? I heard his first name was David."

The girl sorted through the cards until she found it and handed it to Gigi. "See, there on the bottom, he checked 'I do not desire baptism at this time.'"

"Did you look closely at this card?" Gigi asked in amazement. "This man's name was David Stein."

"David Stein?" Jody asked, as if he thought the name should somehow be meaningful.

"*Stein,*" said Gigi sharply. "He was Jewish."

When Gigi's story appeared in print, the backlash was almost immediate. Anna K. Soesbee, the letters editor for the *Dispatch,* made a swift judgment not to publish any of the hate mail and, after the first two dozen were received, even considered throwing them away. Gigi, suspicious of the awkward silence following the publication of what even she considered a controversial article, pressed her for the truth, and Anna K handed over the letters. One that figured prominently was penned by Dr. Crawford LaRue: a three-page, single-spaced exposition of his church's ministry rife with biblical quotations. Gigi suggested that this one be edited for space and be published as a guest editorial, and Anna K took the idea to her boss, who thought it a good idea. Along with it, however, came a statement that the *Stockyard Dispatch,* while willing to provide a forum for dissenting opinions, stood by the veracity of the facts presented by their writer.

The whole affair was deeply disturbing to Gigi. In her view, Chisolm Trail Believer's Outreach Center was manipulating the homeless to pad their baptism and attendance figures and simply cloaked it in the guise of evangelism. No effort was given to really know these people, to listen to them, to care for their real needs—physical or spiritual. It underscored her assertion that the poor were seen as nothing more than objects to be used for someone else's benefit. But it was not the poor who were soulless—it was the ministers of benevolence themselves. So, a homeless man was dead. No arrests were made. There was no advocate for David Stein, who, Gigi imagined, resented the humiliation of his poverty and simply would not submit to surrendering his beliefs for the sake of a plate of beans. She considered delving into whatever details of his life were available and making them known.

Though the killing was the force of the story, Gigi was wide-ranging in her indictments. She disparaged not only what she saw as the self-serving ministries of Chisolm Trail and Restoration but the lack of concern for the needy in general by the churches, many of which boasted fabulous buildings and wealthy congregations. She knew the piece was one-sided; she had deliberately avoided covering the more compassionate congregations. She was not seeking to praise those who merely did what they should have done but rather to expose the hypocrisy that passes for modern religion and remains largely unchallenged by the faithful. She was issuing a wake-up call to those who wouldn't allow her the chance to be heard any other way, and she knew that her objectivity was tainted

Q

by the bitterness of her own personal experience. And Daniel Withers had urged her to do it, which disturbed her all the more.

The letters themselves did not refute her points but instead rebuked her for what one writer termed "vicious invective toward those who sought to do good." There were many Bible verses quoted, but Gigi was numb to this sort of thing, having spent years trying to justify her calling to those who found refuge for their prejudices in the words and phrases of Scripture. Still, after reading through the letters, she reread her story and saw more clearly her judgmental tone. Had she, mired deep in the frustration of her own lost cause, become as arrogant and stubborn as they?

It was the call from A.D. that finally did it. From the first hello she knew something was up. He had been selected to inform her that she had been the subject of a recent meeting of the seminary trustees, who were petitioned to address the matter by some angry influential alumni and supporters of the school. She was being asked to print a formal apology.

From that moment, Gigi Vaughn took as her burden the mantle of the persecuted, the paranoia that has gripped well-meaning ministers from time immemorial, so well described by Jeremiah, who saw "terror on every side." In the hallways of the seminary, parked at a red light, fetching mail from the apartment postal boxes—nowhere could she escape the weight of unseen eyes that may have been watching her, hating her, plotting against her.

Gigi had brazenly hoisted her enmity aloft and brandished it like the colors of a defeated nation. But the war was only just beginning.

Gigi rolled lazily out of bed and shuffled to the refrigerator. She inhaled the cold air as she slouched over the open door, then yanked out a jug of milk for her morning cereal. The door swung under its own power and closed with a loud rattle. As she reached for a box of sugared flakes, an image of a white envelope flashed in her groggy mind. She paused, then looked out toward the front door. There on the floor was the envelope, apparently slipped under the door during the night. She had walked right over it on her way into the kitchen.

The card was neatly handwritten, without salutation or signature:

You are cordially invited to the weekly meeting of
The Enclave
Friday evenings @ 11 P.M.
Colossians 2:8

Gigi returned to the envelope to find an address written on the back. She wondered; the nature of this invitation had the feel of some kind of esoteric society, but the Bible verse seemed to disavow anything sinister. But why the odd hour? She smiled and tapped her palm with the card. This was interesting; she had to go.

"I'm perfectly happy at my church, I hope you know. I'm just doing this for you."

"I know, Anna K. You don't have to keep saying it," Gigi answered with a laugh. "And I appreciate your willingness to come along. Consider it a learning experience."

"I'm a Baptist," Anna K shot back. "I already know everything." She joined Gigi's laugh with her own obnoxious giggle. Anna K was only a few years older than Gigi, still single, very skinny and bookish-looking. She had degrees in library science and journalism and hoped to continue rising through the ranks at the *Dispatch,* work being the main focus of her life. Conservative and reserved, she was drawn to Gigi's flair for the dramatic—to that, and the fact

Q

that she had met Daniel Withers, while Anna K herself, in three years with the paper, never had.

It was a quiet street—not surprising at all given the late hour and location—in the midst of a long line of simple, one-story structures that were nearly all owned by the seminary for student housing. "This is so weird," remarked Anna K as Gigi shut off the engine.

The small house was ablaze with light from within. About a dozen cars were parked in front and along the street. As the women approached, a happy man with long wisps of brown hair combed over his bald pate opened the door. "Welcome!" he said, with the enthusiasm of a well-trained Sunday-school greeter. He swung wide the screen door. "This is the Enclave."

The first room to the left was filled with chatting people, nearly all men in their forties and fifties, with a few Gigi's age. The few women, probably wives, were noticeably attached to certain of them. One of the men stood and walked over to greet Anna K and Gigi; as he did so, the room fell silent. "How do you do, Miss Vaughn? I'm Dale Dole."

Gigi blinked at the sound of the name, just as they clasped hands. "I know you," she said, the words slipping out slowly as they came to mind.

"Oh, yes, well, no doubt you know *of* me," he said jovially. "Though I would ask you to dispel whatever you've heard from your thoughts and come to your own conclusions. I'm not the bad man they say I am. Not *really.*" At this, the room tittered with mild laughing.

Gigi turned her head to Anna K, still looking at Dole. "This gentleman is a former professor, if I'm not mistaken." She turned again to face her host. "This is my friend, Anna K. Soesbee."

"Charmed," said Dole as he shook Anna K's nearly petrified hand. Anna K nodded uncomfortably. "Come in, both of you, and find a seat. We have no agenda this evening other than to discuss your particular—situation."

"I'm right, aren't I?" Gigi asked as she sat in a ladder-back chair someone had dragged in from the kitchen. "You did once teach at the seminary?"

"For several years I did, that's true. That was before they objected to certain of my views. But none of that is important, really. I still count myself among the scholars, though I must commit a fair portion of my time to property and casualty insurance if I want to eat." Again, a rift of laughter rode around the room like a tiny wave, and Gigi wondered if the guests were trained to respond to the various quips of their leader. "This community is gathered for the sharing of Christian ideas without fear of judgment. It exists to allow intellectual stimulation and growth for its members."

"So, you've relocated your class from campus to this little house?"

Dole looked at Gigi through narrowed eyes. "Miss Vaughn, you have been invited here because we know what it feels like to be unfairly attacked by wolves in sheep's clothing. We thought you might benefit from our fellowship."

Gigi relaxed. "Of course. I apologize. But you've got to admit, the invitation under the door, the antiworship hour, the excommunicated leader—the whole thing's a bit . . . " She groped for a word that wouldn't offend.

"Creepy," blurted out Anna K from an ottoman in the corner.

Dole laughed heartily, and the congregation followed suit. "Certainly. But I assure you, this is no cult. We're simply attempting to replicate the experience of the New Testament churches. As you get to know us, you'll understand."

Gigi glanced over at Anna K, whose darting eyes indicated a constant vigilance, just in case.

2.2

G IGI AWAKENED ON SATURDAY MORNING TO A BRIGHTLY LIT DAY with nothing to do, the first one she could remember having in quite some time. She had a date planned with Cody that evening, but the day was clear. It was a good chance to study, do housework, e-mail a few friends, and call her father. The options overwhelmed her as she lay comfortably considering them in bed, until the harsh ring of the telephone forced her to move.

"This is Daniel Withers."

Gigi bolted upright. "Hi," she eeked out of a dry throat.

"Come downtown. We have an important matter to discuss."

"I . . . well, I . . . "

"Ten-thirty should do fine. We can be finished by lunch." A soft click ended the conversation.

"Who does he think he is!" she shouted, slamming down the phone. She sat there for a moment, blood suddenly rushing to her head, and laughed out loud at her own outrage. As she jumped from the bed and walked briskly to the closet, she began to ponder what this business might be about. She bristled with energy at the thought of it.

The traffic was unusually heavy, but Gigi had no difficulty arriving on time. Withers was standing in the lobby, staring at a blank wall formed of glossy black granite blocks.

"Miss Vaughn, good morning," he announced, apparently having seen her reflection in the stone as she approached. He whirled to face her. "Thank you for coming."

"You mean I had a choice?"

"Oh yes, of course! Did I not make that clear?"

Perturbed, Gigi ignored the remark and looked past him at the wall. "Am I missing something, or is the wall really that compelling?"

Withers laughed. "Am I so vain? No, it is the wall itself that consumes me these days. As it has you."

Gigi brushed back her hair and scratched her head. "I don't see anything unusual about it." She looked again. "It's cool. I like it. You've been working on it for a while, right, I mean, wasn't there some big scaffolding over here before?"

"Correct. The wall has been concealed until now," he said.

"Great. Is that it?"

Withers grinned and crossed his arms.

"Well?" Gigi demanded. "You wanted my opinion, and you got it. Another million dollars got you a great wall. I'm really impressed. So," she said impatiently, "is there anything else?"

Withers touched her on the shoulder and led her to the elevator. "Come with me," he said.

"I understand your popularity with the brethren seems to be waning," he said as the elevator lifted them toward the top floor.

"To your delight, I'm sure."

"Don't judge me just yet, Miss Vaughn. By the time they're finished with you, you'll never want to set foot in a church again."

Q

They stepped out of the elevator and walked the long hallway to Withers' private conference room. Gigi's heart pounded in anticipation. Her instincts told her something important was about to be revealed.

"I have always believed that time would one day reveal the truth, Miss Vaughn," Withers continued. "The time has come, and I am the messenger of the revelation."

Gigi felt a chill run down her spine as he directed her to a seat at the end of a long mahogany table. The room was narrow and darkened, with recessed lights in the ceiling glowing like dull eyes. Withers sat across from her and folded his hands in front of him.

"That wall you admired so is but a facade. The real treasure lies behind it."

Gigi perked up, forgetting his earlier insults. "That's where you're hiding it—behind that wall!"

Withers held out his hands as if to deflect her words. "Not so fast. One doesn't just drop the curtain and spring something like this on the world. There's an orderly process to revelation. We can't just have it hit us all at once. That's God's way, in fact, to proceed slowly—don't you agree?"

Gigi sat back, again feeling the chill. She sat on her hands and forced herself to wait.

Withers stood up and began to pace. "The wall, you see, is actually a fairly thin veneer of granite panels. With the proper tools and expertise, these panels can be removed to reveal portions of a second wall, upon which are engraved the words that will quite dramatically change the world." He watched her closely for a response.

"You mean, you've copied the document—on a hidden wall?" she asked at last.

"Yes. And one phrase at a time, it will be revealed—*after* it has been published in the *Dispatch*."

"I see. Your plan is to whet the world's appetite for more—to create excitement . . . "

"Excitement? No!" Withers leaned hard with both hands on the table. *"Panic* might be the more appropriate word."

Gigi blinked rapidly as her brain processed Withers' plan. She felt a bit nauseous. A cold sweat erupted on her skin.

"Ah, yes, I can see you know what I mean," he said dryly, sitting down again.

"OK, just hang on here. You're saying that Q could be damaging to Christianity?" She felt her throat close as she pronounced the words.

"Who, me?" Withers laughed loudly. "I would never presume so much. But there are others with the proper credentials who may have an opinion, of course. I might simply help them to, shall we say, spread the word."

"Why are you telling me this? You know I won't be part of it," she said sharply.

"Of course you will, Miss Vaughn. And you'll do so gladly." He sat back, wearing a smug expression. "Let's look at the facts. You have yet to print the apology that the holy fathers have requested, which we both know you won't do, and you are known to consort with certain heretics in their secret meetings . . . "

"What? Last night—you know about last night?" Gigi was startled.

"Don't be so naive, Gigi. Not about what I know or about this so-called fellowship. The Enclave is well known in this city, and you have only seen the tip of the iceberg in terms of their teachings, and their numbers. There is far more beneath the surface than you realize."

Gigi could only sit silently as he spoke.

"Furthermore, you aspire to a pastoral position, despite being of the gentle gender. You are hardly suitable to play the hero of all Christendom, now, are you."

He leaned forward. "You might as well join the winning team, Miss Vaughn. Mine."

"When is all this supposed to happen?" Gigi said meekly.

"It begins tomorrow, with the announcement in Sunday's paper. A team of scholars has been at work studying the work and have verified its authenticity; their findings will be published next week. Each Sunday thereafter, an excerpt will be published, and a section of the wall exposed. After several exerpts have been published, a complimentary, leather-bound first edition of Q will be sent to the pastors of every Christian church in the United States. Soon thereafter, it will go on sale."

"And what's this got to do with me? It seems you've got this thing planned out to the last detail yourself," Gigi snipped.

"Oh, no, Miss Vaughn. You are a key element in the plan!" he responded, waving his hand in grand fashion. "You see, as these excerpts are published, there should be quite a reaction from the preachers. You know how they can't resist a soap box! It will be your assignment to present their opinions in an orderly manner—a counterpoint, if you will, to our scholars' opinion."

"Be serious, Mr. Withers!" she cried. "They dislike me already, and they don't need your paper to sound off on this thing. They have their own papers and radio shows and TV and pulpits . . . "

"Yes," he interjected, "they do. But the people they want to reach—the ones outside the churches, who already are skeptical—they're reading *my* paper, not theirs."

He made an excellent point. If the unchurched world was exposed primarily to Withers' propaganda, which would likely be swept along by the secular media . . .

"Besides, *you'll* want to know the truth yourself, won't you?" he added. "Like I said, I don't think I'll have to twist your arm. You'll come to your own conclusions, and you can print them. I'm willing to risk that you'll see their true colors before this whole thing is over, and that only helps my cause."

"What if I agree with them about these excerpts?" she asked.

"Well, that helps me also. It's always good to have a dissenting opinion if you're a publisher. People like fairness in media. Of course, ancient documents that cast our modern understanding of Christianity in a dim light have been discovered before, and they haven't made so much as a dent into organized religion. But this time will be different. The whole world will see Christianity put on trial. I have the money and the will to make sure of that."

"Well, then, I'm out!" She stood up. "I don't need a byline in your paper to practice my faith." She walked toward the door.

"It's the only pulpit you'll ever have, Gigi," Withers said over his shoulder in an almost sympathetic tone. "You may think me a monster if you will, but at least I'm giving you a chance to speak, which is more than they will do."

Gigi paused, her hand above the latch. "If I do this thing, there's something more I want from you," she said quietly.

Withers' voice, though barely above a whisper, filled the room. "Really! I didn't think you the mercenary type, but I'm sure something can be arranged. In fact, I'm confident you'll be able to build quite a career from this. Who knows where it will lead? Of course, if you choose to stay in my employ, you'll never want for anything."

"That's not what I had in mind," she answered.

"Oh no? I'm sorry—what then?" He seemed truly mystified.

Gigi straightened and nearly shouted the words. "I want to see it."

Withers stared at her momentarily, then laughed. "My dear, *everyone* will see it! I intend to build a museum dedicated to the rise and fall of Christianity, and the codex will be prominently displayed for all to view."

"You misunderstand me," she said. "I want to see it for myself. Before it is printed and sent to all the ministers, I want to see it, touch it. I want to look at every word."

He regarded her with admiration. "I see. You want to be sure, though I doubt your powers of translation are so well developed as to make sense of the text." He smiled. "But you want to be as sure as you can be. You're a true seeker, Miss Vaughn."

She stared him down, but his smile remained. "You'll allow it, then?"

Withers, curling his smile into a smirk, looked away as if in thought, then back into Gigi's hard stare. He nodded his head and whispered, with a resigned flourish of his hand, "Why not?"

The pizza was divided evenly, part cheese and part veggie. Cody was chatty, energized by the work at the Kitchen, trying to get Gigi caught up on the latest events. Like a third person carrying on an independent conversation with himself, the TV was sending flickers of light in their direction as they sat in the dark, nearly empty restaurant. Gigi was struggling to listen to Cody but found it diffi-cult, distracted visually by the bright colors of the screen, preoccu-pied mentally with Withers' secret plan.

"You seem distant," he said, matter-of-factly.

Gigi's ears caught up with his remark just before he repeated it. "Yeah, I know. I haven't done a thing all day. It's like, I had almost forgotten about the book, you know, until this morning. I was really getting into the writing—I was saying something important, people were reacting. It's a rush."

Cody folded a piece of crust and stuffed it into his mouth. "That reminds me," he garbled. "You're preaching tomorrow, remember."

Gigi was stunned. "What? No—I can't! I'm not ready. I thought you were preaching."

He swallowed and shook his head slowly. "No, it's your turn. C'mon, Gigi. You of all people, forgetting you have to preach?" Her look conveyed complete innocence. "OK. I can whip something up," he said. "Don't worry about it."

She felt an urgent instinct to hug him and nearly knocked him over with the surprise embrace. "Cody, do you think I'm nuts?" she said in a childlike voice.

"Pretty much," he drawled, finally swallowing his last bite. "But that's cool."

The TV continued to shout its mindless message, and they watched, the visual images locking their eyes but freeing their minds to move along random paths.

Gigi took his chin in her hand and turned his face toward hers. "What do you think, really, about the book?"

"What, Withers' book?"

Q

"Yeah."

"Haven't read it."

Gigi rolled her eyes. "Can you get serious for a minute?" She sat up. "Here's this evil villain with all the money in the world who's out to disprove God, and you joke about it." She was smiling as she chastised him.

"You're sitting in the pizza."

"Cody!" She slapped him hard on the shoulder.

He laughed and pulled himself over beside her. "Listen. Faith is a matter of the heart, not the mind. Does it really matter what the book says? I mean, it would have to be a real bombshell to nullify two thousand years of religion. In the end, people believe what they are drawn to. The Gospel is a powerful draw."

She thought about this before answering. "That's not what I'm worried about, though."

He frowned. "What else is there, then?"

"The Church, Cody. You see it, don't you? The Church is hanging by a thread."

"Where do you get that?" he said, leaning back on his hands and stretching his long legs out in front of him. "You're talking about the most powerful institution there is. If this little lost book does present a threat, don't you think the hounds of Heaven will be loosed all over the place?"

"You're missing the point," she argued. "The modern church is man-made. So much of its ministry is self-serving. There isn't enough God stuff there to hold it together under pressure. It wouldn't take much to burst the bubble."

"I totally disagree," he answered emphatically. "Just because you're on this rebellious prophet kick doesn't mean this is the Middle Ages. The Church has flaws, but down deep it's sincere."

She sidled away from him, unaware that she did so. "You don't know this man like I do. He's really got something here. A lot of people will be shaken by this."

"Why? You won't be, will you?"

She looked at him hard, hesitating deliberately.

"Now, tell me something," he said, softening the awkward moment. He pulled up close to her again, only inches away. She locked into his gaze.

"Are you going to eat those?" he said, nodding toward the last two slices of veggie.

She slapped his hand as he reached for the pizza and punched him playfully.

About midway through Cody's sermon, the main entrance door swung open, and four well-dressed men strolled in. Cody paused, greeted them with a nod, and continued. They stopped at the door, surveying the scene. At length they found chairs near the back of the room. Gigi was certain they had come to see her. When the service ended, her assumption proved correct.

"You must be Miss Vaughn," the first man said, a portly fellow with an unbuttoned collar under his tie and a plaid jacket, which looked a few sizes too small.

"Yes, but I'm not sure we've met," she answered pleasantly.

"No, we haven't." There was an awkward silence as he glanced around at the other men. "Uh, we were expecting you to be preaching today."

"Pardon?" she said, with a discernible attitude.

"We called, and a gentleman said you were out but that you'd be preaching today." He hesitated. "We've read your articles," he continued. "We were curious about you."

He said this so kindly that Gigi was momentarily flattered. "Are you—a—pulpit committee?" she whispered excitedly.

The round man's face reddened with embarrassment. "Oh, no, no, Miss Vaughn." He put his hands out as if in self-defense. "Nothing of that sort. But we are deacons. You've been to our church, in fact—Chisolm Trail."

Gigi's disappointment was soon replaced with anger. "Not a pulpit committee," she repeated. "More like a posse, then?"

The man faked a smile. "We don't appreciate this crusade of yours. We've come as fellow believers, to ask you to stop."

"Listen, you brood of vipers!" she threatened. The man stepped back. Out of the corner of her eye, Gigi saw Cody approaching with several men, including Carl. She softened her voice. "What you're doing down there is wrong. Your pastor got to defend your warped view of evangelism in the newspaper, so as far as I'm concerned, we're even."

"You're a very disrespectful person," he said flatly.

Gigi flushed. "I don't mean to be." She felt a rising anger she knew she could not contain.

"You have to stop your attacks," he insisted.

Her blood was boiling. "I'm not attacking anyone!" She clenched her fists and threw up her hands. "I just want to *speak!*" she screamed, her eyes tightly shut.

When she opened them, she was surrounded by Carl and friends, with Cody holding them at bay as they stared menacingly at the men, who had retreated back toward the door. "You have a very interesting ministry here," the round man said sarcastically.

As they turned to go, they bumped directly into Ashley Dunbarton, who surprised them with a wide smile as he stepped aside. He was puzzled by their lack of a greeting and abrupt departure, and he watched them get into their cars. He shrugged and turned back toward the room.

"Uh, did I just miss something?"

It was then that Gigi noticed the rolled up newspaper under his arm.

The tea was almost liquid sugar, and with each swallow it made Carter Rutledge thirstier.

"Mildred, this is by far the sweetest tea I've had in quite some time," he said.

"It's grown right here in Charleston," she answered.

He nodded. "How appropriate to complement such a grand meal. I've always said that Mildred Dunbarton sets the finest table south of Broad." He winked, and she pretended not to notice. They were old chums, both widowed, and this was their ritual most Sundays. Occasionally, they lunched at the Piccadilly.

Mildred usually mentioned the morning message at least once during dinner. It didn't take much for Carter to pick up where he had left off in the pulpit, enlarging on the main points and leading forays into his many social, political, and cultural observations. But on this day she carefully avoided such talk, having a mind to discuss another subject.

"I'm surprised you didn't mention the news this morning," she said casually.

"Hmm?" He held the glass away from his lips and looked at her, as if surprised by the question. "Oh, *that,*" he said finally. "No sense getting worked into a lather so soon. It's not good to be defensive about such things." He moved to resume drinking but paused and spoke again instead. "Have you, um, spoken to Ashley about it yet?" He closed his eyes and savored the last drops of tea.

"No, I haven't called today. He's likely home by now, though. Maybe I could give him a ring—before you leave."

The Reverend Rutledge reached nonchalantly for the pitcher and sought to refill his glass. "Whatever," he said. "I'm sure it's nothing much."

They sat at opposite ends of the table, both thinking the same thing. It was indeed something much. Mildred had lain the paper conspicuously on the sideboard, just a few feet from where they were sitting. Carter was, quite remarkably, out of words. He swirled the ice around in his glass.

"I think I should call," Mildred said.

"Naturally, you should," he agreed. She was already up and walking to the phone.

Cody, Gigi, Tinky, and A.D. stood in the cooking area alone, now that the worshipers had gone. On the counter was spread the *Stockyard Dispatch,* ablaze with the headline: "LOST BOOK OF THE BIBLE RECOVERED." They had each taken turns reading the story in silence.

Dispatch *publisher Daniel Withers will announce tomorrow the acquisition of an important first-century document, which he plans to distribute without charge to clergy nationwide.*

The document, which is to be known as the Withers Codex, was quietly brought to Fort Worth by Withers earlier this year, following its acquisition for an undisclosed price from the private collection of an unnamed antiquities dealer.

The codex, called by Withers "the most reliable repository of information about the life of Jesus ever found," is a book of sayings attributed to Jesus with commentary by the author.

"It is undeniably the very source for the Gospels Matthew, Mark, Luke, and John," said noted Jesus scholar Lester B. Bothwell, who headed a team of experts commissioned by Withers to study the document.

"Scholars have long surmised the possibility that such a work, commonly known as Q, may have existed, because the Gospels have so much material in common," he said. "But no one believed we would be so providentially favored as to find a complete first-

century manuscript that strips away the ideal from the real to bring the historical Jesus into such clear focus."

A press conference will be held in the lobby of the Withers Tower at nine o'clock Monday morning to disclose further information about the codex and its imminent publication.

They were all looking at Gigi.

"I have no idea what to do now," she said.

"There's nothing we can do, except wait for this thing to unfold," said Dunbarton with a weary sigh. "If Bothwell is involved, this can't be good. Based on what you told me about Withers' plans, we'll need to be prepared to make a quick response."

"How can we do that when he won't release the full document?" cried an exasperated Gigi. "By the time the whole thing's in print, he will have already interpreted it for the whole world. If he publishes a sentence or a paragraph . . . "

"That's irresponsible scholarship!" shouted an agitated A.D.

"I think we all know," Cody quipped, "this isn't about scholarship. It's about *spin.*"

"Exactly, and he has the means to do it," Gigi added.

Dunbarton crossed his arms. "So what are you planning to do about it?" he demanded.

The three of them beheld him cautiously. After a moment Gigi said, "Dr. Dunbarton, are you OK?"

A.D. gathered himself and took in a deep breath. He could feel his face tightening with anger. "Look, it's just professional jealousy, that's all."

"I don't think so." Gigi's eyes narrowed to a squint. "It's got to be deeper than that to get you so upset."

He said nothing but squeezed his thin frame more tightly and stared down at his wing tips.

"Alright. Knotty's theory," he said.

Cody and Tinky looked at Gigi for a clue to the remark. "*What* theory?" Gigi asked.

A.D. huffed loudly. "OK. Remember that e-mail from Ravenswood you showed me?" She nodded. "Well, in there he said Professor Knotty, who supposedly discovered this document originally, believed it was *not* the source document for the Gospels, as Bothwell claims. Why do you think Knotty would think this way?"

"Because it was different in some way?" Cody tried.

"Obviously. But in what way?"

The three of them stood there, puzzling.

"Well, it would have to be contradictory. This would explain why the Society didn't want its contents revealed."

"But we already knew that, professor," complained Gigi.

"Yes, but think about what this means. We have a contradictory account. The key is, who wrote it, and why?" He was energized now, in full lecture mode.

"Do you think the authorship is given in the book?" Cody wondered.

"Doubtful," Dunbarton replied. "But Knotty must have had some inkling of his identity; the e-mail sent to Gigi said that he believed Matthew knew the writer personally."

"I remember that," Gigi said. "He must have been grasping for something, you think?"

Q

"Maybe. But I've been turning this over and over in my mind for weeks. Finally, something hit me." He looked around the room. "Cody, where's your Bible?"

Cody walked over to the upside-down plastic trash can that served as the pulpit, where he had left his big Bible.

"*New King James.* Excellent," said Dunbarton.

He flipped through the pages and placed the book open on the counter, pointing to Matthew 8. "Look here, at verse 19. Some of the translations don't pick this up, but it's very plain here."

They all peered down into the page like vultures. "See this phrase Matthew uses: 'a *certain* scribe,'" Dunbarton continued. "In Greek, the modifier means 'one,' the way we might say, 'one scribe, in particular' did such and such. The translation *certain* carries the idea quite well. Matthew doesn't name him, but he might have been well known, or at least known by Matthew. He was understood to be different from other scribes, unusual in some way, perhaps in a negative sense. That's how I read it. For instance, Tinky, you might say, '*Certain* people think they know everything,' and look in Gigi's direction. Well, that's a kind way of pointing out some flaw to be associated with Gigi. This could be what Matthew is doing here with this scribe. The rest of the text seems to bear this out."

"How so?" mused Tinky, suddenly engaged.

"Because he's a scribe, and he asks to follow Jesus. That would be unusual," noted Cody.

"Correct," said the professor. "And what else?"

Gigi's eyes opened wide. "He's refused. Jesus won't let him come."

"Because . . . ," the teacher prodded.

"Because he can't handle the sacrifices required. That's clear from verse 20."

"Very good. So," stated A.D., "we have a *certain* scribe who knew Jesus, who pledged to follow him but was sent home. He must have been dejected, even angry, wouldn't you say?"

They nodded in agreement.

"Now tell me," he concluded, leaning back against the counter. "Exactly what is it that scribes do?"

"They—write books," answered Tinky.

It was a startling revelation to think that someone opposed to Jesus would be the first to write down his sayings. It was true that evidence in the Gospels suggested the Jewish leaders did have some idea of the specific things Jesus was saying, for they eventually sought to condemn him by his own words. Was it possible that they had some kind of written source? Could this would-be follower have been a spy, a sort of ancient undercover agent for the authorities? If so, it is obvious that Jesus would reject his proposed discipleship, since he knew the hearts of all men. But that wasn't the reason Jesus gave. Furthermore, blackballing him from the inner circle wouldn't have kept the scribe from trailing along, reporting the events as they happened. Or perhaps he was sincere in his desire to follow, and the rejection set him against Jesus, as A.D. seemed to suggest. Strangest of all, if this scribe did know Matthew, as Knotty proposed, wouldn't he naturally have had conflicts with Matthew's chosen profession of tax collector for the Romans? The story of Matthew's call by Jesus is told in the next chapter, apparently *after* this episode. So on what basis would he be sincerely drawn to Jesus? Certainly Matthew wasn't evangelizing scribes before his own call to discipleship!

The issues were difficult to sort out, and as Gigi pondered them, she felt that she was losing her grip on the situation once again. It was she who had stumbled upon this international scramble for the lost book, because she herself had so much insecurity about modern religion and had hoped for answers and assurances of her own calling. She had never in fact gotten close to anything but danger, and now she was being ostracized by the Christian community. For all she knew, the seminary might ask her not to register for classes in the fall. And it appeared that the lost book itself, far from being "the answer," would only create even greater questions for even greater numbers of people.

In the meantime, however, she had discovered some things about her own commitment to ministry, rekindled her passion for real religion as the New Testament writer James defined it—"to visit orphans and widows in their distress, and to keep oneself unstained by the world." And yet, despite her valiant stand for righteousness, she felt more corrupted by the world than ever before. Was she doing the right thing for the wrong reason? Was she orbiting foolishly close to Daniel Withers? What was really motivating her—to find God's truth, or her own?

The rectangles of light which illumined the Withers Tower flickered into black one by one as the night encroached and men and women—who knew nothing of the fitful preoccupation of the dark man above them on the top floor—left their offices and cubicles for home. He would soon be alone in his building, and for this he waited, not because there was any hope of discovery but because he felt better knowing there could not be any. He stood by the window, alone with his thoughts, until he walked into the chamber he had modified just for this one purpose, to gaze undisturbed at his prize.

Withers ran his hand lightly over the coarse leather cover of the codex. He mused: this one work had survived twenty centuries, whereas no other had, not even any of the biblical writings themselves. It had been hidden in a cave for most of that time and then in the cold floor of an ancestral manor—where he himself had walked, not knowing about it until Ellis Cole had revealed it to him. These brittle pages had reposed quietly in a small vault hewn from the rock just beneath their feet—waiting all this time, it seemed to him, for him and him alone.

It would be difficult to sleep. In less than twelve short hours, he would be standing before a packed lobby downstairs, introducing the scholars who were by now arriving at the luxury hotel down the street, checking in with their notebooks and polyester jackets, despite the warm air, muttering to one another—and possibly themselves—of the treasure that so few living had been privileged to see. They would be sleepless this night too, for the pleasure of notoriety had seduced them, swallowed them whole.

All but Bothwell. Withers pictured the scholar ruminating in his bed, not over his imminent fame—for in some rather limited circles he had enjoyed that already—but over the book itself, the pearl of great price that had elevated him so. He would be focused, reverent, speaking in hushed tones, hunched behind the mike, his wisps of white hair sprawling abstractly over his large ears, his bushy gray brows knitted in a thoughtful arch. He would relish each word he would be so favored to utter, that he himself might humbly share the stage with this old sheaf of letters. Withers laughed at the thought of it.

He envied Bothwell in some ways, because the seasoned academic seemed sincere in his opinions and satisfied by them. He was a scholar of no small standing, in part because he so passionately believed in his theories, which, it seemed to Withers, were simply explanations derived to dash men's hopes. And yet this empty rationalizing, this pricking of the believers' balloon, somehow brought meaning to his life, as if to say, *See, it is as I said. It cannot be true; it can all be explained.* This book would now testify, in his mind, that he was right and had been all along.

Reason must be the deadly enemy of faith, or at least it would seem so to any thinking person. But the faithful will hear of no logical explanations; they wish to keep believing in spite of what you tell them. The cynics are just as firm in their logical reasonings, fearing the uncertainties of faith, or perhaps the absolutes of it, choosing instead the way of practicality, which is comforting because it can be seen, touched, known. And now at last comes this ancient writ, which also can be handled and smelled and read—and it comforts those who fear the plunge a life of faith requires.

So why trouble the faithful at all, if they choose such sublime deception? Why drive home this one final nail in the coffin built from the timbers of reason? *To see what will happen when the lid is slammed shut,* Withers mused. *To see if they shall rise again.*

He checked the temperature settings and walked deliberately from the chamber, turning the key in the lock behind him. Alone once more in the stillness of the sealed room, the book waited silently for its long-awaited resurrection.

2.3

DANIEL WITHERS RODE IN HIS PRIVATE ELEVATOR DOWN TO THE lobby. He was wearing an uncharacteristically preppy khaki suit, crisply pressed as always, chosen both to mark the arrival of the warmer weather and to cast him in a favorable light. Although his name was a household word in the Southwest, he imagined that few had bothered to remember his face from those occasions when his picture appeared in one of his publications. This would be his first exposure to the public eye of the nation, and he wanted to make a positive impression.

The doors opened so quietly that they could not be heard. Withers strode out, hard heels on the glossy stone tiles announcing his ascent to the podium from behind the large, noisy crowd. Their voices fell away as he passed; faces turned to watch him in silence as he made his way forward. Cameras swung into position and began to click and roll. Withers nodded to the three individuals seated on the rostrum, which was decorated with foliage and easels draped in velvet cloth. Behind them a tall curtain hung motionless against the newly prepared wall.

He glanced casually at the crowd and then searched for the nearest camera, deciding in a few seconds that it was best to speak directly over the heads of the men and women who stood before him. "'The kingdom of heaven,'" he began, "'is like a treasure hidden in the field, which a man found and hid again; and from joy over it he goes and sells all that he has and buys that field.' And so it is that such a treasure shall now be made known, having been brought here at no little expense, so that my joy might be shared with all of you. For what we begin here today will inaugurate a new age of thinking about those deeply held beliefs that both inspire and disturb us. It will unite us in knowledge and place us on solid ground."

Withers looked over his shoulder at the three invited guests, two of whom were smiling broadly. He then turned back to his audience, unbuttoned his jacket, and continued in conversational style.

"The Lost Book of the Bible," he whispered, waving his hands in spooky fashion. The crowd, stiff and uncertain up to now, relaxed with an almost audible exhale in response to the speaker. "It sounds incredible, I know," he said. "But think about it—we have four Gospels, but none of them are originals, just copies of copies. Even the most faithful among us have some difficulty with that. And what of the miracles—walking on water, making wine from water, quieting down storm-tossed water—these kinds of things? Miracle workers aren't often arrested, abandoned by their followers, and executed, are they? It would seem to many of us that, just possibly, the gospel writers—well, may have *added* some things." He winced as he said it, perhaps anticipating an angry response. But the crowd, made up mainly of reporters and academics, simply recorded his words on their tape machines and pads, without emotion. Their lack of profound reaction irked Withers somewhat. Did they think this was just another story?

He walked to the easel. "The Withers Codex, as it will heretofore be known, is the oldest manuscript concerning Jesus ever to be discovered." He carefully removed the velvet cloth and dropped it onto the floor, revealing a large photograph of an ancient-looking pile of yellowed pages tied with a coarse leather cover. "For reasons that should be obvious, the codex itself is kept in a environmentally controlled location designed to minimize further damage, but in time it will be appropriately and publicly displayed." He walked back to the podium.

"A team of world-class experts has studied every word of the text and has confirmed its authenticity. To my right, please welcome Dr. Postell Cheltenham of Edinburgh and his colleague, the eminent Dr. Lester B. Bothwell, retired, of the University of South Carolina, who chaired the team. Dr. Cheltenham will speak to the age of the document, and Dr. Bothwell will discuss the factors leading to our assessment of it as an authoritative source for understanding the beginnings of Christianity."

Withers walked briskly to the opposite side of the rostrum and exchanged seats with Cheltenham, who rose hesitantly and crept to the podium with a gait that exposed the effects of every one of his eighty-three years. He was a very small man, hunched and peculiar, with knobby ears and dressed in thrift-store garb: a frayed, yellowish polyester jacket with extremely wide lapels, a check print shirt, and brown knit tie. He was not the type of man one argued with about obscure extrabiblical manuscripts, having devoted all of his adult life to their study.

Cheltenham removed a wrinkled hanky from his back pocket and wiped his nose. "I am honored," he croaked, "to have been given the opportunity to participate in such company as Lester Bothwell, whom I have known and admired for many years. For you see I am but the apprentice and he the master in this enterprise; I am concerned with such things as jots and tittles, if you will, and he with the truth of the texts." He glanced furtively at Bothwell, who nodded in appreciation. Both men knew only disdain for one another, but the opportunity for fame breeds strange companions, even in the academic world.

Q

"I am what is known as a paleographer." He scanned the faces of his audience for some form of visual recognition that they might be familiar with his field but found none. "My expertise has been to study the handwriting found in ancient manuscripts, and to thereby date them or perhaps even authenticate them. Now we have here a document that Mr. Withers purchased under the assumption that it dated from the first century, and I can say without reservation that it is indeed that old and can in fact make some fairly confident assumptions about its origins."

A nearly imperceptible rustling could be felt from the crowd; Cheltenham knew not whether anticipation or tedium had caused it. "Now before we consider how old this manuscript is, we must determine how young it is—that is, can we find anything here that tells us it could *not* have been written earlier than such and such a date? And we see that this document is actually a series of documents, stacked together, folded, and originally bound into a leather cover. This is called a codex, a method of preparing documents that came into fashion about the time of Christ. Therefore we can say with some certainty that this is at least a first-century document—but how early was it written?

"You know of course of the famous Dead Sea Scrolls," the paleographer continued, "which many believe were originated in the community of Qumran, though there is some evidence that certain of the documents that have been recovered were transported there from Masada or perhaps from Jerusalem at various times. What we do know is that the physical environs of the Qumran community were destroyed at the time of the Jewish Wars, or in the early '70s. Therefore if the Withers Codex were written at Qumran, it must be earlier than those events. Now this becomes interesting, because this document contains sayings attributed to Jesus, and to identify it with the Essenes of Qumran is challenging, because no New Testament writings—not even a tiny scrap—have been found there to date. So if it were written at Qumran, how could it have influenced the writing of our Gospels? There is only one way, and that is if there were other copies. On this point I must elaborate somewhat.

"Most ancient writings were applied to a material known as papyrus, or reeds which grew in the Nile Delta and other similar regions. Strips of papyrus were placed side by side, and more strips were lain perpendicular to these, and the whole thing was covered with a type of paste. When it dried you had a smooth writing surface. Longer documents were rolled into scrolls, which the reader unraveled as he went along. But papyrus will crack if folded, so it was not suitable for the codex form.

For this reason our writer used parchment, or sheepskin. Now I must say this is significant for two reasons. First, it suggests that the writer intended that his codex be used for reference, that is, it is quite bothersome to quote or copy from a long scroll. Second, there was plenty of parchment at Qumran, because it can be re-used—cleaned and written on again. I don't think the good brothers would fancy trekking off to Jerusalem every time they spilled the ink or misspelled a word!" He wheezed a laugh, amused at his prepared joke.

"But this is not all, you see, for beyond the physical characteristics of the codex itself, there is the inscribed text, which is nothing short of fascinating." He limped over to the easel and removed the large photograph to reveal another showing a page from the book, though the script was too blurred to make out the characters. "Now, as you may be able to deduce from this rather fuzzy picture, we have two languages here—the main text, written in Greek, and notes written in the margins, which are in Aramaic. It is a paleographer's dream!"

He shuffled back to the podium. "Paleography, you see, is vitally interested in connecting the dated writing of one document to the undated writing of another. For instance, if we have one manuscript which records an event—say, an earthquake, the date of which is given in the document itself or determined from other historical sources—we can then compare it to other documents and assume they were written around the same time and possibly from the same location. You see, writing styles—the shape of letters, the use of phrases, the actual arrangement of the words on the page— can be placed in specific contexts. There was no font selection, so to speak, available then—a scribe knew what he knew from what he had seen. Now, the first thing that hits you about the Withers Codex is that it bears striking similarity to what we find in the oldest copies of two of the Gospels, in some cases word for word transcription. So it would seem that it was a source for the Gospels or that it was copied from the Gospels. Our committee advocates the former, since we have also verified it as a text that originated at Qumran, and most scholars date the earliest Gospel, Mark, from the mid-'60s on, and the other two synoptics, Matthew and Luke, later still. That means our codex—if it is a Qumran document— would have to be earlier than Matthew and Luke, since Qumran was destroyed by the Romans about the time or even before these works were written."

He glanced back at Bothwell again, who wore a forced smile, and Cheltenham thought perhaps he had stolen some of the professor's thunder. Though delighted with this assessment, he decided to get right to the point. "Now, ladies and gentlemen, I have been looking at ancient manuscripts through an expert lens for almost seventy years. And having looked at this one, I believe that it did originate at Qumran and that in fact it was written by the author of another of the Dead Sea Scrolls—the Hymn Scroll."

He expected a gasp, or perhaps at least a twitter, at the mention of this particular scroll, but the audience simply looked on in vacant wonder. It was tedium, he thought, to be sure.

"The, ah, Hymn Scroll, was among the first seven scrolls recovered, and what we have of this work has been published and studied by scholars worldwide. When my findings are published on the Aramaic text of the Withers Codex, I am quite sure that the academic community will largely agree with me that, paleographically speaking, there are unmistakable connections to the Hymn Scroll and that they were, perhaps, even inked by the same hand."

A reporter in the second row asked, "How old is this Hymn Scroll?"

"The widely-held date for the Hymn Scroll is early first century," answered Cheltenham. "Therefore we should find an early first-century date for the Withers Codex as well.

"Of course we have also chosen to apply scientific methods to these ancient works," he continued, wiping his nose again, convinced now, having dropped all of his bombshells, that the audience was unschooled in matters of such importance. "You are, I hope, familiar with carbon 14 dating procedures, which I shall review briefly for the uninitiated." He spoke matter-of-factly now. "Carbon 14, also called radiocarbon, is a type of carbon that is present in all living things, for it combines with oxygen and is absorbed into plants, which are eaten by animals, and so on and so forth. Carbon 14 is unstable, and as soon as the living organism in which it is present dies, it begins to decay. Now Carbon 14 has a half-life of 5,730 years, or thereabouts, which means that this is how long it takes for half of the radioactive isotope to disintegrate.

Q

Using this method we can therefore come to fairly confident conclusions regarding the date of ancient manuscripts.

"In recent years a new approach called Accelerator Mass Spectrometry has been devised, which allows us to simply count the residual isotopes therein. These methods have been applied to the Withers Codex, and our paleographic assumptions have been thus confirmed; this manuscript can be said to have been written between A.D. 40 and A.D. 65. These would be somewhat later dates than we had assumed for the Hymn Scroll but remarkably close given the two thousand year hindsight with which we are forced to view these matters." His initial excitement gone, long exhausted by his age and limited capacity for such things and the lack of enthusiasm shown by the gathering, Cheltenham folded up his papers loudly and returned to his place on the rostrum.

Lester B. Bothwell jumped as if just awakened and moved on bandy legs briskly to where Cheltenham had stood. He was dressed in khakis, a light sweater of baby-blue cashmere, and new brown round-toed boots, which he had purchased some weeks earlier on the very day he arrived in Texas. They hurt his feet.

"I think I speak for all of us that Dr. Cheltenham has provided a solid platform from which we may responsibly interpret this newly discovered work, and for that we are indebted and grateful. Thank you, Postell," he said, turning back to the previous speaker. Cheltenham waved his hand casually and leaned back in his chair, wondering why anything further needed to be said.

"Before I delve into the assessment of the Withers Codex," Bothwell began, "I would like to put its significance into proper historical perspective."

Withers looked toward the back of the lobby and saw a handful of people slip quietly for the doors. This press conference, which

251

he intended as a dramatic and portentous announcement, was rapidly losing strength, awash in the droll reveries of the dueling academics. Perturbed, he considered taking over the show.

"In the year 1844, Constantin von Tischendorf visited Saint Catherine's Monastery on Mount Sinai, and strolling in the library, ran across a basket of manuscript fragments, which proved to be copies of the Old Testament written in Greek. Upon his inquiry, the librarian said that the fragments were being burned for fuel and would soon be gone. Tischendorf took these with him—forty-three pages in all—back to the University of Leipzig. In 1853, he returned to the library and found nothing. In 1859, he went back again and, through a process of careful examination of one of the monks, was introduced to what has come to be called the Codex Sinaiticus—the Bible of Sinai—a complete fourth-century edition of the Holy Bible, which today resides in the British Museum. As exciting as that discovery was, it pales in comparison to this," he pointed to the photograph on the easel, "the revelation of the true story of Christianity's origins, the *quelle* itself." His voice trembled as he spilled forth the words.

"The word *quelle,* ladies and gentlemen, is German for 'source.' In the years before Tischendorf made his famous discovery, German theologians were puzzling over the arrangement of passages in the Gospels of Matthew and Luke, which seemed to indicate heavy borrowing from Mark, thus establishing Mark as the first of the written Gospels. But one scholar looked further. In 1838, Christian Weisse—of, interestingly, the University of Leipzig—saw other similarities in Matthew and Luke, largely the sayings of Jesus, none of which appeared in Mark. From this he deduced that another source must have existed, which came to be known as Q, based on the word from which the concept sprung.

Q

"We know from our tradition that the four Gospels represented an attempt to standardize the Christian party platform, and therefore the use of anything else would have been discouraged by the ecclesiastic authorities. These embellished Gospels, then, rendered the rough drafts of truth meaningless, and these sources ceased to be copied and faded from circulation. Any hope of our finding an early copy of Q—if in fact it even existed—was slim indeed. Then, in 1945, along the Upper Nile in a place called Nag Hammadi, thirteen codices—similar to the one in the photo here—were discovered, including one called the Gospel of Thomas, which was comprised exclusively of sayings, some of which are approximated in Matthew, Luke, and . . . ," he pointed again, "the Withers Codex!"

A hand was raised abruptly in the middle of the crowd. Bothwell leaned over the podium, squinted, and smiled.

"Ladies and Gentlemen, one of my former students and a not-too-shabby scholar in his own right, Dr. Ashley Dunbarton, has indicated his desire to speak." Bothwell extended his hand to scoop up the question.

From her place on the rostrum, Gigi perked up.

The thin man in the blue oxford-cloth shirt spoke as if from the bottom of a well, his voice thin and shrill in response to the amplified tones which resonated from the podium. "Dr. Bothwell, how can you be sure Matthew and Luke utilized this book Q and not the other way around?"

"Oh, well that's quite simple, Ashley. I suppose the author could have copied the sayings from the Gospels, but as we have already heard, the paleographic and AMS dating suggests this document is earlier than Matthew and Luke. Furthermore, in addition to the sayings, we have these Aramaic notations, which indicate that the author was clearly an eyewitness to these events."

"Why is that?" Dunbarton interjected. "Dr. Cheltenham said the sayings were in Greek and the notes in Aramaic. This seems odd. Couldn't someone have made these notes on another's manuscript?"

"No, I don't think so," Bothwell answered thoughtfully. "Remember, this is parchment. The words could have been erased from the pages if someone had wanted to do so. More likely, he would have destroyed the sayings book if he had found it objectionable. Besides, the textual analysis strongly suggests the sayings and the notations were made by the same writer. You would agree if you could examine the document for yourself."

"And will I have such an opportunity; I mean, will the codex be published in entirety?" he interrogated with a suspicious tone.

Bothwell, sensing resentment in his former protégé, answered formally. "It is my understanding that it will, Dr. Dunbarton. Mr. Withers will undoubtedly address that issue. Is that all?"

A.D. looked nervously around. "Actually, no. You haven't adequately explained the two languages."

Bothwell smiled. "That would be elementary. To the writer, the Greek text of the sayings would communicate the words that Jesus said. By choosing to write the notations in Aramaic, he was reinforcing his opposition, as in 'This is what *I* say.' Similar, it seems to me, to what Jesus was saying in the Sermon on the Mount, do you follow?"

A.D.'s face was reddening. Gigi could not hide her disappointment that his efforts at challenging Bothwell were only strengthening the liberal scholar's position.

"But Lester," he pleaded, "are these notations to be believed over the Gospels themselves? There were plenty of reasons people had to try and discredit Jesus. Perhaps this book was written to do that."

Q

Bothwell leaned against the podium and folded his hands together. "My dear Ashley," he said in a suddenly sympathetic and almost fatherly voice, "I see your point, of course, but you strain to make it. It is hard for you to kick against the goads! Your scholar's mind struggles with your Christian spirit. But you must accept what is here. This is Q! We have known it ere we have seen it. Tell me, if you were to write a book to discredit Jesus, would you risk the further diffusion of his powerful sayings, even with your own commentary? Of course not! You would simply write your treatise. And consider this, now, my friend: if you wanted to write a polemic—a denouncement of the God-man Jesus, wouldn't you have included the one crucial event that turned him from wise peasant into Messiah?"

He waited for a response. Gigi sat on the edge of her chair, her heart racing.

"Of course you would!" Bothwell answered himself. "Then why is there no account of the passion? Why no cross? No resurrection?"

A murmur, quite loud this time, filled the spacious hall.

"That's correct. There are no resurrection texts here. Only sayings. Only the wise peasant. An intelligent, controversial, charismatic man is revealed here . . ." He paused. "But a man nevertheless. Nothing more."

At this, the audience erupted into motion and babble, as if struck with a cattle prod. Bothwell, pleased with himself but disappointed that he had been forced into being so blunt, wandered back to his seat. Withers rushed to the microphone.

"If I may have your attention for just one more moment, please," he squawked, exuberant. The crowd hushed. "On Sunday . . . " He waited for total silence. "On Sunday, we will publish an excerpt from the codex, and a second the following week, and a third after that. Our intent is to generate interest in the work, to give the world time to absorb the shock of what it means. We do not wish to injure those who believe but simply to inform their faith. We desire only to place Christianity in its proper historical context. We will then publish, at our own expense, copies of the codex to be distributed to every pastor in the country. We will also construct a museum for the work itself, so it may be appreciated by all."

Way in the back, a chubby hand was thrust high and waved to be noticed. Confident, Withers acknowledged the man with a nod. "Yes, sir, in the back there—do you have a question?"

The man made his way through the masses to the front, right below the rostrum. "Yes, sir, I do."

Gigi sat up again. The accent was decidedly British. The man was dressed in tweeds, despite the heat. He was a caricature of an English gentleman.

"Is it possible that the resurrection isn't mentioned because the book is incomplete?"

Withers looked back at Bothwell, who stood to answer.

"It is highly unlikely," he said.

"I see," the gentleman said. "I seem to recall from my studies that the hypothetical Q contains approximately 225 verses shared by Matthew and Luke. Does the codex contain 225 verses?"

Bothwell blushed. "No, it doesn't. Some are missing, it would appear."

"Oh yes," agreed the portly man, "of course. Now, Mr. Withers," he mused, "from whom exactly did you obtain this precious volume?"

Withers stiffened. "I'm not at liberty to say," he said firmly.

Q

"Perhaps it is not important, then," the inquisitor commented with a shrug. "But it would seem to me that, well, since you purchased it from someone who wishes to remain anonymous, there may be questions about the other portions of the book that have not been included. One wonders what those pages might contain! Might they still be available for sale, sir?"

"I can't really say," Withers answered calmly. "I'm sure the audience is hardly interested in such things. Perhaps we could visit later." He paused. "I didn't catch your name . . . "

"John Ravenswood," the Englishman answered sharply.

Gigi felt a chill. The crowd fell silent, stunned by the angry retort.

"I should say that your little book is indeed a great find, Mr. Withers," Ravenswood continued, "but by no means should we accept it as the final word in this matter." He turned abruptly and made his way back through the people, who this time stepped aside to let him pass. No one spoke a word until he had exited the building.

"I suppose it does not need to be stated that some may find this whole experience rather unsettling," Withers counseled. "We are, of course, sensitive to that. For this reason I have asked one of our brightest young writers, Miss Gigi Vaughn, who, by the way, is also a seminarian and preacher here in our community, to investigate and publish reactions to the excerpts." He nodded in Gigi's direction, and heads followed his glance. Gigi sat, almost afraid to look at them, tight-lipped. "We will be responsible in our coverage of this important issue."

With that, Withers raised his arm, and the curtain behind him fell away, revealing the granite wall. "Upon this wall, the pure truths of a historic faith will be engraved for posterity. It is our hope that all those who prize reason will find this a sacred place in days to come. Now I thank you for coming and bid you good morning." He descended the rostrum as the crowd dispersed, chattering loudly like a herd of disturbed cattle, and waited to congratulate Bothwell and Cheltenham on their fine orations. While still shaking Cheltenham's hand, he turned his head toward Gigi, who was still frozen on the platform, and winked.

Carter Rutledge scratched the back of his neck as he beheld the large banner being hung in the conference room of the Holy City Christian Ministers' Alliance, whom he served as president. The banner was red with white letters, two feet high, which asked: WHAT ARE YOU WAITING FOR? At that particular moment, Carter was waiting for Gil Tucker, pastor of the newly formed Castaways' Church on Daniel Island, to arrive. The student volunteers had picked up the banner that morning and knew immediately that it wouldn't fit in the conference room. A stout girl standing on a chair finally dropped her arms in exhaustion and let the banner trail on the ground.

"I don't think this is going to stay up," she said to Rutledge.

"He said it was the key to his church's ministry," the pastor of Seventh Baptist Church replied. "But you can just let it drag, I suppose."

Delighted, the girl hopped down from the plastic chair.

"On second thought," Carter added, "maybe we should try one more time—just wrap it around the corner, OK."

Q

"Hey, Carter!" Gil Tucker exploded into the room, carrying a notebook computer and a stack of large, full-color brochures that looked like athletic programs. He stopped. "Uh, where's the video?"

"I'm sorry?" Carter asked, still a bit startled at Tucker's entry.

"No, I'm sorry," Tucker said. "I shouldn't have assumed you guys would have a projector down here. We could have sent someone over to set up the presentation, if I had given it much thought . . . "

"So," Carter announced, extending his hand, "it's great to have you today. I hear the Lord is doing a mighty work through your ministry."

Tucker shrugged. "It's been unbelievable. It's just God's vision at work. That's all I can say."

"Well I hope you can come up with something more than that!" Carter joked. "I've figured you for about thirty minutes and then some questions."

"You mean, *talk* for thirty minutes? I'm not used to going that long."

"Oh?" Carter said, not sure how to take the comment. "And you call yourself a preacher?"

It was intended to be funny, but Gil Tucker just looked confused. "I usually speak for about fifteen and a half minutes, if that's OK," he answered seriously.

By this time, several ministers had already entered the room and were looking curiously at the casually-dressed Tucker.

Carter took Tucker aside, sensing he might not relate well to the group, and said, "Gil, you might want to soft-pedal your approach this morning. I know you've got great ideas and your church is growing rapidly, but some of the things you do might be perceived as threatening to folks from more traditional churches. This is Charleston, remember. I think you'll help them see your point of view better if you can try to relate to where they're coming from—do you get me?" He clutched Tucker's arm in a brotherly way.

"I think so. Like when we used fresh coconut shavings for the communion service on the beach, that might be too much, right?"

Carter nodded and patted his shoulder.

"It helps to communicate our vision, though," Tucker said.

"I understand, Gil," said Carter. But he really didn't.

The Holy City Christian Ministers' Alliance was only four years old and still recruiting members. It had been formed in response to the increasing tendency for the various denominational meetings to get bogged down in their particular petty controversies. It began as a study group of five pastors who were seeking to grow in their ministries by learning from each other's successes and failures. Carter Rutledge had led the group from its inception.

After several minutes of greetings and announcements, Carter introduced the monthly guest speaker. "We are privileged today to have Gil Tucker of the brand-new Castaways' Church to speak to us about his work out there on Daniel Island." The two dozen men, all in coats and ties, eyed Tucker as Carter spoke.

"Is your name really Gilligan?" someone shouted from the back. They all laughed.

"Naw," Tucker answered from his seat. "It's Gilbert." This evoked more laughter and left Tucker slightly embarrassed.

"In about six months, Gil's church has grown from a prayer circle of six couples into a congregation of around six hundred," Carter continued. The laughter subsided. "We could all learn a lot

Q

from this young man. Please welcome Gilbert—he emphasized the "bert"—Tucker of Castaways' Church."

Polite applause greeted the pastor as he changed places with Carter. "Thank you, Reverend Rutledge, for your kind words. But we're not up to six hundred yet. We had about five-forty last week."

Carter smiled. "We always round up, my boy," he advised. There was more laughter, this time even from Tucker.

"I guess all you might know about us is what you see behind me on the banner, which is what we call *the question,*" Tucker began. He was wearing olive khaki pants and a navy polo, his hair a disheveled brown mop above delicate features. "And it's true what you may have heard about the *Gilligan's Island* theme, believe it or not. All I want to do this morning is give you some background on why I think our church has been so successful so quickly.

"It started in the home of one of our couples almost a year ago. We had absolutely no idea at that time that our little group would become a church. We had just finished our prayer time; and someone turned on the TV, and there was this episode of *Gilligan's Island* on one of those vintage TV rerun cable stations.

"Melissa Johnson—who is our youth pastor now and whom they call Mary Ann—said something like, 'Can you imagine waking up every morning with no hope, like so many nonbelievers do? They're like these castaways, stuck on this island, trying everything they can to improve their situation—doing desperate, silly things, and never getting anywhere!'

"We all just looked at each other and started building on the metaphor. We began to see the characters on the show differently. Instead of hopeless people, we saw them as actually *hopeful*—driven to do whatever they had to do in order to get home. This hope kept them going. I came up with the question: *What are you waiting for?* Everyone had to answer it. We discovered that we were waiting for a lot of things but not doing much to get them accomplished. We were waiting for God to do something in our lives, but we weren't participating in his work. In fact, none of us were very faithful church members. We weren't living like hopeful people.

"It dawned on us that God wanted us to take the message further, to ask the question of others, especially disfranchised churchy people like ourselves. So many people have an excuse to stop serving God. What if we started a church that took those excuses away? So our ads ask the question: *What Are You Waiting For?* The implication is to quit waiting for God to do something— he's already done plenty. It's time to get busy with our faith.

"The fact that my name is like Gilligan's made us feel like God was trying to teach us more from this particular TV show. At the heart of our church are five vision points. Together, the first letters spell 'HEART,' so they're easy to remember."

Tucker felt like he was losing them. The skepticism was all over their faces. He fumbled with his hands, not knowing where to put them. He missed the video system he was accustomed to using whenever he spoke.

"The first vision point is *hope for a better future.* We believe this is what everyone wants. In our church we emphasize self-improvement. If you want to be a better parent, in better shape, more spiritual, whatever it is, we encourage that. We set up mentors to help people with their personal goals.

"Next is the *explorer mentality.* The castaways are always setting out from the camp, looking for something to better their lives or get them off the island. We believe in stretching people's minds and spirits. We challenge them.

Q

"Third is *acceptance of others*. On the show, seven stranded cast-aways are stuck there together all the time. They need to work together to make good things happen for the community, since conflict invites hardship. The only way they can do this is to tolerate and appreciate each other's individual gifts and personalities. We come out strong against any kind of judgmental attitude in our church.

"Fourth is *relaxation*. The castaways had lots of time on their hands. They were forced into it, of course. These days, people are so busy and stressed. Our church spends a lot of time in recreation, and we create a casual atmosphere in everything we do.

"Finally, we have *thirty-minute worship experiences*. The TV show is a half-hour, and most people can pay attention that long. I preach for fifteen and a half minutes, which is just under the substantive length of a sit-com, less the commercials. The rest of the service is made up of singing and drama. We have three services on Sunday morning at the top of each hour and two on Friday nights at seven and eight. We have what you might call Sunday school on Wednesday nights for different ages, but not many people attend that. Of course we sponsor cell groups in private homes. The rest is made up of special events—we do a lot of things at the beach, and those activities do last longer—but that's basically our program."

He looked down at his watch; he had been speaking for about eight minutes. He glanced over at Carter, who wore a serene expression, as if he was thinking pleasant thoughts or expecting the real stuff any moment now. But for all of his boldness on his own turf, Tucker scanned the room full of wizened men of the cloth, and all he wanted to do was get out of there.

A hand went up in the front row. Tucker gladly recognized the individual and invited him to speak.

"What's your theology?" the pastor asked solemnly.

Tucker sniggered at the question, not sure he was expected to answer it. The man in the front row stared at him sternly.

"Well, if you are referring to doctrine, we don't really make much of that. Mostly we're interested in just helping folks get through the day. As far as theology goes, I guess you'd say we're conservative in belief but liberal in methodology."

The answer didn't satisfy. "Conservative? Coconut Communion in string bikinis is conservative?" another man snapped.

Tucker shot a look over at Carter, who just shrugged. "I don't recall any string bikinis out there," Tucker said, grinning. "But I see that as a methodology issue anyway, not really a theological one."

"I'm sorry, Reverend Tucker, but our Savior's death on the cross isn't exactly my idea of a day at the beach," the first minister said. Someone offered an *amen.*

Tucker cleared his throat. "Look, I was asked to share my vision, not defend it," he complained. "It so happens that our church is reaching people, which is more than most of you can say about your churches."

Carter stood up. "Let's calm down a minute," he said paternally. "We have to remember that there's a cultural gap here. A lot of you can't get by the cultural issues to see the essence of Gil's ministry. We all agree that the church is about making disciples, right, Gil?" He smiled warmly and sat down.

"Exactly," Tucker affirmed. "And we do that in our small groups."

"How?" someone asked.

Tucker swallowed. "That's a question for Alan Simpson, our associate pastor. We call him Professor. He handles the small group ministry."

"We don't need a clinic; just tell us how you monitor their spiritual growth."

Q

Tucker chewed on his lower lip. "We leave that to the leaders. They set the time for the meetings, choose the curriculum, and so on."

The same man looked aghast and said, "Well then, how do you know what is being taught? Is there any accountability?"

Tucker was relieved at the question. "No, actually. Remember the third vision point? We are accepting of others. We don't judge them."

At this, there was a loud murmur loosed in the room.

"How do you know they're ready for baptism?" someone asked, hoping the easy question might get the young pastor out of hot water.

"We just invite them to get baptized at our beach meetings. A lot of people do it. We don't count them or ask them their full names. It's personal, the way we see it," he said.

"Excuse me, Gil," said a man about his own age who stood from his place in the second row. "I'm Rusty Rowe from Mission 419 just a few blocks from here. I'm on your side, but I see where these guys are coming from, because I deal with these issues with my people every day. Our church started as a mission to reach non-Christians, but somehow all we have ended up with is dissatisfied church members. They've got a lot of religious baggage, and it takes time to get through to them with new ideas. So here's what you've got to explain. You said you wanted to start a church that would eliminate the excuses people give for not attending. It looks to these pastors like you eliminated the actual commitment and just made everything kind of light and fun so that people would come. What they want to know is, how do you know if your church is really changing people?" He sat down, apparently feeling like he had redeemed the meeting for everyone.

Tucker thrust his hands into his pockets and thought for a moment. "We don't, Rusty," he said at last. "But God does. We just lead them to the truth. It's their job to take what they're given and use it according to God's will for their lives." There was no response to this, so he continued. "Let me ask you gentlemen the same question. If nobody is joining, how can you all say your churches are doing it right? Are your churches really changing people?"

"God changes people through his Word," said a tall, distinguished man with a clerical collar. "You want to attract them to your church, and that's fine, and I agree with you that they're responsible for their response—as long as you're faithfully declaring the Word."

Several *amens* rumbled forth in low voices. "I do that, sir," Tucker said. "I'm so glad you pointed that out. I think sometimes they come for the entertainment, for the novelty of what we do. But the Word has power, and if they're exposed to it long enough, they'll be forced to encounter God's claim on their lives. We try to lower the barriers to get them in, and we want church to be a positive, enjoyable experience; but in the end, they have to face up to the truth if they want to change. Everybody has got to get off the island."

Carter stood and walked over to Gil Tucker and put his arm around him. His instincts told him this was probably as close as the meeting would come to agreement. "We can all agree on two things: one is the primacy of Scripture in all that we do, though we sometimes interpret it differently. The other is that it's just about time for lunch."

"What are we waiting for?" shouted someone to a roomful of laughter.

"Just a minute," came another voice. "We speak about our commitment to the Word, and we take it for granted. Brothers, the Word is under attack today." He pulled a newspaper clipping out of his pocket and held it up for all to see. Several of the men grunted in disgust, knowing what the article said without having to read it. "I think we need to talk about this, because there are going to be some questions."

2.4

From Q, the Prologue:

> *¹ The words of Jesus, greatest of all [teachers], in whom the weak and the friendless had so desperately [hoped]:*
>
> *² May he live again in [these] [sayings], for which this devoted scribe has also paid so terrible a price.*

"IT'S WORSE THAN I THOUGHT," ASHLEY DUNBARTON SAID, PUSHING the Sunday edition of the *Dispatch* to the other side of the breakfast table. "And it smacks of Bothwell. But it's not devastating. I skipped church this morning to work on . . . I know, Mom, but people would have had questions, and I just . . . yes, I realize that." He closed his eyes, listening impatiently. "Of course there are. The brackets are key to the whole thing." He paused again to listen as his mother spoke through the telephone. "Yes. I think that was good. But we'll need more than that, I'm afraid. Tell Carter I'm working on it."

He turned aside to send his mother his love, which embarrassed him slightly but which Gigi and Cody found endearing. "She says her pastor in Charleston preached on the subject this morning but not on the text itself. His point was that Jesus is a present reality, a living being with whom we have a personal relationship, not a name in a book or merely a historical figure."

"How very Baptist of him," Gigi quipped.

"Now, hold on, there," A.D. answered. "That's actually the key to this whole thing. Christians know Jesus on a personal level. Whatever is in this old document can't nullify that."

"But that isn't the problem, is it?" Cody insisted. "We three around this table know that Jesus is alive, but those who don't will surely be put off by the demythologizing that's going on here. You know, if Jesus is God, I might give him a try, but if he's just a great teacher, well, so were Buddha and Groucho Marx."

"You mean Karl Marx," Gigi added.

"Actually, no, I was thinking of Groucho," he replied. "I mean, without the divinity, the authority of Jesus over someone's life is simply a matter of personal preference. They can live by the words of John Lennon if they want and be content with that."

"Imagine!" said Gigi.

"I'm glad you two are so relaxed about this, but we have some serious problems to address here," A.D. scolded lightly.

"But what Cody said *is* very serious," Gigi said. "And not only for those outside the Church. What about those inside?"

"The ones who don't have this personal relationship with God," Cody agreed, nodding.

"The ones who say they follow Jesus, but it's really conventional wisdom, the contemporary world view, the corporate culture, and so on," Dunbarton added.

"The Church stands to take a big hit here," Gigi warned, "and this is just the opening shot."

"Yes, but look at this text for a minute," the professor said, reaching for the paper. "See these brackets? They represent words that the translators, in this case our friend Lester Bothwell and his esteemed committee, couldn't quite make out. In these kinds of studies, such words or phrases are often referred to as 'hypothetical reconstructions.'"

"So even though they can't make the word out, there are enough letters there to translate it?" Cody wondered.

"Yes and no," A.D. responded. "You would think that the translators would be responsible enough not to reconstruct words from context alone, but sometimes they do."

"If that's the case with this passage, then that word *teachers* could be something entirely different, like *prophets* or *men,* or even *lords?*" Gigi asked hopefully.

A.D. winced. "Perhaps. But doubtful. Remember that we'll all get a look at this manuscript at some point."

"Sure, but by then the damage will have been done. It's hard to reverse popular opinion once it takes hold," said Cody.

"Let's hope things don't get that far out of hand." Dunbarton looked hard at the words again. "The first line presents no problem, really. There's nothing here that causes concern. In fact, it's a flattering portrait of Jesus as we know him. Nothing that is said here is untrue. The fact that he is the greatest teacher doesn't say he is God, but it doesn't say he isn't, either. And the objects of his compassion, the 'weak and the friendless' are the kinds of people we see Jesus caring for in the Gospels, especially in Luke." He paused. "The next verse, however, is somewhat troubling."

Frowning, he continued. "If we take the verse at face value, it suggests several things. First, it seems to imply that Jesus is dead at the time of this writing. Do you see that in 'May he live again'? Now, this is where I suspect some mischief might be going on. You see, liberal scholars like Bothwell have long taught that the historical bodily resurrection is sheer fantasy, that Jesus never arose at all. They say that the resurrection story is a way to profess that Jesus lives in a spiritual dimension through his followers. It is as if he is really alive, because we have memorialized him by our acceptance of his teachings. And Bothwell would say that the author of Q is saying just that. 'May he live again in these sayings.' It's a perfect fit for liberal theology—too perfect, it seems to me."

"Isn't that what your mom's pastor was preaching about, though?" Cody wondered.

"It is, it is," said A.D. "But the relationship he was speaking about is based on fact, not fiction, and that's the difference. We can have a relationship with Jesus because he really exists, not because we've immortalized him in literature and it's *as if* he really lives. Without a bodily resurrection, our faith has no basis in fact."

"But there are brackets here, and that could alter the meaning," Gigi observed.

"Yes, and that's the challenge presented to the interpreter. 'May he live again' is not too damaging if what follows enlarges on the writer's meaning. For instance, 'May he live again as he said' might be OK in that the writer is writing before the Cross and has somehow grasped the implications of Jesus' intimations of a future resurrection. But the desperation of the followers in verse 1 suggests that the writer knew that Jesus could not give them what they wanted—though that could mean anything: food, freedom from Roman oppression—any number of things. I don't know." He let out a deep breath. "It's difficult."

"And the end of verse 2 seems to blow your other theory," Gigi said resignedly.

"Yeah, I figured you would catch that," Dunbarton acknowledged. "You're referring to my idea that the author was an opponent of

Q

Jesus writing to discredit him. Well, our enemies don't often suffer for our causes, do they?" His frustration was disturbing to Gigi, who looked up to him so and liked to believe he had all the answers.

A.D. snatched up the paper and held it tightly. "There's got to be a reason!" he shouted.

Cody cast a knowing look at Gigi.

"You see, the problem with questioning the reconstruction is finding words that link the author's suffering to Jesus' living again. Even if Bothwell comes up with 'these sayings' from context only, what else can possibly fit?"

"Look, but there's something else here . . . " Cody was still thinking as he spoke. "If this guy was so devoted to Jesus and all, how did this manuscript ever come to be published?"

Dunbarton looked at him quizzically. "You're saying—if Jesus was killed, and the scribe was one of his public supporters—no, no, I don't agree with you. Remember that this document supposedly came from the caves near Qumran, like the other Dead Sea Scrolls. We have no real evidence that Christianity ever reached the Qumran community. It could have been written secretly by this scribe and brought there at some point, so that it made its way into the caves when the Romans closed in. That's plausible, I'm afraid."

"But you would admit that if the authorities knew about this document, they would have wanted it destroyed, right?"

"I suppose so."

Gigi entered the discussion abruptly with a flash of her hands. "Hold on! That's it! It makes perfect sense."

The two men beheld her curiously.

"The scribe was a devoted follower. He himself was one of the *friendless* he mentions in verse 1. He was persecuted for following Jesus and fled to the desert, where he wrote this book. He didn't mention the resurrection"—her huge eyes glimmered—"because he didn't know about it!"

The professor looked at Cody with narrowed eyes, then back at Gigi. "You might be on to something—but—there are still some problems . . . "

Gigi threw herself hard against the back of the chair. "Like what?"

"OK, listen, I don't want to dampen your flame, but we're at a big disadvantage here. All we have to go on are these two verses and what the committee has told us about the codex. Believe me, they wouldn't be so convinced that this is such a blockbuster if it were so easily explained. There are sayings to follow and the scribe's personal notes. Those notes must be where the real explosive stuff is. But your theory . . . ," he stroked his chin, "does have merit—except for one other question."

The two students waited, breathless.

"It throws a shadow of doubt on the integrity of Matthew and Luke. Let's say, for instance, that this codex is the real story. Matthew and Luke clearly could not have used it as a source without altering it significantly."

"Editing out the bad stuff," said Cody.

"Exactly. Of course, that's what Withers is putting forth right now, that the Gospels are fanciful accounts, and not truth at all. Before this is all done, he'll be saying, 'Here's my Gospel, and here are the others. Choose mine or the other four, but not all. They're mutually exclusive. Both can't be right.'"

"Sure they can," said Gigi.

Q

A.D. crossed his arms defensively. "How so?"

"Easy," she said. "There are two Qs, maybe even more."

"But Gigi, they will argue that the similarities in the sayings are such that they rule out any other possibility but that this is the one true source. We must be prepared for that."

"OK, then, there are two Qs, both by the same writer. This one was written later. It was a revision of the rough draft, which may not have included the notes. If Knotty's theory is correct and this scribe knew Matthew, that would not be hard to accept, would it? He made notes; Matthew used them. He fled to Qumran and wrote memoirs. Maybe by then he had grown bitter after years of exile. It's quite simple, really. There have to be two Qs."

The men sat silently, thinking. A wry smile curled around Cody's mouth. "That is so cool," he said.

Dunbarton shook the paper in his hands. "I don't know. It seems impossible—to get out after the trial, or even the Cross, but before the resurrection? Hard to imagine. And how would the first edition have survived? Matthew ran in fear like the rest of the disciples when the hammer came down on Jesus. So everybody's running away; nobody is believing anymore—of what value then are the parchments? Who would risk hanging onto them? Where would they be kept, so they could be conveniently retrieved once everyone saw the light? Then we have to believe that the word of the resurrection spread to everyone—but not to this scribe?" He shook his head negatively.

"He was friendless, like I said," Gigi answered.

Dunbarton rubbed his forehead. "It doesn't represent good textual criticism. It won't hold up."

"Forget the fancy methods for a minute, Dr. Dunbarton," she advised. "I'm appealing to logic. This is how Sherlock Holmes would go about it. What was his approach that he said so many times? 'Eliminate the impossibilities, and whatever remains, no matter how improbable, must be the truth,' or something like that. My theory appeals to logic. It explains these verses."

"It takes a lot of faith to believe it, though, sweetie," said Cody.

"Not to me. I think it takes more faith *not* to believe it. The apostles died for their faith, every one of them. Something happened to change them so dramatically, and we believe it was the undeniable truth of the resurrection. This poor scribe just didn't get the message, that's all. Now comes this posthumous publication, with no attestation from any other source, with no real background on where it came from, and we're expected to embrace it as gospel truth—and deny two thousand years of Christian experience? No, I think it's a good theory. In fact, I'm certain that's exactly what happened."

"It would help if we could get our hands on the rest of this codex before the spin doctors twist its meaning all out of proportion," Dunbarton muttered.

"Be patient," Gigi said confidently. "I'm working on that."

The men looked at each other worriedly, afraid to challenge her anymore.

The campus of Restoration Fellowship sprawled across the prairie on the west side of Fort Worth, along the road to Weatherford, where just a few years before, there had been no development save the mall on Hulen Street and a few shopping centers. Now, although the land had been engulfed by restaurants, large specialty stores, and residential subdivisions, the church continued to sit just beyond the suburban sprawl, like a city one approached with awe and apprehension. On Sundays, cars streamed forth in a seemingly endless convoy and filled the remote lots named for the spiritual gifts, identified by colorful banners proclaiming "hospitality" or "administration," for example. The idea was that once you had discovered your gift, you would park in the assigned lot, and therefore the church proclaimed its wholeness and balance by the placement of the automobiles the worshipers left outside. On Sundays teachers were expected to arrive first in their classrooms; but on Wednesday nights or for meetings on other days when far fewer people were present, the "mercy" people might slip into the "teaching" lot, which was closer to the building. The biblical gifts of tongues and interpretation were not represented by lots, since the church did not emphasize those gifts, and tales drifted around the seminary of Pentecostals who had driven aimlessly around the church, looking for their place and, finding none, got the message and left.

Bobby T. Raeburn was first on Gigi's list; in fact, he had called the paper seeking an audience. He allowed himself to be interviewed in his study, and though he never moved from behind his massive desk, Gigi was so distracted by wondering if he had worn his famous red boots that—right in the middle of some windy story about an oil rig gone dry—she interrupted him to ask. He was startled but pleased that his trademark was so well known, and placed his feet up on the desk. Then, with his red boots thus gloriously displayed, he continued with the story.

"We can take something for granted for so long, and then all of a sudden, the well dries up and we're left there with empty pockets and have to start diggin' again real quick. That's what's happened with the Bible, Miss Vaughn. We got people with dozens of Bibles sittin' on shelves and under coffee tables in their houses who never even read them. Now there's this big controversy, and we're all uptight over it." He shook his hands like a Halloween spook. "The Bible isn't real to these folks, or at least it hasn't been before. It just gives them comfort sitting on the shelf in case they need it. Now, this Withers thing will make them pick up their Bibles and read them. Then the Spirit of God will do his work, and you'll see mass conversions from church people."

Gigi tried hard to hold back a smirk. "You aren't very worried then? You don't see the Withers Codex as a threat to Christianity?"

"Naw! C'mon, are you kiddin'?" He chortled a bit. "Listen here, this is a good thing. Every time the devil goes after God, God has an answer. That's the lesson of the temptations, in Matthew 4."

"But—I don't see how that relates . . . "

"Aw, c'mon now, Miss Vaughn!" He put the boots down and sat bolt upright, leaning on the desk. "This is just another devil's trick. He attacks our intellect, see. He gets us thinkin' too much." He tapped his head with his finger and squinted, as if he were revealing some sinister secret only he knew. "He's trying to lure us away from God with his lies."

Gigi tried to respond. "But common sense dictates that we at least address . . . "

"I addressed it Sunday, in fact. Did you happen to be here?"

"No, actually, I . . . "

"That's OK. We have a great seminary department; you ought to try it." He paused. "You still go to Southwestern, right?"

"Last time I checked I was a student there," she quipped.

"Yeah. The Christian Pharisees are out to get you, I heard. Don't pay attention to them. They don't care for me, either."

"Jealousy," Gigi commented.

"You know, you're absolutely right. Absolutely. They can just wag their pointy fingers all they want. I've got thousands of people comin' to hear me preach. There's got to be a reason for it."

Gigi smiled at his choice of words. "What's your theory? About your success, then."

"Oh, well, that's simple. We preach the Word, and we help people. We tell them about Jesus and do what Jesus did. That's it."

"You don't think your personality might have something to do with it?"

"Oh, sure it does, but that's not the main thing."

"Perhaps the prestige is part of it too?"

"Mmm. Maybe. But people don't make commitments just for prestige."

"Can I say something?" Gigi asked.

He sat back, and the leather chair squeaked. He folded his hands across his belly. "Go ahead."

"You're just loving this, aren't you."

He laughed. "What do you mean, sugar?"

"The attention. And please don't refer to me as a condiment."

He looked puzzled but decided not to pursue the question.

"Let's face it, Reverend. You have this big church out here that could probably grow if you got up in the pulpit buck naked and sang 'The Yellow Rose of Texas' . . . "

"No doubt it would!" he said laughing and rocking and squeaking.

" . . . and the new book, and the ROC. You're a household name, and people are beginning to hear of you outside of Texas."

"Are you saying I shouldn't enjoy my work? Why? If God is blessing . . . "

"You're missing my point," she said sharply but in a gentle tone. "You are so insulated, sitting atop this empire of yours, that this Q business is nothing more than a chance to get your name in the paper again. Your people—the thousands who come to hear you—they really like the whole business of being your subjects. It makes them feel good about themselves. It's not about God at all; its about being part of the club. That's what I think. And I don't know if the devil will bother picking at whatever's in your brain, but if I were you, I'd try to come up with an answer one of these Sundays, before the whole thing comes crashing down."

The minister was shocked and speechless.

"To put it plainly," she concluded, closing her notebook and stowing her pen in a pocket of her purse, "I don't think your people are grounded enough in their faith to weather the storm that's coming. Ignoring it is a grave error. Once the feel-good part of the Restoration experience is questioned by their rich friends and neighbors because of all this, there'll be no reason to come here, other than to be laughed at. They'll just find another club, where they can wear their membership on their sleeves like a badge of honor, instead of a badge of shame."

She stood up to go, amazed and strangely satisfied that he still said nothing, apparently continuing to process the information, which was an entirely new message in his ears. "Please don't misunderstand me," she said. "You've accomplished a great deal here. I'm sure there's a lot of good that's getting done. But you're overestimating your influence over your flock and underestimating this

Q

so-called devil's trick. And, knowing this particular devil as I do, I can't emphasize the danger strongly enough."

Gigi left him there, thinking, apparently not offended by her words but mystified by both their substance and their source. She assessed the interview as one-way communication on both sides. Her legs were heavy as she made the long walk out of the building and across the empty parking spaces in the afternoon sun to a far lot, where a huge red and gold banner hung atop a high pole, emblazoned with the word "Prophecy."

The seed was already planted in Gigi's mind to offer her theory about Q in the feature story she had been commissioned to write; the problem, of course, was Daniel Withers, who fully expected her to print the objections of the more outspoken leaders of the churches, to give voice to their loud, rather naive protestations. Should she deviate from the script, he might remove her privilege, and she couldn't risk losing it. As long as she could speak, even through the muffled megaphone of the *Dispatch*, she might be able to do some good. And as long as she remained close to Withers, she might even accomplish more.

The churches, of course, weren't making it easy for her. The seminary trustees had announced that a thorough examination of the matter would be conducted once the complete manuscript was released, and a monograph laying out the official position would be published later. This was typical and probably wise, though Gigi lamented that it played right into Withers' hands in that he would get plenty of free press to spread his views over several weeks, or for as long as he wanted. One of the flaws of modern Christendom, Gigi thought, was its attitude of invincibility; it saw only good in itself and rested in its tradition, assuming it would always stand. Gigi herself believed it would indeed stand but in a far different way. She saw the Church as a movement, not as an institution, which at present seemed to be in grave danger, despite the arrogance of its keepers. The movement would continue, as it had in so many places around the world when the institutional church fell under attack. So it would happen here, and Gigi wondered if that would not be all that bad.

She could not bear to write the opinions of Bobby T. Raeburn. Crawford LaRue, predictably, refused to return her calls. Angry messages from pastors filled her voice mail at the *Dispatch* offices. No one, it seemed, trusted her with their opinions. Other than Raeburn, only one other Christian leader (though some would shudder to think of him as such) seemed eager to speak with her: Dale Dole of The Enclave. She hesitated to return his call, and the more she hesitated, the more she knew she never would.

Desperate to write something that would help the faithful and hold Withers at bay, she considered literally inventing opinions that might give rise to intelligent speculation, though she feared being found out. Besides, she was too much the servant of her own morality, and she was loath to deceive, even for good. Then, while rustling around in her neglected pantry for a stale bagel, she got a grand idea.

The lunch crowd in Yesterday's Muffins was loud and lively. Gigi entered, notebook computer tucked under one arm and a stainless steel travel mug in her opposite hand, and scanned the patrons for an easy mark. She bought a house coffee and transferred it to the mug, then walked over to a table where a bearded young man in jeans, oversized black T-shirt, and sandals lounged, reading the newspaper.

"Anything interesting in there?" she asked.

Q

The greeting startled the man, who blinked rapidly in response but said nothing immediately. Instead he flicked his eyes left and right, wondering if she might be addressing someone else, then took in Gigi's full figure, and suddenly sat upright.

Gigi put the notebook down on the table. "I write for the *Dispatch*," she said. "Do you mind?" She pulled out a chair tentatively.

"Oh sure, I mean, no, it's fine—go ahead," the man stammered. He plucked at his unkempt beard in nervous fashion.

Gigi smiled and swung her thick hair back. She crossed her arms on the table and faced him. "Have you read about the lost book of the Bible?" she whispered.

"Oh, yeah, I read that." The man's face indicated his extreme disinterest, with a trace of disappointment.

"Well—what do you think?"

The man looked bored. "I don't really have an opinion." He paused, expressionless. "Is that all you wanted to talk about?"

Gigi worried that she had gone about this all wrong and that having played on the poor guy's emotions, she might get brushed off. "Honestly, yes. But I don't expect you to talk to me. I was just hoping, that's all."

The man watched her face intently, until at last his features softened. The ploy worked.

"It's totally offensive to me, if you really want my opinion." Gigi raised the screen but kept her eyes firmly on his as he spoke. "This whole big media hype over something somebody wrote two thousand years ago. It's all crap."

"Crap?" Gigi's fingers couldn't move above the keyboard.

"Yeah. The Bible's outdated anyway. Nobody really believes all that stuff in there. So what's the big deal about one more old book about somebody else's religion? I don't get it."

"So, you're not a religious person, then?"

"I'm a spiritual person but no, not religious."

"What's the difference?"

He huffed, perhaps perturbed at her fake innocence. "Spirituality is about love and God and higher ways of thinking. Religion is all rules."

"You don't attend church?"

"Church is for religious people."

"You don't read the Bible?"

"No. I have my own ideas about God. Why should I plug into some dead guys' ideas?"

"You're talking about Jesus?" She was growing more interested in the man as he revealed his views.

"No way; Jesus was cool, but these guys who wrote the Bible, they were pretty much out of control, you know. They used Jesus to advance their own agendas, like . . . " he smirked.

"Like what?" she asked, eagerly awaiting the answer.

"Like y'all in the media."

Gigi laughed. "So I guess you don't believe everything you read," she said.

"You could say that. But I still read everything y'all write." His body language had changed; he was far more relaxed now than he had been a few minutes earlier, and Gigi took advantage of it.

"You must be a seeker, then," she observed.

He thought about this for a moment. "Yeah, you could say that."

"Truth is important to you."

He grew slightly uncomfortable. "Yeah."

"Are you going to read the codex when it's published?" She had closed the screen, hoping it might encourage him to speak more freely.

"I might."

"Why?"

He swallowed and leaned toward her. His face was serious, revealing some hidden hurt. "Because I would like to think there might be something to believe in after all."

"That's interesting," Gigi said. "I was under the impression that the codex would do just the opposite."

He shrugged. "It's all in the way you look at it, I guess."

They talked for almost an hour. He bought her a refill and tried to get her phone number. Gigi felt that he was enjoying the conversation, and at the appropriate moments she tried to steer him toward the Gospel. She took a subtle approach, trying to get him to answer his own questions or at least to see that he had no answers. To him, God was hidden in the heavens, and his representatives on earth were at best well-meaning though bumbling servants, way off the mark. He clung to a faith in a higher power, which logic seemed to dictate existed; he wanted to believe there was some point to his life. He felt ignored, unappreciated, even rejected. It was strange that Gigi had not considered his point of view before. This man had long since abandoned modern religion, so Q could not undermine his belief system. Rather, it held promise for him that somehow its discovery might expose some obvious but long-obscured eternal truth that would help him make sense of his life.

It was disturbing to Gigi to realize how organized religion had alienated so many people in one way or another. Was anyone really to blame? For some reason, this man had not felt comfortable embracing traditional beliefs or the social customs of the religious community, which served as his reference point for understanding God. Possibly, he had bought the late twentieth-century dogma that everything is relative and that absolute truth does not exist; if so, he would be unwilling to make any lifestyle concessions just to be accepted in a church. Maybe he had been persecuted for some spurious reason or much worse, ignored. Perhaps it was his repeated disappointment with the stark humanity of Christians in general and their leaders in particular, who played the hypocrite and were caught. She concluded that this must be it—the impossibly high expectations of Christianity against the vivid reality of the fallenness of its adherents—that offended nonbelievers the most. Ironically, what should have led them toward the Savior had the effect of driving them away.

In all this, however, God came out clean, unscathed, the true icon of perfection, pure love, and justice. To most, if not all, God was still the ideal being or concept or standard; it was simply those who had constructed the machinery with which to apprehend him who were hopelessly flawed. Q, therefore, could not move God from his lofty position, but it could inflict irreparable damage upon the religious community, which was already seen as narrow-minded, intolerant, self-righteous, or worse. This might not turn out to be all that bad, to destroy the temple and raise it again; but if taken to its final conclusion, it could spell doom for the Gospel itself. For if the divinity of Jesus were called into question and license were given to those who at present restrained their skepticism for the sake of convention, there could be no recovery. If Jesus was a man and is not God, then the elaborate scheme that has been carefully erected upon and around him for two centuries would be seen as baseless. The world would be left with a generic, toothless sovereign who was flexible in his judgments, if he executed any judgments at all, an idea, a concept, an invention of the individual man, without Jesus there to explain him.

As she drove through the city toward home, these thoughts continued to darken Gigi's mind. Now she understood more clearly why the Society of Saint Matthew had kept Q hidden for so long. It was not that they had a stake in Christianity and wanted it preserved, but it was rather that they believed deeply in Jesus and could not bear to have his name degraded by modern thinkers. Their faith never wavered; they simply sought an explanation of how this document came to be and why. They were possessed by the fear that this ancient manuscript might give a million people— or one person—an excuse not to believe. They knew, as Gigi knew, that there had to be a reason this document was written.

Suddenly, she came upon a billboard with Dale Dole's face pasted on it and the words, "The New Face of Christianity: A Frank Discussion of the Role of Faith in the Modern World." The sign indicated the meeting would take place next week at the convention center, with no admission fee charged. It was sponsored by the Enclave.

Gigi was incensed. She punched the gas and gripped the wheel tightly in anger at the thought of what further damage Dole and his cronies might inflict on the faith. Flying down a service road parallel to 35W, she was distracted by a white pickup that had pulled over on the shoulder, emergency lights flashing. She was in no danger of hitting the truck but slammed on the brakes anyway, a reaction she would later say was unquestionably providential. Fortunately, no cars were behind her, and she eased off the road, in front of the parked vehicle. In her right-side mirror, she saw them: a man, fifty-ish, in jeans and denim shirt, leaning over another man who lay motionless on the ground.

"Did you hit him?" Gigi called out over the roar of the traffic as she slid along the side of the Nova and jogged to the two men.

"No, but the guy two cars in front of me almost did. Believe it or not, I think this fella's OK. Maybe it's the alcohol numbed him a bit—you can smell it from here."

Gigi approached and knelt by the prone man. She put her hand on his shoulder and squeezed gently. His head waggled like a turtle's, and he blinked his eyes open before they settled half-closed.

"You OK?" she asked, squeezing harder.

The man jerked his limbs and turned to face her. Seeing the big man standing over her shoulder seemed to scare him, and he scooted away like a crab.

"Poor fella's terrified," the man said. "Hey!" he yelled. "We're just tryin' to help you. No need to run off now."

Despite the appeal, the victim scrambled away and retrieved a cardboard sign the other man and Gigi hadn't seen before. Suddenly, the man started running, and the other ran to chase him, overtaking him about twenty yards down the road. They talked for a moment, and the man with the sign dropped his head and nodded in response to what the other was saying. Then, they walked (and staggered) slowly back to Gigi. The man with the sign flashed a coy smile at Gigi and hopped into the truck.

"What did you say to him?" Gigi asked.

"Told him to quit the alcohol and I'd give him a job. I'm in construction; there's always work for the willing. That's what his sign said, 'will work.' That's it, just 'will work.'" He laughed.

"That's great!" Gigi exclaimed. "Listen, I work at the Kitchen, a men's shelter not far from here. If you can get him there after work, we'll take care of . . . "

Q

"That's OK, miss," he said, interrupting. "I'll take this fella home with me. I've got room. In fact, I'll take him to church with me tonight."

Gigi was impressed. "It's not every day you meet a Good Samaritan on the interstate." She extended her hand. "I'm Gigi Vaughn."

"Mack Jeffers," he said, completing the handshake. He was a burly man, nice looking, with graying temples and stubble framing ice-blue eyes. "Seems I know that name from somewhere . . . "

"Probably from the newspaper. I write part-time for the *Stockyard Dispatch*." There was a visible physical reaction when she said this, subtle but definitely there.

"You know my work?" she asked, hoping he didn't.

"I know the paper, of course. And Daniel Withers." His words were sharp.

"Doesn't sound like you're much of a fan."

The man grunted. "The man's evil, that's all. I know it first-hand. What he's doing now, with that so-called Bible book? You know it's gonna be all lies. The man hates God. Can't compete, I guess."

Gigi looked beyond him. The drunk's face was pressed to the window. He was sleeping comfortably, or dead. "How'd you come to know Mr. Withers?" she inquired.

"Used to work for him. The Withers Tower." Jeffers turned back to the truck, his eyes following Gigi's, then back to face her. "I built it."

It was a very hot day, and at that moment the heat seemed oppressive to Gigi, but after a few seconds, she sensed that the emotional shock of Jeffers' words was the source of her swoon and not the Texas sun. If ever she was to see God opening a door, this was it.

"I would assume, then, that you might have plans of the building somewhere?" she said, shielding her eyes.

He beheld her suspiciously. "Why?"

Gigi squirmed a bit and stuck her hands in her pockets in an apologetic stance. "Well, as you know, it's a very big building, very nicely built, by the way, and it's easy for things to get misplaced, and . . . ," she watched for his reaction before continuing. "Well, let's just say that somebody has lost something in there, and I'd really like to find it if I can . . . "

"Why don't you just ask Mr. Withers?" he said smugly. It was clear that he wanted Gigi to come right out and say what she had in mind.

She sighed. "Tell you what, Mack. Your new employee seems to be content right now." They both looked at the sleeping man, whose cheek was flat against the glass. "If you've got a minute, we could sit in my car, and I'll tell you all about it."

He looked at her warily, then smiled.

Two hours later, Gigi was walking briskly across the seminary campus, hoping Professor Dunbarton would be in. He usually kept office hours on Wednesday afternoons, even in the summer, which he used to prepare for teaching responsibilities that evening in his church or wherever he was serving as an interim pastor or guest speaker, if he had no appointments with students. The textual criticism class was unusually hard, and Gigi assumed some struggling seminarian might be there. If so, she would wait. She had to tell him what she was planning to do.

It was risky, of course, and he would discourage her from actually carrying out the mission. She wondered if that's what she wanted down deep somewhere—a rational person to tell her she was crazy to try this. Cody would surely take this position, but she wouldn't tell him about it, because he wouldn't even think it through. It was fine for him to be concerned with her safety, but he wouldn't even consider the value in what she was proposing. Tinky would do the same and so would her dad. It was better to try A.D., who would tell her to forget it but who would at least appreciate the importance of what she was so foolishly attempting. Instead of criticism for stupidity, she would get praise for bravery, and she liked that. For Gigi, though, discouragement usually had the opposite effect; to tell her she couldn't do something would only strengthen her resolve. Yes, she was crazy; but yes, it was important; and no, she shouldn't do it; but no, she wouldn't turn back now. Not now, after the incredible chance encounter that afternoon.

A.D.'s office door was slightly ajar. Without knocking, Gigi burst inside, catching the professor off guard as he sat behind his desk amid a shipwreck of papers, folders, and books. She considered too late that her rather close relationship with her teacher led to an inappropriate informality and that she should have knocked, but she was in the room now and there was no sense to stand on protocol when the salvation of millions was at stake.

"I have to ask you a question," she said quickly.

"Gigi, I really can't . . . "

She hardly acknowledged his discomfort. "Just a question. It won't take but a minute. I know the answer already, but I have to ask." She was nearly out of breath from the fast-paced walk and the growing excitement.

He stood behind the desk. "Really, Gigi, now isn't a good . . . "

"If you had the chance to look at Q, could you determine if it were the real thing?"

He cocked his head to one side, sensing where this was going. "I suppose I could, with time and the proper resources . . . "

"Excellent!" she shrieked. "I'm going to get it for you!"

He put his hands on his hips and rolled his head around in exasperation before responding. "You and I both know that's not possible. Look, maybe we should discuss this some other time." He walked casually around the desk toward her, giving her the distinct impression he was anxious for her to leave.

"Wait a minute, Dr. Dunbarton," she begged. "Just hear me out. You won't believe what happened today! I was on my way home . . . "

"Gigi," he said firmly. "I have an appointment."

She looked at him quizzically. This was strange, indeed. Something was different about him; he had never taken such a tone with her. What was it? She looked around instinctively, not knowing why. At last her eyes fell upon something that registered in her brain—a little detail, long forgotten, a riddle suddenly solved.

On the two-drawer file cabinet near the window sat several envelopes made of dark brown cardboard, each with a flap and a thick, cloth-covered elastic band.

Before she could speak, someone entered the room behind her.

"Ah, Miss Vaughn!" the gentleman said. "So sorry I had to leave suddenly the other day without actually having the chance to make your acquaintance, but I was somewhat miffed at the whole affair, you might say. My, it is wonderful to see you face to face!"

Gigi could only stare blankly at the man, hypnotized by the warmth of his smile.

"Forgive me, my dear," he said with a sweep of his hand and a bow of his head. "I'm John Ravenswood, of England."

2.5

From Q19:

Whoever troubles one of these little ones who believe [in me], it would be good for him that a heavy millstone be hanged on his neck and he be drowned in the depth of the sea.

> *It was impossible for him to know what I had done but that one [of the disciples] had given me away. This shamed me beyond all necessity, for I had no hope now of ever being accepted among them. And so, with his hands resting upon the innocent child's shoulders, he watched me steadily [as he spoke]. That any or all of the befuddled disciples knew these words were intended for me I cannot say, for they were surely [absorbed] in their own petty jealousies, as they often were. But I shall never forget his burning gaze, for with it came a dread such that I had known not before.*

THE PUBLICATION OF THE SECOND EXCERPT OF THE WITHERS CODEX promised to be even more damaging than the first had been. Anna K. Soesbee, sitting cross-legged on her sofa in her tiny apartment south of downtown, sipped her heavily flavored coffee and wriggled under her afghan. It was just past dawn and not particularly cool, but Anna K was always cold, as if her frail body had no capacity for storing any heat of its own. She had been awakened by the ringing phone at her bedside, startling her from a dead sleep. It required several rings before she reached over to answer, not because of the hour or the sudden interruption of slumber but because it hardly ever rang, and she could scarcely believe the call was intended for her.

The urgency in Gigi's voice demanded that she clear her head quickly. "Have you seen the paper?"

"No, I . . . "

"Go get it. I'll be there in less than a half-hour."

Anna dressed herself in gray sweats and tied her hair back with a rubber band. She hurried into the kitchen and switched on the coffee maker, which had been programmed to start brewing at 7:30. Then she opened the front door and hopped with bare feet onto the concrete floor of the landing, snatched up the Sunday *Dispatch,* and darted back into the apartment.

This time, Lester Bothwell had submitted an interpretation of the text and notes.

We are familiar with these words of Jesus, of course, from Matthew 18:6 and Luke 17:2. There is no parallel account in Mark, since Q—or perhaps now more properly referred to as WC for Withers Codex—would have served as a parallel source. What we have not heretofore been told is the context from which we should shape our understanding of the saying.

In Matthew, Jesus speaks to address the disciples' question about greatness in the kingdom; in Luke, the statement arises without pretext, almost as an independent teaching.

Q

But now, thanks to our Heaven-sent scribe, we can know from his personal observations more about why this remark was uttered and what it means.

The truth should not surprise us, though it gives us pause. When considering the reality of what is presented here against the overall ministry of Jesus, one finds an astonishing pattern that should have been obvious but has been subconsciously eliminated from all possibility because of the divine nature, which we have ascribed to Jesus for so long.

The notations left to us by this dutiful scribe portray Jesus in his true light. He was, indubitably, a cult leader, much like those common to all religions and consistent with those characteristics displayed in the notorious figures in more modern times with which we are all too familiar: Moon, Jones, Koresh, et al.

Anna K removed her glasses and rubbed her eyes. She tuned her ears beyond the apartment walls and listened for traffic, fearing that somehow the words she had just read might have struck such a blow that the churches would be empty on this morning. She heard nothing and caught her breath before realizing that it was still too early for even the earliest of services. Relieved but still deeply grieved, she returned to Bothwell's report.

That Jesus falls firmly into the tradition of these leaders, or more accurately that they follow the tradition established by him, is clear from the observer's recollection of events. It would seem that he had attempted in some way to create controversy among

*the disciples, possibly to undermine Jesus' authority
over them or to expose his ulterior motives.*

*Note that he refers to them as "little children," a
term commonly employed by those who seek to numb
the minds of their followers, who must be conditioned
to obey and never question their leader. Having been
so brainwashed, it is logical that the disciples might
not have understood the true motivation behind the
words but instead puzzled over them as they did over
many such obscure lessons, as we do even today.*

*It would naturally have been an exclusive group
over which Jesus held a mesmerizing power, and those
who sought to break it were anathema indeed. This is
a direct warning—a threat, if you will—directed
toward this scribe or anyone who might tempt away
the weak-minded men upon whom their leader preyed.*

*All the marks of the cult are here: the gathering of
the easily-led and disenfranchised to one charismatic
person, the extreme loyalty required by said followers,
the insecurity of the leader, and the jealous paternalism
hinting of extreme, justified violence toward anyone
who might get in the way. Perhaps most disquieting of
all is the scribe's recollection of the hypnotic, bone-chill-
ing stare of the one characterized by generations as
meek, lowly, and gentle of heart.*

Quick footsteps approaching outside reached her ears without
warning and nearly caused Anna K to spill her coffee. Frantic, her
heart pounding from what she had read, she jumped up, casting
paper and afghan aside, poised to flee like a rabbit in a thicket,

Q

knowing the threat was rapidly approaching but not perceiving from whence it came. In seconds her mind cleared and she clutched her hand to her throat as Gigi banged on the door.

"I didn't know anything about this, really I didn't," apologized Anna K as she opened the door. Gigi smiled and nodded. "That didn't even cross my mind. What—did you think I was mad or something?" She was unusually chipper and bounced inside with a roll of blueprints under one arm.

Anna K shrugged and said nothing. Gigi dumped the blueprints onto the kitchen table and turned to face her. "Let me ask you a question," she said in a challenging tone. Anna K blinked, waiting. "Do you really think there's anything intellectually honest or ethical about what he's doing?"

"Who—Mr. Withers?"

"Yes! Bothwell may be all wet, but he's not doing anything sinister. Put yourself in his place: here's a gazillionaire with this manuscript, and he offers you the chance to blaze a new trail of scholarship—wouldn't you take it? Withers knew just what Bothwell would do. It's a foregone conclusion based on his record. But he's got the credentials Withers needs, and he's articulate. He was a perfect choice. Withers is exploiting Bothwell to serve his own twisted needs—the same way he's trying to exploit me."

"I don't . . . " Anna K stopped in midsentence because Gigi didn't seem to expect an answer. Instead she helped herself to a cup of coffee and sat down at the kitchen table.

"I want to tell you something, Anna K," Gigi confessed. "I'm in the middle of this for a reason. I've always been something of a rebel, I guess, but I have this passion for justice that gets me into trouble. I can't just accept things as they are. It's a long story, but I found out about this book by accident, and ever since I haven't been able to wait to get my hands on it. At first, I thought it might answer some big questions about Christianity—you know, fill in some gaps, maybe solve some conflicts. We fight about so much, I guess I thought . . . well, I don't know what I thought."

Anna K pulled out a chair and sat down. "It takes a lot of faith to do what you did," she said. "And to do what you're doing."

Gigi shook her head. "That's just it—why am I doing it, really? I wanted God to vindicate my positions, that's why. I wanted to prove people wrong. Here I am, so critical of self-serving religious hypocrites, and I'm doing the same thing."

"No, no you're not," Anna K answered. "You see that things aren't right. You have faith in God that he wants to change them. And so you do what you can to be used by him for that purpose."

"Well, I appreciate that, but I'm in too deep now. I got close to this evil man, so I could maybe see this book, you know, if it really exists."

"I see nothing wrong with that. Maybe it doesn't."

"Oh, it exists alright. I know someone who has seen it. But that's not the bad part. Withers knew that's what I wanted and used it as bait. He let me believe that I was using him to do something else at the same time . . . "

"Preach?" wondered Anna K aloud.

"Exactly. Through the articles. But now it's all turned around. The Church sees me as being on his side. It's terrible. I started out wanting to help the Church, and now, I'm the enemy."

Anna K sat quietly, not knowing how to comfort her. The cheery excitement she had witnessed a few moments ago seemed to have vanished in Gigi's self-evaluation.

Q

"So now—well, I feel powerless, like there's nowhere to go from here. My credibility with the Church is gone, so I can't really make an impact by writing for the paper, especially now, when I'm forced to represent the Church's point of view. There's nothing there, Anna K. I can't defend them when they have no defense. I had in my mind that I could vindicate myself by getting to this book and somehow clearing things up, because it's obvious that Withers is bent on destroying people's faith in God. He's trusting that his media barrage will shape their opinions, and I'm worried that this crisis will expose just how flimsy our religious facade is. But then, I thought, *That's just another self-serving pursuit. Go ahead and be the hero, Gigi, and see if God can borrow some of your glory.* So I thought I should just quit, go back to California, forget about the ministry and this whole thing, do something else."

"Doesn't sound like you," said Anna K, smiling.

"No, sure doesn't. But I didn't ponder it long." She leaned forward. "I met this guy who built the Withers Tower, and he gave me the plans." She pointed her head in the direction of the roll on the table, and Anna K's eyes followed. "It was like a confirmation from God."

"What? I don't get it." Anna K squinted, trying to understand.

"The book. The codex," Gigi tried to explain. "I'm going to steal it."

Anna K's eyes widened behind the lenses. "Gosh, Gigi. Why?"

"For one, to let some real scholars take a look at it and give a complete evaluation. See, nobody knows what this thing really says. We have to just sit here helplessly while the media takes shots at us every Sunday. That garbage Bothwell wrote—that's just a little of what's to come."

"I thought you said you knew somebody who had seen it," Anna K said.

"Yes, I do. You've seen him, too, at the press conference: John Ravenswood. But he hasn't seen it in decades, and he's not a scholar himself. In fact, his little group that held on to this secret had dwindled down to one other person, and when he died unexpectedly, that's when Withers got involved. The man who first studied this book was something of a drug addict. There's a lot of speculation about it even today, and there are supposed to be a few hand-picked scholars out there who have copies of this druggie's notes and are trying to make sense of them. But the manuscript needs a fresh look, that's for sure."

"So Withers is beating everyone to it and trying to shape public opinion," Anna K said.

"Right," replied Gigi. "And who knows how bad this will get? He says he plans to publish it and that he'll put it on display, but will he leave some things out? Will he alter the text? The man's got unlimited funds and state-of-the-art technology. We know his agenda. We can't let him get away with it." The excitement was back in her voice.

"So, I'm guessing you're here because you want my help."

Gigi smiled and reached out to unfold the roll of plans.

"There's only one way to deal with this, and that's to confront these people head on." The man who spoke was fat with a white short-sleeved shirt, red suspenders, and a red tie. His navy blazer defied buttoning. His wife, a small woman with gray hair blending into common features, said nothing but nodded occasionally without pausing between forkfuls of macaroni and cheese.

"It's a liberal plot, that's all it is, and I say we march down to Fort Worth with about a million Baptists to protest," he insisted.

An older man dressed in a brown suit at the next table seemed interested in his banter but not particularly pleased with the tone. "Excuse me, but are you discussing the codex?" he asked.

The heavy man moved his bulk with difficulty to speak directly. "Yes, and I take it you're just as outraged as I am?"

The gentleman smiled and nodded. "I am. But I also think we should wait to see where this is going. It could be we will all learn something out of this."

"How can we learn from something that is unbiblical?" said the heavy man, his voice rising above the din of the cafeteria. "That sounds like something that would come from some liberal preacher. Where do you go to church?"

The other man laughed, not realizing he was serious. "Seventh Baptist."

"Well, that explains it, then! I used to go there, when was it, honey?"—she paused, said nothing, and continued eating as he answered his own question—"back in the early nineties, I think. That's where that fellow Rutledge preaches, right? That's why we left."

"I don't think it's very Christian for us to be running down pastors, do you, Hal?" The voice came from behind the table. It was Martin Black, pastor of First Baptist, peering down reprovingly but with a gentle manner.

The big man turned toward the voice. "Hey, Pastor!" he said cheerily, then frowned. "You been listening in on this?"

"Actually, no, I was just on my way to pay the bill, and there you were, big as life." He smiled and winked at Hal's wife, who blushed and got some macaroni caught in her throat.

"Well, we were discussing that new lost book of the Bible. You got an opinion on that?"

At one time Hal had been a member of First Baptist for about a year and had demonstrated a high degree of loud intolerance for intelligent thinking in that short time, and there was no way his former pastor was going to engage him in debate in the middle of Picadilly Cafeteria. He leaned down as if to say something profound, and Hal leaned in to listen.

"Don't look now, but Carter Rutledge is walking over here; why don't you ask him?" He smiled, patted Hal on the shoulder, waved to Carter, and disappeared.

The senior pastor of Charleston's Seventh Baptist Church approached the large man with a quizzical look on his face, as if he was trying to place how he knew this man. When the penny dropped, he looked with mocking anger toward Martin Black and addressed the large man with a casual greeting.

"Good afternoon, sir, you do look very familiar. I'm Carter Rutledge. Didn't you attend our church at one time?"

In minutes, a crowd had gathered around Hal's table, and a lively discussion ensued. There were a few more folks from Seventh and several from Mission 419, where Hal had most recently placed his membership and spent most of his time there torturing his young pastor.

"Just shut up, Hal," another heavy-set man said at last. "Nobody wants to hear your redneck opinions." The speaker had only recently crossed swords with Hal over a proposed pulpit guest at a church business meeting.

Hal jumped to his feet. "What about you and your high and mighty ideas, eh, Joe? Why don't you tell these good people about that flaming liberal friend of yours who wants to serve communion to the queers right down at our church!"

"He wants to start a ministry to victims of AIDS," Joe shot back. "And Rusty's all for it, if you must know. I guess this means you'll be moving to another church pretty soon—if there are any left you haven't joined."

Hal walked right up and got in Joe's face. Their fellow church members reached in to prevent further aggression, but their hands only seemed to bless the violence that erupted. Hal's wife, having freed her clogged airway, scooted behind Carter for safety as the two men crashed onto the table. Hal rolled over the food and came up with smashed macaroni and cheese pasted to his back. When he was pulled off Joe, Joe got to his feet and rushed at him again, sending drinks flying and dishes crashing to the floor.

Mildred Dunbarton walked up to the crowd as the men were being separated. "Children," she muttered, disgusted, not recognizing the irony in her assessment.

Rusty Rowe walked through downtown Charleston in an attitude of prayer, as he often did, though, as usually happened, the sights and sounds of this magnificent and enigmatic city distracted his focus. He had been sent here to start a church, which he had done, following the prescribed guidelines of the denomination and with the full support of the local congregations. The goal was to establish a congregation that could reach the rich and the poor of the peninsula at the same time, a truly multi-cultural thrust.

It was felt that a building was needed immediately to create an identity, and a suitable location was found at 419 Proprietors' Lane: a peeling stone edifice that had undergone multiple renovations spanning nearly a hundred years with one distinctive feature left untouched, the number 419 carved into the cornerstone. Seeing this, Rusty turned to his Bible and verse 4:19 in Matthew's Gospel: "Follow me, and I will make you fishers of men." It seemed an appropriate focal point for the new endeavor. As Jesus had intentionally sought men along the Sea of Galilee to walk with him and learn God's ways, this church would do the same where the Ashley and Cooper rivers emptied into this picturesque harbor, which had drawn those from all walks of life for so long.

As it happened, there was a complete acceptance of the pastor's vision, but the early going was difficult. The services were intended to be understated, contemporary presentations of the Christian faith featuring computer-aided graphics and drama. Unfortunately all who came were lifelong believers who were unhappy in their churches, and it was apparent that the young mission was in danger of being swept away into controversy. Issues were raised concerning the style of worship, and Rusty attempted to adjust but the building had aesthetic limitations, which hindered the kind of worship experiences the new members seemed to prefer.

Recognizing the drift away from his vision and toward a replication of what was already being done, Rusty took on a more autocratic leadership style, and conflict resulted. Desperate to reach into the impoverished crannies of the city with the Gospel, he launched street-corner Bible clubs using student volunteers from the local colleges, along with literacy training, and opened the building on Friday and Saturday nights as a kind of youth center. He received almost no support from his Sunday morning members,

Q

who harbored such a resistant spirit that those inner-city prospects who were interested in learning more about the church remained outside the front doors during worship, intimidated by the crowd inside. Frustrated, Rusty established two services for the two groups. If the truth be known, he preferred the ministry to the predominantly black congregation, made up primarily of children and young mothers; they seemed to benefit from the work and brought a spirituality to the dingy building that excited him. By contrast, he grew to resent the other group, and it showed. In time, they began to withhold their giving but not their attendance or opinions.

The letters were perhaps the most disturbing aspect of the conflict. Though anonymous, a continuing theme could be found in nearly all of them. One defiant writer cited Acts 4:19, misapplying Peter's words, "Do you think God wants us to obey you rather than him?" to the pastor's leadership. Another used 1 Corinthians 4:19, taking the persona of a denominational executive (as if a denominational executive would write an anonymous letter!), saying, "I will come soon to find out if all this big talk really represents God's power." Still another found support for his position in Ephesians 4:19, which ascribed to Rusty those unbecoming attributes found therein: sensuality, impurity, and greed.

All of this affected the young pastor profoundly, placed a dreadful strain on his marriage, and for a time nearly jettisoned him from the ministry. It was fortunate that Carter Rutledge, pastor of one of the sponsoring churches, had noticed the situation and provided encouragement, not just with his personal time and wise counsel but with several of his more progressive members to assist the work of the "second" congregation.

The local paper had been bristling with editorials concerning the Withers Codex for over a week, and local ministers were beginning to speak out. The general opinion in Charleston was to ignore it and wait for it to go away. As he approached the weather-beaten hulk of Saint Phillips Church, Rusty blended in among the tourists to eavesdrop. He leaned along the wrought-iron fence as they drifted to and fro, standing on the sidewalk with their tour maps, pouring in and around the church like ants busily settling a new hill. In all of this, there was no talk of Q.

It was a cloudy day, and Charleston looked its age. Rusty considered how the historic churches might fare when all this was over. Standing across the street next to a group of basket weavers, admiring the white dignity of Saint Michael's, he realized that for many, nothing would change. Jesus had said that when lifted up on the cross, he would draw men to himself; today, they were drawn by so many other things—prestige, the right social circles, entertaining preachers, friends in high places, and cheap grace, the kind Bonhoeffer described, the kind that costs nothing. Though Jesus be slandered and his divinity dragged through the dust, it would not affect many of the old churches, for their tradition rested on much more than him. But to the poor of downtown Charleston, who huddled in the shadows of this living history museum like hopeful extras, these understated cathedrals were high and lifted up, far from them, impossible to reach, like God in Heaven, save for the love of Jesus.

Rusty walked along the Battery and looked out at the open sea. He loved this city, though it frustrated him. Its beauty was deceiving, and its charm was borrowed from a previous time, reconstructed and gloriously established as a truth that may never have been true. Pride, honor, stubbornness, valor, a smile and a handshake to welcome you but not permanently, because you're not from here; you're invited to dinner but buried across the street. A place where style is more prized than substance and form eclipses function, where just below the surface resides a fear that we might be found out, that all the glory might be lifted off like a roof in a violent storm, exposing who we really are, standing as beggars in cottons and khakis, paying lip service to a God we so desperately need.

The Fort Worth Convention Center was dimly lit, with all attention focused on the stage furnished with a few metal folding chairs and a microphone stand in the center. Dale Dole wandered out first, followed by Lester Bothwell and a few other men conspicuously dressed in the erudite fashion of academics. The auditorium was perhaps half-filled, with the crowd scattered, leaving large gaps. Presumably these were the house groups which comprised the Enclave, all joined together to celebrate the emergence of a more modern understanding of Christianity. This would be Lester Bothwell's first opportunity to speak, and he beamed as Dole introduced him, now growing comfortable with the celebrity status that was surely coming.

The first half-hour consisted of Dale Dole presenting his "modern understanding of Jesus," which Gigi had heard him explain before—though not in so much detail—that night with Anna K at the small house on the south side. There were several hundred more people in attendance, and their voices rose in boos and hisses with increasing frequency. Ushers roamed about the large hall inviting them to leave, which they gladly did. When Dole had concluded, he announced a brief intermission, which would be followed by Bothwell's previously unannounced appearance. As the men returned to the platform, Gigi noticed that only a few of the news teams had remained, and seeing them rushing up the aisle across the auditorium, she followed out of curiosity, leaving A.D. and Ravenswood to hear what further revelations the scholar might impart.

Outside, the street was alive with commotion. Protesters had appeared with signs walking back and forth, and interviews were being conducted in several locations. Observers were beginning to gather, and police were setting up wooden barricades. Singing broke out in places, though the choruses could not be sustained and the harmony of each song soon fell away before another commenced. Gigi saw Crawford LaRue talking into a camera; behind him were several teenagers waving and goofing around. She made her way to within a few yards to listen.

"The Bible is God's Word, and these people who are undermining it cannot be considered true Christians," LaRue was saying.

"And you, of course, are," the reporter said, pushing the mike back in front of LaRue.

"I am, though I say so with humility. We are all sinners, saved by God's grace."

"Then why do you protest these sinners inside? Why don't you enter into a dialogue with them, perhaps a debate?"

"Because there is nothing to debate!" LaRue shouted. "They have as their agenda to water down the Gospel into nothing. It is an excuse to avoid taking Jesus on his terms. We have no portion with such people."

A voice arose from the crowd near Gigi. "You hate them, the same way you hate the Jews!" he shouted in an unmistakable reference to the death of David Stein. A loud murmur and sharp unintelligible exchanges followed. Gigi winced at the epithets she could hear being hurled at the preacher and hoped he wouldn't react.

Q

"No! We do not hate, we only disagree!" LaRue insisted. His amplified words silenced the crowd for a moment. "'Would to God that they become as I am,' Paul said."

"So a true Christian must be just like you?" the reporter interjected.

"Not exactly—but we believe our way is right. We are not ashamed of the Gospel. We will not stand by and see it attacked."

"The world would be better off without your kind in it, you bigot!" a man shouted.

LaRue tried to calm himself, but other shouts filled the air.

"You're a narrow-minded nitwit!"

"We don't want you telling us what to do!"

"Free your mind! Free your mind!" This last one seemed to gather momentum as many voices joined in. The chant overpowered LaRue's ability to respond. The reporter extended the mike toward the surging crowd and the cameras swung wide to film the scene. Gigi suddenly found herself caught in the middle as marchers ran toward the disturbance and clashed with the throng, waving their signs aloft like medieval banners in hand-to-hand combat. Gigi fell; someone stomped on her arm, and another tripped over her. Punches were flying, and she cradled her hands over her head for protection. She could hear the police megaphones threatening arrests. There were screams; Gigi tried to rise but was knocked over, her knee crashing into the pavement, causing her to cry out in pain. She closed her eyes tightly in fear and prayed. In that instant she became aware of strong hands gripping her ankles, straightening her legs and dragging her for a short distance, then reaching under her and carrying her away from the melee. Half in shock, she kept her eyes tightly closed as her rescuer ran from the crowd.

"That's a bit of a sticky wicket back there, but you'll have no worries now," he said, breathless.

She knew the voice and opened her eyes wide. "Jeremy!" she cried.

He held her close and cradled her bruised body as he placed her in the backseat of the car, where Ashley Dunbarton and John Ravenswood sat in front, watching the riot from a distance. "She'll be all right," Jeremy said, hopping in beside her. "A bit nicked up is all."

Gigi stared at him, speechless. Her jeans were torn and her knee was bleeding.

"Have you any idea what set them off?" Ravenswood asked.

Gigi forced herself to focus. "I . . . I don't know. It was an accident waiting to happen once LaRue got in front of that microphone." She reached out and clutched Jeremy's arm, amazed, and he laughed.

"As you can see, I'm quite alive, and I must say I've been fairly content living in your professor's home, though I've grown weary of take-out cuisine," he said. "The man simply has no culinary talent."

Dunbarton chuckled to himself and started the car. He turned the mirror to look into Gigi's eyes. "I tried to keep you out of this. Over and over again I tried," he lamented. "You have a knack for finding trouble, I'm afraid."

"More like a nose for danger, it would seem," Ravenswood added.

"It's not a terrible trait, I suppose," Dunbarton said, turning the wheel sharply and driving away. "It will make you a great scholar someday."

"Or a great thief," added Jeremy.

"We're a car full of snoops, then, would you say?" said Ravenswood. The three of them laughed heartily at this, glad to have the girl safe and relieved that the secrets were out at last. Only Gigi could find no joy in the moment, no matter how temporary it might be. She watched sadly as the car retreated from the scene, which fell away from her sight but promised to return for all to see on televisions nationwide.

On a large table in the dining hall of the Kitchen, several sheets of blueprints lay open and were kept from curling by cans of beets and green beans placed on the corners. It was a few hours before the evening meal, and Gigi, Dunbarton, Cody, Jeremy, Ravenswood, and Anna K sat poring over the diagrams while Tinky cooked. None of them had any experience with architectural drawings except Ravenswood, and his was severely limited. Jeremy suggested Mack Jeffers be invited to review them in detail, but Gigi preferred to leave him out of it; there was no traceable connection between them at the moment, and she felt it should remain that way for obvious reasons. Several questions were put to Anna K, who unfortunately had minimal knowledge of the building beyond her immediate work area. Only Gigi had been to the top floor for her meetings with Withers, and her memory was naturally not photographic.

"There are two possibilities, I think, based on what Gigi has told us," said Ravenswood, stroking his chin. "Either the codex is hidden behind the lobby wall or somewhere high above in the private offices where Mr. Withers resides."

"You know, the more I think about it, I doubt there's anything behind that wall except the engraved words—that's what he meant, not the book itself."

"It could be that he has it somewhere else, possibly at home or in some secured area," Cody said.

"No. No way," Gigi said. "Remember when Jeremy was after it? He wouldn't have taken it home—too dangerous. As for another location, I doubt it. He would want it close to him, as close as possible. I think it's up there, in some vault or something."

They shuffled through the large sheets looking for the layout of the top floor. It was not very complicated, with large rooms around the perimeter and an interior corridor all the way around, framing the main elevators. On one side was a private elevator reserved for Withers only; beside it was his office, connected to a large conference room, which Gigi remembered.

"That room is unusually large," Jeremy said of Withers' office.

"Like his ego," quipped Gigi.

"Yes, but . . . " His voice trailed off as he thought. "Do we have a plan of the floor just below this?"

Cody and A.D. rustled through the paper. "This one's a typical drawing of floors thirty to fifty," Cody said. "The top is the fifty-first."

Jeremy studied the drawing, then placed the two side by side, rearranging the cans to hold them down. "See there," he said, "below where Withers' office is."

They all looked where he pointed. "See that? It's a wall sealing off that little room labeled 'storage.' And there's an entrance from the corridor."

"But not on floor fifty-one," observed Cody.

"Exactly," said Jeremy. "Now, that wall is concrete; it goes all the way down. It is likely above, on Withers' floor as well."

"That would mean that it takes up a portion of Withers' office," said Anna K excitedly.

"But there is no doorway shown off the hall," said A.D.

"What does that tell you, hmm?" crowed Jeremy. "It's got to be there—a secret room, or a vault of sorts, for valuables. Accessible somehow, undoubtedly through Withers' office. It would be quite normal for the paranoid sort of person Gigi says he is."

"A secret room!" Anna K's remark, though suggesting to the others that she was just catching on, actually indicated her immense excitement that such an intriguing thing could be going on in the building where she worked.

They looked at the plans quietly, the only sound coming from Tinky's clattering over the stove. "Now all we have to do is get in there. We'll need tools, and—what about alarms?" Gigi asked.

"There will be a plan somewhere, probably in the office. But I'm afraid we shan't have time to find it and decipher its mysteries," Jeremy said regretfully.

"But alarms are tricky and highly sensitive," said Ravenswood. "If this were really a secret room, he would not desire anyone to know of it or to think about it as such, not repairmen, not anyone. Trust me; I know about these matters."

"It's a risk we'll have to take," Gigi said.

"I'm game, then," said Jeremy confidently.

"Vaya con Dios," boomed Tinky from behind the counter. "But before you rush off to save the world, how about helping me out with the baked chicken."

The phone rang nineteen or twenty times, perhaps more. Mildred's rule was six rings under ordinary circumstances, eight if it were the last attempt for a significant span of time. Around the seventh or eighth ring, she was distracted again by the drama unfolding on her television screen and lost track of the count. No matter; her son was not at home.

He would certainly have been at the convention center, and she feared for his safety. She did not even try to find him among the protestors, since that was certainly not his style. Though convinced that he was not in the center of the fracas, she would not feel at ease until she spoke with him. Logic dictated that he was alright, but a deeper distress gnawed at her: the dreadful awareness of how this episode would be played out in the press in coming days.

She hung up the phone and watched as an ambulance pulled away from the scene, which looked like the aftershock of some freakish rock festival, with so many animated, out of control people and the red and blue flashing lights. As the camera pulled away to show the breadth of the disturbance, a reporter entered the picture and commanded attention.

"At the center of this controversy lies a fascinating manuscript called the Withers Codex, which is purported to actually predate much of the biblical literature concerning Jesus," he said in a nondescript tone. "It is being published one small portion at a time, a tantalizing process that has sparked nationwide interest and now, apparently, even violence."

He held a folded newspaper in front of him. "As reported in a recent feature article by Gigi Vaughn in the *Stockyard Dispatch,* and I quote, 'One wonders what it will take for the Church to awaken and spread its wings to embrace those it has thoughtlessly left out in the cold, who continue to believe that something better exists, though they know not where it can be found. Instead of compassion, they have been met with persecution. Instead of being invited, they have been excluded. Instead of grace, they have been granted law. A harsh and unforgiving standard it is, for it isn't even

Q

God's but man's, and it is rife with hypocrisy. One wonders: what will it take for the Church to awaken, to stop preaching and start listening, to repent and follow the Master and learn the way of the Cross?'"

The reporter dropped the hand that held the paper and lowered his eyes momentarily, pausing for dramatic effect. "We don't know what the final assessment of this ancient text will be; some speculate that it will spell the end of Christianity as we know it," he said soberly, looking away. Then he stared hard into the camera. "One thing is sure: if today is any indication of what may follow"—he turned to look back at the chaos—"Christianity doesn't seem to need any help."

2.6

From Q23:

From the day John the Baptizer began to preach, the kingdom has advanced mightily and [forceful men] seize the opportunity to enter it.

Many times I faltered on my journey from the Dead Sea, but determined was I to face him once again and to put forth the question we had pondered in the darkness [of the fortress]. He answered me harshly, and spoke unto the crowd, many of whom had known John, [with a passion both] exhilarating and terrifying. He scolded the cities of Galilee for their faithlessness and decried their misunderstanding of his [works], and it occurred to me that his will was indomitable, that he would accomplish all that he intended. As John had boldly led the people to him, he now would lead them [further], but to where I could not discern. His manner disturbed me, and yet [I have no doubt that] I would have sought to follow him still had he not commanded me thus to Machaerus, to report what I had seen and heard.

GIGI LAY ACROSS THE CARPET, PROPPED UP ON HER ELBOWS, READING for the fourth time the scribe's enigmatic words, trying to decipher, with Bible opened, what he might have meant to say.

Q

The verse was a difficult one to interpret, appearing in different forms in Matthew 11:12 and Luke 16:16, and the scribe's version represented yet a third recollection of the saying. She rubbed her forehead, straining to think, lamenting again the disadvantage of not having the scribe's Greek text to compare with the others.

Bothwell's comments were even bolder than on the previous week, and Gigi wondered whether he had abandoned all aspirations to intellectual honesty in favor of the zeal for trailblazing so typical of liberal scholars. She had no idea what kind of effect his dismantling of the traditional understanding of gospel truth might be having on the Church but feared the worst. The masses, who were skeptical of organized Christianity before, now had an excuse to be skeptical of Christ himself, and without the means to refute this propaganda, she could only watch and wait. Any attempt to put forth a legitimate response would probably be overshadowed by the vain and ill-conceived antics of Bobby T. Raeburn, Crawford LaRue, and a host of other egomaniacs around the country who were behaving just as foolishly. It pained Gigi to think of it, almost as much as it pained her to read the words.

We in the scholarly community are most indebted to this scribe for splashing light upon a previously obscure saying, which both Matthew and Luke (or those who compiled their gospel accounts in their names) almost certainly misunderstood.

The pericope as a whole is strange, and the fact that it is followed by the famous "woes" against Chorazin, Bethsaida, and Capernaum is stranger still. In the scribe's dark description of Jesus, one might find allusions to emotional and/or mental instability, and this has been suggested before but only in hushed tones by those on the fringes of the academic world.

John is in prison, and the scribe has just returned from there; his question must have stunned Jesus, for he needed John's credibility to succeed. He responds, therefore, with a violent verbal assault upon the innocent scribe, and then, as if to intimidate his hearers from casting further doubts as to his legitimacy, he blasts the Galileans for their lack of acceptance of him!

This saying, then, can only be meant to compare himself to John—to borrow, if you will, from John's popularity; as John was unconventional and perplexing, so is Jesus, yet both are aggressive in pursuit of God's will.

I see perhaps a tinge of paranoia here, possibly even fear, that Jesus himself might be hauled off by the authorities, yet he does not shrink from his bold vision. Such was the inscrutable power of the man, then and now.

Still, the irony of the appearance in our modern time of the true nature of this saying is striking, for those who wield their faith like a sledgehammer often win the day over the more gentle, inquisitive sort, who are frequently bludgeoned for simply admitting they struggle to believe; yet they do so, it does appear, with good reason.

The more she read, the angrier she became, until with a fierce, cat-like pounce, she shredded the paper and left it in tatters on the

Q

floor. She rolled on her back and stared helplessly at the ceiling, its white whorls of plaster blurring in her moist eyes.

The telephone shattered the silence.

Gigi moved slowly, raising herself to her feet with great effort, finally reaching the phone after so many rings that she was surprised the caller was still there. The voice was chillingly familiar.

"I'm very disappointed to find nothing from you in today's paper," Withers hissed. His voice oozed with irritation.

"I . . . I . . . " Gigi could not find the words to respond.

"A riot, Miss Vaughn, and you give me no coverage from a religious angle. It is unacceptable."

"I couldn't . . . I . . . I intended to write something, but . . . wasn't there enough coverage on that?" She asked the question honestly.

"Insight! I need insight, not just facts!" he bellowed. "That's what I'm paying you for!"

"Yes, sir, well, I'm sure I can come up with something next week . . . "

"No! This week!" he demanded. "Come to my office at nine tomorrow morning, and we'll discuss your next piece." With that, he hung up the phone.

Gigi slammed down the receiver in disgust. How much longer could she take this? And then, as she marched into the den and saw the newspaper spread over the floor, a thought struck her. Racing back to the phone, she called A.D.

"Professor?" she asked anxiously, before he could even say hello.

"I knew it had to be you. No one else would be calling this early. I guess you read this week's headlines from hell," he yawned.

"Naturally. But that's not why I'm calling. Get Jeremy up. I'll be there in ten minutes."

She was already off the phone and getting dressed before he could answer.

Without provocation, the congregation settled in comfortably for the sermon, opening their Bibles to the selected passage in the bulletin, relaxing in the pews in preparation for the weekly feeding like baby birds in the nest. Carter Rutledge looked out over them like a disappointed grandfather, feeling powerless to redirect the course of their lives but nevertheless determining to try. Ushers in dark suits came forward, their polished dress shoes crunching lightly on the scarlet carpet like rubber boots on compacted snow. The mystified congregants watched as they ascended the platform and removed first the pulpit and two of the throne-like chairs, reserved seats for the staff ministers who were now skittering away ahead of them, leaving only Rutledge seated on the left, holding a large, camel-colored leather Bible tightly to his chest like a football, as if fearing it might be taken too.

Suddenly, a female choir member stood in the chancel and slid along the front row behind the rail, walking through the mahogany swinging door and straight up to the front of the platform, followed by a young man from the tenor section. She was carrying a plastic pail and shovel; both were barefooted.

Reverend Rutledge felt queasy, suddenly regretting the phone call to Gil Tucker, the ensuing discussion of texts for the coming Sunday, and Tucker's offer to 'whip something up' and send members of his drama team to Seventh Baptist. Carter accepted because he didn't know how to tactfully decline.

Q

The young lady placed her pail and shovel on the floor, then unzipped her robe, revealing more skin than had ever been exposed inside the hallowed walls of Seventh Baptist Church—or in any Charleston sanctuary for that matter. Once completely out of the robe, she fluttered it down on the carpet the way one might spread out a towel at the beach, kneeling in her lime green swimsuit. Then, amid stifled gasps and murmurs (along with the silent yet tangible attention suddenly paid by the usually-somnolent men in attendance), she sat on the edge of the robe and began to pantomime the building of a sandcastle, humming a tune, which Carter interpreted as "The Church's One Foundation." He rubbed his head, agonizing over the spectacle, afraid to look and more afraid of being seen looking. At last she stood up and crossed her arms with pleasure. "What a lovely sandcastle I have built," she announced.

As if on cue, the young man violently tore off his own robe and leapt forward, a well-muscled maniac in red surfer shorts, pouncing on the spot where she had been working, leaping savagely and shouting indecipherable things like a mad gorilla, accompanied by shrieks from the girl. After a dozen or so stomping motions, he scrambled back to where his choir robe lay, snatched it up, and raced out of the sanctuary.

The girl turned to the stunned worshipers and said with poorly acted emotion, "I shouldn't have built a castle. I should have built a church." And with that, she quickly donned her robe, retrieved her pail, and returned to the choir loft. From the side door followed the young man, now suddenly sane like the exorcised man of Gadara, who took his former place as well. A blushing usher came forward with the pulpit and set it upon the platform as Carter stepped behind it. The plastic shovel still lay on the carpet, a brazen reminder of what had just transpired.

"We are indebted to the Reverend Gil Tucker of Castaways' Church on Daniel Island for loaning us two young people from his drama team and for their fine improvisation on this morning's theme," he said ministerially, looking back and nodding at the smiling actors, too embarrassed in fact to face his own congregation. A large man in a golf shirt stood in the back of the church and applauded, and a relieved laughter followed with scattered claps and cheers. The tension thus broken, Carter calmed himself and launched his message.

"'I should have built a church,' the young lady said. Why? Because a church, dear friends, is built on the solid rock of Jesus Christ, and it can never fall. A church by definition cannot be built on anything else and still be a church, though it might look like one and though it might be called one. We are overrun with such so-called churches today, and every one of them stands dangerously in the path of a coming storm."

He cleared his throat, still shaking off the shock of what had preceded. "Jesus concluded his famous Sermon on the Mount with the parable that forms the basic thought of my message today. The sermon, of course, had been full of many controversial statements, such as, 'You have heard it said . . . but I say to you,' and the like. He has been challenging them by his words. And he concludes by saying that hearing and obeying these words is like constructing a house on such a sure foundation that, when storms come, it will ever remain. But to ignore his words is likened to the building of a house on the sand, which cannot ride out the storm because its foundation is flawed. We will consider this morning one aspect of this teaching which relates to the current storm that has ravaged our congregations in recent weeks—the controversy surrounding the Withers Codex."

Q

The people were sitting in rapt attention, having been lulled from their dreary daydreaming not only by the shocking vision in lime green but also by the reference to the codex, which, it appeared, their pastor was finally prepared to address directly. Carter noted their active listening, though he acknowledged having already lost several of the boys in the youth group, who looked past him at the girl in the choir loft with that vapid adolescent expression that could only mean one thing. He wondered how many of them he would lose to Castaways' the following week.

"I say ravaged because . . . ," (he immediately regretted repeating this particular word, which made some of the starry-eyed boys fidget uncomfortably), "an independent research group has published the results of two surveys which justify my concern—not that the codex has damaged the Church but rather, that it has exposed some damaging truths about the Church." He paused for effect but sensing none, continued quickly.

"The first survey questioned Americans at large. Its first question was: 'Do you think the Withers Codex is an authentic first-century work?' Almost 90 percent said yes.

"The second question: 'Do you think the Withers Codex was used as a source document for the gospel writers?' Over 79 percent said yes.

"A third question: 'Do you think the Withers Codex presents the earliest and therefore most accurate description of the life and ministry of Jesus?' My friends, 76 percent of those surveyed said yes."

Carter scanned the faces of his hearers; they were listening intently but were for the most part expressionless. He spoke louder, with an ominous tone. "A fourth question: 'Do you intend to make a personal study of the Withers Codex once it is published in book form?' An incredible 87 percent said yes."

The preacher folded his reading spectacles and slipped them into his lapel pocket with practiced ease. "The last question is the show-stopper. 'Do you believe that the Withers Codex will alter the traditional view of Jesus Christ as the Son of God?' Forty-one percent said yes. That's a lot of people, folks. But note the way the question is phrased. They were not asked about their personal view of Christ but for their opinion on the view of Christ in general. A note in the survey explained that the question was framed this way because they were measuring perception, not reality. A person cannot comment fully on something he hasn't read, but he can give an opinion on how he thinks others might react. He bases this opinion on what he hears others saying and what he is getting from the media. It represents his perception of things, and over forty-one percent of the people think the Withers Codex will change the way we all see Jesus. I suspect that, if the coverage of this issue continues as it has been going, this number will only increase."

Carter relaxed and rubbed his chin thoughtfully. "A few things can be inferred from these results. First, there is a tremendous interest in Jesus. That's good. Second, there is a readiness to accept the official position about the codex put forth by its publisher and his scholarly team, prior to its publication. That's not so good, because it reveals the powerful impact marketing has on our thoughts and minds in American culture. Third, the eagerness to embrace this purported lost book of the Bible suggests a dissatisfaction with the status quo in religious thinking on the part of many people. This is very bad—it indicates that we in the Church are not giving them satisfying answers. My proposition in this message is that we're giving them a lot of things—security, social acceptance, fellowship, recreation—but we're not giving them Jesus. The one we're preaching just isn't believable, and so they're looking for another one.

"Perhaps they have trouble with the miracles. Perhaps they are offended by the Cross. Perhaps they are unwilling to surrender their lives to God. One thing is certain: none of this will ever make sense to them until they meet the real Jesus, the one who died and rose again and lives today. They haven't seen him in us. They don't know what he can do."

Carter looked intently at his people. He narrowed his eyes and leaned over the pulpit. "What I haven't told you is the religious background of the people who were surveyed. Over half described themselves as regular church attendees. Apparently many of us inside the Church have as many doubts as those who never darken the door." At this, a slight twitter arose in the pews.

He drew out the spectacles and set them above his nose. "I mentioned a second survey earlier. It is nothing more than a simple tabulation of data. It reveals a 7 percent decline in church attendance in each of the past two weeks. A 7 percent decline."

Carter paused after this and read the parable again, the leather-bound Bible draped over one open hand. "A storm is coming," he concluded, "and it threatens us all, because our lives, and subsequently our churches, are not built on the right foundation. We have erected steeples on top of sandcastles, and we soon may be washed away."

He closed the Bible and walked to the side of the pulpit, hands in his pockets. "Let me speak frankly to you. I don't know what this Withers Codex really is. I do know, however, that the running commentary in the news is clearly biased against Christianity. Dr. Bothwell and his ilk are well-known liberal theologians. You can come to your own conclusions on the matter, and I hope you will. As for me, I will reserve judgment until I know more about the manuscript and more people have had a chance to study it, such as our own Ashley Dunbarton of Southwestern." He smiled at Mildred, who was sitting down front in her usual place.

"There's something else I know. Jesus is a real person to me. He isn't merely a historical figure, a man who lived long ago. He isn't a cult leader or an opportunist or an eccentric religious nut. He is the living God who became man and dwells in us through his abiding Spirit. I know this, because I know him.

"We have a tendency, I think, to elevate the Bible to a place higher than Jesus. The fact is that the Bible simply points to Jesus. You can memorize every word in the Bible and still not be saved. We have exchanged the Word of God for the words of God. We fight about what the Bible said and about its inspiration, its authority. But even without the Bible, we would still have Jesus. Adam knew him. Abraham knew him. Moses knew him. All without a book by which to learn him. And that relationship altered the course of their lives.

"So now comes an old book with a new angle on Jesus. No cross. No resurrection. Observations from an unknown reporter. Perhaps the media was just as biased then as it is now! Who really knows for sure? You can read the reviews and dismiss Christianity as fantasy, and you probably will, if you don't know Jesus."

Carter was back behind the pulpit now, but he spoke apologetically, not with the usual force. The sermon was taking on the quality of a testimony, with an honest, heart-felt, this-is-just-the-way-things-are kind of tone.

"John's Gospel says that in the beginning the Word existed, before anything else, he, Jesus, the Word, was there. The writer of Hebrews refers to Jesus as God's final Word. When you read the Bible, you are only reading about him. When you live the Bible, you are walking with him, and that's what a true Christian does. The Bible is not the true foundation of our faith; Jesus is.

"Christianity has become so many things that we can hardly recognize it anymore. We like to be entertained, and that's good; but that's not all there is. We like to be reassured by coming to church regularly, and that's good; but that's not all there is. We like our traditions, and they do have value; but they can limit our understanding and numb our hearts to what the Spirit wants us to do. We like our causes, our political arguments, and they're important; but our motives get all mixed up, and suddenly it's us versus them, the Church against the world. But God loves the world. Why don't we? God sacrificed everything for a world that rejected him. Why don't we? God walked into the world and touched it with his grace, personally and intimately and tenderly. Why won't we?"

The church sat motionless before her pastor's pleading. "I guess what I'm saying is that real Jesus-people do what Jesus did, and that's where the power is. Christianity is not an intellectual exercise but a way of life that brings eternal value and blessing, not only to us but to others. We should be caring for people, counseling them, standing as their advocates rather than their judges. The greatest argument for Christianity is the Church, but the greatest argument against it is also the Church. If we have not done these things, we have not known Jesus. And if we have not known Jesus, our witness is false and our foundation is flawed. One mighty wave will carry us away.

"It is time to wake up and do some serious introspection. Have we built our lives and our churches on the rock who is Jesus or on something else?" He visited his most urgent gaze upon the still worshipers. He walked across the platform and picked up the plastic shovel the girl had left in her haste to exit the stage. "Time will tell, dear friends," he warned, inspecting the shovel as if it were a curious relic from the past. "Time will tell."

Monday morning brought with it a heavy rain, to the great glee of the television prognosticators, who had been predicting the much-needed deluge for several days. Gigi drove cautiously through the clogged arteries of south Fort Worth on her way downtown, all the while contemplating the rather skeletal outline of Plan A, anxious over the fact that its success hinged on her ability to perform as she had so confidently promised, despite so many unknowns. All the assumptions would need to be true: that the codex was indeed located adjacent to Withers' office, that it was accessible from there, and that any elaborate alarm would be disconnected during daytime hours. Beyond this, Gigi would have a limited amount of time to get the job done and get out of there without being discovered.

The parking garage was already nearing capacity, and Gigi drove around several times, in her anxiety passing the few open spaces that remained. Finally she found a spot, exited the car, and smoothed her clingy yellow cotton dress. She looked around and saw no movement; above and below her she could hear the rumble of slow-moving vehicles, faintly discernible through the pounding torrent. She reached into the car for her book bag—inside of which she had placed a folded canvas bag in which she planned to place the codex—and slammed the door shut.

A narrow walkway led to an elevator from which the Withers Tower could be accessed from street level. She entered and rode alone down several levels to the first floor, then headed through

Q

the covered walkway to the side entrance of the lobby. Inside, the three passages already printed from the codex were inscribed on the huge wall. She paused to read each one, then approached the reception desk, making sure she smiled brightly at the middle-aged security guard who stood nearby, just in case. She wanted to be remembered.

A few buzzes of the phone later, Gigi was riding the main elevator toward the top floor in the company of a young male intern. She fixed her eyes on the rapidly changing lights above the door, knowing all the while that he was watching her.

Jeremy cursed the rain as he exited the car, his stiff loafers landing squarely in a deep puddle, soaking his feet.

"I'll meet you on Throckmorton in forty minutes, in front of Barber's," Dunbarton called out. "If you don't see the car, just pop in there and wait. I'll be circling the block."

He nodded and hopped up on the curb, turning to wave at A.D. as he sped away. Then he walked through the front doors of the Withers Tower. Immediately, he saw Anna K. Soesbee waiting in the lobby.

"Rolfe!" she called out excitedly, and it took a moment for Jeremy to realize it was he she was addressing. He smiled and walked up to meet her.

"Rolfe?" he whispered.

"Isn't it English?" she asked, frightened. "I thought it might go with your accent if somebody asked . . . "

"Shh," he cautioned. "No need to panic. Rolfe it will be." His smile calmed her and she returned it.

The lobby was beginning to thin out as the final rush of workers lined up in front of the elevators. Jeremy was dressed in a charcoal pinstriped suit with a silver satin tie and carried a large molded briefcase. He blended in well. Few people took notice of them, hurried as they were to get to their offices. The pair waited, talking about nothing, moving slightly as needed to remain just out of earshot of the nearest person.

"What's in the briefcase?" she asked.

"Lunch," he replied, grinning.

Finally, once the workers had all gone, Anna K walked calmly to the elevator and mashed the down button. As expected, the doors opened to an empty car.

Once the doors had closed, Jeremy reviewed the plan. She was to take him on what would look like a routine tour of the presses in the basement, then slip away when he gave the sign. He would do the rest.

The precautions proved unnecessary because no one else was present in the hall where long glass windows separated the observers from the huge machines. Jeremy studied them intently through the panes as they made their way along, with Anna K explaining what she knew, which wasn't much. The machines made a hypnotic sound, which Jeremy thought must have been quite loud on the other side of the insulated glass. They came to a locked, unmarked door at the end of the hall. Jeremy looked back; no one was there.

"Stand here, to my left, please," he said.

She obeyed, realizing he intended to use her as a screen while he picked the lock, just in case someone should appear at the other end of the hall. In a few seconds she heard a click, and he turned the knob and cracked the door. A sound like a locomotive burst into the hall.

Q

Anna K looked hard into Jeremy's eyes, her heart racing. "Go!" he whispered, smiling. She immediately turned and skipped back down the hall. "Walk!" he called out as softly as he could and still be heard. Without looking back at him, she slowed to a regular pace. He laughed to himself, gripped the knob to open the heavy metal door, and slipped inside the press room.

Daniel Withers was standing directly in front of the elevator doors as they opened, his arms crossed on his chest, his suit coat buttoned twice. The intern didn't see him at first because he was still watching Gigi, working up the courage to speak. "Good morning," Withers announced with the same contemptuous tone he had used on the phone twenty-four hours earlier. The intern jumped back a bit, startled by the sudden appearance of the most powerful man in the Southwest, and fell back toward the wall, completely ignored by both Withers and Gigi. She walked out and followed Withers in quick steps down the corridor as the elevator doors closed behind them and the intern descended in solitude, his opportunity lost.

"Can you have something decent for me tomorrow?" quipped Withers.

"I'll try."

He stopped suddenly and faced her. "You'll try?"

"I will," she said firmly. "If you don't mess around with it and make me rewrite it."

He laughed and resumed walking. "You know me, Miss Vaughn. Don't listen to the gossip so much. I haven't changed a single sentence of your work. In fact, I don't even see it until it appears in print." They finally reached a large door of inlaid wood panels. "Besides, things are going so well, I have no reason to." He grinned, reaching for the door handle. A secretary's desk with empty chair and some ornate bookcases dominated the little room.

"Are we going to your office?" she said, thinking out loud.

He said nothing but walked toward French doors fashioned like the outer one and pushed them open. The first thing Gigi saw was an incredible panorama of the city through two glass walls joined in the corner; it was breathtaking, despite the rain. Instinctively she glanced at the far wall, to see if anything might give evidence of an entrance to a secret room.

"Please, sit," he invited, and Gigi understood that this meeting was nothing more than an opportunity for Withers to show off. "Tell me about the riot," he said, settling back in a gray leather chair. His desk was made of chrome and glass; the carpet was jet black and the wallpaper stark white. Gigi leaned forward in a chair upholstered in violet crushed velour. "I wouldn't exactly call it a riot," she answered. "More like a disturbance."

He waved her comment away with his hand. "Whatever." He didn't realize she was stalling for time. "I heard you were almost injured."

Gigi laughed honestly. "C'mon. I'm tougher than that. Takes more than a bunch of religious bigots to stop me."

The remark seemed to please Withers. "Was it that obvious to you that they were the cause of it all?"

Gigi sat back and looked around casually, as if she could get used to such luxury, though it certainly wasn't her style. "Hard to say. There was a lot of heckling back and forth. But what they did was inexcusable, that's obvious."

Withers folded his hands on the desktop. "How are you handling this, really? You seem to be hardening against the religious community, though I should say I'm not surprised."

Q

Gigi asked a question before answering his. "No?"

"No," he said. "You're a bright young woman, and you were already holding a grudge when I found you." Found me? Gigi thought. "It was only a matter of time."

Withers was so relaxed that it disarmed Gigi a bit. The angry tone was definitely gone. He was enjoying this, having her up here in his office, and gave the impression he had nothing better to do than to chat. "But I'm curious. What exactly was it that pushed you over the edge?" he wondered. His arrogance was insulting.

"Wait a minute, sir. I'm still a Christian. And I still love the Church, even if I express it in criticism," she declared.

"Well! Isn't that quite a statement!" he exclaimed. He talked with his hands like an Italian fisherman describing the one that got away to his bored wife. "You would never know it to read your work," he quipped, knowing it was a weak response.

The intercom buzzed. Irritated, Withers pushed the button. "What?" he snapped. "I'm in a private meeting."

The woman's voice sounded mechanical. "I'm very sorry, sir. There's an emergency."

Withers squinted and asked her for the details.

"It's the presses, sir. Several of them have stopped running, apparently all at once. I was told to inform you."

Withers punched the button again with disgust. "I'll be back in a few minutes. You can be working on your story while I'm gone." He flashed a sickly smile and scooted around the desk to a cabinet near the door; opening it, he removed a key ring hanging inside, then threw open the French doors and marched out. Gigi saw him reaching for another set of keys deep in his pocket. He slammed the door to the outer office and locked the deadbolt from the other

331

side. Gigi sat silently, listening to his rapid steps down the hall and the whirr of the private elevator nearby.

She jumped to her feet. There were no pictures on the wall behind which the secret room should be located. She felt carefully for a latch or some button behind the wallpaper. Nothing. She stepped back and looked at every inch of it intently. Then she began to pound upon it for something—anything unusual. It was useless. The wall was solid.

Spinning in the room, Gigi scanned every object for a safe. She darted to the opposite wall and looked behind a portrait of an austere-looking gentleman, but nothing lay behind it. Crawling on her hands and knees, she felt for a latch or a hinge of some kind that might indicate a trap door. Then she flew to the desk and searched it for a lever, like one she had seen in an old movie. Frustrated, she ran to the cabinet and looked inside; it was filled with liquor. There was a drawer below, which she pulled out to see an ebony cigar box. Inside she found several keys in a variety of sizes.

The whirr of the elevator returned. Gigi snatched up the keys, immediately wishing she had worn jeans instead of the tight-fitting dress. She closed the box, pushed in the drawer, shut the cabinet door, and got back in her chair just as she heard Withers turn the deadbolt on the outer office door. She reached down and pulled a pad from her book bag, on which, fortunately, she already had made notes about the forum at the convention center; as she did so, she dropped the keys to the bottom of the bag. The French doors flew open, and Withers found her scribbling.

"It was the fault of those maintenance people!" he said, barely keeping his voice below a roar. She could see he was sweating heavily, perhaps from the combination of exertion and anger. "It will be days before we get those things running."

Q

Gigi looked up as he walked to the glass wall, his back to her. "Does that mean we'll have no paper?" she said innocently.

"Of course not!" he shouted, still looking out the window. "We don't print the paper here. We have a plant on the north side, a modern facility, for that. Those are the old presses in the basement. We're using them for the first edition of the codex, the one we're mailing to the ministers. We're doing it the old fashioned way; we thought it would be quaint."

"No big deal, then," she said. "At least my story will get out."

"Hmmph," he grunted, taking his seat. Strangely, he started laughing. "I told them to service those presses months ago," he mused. "While I was down there just now, I made them check one of the broken ones thoroughly." He continued to snicker, as if he were talking to himself.

"And . . . ?"

Withers shook his head. "You won't believe what they found, jammed down in the belt drive. Of all things—an empty can of beets."

Two hours later, Gigi arrived at the Kitchen, where Cody and Jeremy waited with Tinky and A.D. Jeremy had already changed back into his boots and army jacket. According to the plan, Gigi had called A.D. from the car and explained that she had found nothing, so the rest of the plan was abandoned and the mission put temporarily on hold.

"I was sure it was there," said Jeremy, annoyed. "You found nothing, Gigi? Nothing at all?"

"Nothing," she said, wearily. "Except these." She retrieved the keys from the bottom of the book bag.

"Interesting," Jeremy observed, taking the keys and holding them up for a closer look. "A few of these are unique indeed." He turned quickly to Gigi. "Do you know what these are for? How long before he realizes these are gone?"

"To answer the first question, I have no idea. I found them stashed away, probably spares. He has a key ring he keeps in his pocket and another key on a hook inside a cabinet by the door. He used it to lock the office door when he went down to inspect your mischief."

"No, that's not right," Jeremy said. "You saw him take a key ring from his pocket?"

"Yes."

"Then why wouldn't that one hold the keys to the office door? No, I think he took the other key ring because he didn't want you to find it."

"Do you think we have a copy among those?" she quizzed.

"Possibly. He doesn't keep it on his ring for fear of leaving it somewhere, and yet he doesn't keep it secured inside his office. That can only mean . . . ," the rest of them stood by silently while Jeremy thought out loud, "it is a secondary key. That's it! He keeps a key with him that opens something, and this other key can then be used." He looked down at the keys in his hands. "Pray to God that we have the right ones. From the looks of these, they go to some very sensitive locks, perhaps alarms. We may even need them all to get where we're going."

"And where's that?" asked A.D. wistfully.

"Oh, trust me, Professor," said Jeremy with a glimmer in his eye. "If it's there, I'll find it." He put his hand on Gigi's bare shoulder, irritating Cody immensely, and shook the keys in his other hand. "Get ready, missy," he said to Gigi. "It's time for Plan B."

Q

The rain had finally abated by six that evening, leaving the streets glossy and fresh despite the humidity. Gigi dropped Jeremy off down the street and parked the Nova in the parking garage adjacent to the Withers Tower. She took the route, which had become familiar over the past few weeks, and practiced a nervous, jerky walk into the side door of the lobby, just in case anyone was already watching.

She entered the building and looked back conspicuously. She was wearing the same yellow dress from the morning visit and carrying the same book bag. Her black clogs echoed in the huge space, the sound much more pronounced because so few people were present. Approaching the reception desk, she stopped short and clutched her hand to her mouth in distress to find it unattended. All of this, of course, was intended to draw the interest of the security guard, a pudgy middle-aged man with a huge nose, who usually remained until six-thirty, when the building officially closed.

"Can I help you, miss?" he asked pleasantly.

"Oh, I'm sorry—has the lady who usually works here gone home already?"

"I'm afraid so," he said. "She leaves at six on the nose every day. You just missed her." He hesitated. "Is there—anything I can do for you?"

Gigi acted as if she didn't hear him and looked back at the side door again. By this time Jeremy had entered the lobby from the main entrance and was looking casually at a large directory of offices along the far wall. Gigi appeared to be panic-stricken, causing the guard to step forward in concern.

"You alright, miss?" he said.

"Oh, sure," she said, laughing nervously. She swept back her dark hair from her face. "Is, um, Mr. Withers here, do you know?"

"No, he's gone too. A speaking engagement of some kind, I think. Lots of people talking about it today."

Gigi knew, of course, exactly where Withers was. Since the press conference, he had become even more of a celebrity in the Metroplex and never refused an invitation to soak up the limelight.

She sighed audibly and paced to and fro with small steps. Then, she abruptly walked straight up to the guard. "OK, I need help, then," she said urgently. "I think I left my notebook in his office this morning. I have to turn my story in tomorrow, and, well, I can't seem to remember everything. It was good too! It's got to be up there. I was hoping I could catch him in but . . . " she looked back the way she came, causing his eyes to follow. "I thought somebody was following me on the way over here, so I circled awhile, then I heard footsteps in the garage . . . " She stopped and drew in a short breath. He raised his hands to calm her. She jumped in fright at some unseen threat, and he stepped back.

"OK, just calm down. I'll take a look."

He walked across the lobby. Gigi swung her head around to see if Jeremy might still be in sight. He was gone.

"Nobody there, miss," he said confidently. "Man, you're really spooked."

Gigi faked a smile and nodded several times. "Thank you, I appreciate your understanding." She crossed her arms as if she were cold. "Do you think Mr. Withers will come back here tonight? I can wait. I'm not too crazy about going back to the car quite yet, anyway."

His eyes spoke sympathy. "Tell you what. I get relieved in about fifteen minutes. I know who you are, Miss Vaughn. Most everybody

Q

does around here, whether you realize it or not. I'll let you in up there so you can find your story, then I'll walk you to your car when the new shift takes over. How's that?"

Gigi stepped even closer and began to hug him but pulled back her arms just in time. "You would do that for me? That would be great."

Jeremy noticed the small keyhole near the private elevator immediately, though it blended in with the decor, as did the elevator itself. The design was a study in discretion, to be sure. There were no glowing buttons or lighted floor indicators on the wall. He picked the correct key the first time, inserted it, turned it clockwise, and yanked it out as the door opened. Perfect.

If he remembered the plans correctly, Withers' office would be just outside the elevator and to the right. The codex had to be sealed off inside that office somewhere, though Gigi had found no evidence of it. Thus, Plan B was born; it would take a professional to pull this off.

She had acted her part well. No one could resist helping her with the act she was putting on. From what he heard in the lobby, the guard was totally absorbed in her plight. Jeremy had approached Withers' private elevator unnoticed and was now well on his way. He reached into his pocket for the keys, which he had hung on a metal ring for convenience. He had less then ten minutes now to overpower the guard, find the room, steal the manuscript, and get Gigi out of the building before the new security team arrived. He smiled, thinking of the peril.

He was ahead of Gigi and the guard, and if things went as planned, he would be waiting near the main elevators at the other end of the hall when the doors opened. He would overpower the guard, and he and Gigi would fly to Withers' office. Should the plan fail and the document not be recovered, the mugging would be attributed to Gigi's mysterious stalker. Should the plan succeed, it wouldn't really matter.

The elevator hurdled its way to the top floor. He watched the numbers change almost too rapidly to identify them, and then the car began to slow down. He was almost there. He stared at the door, not wanting to lose a second sprinting down the hall. Then, his peripheral vision being expertly trained as required by his profession, he noticed another keyhole along the elevator wall to his right. He cocked his head in the British way and considered it, as the elevator came to a stop.

The door opened, and Gigi stepped first into the hall, grimacing in anticipation of the assault by Jeremy upon the unsuspecting guard. They had argued about this part of the plan, but he insisted it had to be this way. Bribery was not an option, and they could never get past him unseen. With no support from Cody or A.D., she felt pressured to go along. Still, her body tensed with guilt over it, and she very nearly turned to push the man back into the elevator car before Jeremy could pounce.

"Been up here a few times, to Mr. Withers' office," the guard said, stepping out after Gigi. "Beautiful view up here. Never have seen it at night."

Gigi winced. When was Jeremy going to strike? She whirled around, stopping the guard in his tracks.

"Whoa! I almost knocked you down. You gonna be OK, Miss Vaughn?"

"Oh, I think so. Just a little jumpy." She looked past him. No Jeremy.

Q

They entered the office, and the guard walked straight for the glass wall, where the lights of Fort Worth twinkled in the twilight. "Not exactly dark but pretty as a picture," he said.

"There it is!" Gigi shouted. He turned to see her smiling and holding a spiral notebook, which she had deftly pulled out of the book bag. They took in the view together for a few minutes before the guard checked his watch. "This is real nice, but we better go on down." She nodded and headed out of the office ahead of him, bewildered at Jeremy's absence and suddenly worried that Plan B might have been their last and only chance.

Jeremy listened to their muffled voices through the wall. She would never believe it, and he hardly did himself. The room was definitely there, for he was standing in it. An access panel in the elevator car had opened to a hidden hallway, unheated and unfurnished, on the top floor which led to a door of industrial proportions. He had used two keys, and two were left. One of them must have been for Withers' office; the other one belonged to the inner sanctum.

The room itself was not particularly well conceived and almost looked temporary. He could tell immediately that it was thermostatically controlled for temperature and humidity. The lights were hanging in the unfinished ceiling, glowing dimly. Shelves along the wall held boxes and newspapers of various kinds and rolls of blueprints. Resting comfortably on a metal table in one corner of the room was a wine crate covered in tattered cloth. Lifting the ancient shreds carefully, Jeremy found the treasure he was seeking. His brows arched in delight.

The empty briefcase proved to be just the right size. As gently as he could, he removed the stack of parchment with its leather cover. The brittle paper flaked off in tiny bits, but no serious damage was done. He pulled a few newspapers from the shelves—realizing at that moment that this must have originally been intended as an archive room of some kind—and lined the briefcase with them, so the codex would fit snugly. Then he returned the way he had come, through the heavy door, down the concrete walk of the hidden corridor, squeezing through the open panel in the side of the elevator. Upon closing it, he pushed the lobby button and began a rapid descent.

The lobby was clear. Jeremy strolled right toward the front doors and greeted the after-hours officer who had just entered and was initializing the first stages of securing the building for the night.

"Good evening, sir," the uniformed man said. "I didn't see you coming down the elevator." He held the door open for Jeremy to exit.

"Cheerio," said a smiling Jeremy as he passed.

Gigi drove around the front of the building a second time, frantically looking for Jeremy. She saw him emerge from the front of the building and roared the car forward to pick him up.

"Where were you!" she demanded, stomping on the gas.

He tapped on the briefcase on his lap as he fumbled to latch the seatbelt. "Could you slow down a bit? It's bloody bad enough this driving on the wrong side of the street."

"I was in, Jeremy! I thought you were already upstairs. What happened?" She was still racing along, and he could hardly speak from fear.

"I thought you were opposed to violence," he said. "He seemed like a nice man, so I changed my mind."

"You changed . . . " She was indignant, nearly speechless. "What do you think you were doing?"

Q

"Excuse me," he said as the car bumped along. "But I don't think this is the way to the airport. By the way, did your nice bobby help you get what you were looking for on the top floor?"

She stared at him, incredulous, not slowing down.

"I suggest you turn around," he advised. "Oh, and did you call ahead already?"

"No, of course not. What . . . ?" He was fumbling with the latch on the glove compartment.

"Who told you to lock this thing?" he yelled, laughing, remembering the day they met.

"Jeremy! What are you talking about?"

He gathered himself and spoke calmly. "Stop the car now, and give me the key to the glovebox. I have to make a call." She obeyed, confused.

"Next time," he said, "wear something with pockets for things like secret keys and such, or at least save room in that silly duffel of yours for your cell phone and cans of beets—you know, the usual things." He was laughing again, apparently at some private joke.

"Have you lost your mind?" she said, amazed at his bizarre behavior.

"Oh, no," he said, dialing. "I've got my mind alright, and that's not all I've got." He tapped the briefcase again, grinning at her, until her eyes locked on to his, and she laughed with him in joyous disbelief.

It was beginning to rain again when Gigi and Jeremy arrived at the airport. Ashley Dunbarton and John Ravenswood were already on board the small jet, poring over reference works, much of it photocopied from books to save space, although A.D. could not bear to leave behind several essential volumes. Gigi's prepacked suitcase was already stowed away, having been brought by Cody, who was standing outside the plane in the drizzle, waiting. He recognized the car from a distance despite the darkness and walked out to meet it. Jeremy took some obvious hints and left them alone to say their good-byes, which, though temporary, were painful nevertheless.

Jeremy stuck his head inside the cabin. "Ho there!" Ravenswood called out. He walked, duck-like, in a bent posture to greet him. "There is excellent news from England, Jeremy! Excellent news!" Jeremy was taken aback by his colleague's unusual excitement but could not wait to listen to whatever this news was. Instead he handed the suitcase to Ravenswood, who grasped it in two hands like the treasure it was. "Has Miss Vaughn arrived safely as well?" Ravenswood inquired.

"Of course, sir," Jeremy said. "She'll be along in a moment." He pointed his head in the direction of Gigi and Cody, and Ravenswood craned his neck to see.

"Of course," he remarked knowingly. "In all the excitement, we tend to forget what's really important in life, eh?" Somewhat embarrassed, he ducked back inside the plane.

Jeremy made as much noise as possible to announce his return to the car, and the couple finally separated, Gigi handing the keys to Cody. He hopped in and drove slowly away as Jeremy accompanied Gigi to the jet; she paused to look back, delighted to see that Cody had stopped the car to watch her take off. By now the engines were roaring. Gigi waved and vanished from view.

A.D. had already opened the briefcase and was gently turning the pages of the work known to scholars for a century and a half only as Q. Gigi sat opposite him next to Ravenswood and clicked her seatbelt into the locked position. "You have plenty of time to play with that," she said. "Why don't you put it away until we get off the ground?"

"Plenty of time?" he complained, not looking at her. "The time, in fact, is limited. This is stolen property, remember."

"Not yet it's not," she answered smartly. "Nobody knows it's gone."

"Please, I see no reason to use the word, 'stolen,' Professor," said Ravenswood. Then to Gigi he said, "The proper term would be reclaimed."

"Fine with me. I just hope the authorities see it that way," she said.

Ravenswood chuckled. "I do believe they will," he said, his cheeks red with mirth. "That is, of course, if anyone finds out it was ever missing."

The jet was accelerating along the runway, quieting the passengers for the moment. Then, the nose lifted and the plane was airborne. Gigi looked down at the Nova sitting alone in the rain, almost regretful over the whole affair, while Dunbarton cradled the ancient book opened on his lap and scrutinized the first page, which was bathed in the bright beam of the overhead lamp. He leaned forward, not the least bit disturbed by the bumpy takeoff. "Amazing," he was saying to himself. "Truly amazing."

"Mr. Withers," the mechanical voice intoned, "there are some people in the lobby here to see you."

"Who are they!" he demanded, irritated at the presumption of these uninvited guests.

There was a short pause. "It's a Detective Sartain with the Fort Worth police," the voice said. "He would like to have a word, sir."

"Of course," Withers said, suddenly excited. "I'll be right down." He marched out of the office and into the elevator, delighted at the quick response. In a few moments he was strolling into the lobby, where Sartain and two uniformed officers waited.

"Have you any information about our beet-eater?" Withers said, laughing. "As I told the girl on the phone, we prefer our vegetables fresh around here!" He smiled and extended his hand. "Daniel Withers," he announced.

Sartain looked down at Withers' hand, then to one of his colleagues. He reached toward his back and under his coat, pulled out a set of handcuffs, and quickly cuffed one of Withers' wrists. The officers grabbed Withers by the shoulders and swung him around to allow Sartain to cuff both hands behind his back.

"What . . . ?" The stunned Withers was flushed with confused rage.

"Daniel Withers," Sartain began. "You are under arrest. You have the right to remain silent. Anything you say . . . "

"What are you people doing?" Withers gasped. "Don't you know who I am?"

The two officers turned him around again to face Detective Sartain, who had not stopped reciting, "If you cannot afford one, an attorney will be appointed for you by the court."

The officers tugged at Withers' arms. The tall executive, suddenly sweating profusely in his dark suit, shook violently in protest. "I said what are you doing to me? With what am I being charged?"

The officers squeezed Withers and subdued him; he responded to their force quickly because he was not accustomed to pain. "I'm sorry, didn't I say?" Sartain quipped, enjoying the situation immensely. "You are charged in the murder of Benton Cole in England, sir."

Q

Withers could only stare in astonishment as Sartain related the story of how a constable had arrested a well-known hoodlum in a London pub for drunk and disorderly conduct, how they had been tipped off by the proprietor, who had overheard the man bragging about several recent crimes. Withers listened intently, not quite sure how this involved him until Sartain related that the man had been drawing cash from his jacket for his drinks when suddenly, in his inebriated state, he pulled out what appeared to be a wallet instead. Only it wasn't a wallet at all but a leather bank bag, which of course the proprietor saw plainly, prompting him to slip away and make the call. Withers' face became pale as Sartain explained how the constable arrived and found personal checks still in the bag—the Easter Sunday offering from Benton Cole's church that had disappeared from his car when he had been shot. He went on to explain that they arrested the man and searched his apartment, finding a pistol that when tested, proved to be the one that had been employed in the murder.

"Shall I go on, Mr.Withers, to explain how the British authorities were able to link this petty thief—thanks to telephone records and unusually large deposits—to Ellis Cole, the same whose father had been killed with this particular revolver on his way home from church. How in exchange for leniency, he has implicated you?" Sartain was speaking deliberately loud, and a small crowd had gathered in the lobby to watch.

"I wish to speak to my lawyer," Withers hissed. "You have no right to accuse me, and you will regret it."

"Let's go," Sartain said, nodding to the officers, who pulled Withers along much faster than he wished to go.

"Would you like more? I never run out of shrimp and grits when Ashley's home."

Gigi was both amused and delighted at the attention she was being given by her professor's mother, who was scurrying about the kitchen, talking incessantly about Ashley's predilections. "Sure, but save at least a little for him; he should be getting up soon."

Mildred spun around. "Oh, no, Gigi; he didn't come home last night. Didn't he tell you? He stayed at the church, working."

"He what?" The prospect of shrimp and grits notwithstanding, Gigi tossed her napkin on the table and jumped out of the chair. Running back to the guest bedroom, she yelled before Mildred could answer, "Can I use the phone?"

Twenty minutes later she was seated in Mildred's Cadillac, still fuming. She hardly heard Mildred proudly pointing out the features of her native city as they drove through the historic district to Seventh Baptist Church. "We have First and we have Seventh," she said, pulling into the large parking lot. "All the others in between are gone."

Gigi smiled at Mrs. Dunbarton and thanked her warmly for the hospitality, masking the outrage inside. They exchanged a girl hug, and Gigi hopped out.

When Eva, the pastor's secretary, walked into the conference room with Gigi, the men stopped their chatter and stared. Only A.D.'s voice could be heard. "Don't be angry, Gigi. It's not that I wanted to leave you out, it's just that you were so exhausted; I just couldn't haul you over here. Believe me, the night's sleep couldn't have hurt. Besides, I wanted it to be a surprise."

Gigi scanned the room. It was richly furnished in royal blue carpet and window treatments, with a white marble fireplace and a

Q

mirror framed in gold leaf above the mantle. Queen Anne furniture graced the sitting area; behind it was a large conference table strewn with sheets of parchment, with books and papers stacked in piles on the floor all over the room. Ravenswood was there and Jeremy and several others. She carefully studied the pleasant faces of the Society of Saint Matthew as each stared at pages or stood with open books, pausing to behold the brave young woman they had heard so much about. One of the men was leaning over the conference table with his back turned to Gigi. A faint click drew her eyes toward him as he stood and slowly turned to face her.

"Dad!"

Gigi ran into her father's embrace as he swung the camera away to receive her.

"We thought your father a fitting choice to photograph the parchments. This will enable us to continue our research, since we must return the original as soon as possible," Ravenswood said.

"When did you get here?" Gigi asked, amazed and thrilled.

"About the time you were rolling out of bed," he said, his eyes twinkling. "Mr. Ravenswood has had me on call for quite some time, actually." He took her head in both his hands. "It's so good to see you," he said, his voice cracking.

Gigi was doing her best to fight off the tears. "I can't believe this," she repeated several times.

"It was Cody's idea," said A.D. "He and your father have become quite chummy over the phone over the last several weeks. He figured somebody needed to tell him what you were up to."

"Were you worried?" Her question pricked an emotion Gigi's father had hoped would not awaken.

"Naturally," he said. "Scared to death, in fact. But you seemed to be in good hands. Besides, I knew there would be no stopping you. You're your mother's daughter, you know."

At this, Gigi could hold back the tears no longer. They renewed their embrace, and this time some of the scholars in the room began to whisper, pleased at the touching reunion but more eager to unlock the mysteries of Q.

"Let me introduce you to the Society," Ravenswood said. "And we'll show you the conclusions we've reached so far. Then, we must send the codex back to Texas with Jeremy. For your safety, we think it best that you stay in Charleston for a while, just in case Mr. Withers realizes what has happened. It shouldn't be long, though, before he will be in no position to threaten any of us. We shall have to make the best of it here in this lovely city. Once these photographs are developed, you and your father are invited to play tourist for as long as you wish, at the Society's expense, of course."

Gigi shook hands with each of the men, accepting their gratitude and appreciation for all that she had done. Several had British accents, and all were odd sorts, eccentric in deportment, even for academics.

"We thought we should never have to address this subject," Ravenswood said. "All that these men had seen up to now were Doctor Knotty's notes. Of course, we know that the work is not complete, that some of the pages are lost. We were hoping that we might find something to make our interpretation easier. But now, having been forced into the light, we have no choice but to face up to the task and bring forth our findings with an open mind."

Gigi looked reverently at the ancient papers. "Have you determined yet if it's . . . " her voice faltered. "Are you sure that it's . . . "

Q

"Authentic?" A.D. said, finishing her thought. He sighed. "At this point we are agreed that it most definitely is."

Gigi looked at him in wonder. "All of it?" she asked.

"Every word," he said.

By late Tuesday afternoon, Daniel Withers was teeming with fury. After a brief hearing, he was released from custody on a $500,000 bond, though warned not to leave the area by both the judge and his attorney. He rushed back to the Tower, staring straight ahead as he stormed through the building, ignoring the stricken faces of his employees as he passed. Streaking toward his private elevator, he rode in murderous resolve to his office, from which he retrieved the key from the cabinet and headed back toward the secret archive room.

Just as he feared, the codex was missing.

Enraged, he ran to his desk and slammed his hand down on the intercom button. "I need to see Rizzo immediately!" he screamed. "And as soon as he leaves, call Detective Sartain at the police station and explain that I've been robbed."

Rizzo was sitting in his gray sedan, eating a sub sandwich when the call came in. It would only take five minutes to get to Withers Tower, so he finished his dinner calmly before responding. These situations were never pleasant. Rizzo secretly despised Withers, but an unfortunate mistake had found him banished from the police force, and he proved to be a miserable failure at running his own detective business. Withers paid him very well, primarily to watch people, usually businessmen he wanted to discredit or destroy. One job for Daniel Withers amounted to six months compensation in full-time private investigation. The only catch was that whenever Withers called, Rizzo had to go, regardless of whatever anyone else might be paying him to do.

He drove deliberately to the building, subconsciously grinding his teeth. As he had proven capable in small assignments, Withers had entrusted him with more serious jobs, sometimes dangerous ones. He had heard that Withers was not above anything, and that worried him. Rizzo was tempted many times to quit, but unfortunately he knew too much already, and Withers had many thugs in his employ.

The dark man was seated behind his huge desk in his palace of glass and chrome, the high-backed chair turned to face the window. Hearing Rizzo enter, he spit out the name that in just a few short hours had become so distasteful that he could barely utter it. "I want you to bring me Gigi Vaughn."

Rizzo had tried to put the possibility out of his mind that this summons had something to do with the pretty Asian-American girl. Through gritted teeth he said, "You want me to bring her here?"

Withers swung the chair around to face him. "I want you to bring her here first," he said. He glared at Rizzo, who stood stiffly, his fingers curled tightly into fists as they hung at his sides, fully aware of the man's intent. He nodded and walked out.

Detective Sartain was announced a half-hour later. When he entered Withers' office, he complained that he was off duty at this hour but came out of concern for Withers, who seemed so traumatized by the incarceration. He dripped with sarcasm as the condescending words rolled off his tongue.

"My property has been stolen," Withers stated defiantly. "A very valuable item—priceless, in fact. Shall we see how well you investigate a real crime?"

Q

He brushed past the detective and led him back into the hall. He turned the key to open the elevator, then pulled out the other key, which he had kept in his pocket, and removed the panel leading to the secret room.

Sartain arched his eyebrows in surprise. "How interesting," he quipped.

They approached the heavy door. "I have used this room to store valuable papers, which is why it is climate controlled by a state-of-the-art automated environmental system. Please don't touch anything, if you don't mind."

Sartain rolled his eyes at Withers' pompousness but couldn't wait to get inside the room. Withers pushed open the door, and they stepped in; the detective scanned the shelves instinctively. Withers walked to the wine crate, lifted the fabric, and stepped aside. "Here," he said, "is where I kept the Withers Codex. I'm sure you've heard of it. It is a one-of-a-kind document, a book which belongs in the Bible, or shall I say, shall soon supplant the Bible as a source of religious knowledge."

Sartain walked to the crate and peered inside. "This codex, is it the one everyone's talking about lately—like in the picture down in the lobby, a journal with a beat-up leather cover?"

"Yes, that's the Withers Codex in the enlarged photograph. You may take it with you if you like for identification, after you've dusted the room for fingerprints."

"I see no need for that, Mr. Withers," he said, laughing. "You're book's right here."

Withers blinked and stared down into the crate; his lips quivered in astonishment and anger.

Downstairs in the lobby, Jeremy stuffed his gloves into his pockets, dropped several keys into a padded envelope, and walked across to the reception desk, still stiff from the lack of sleep and air travel. He borrowed a marker from the woman and jotted a name on the envelope and sealed it. Handing it to her, he smiled and said, "Will you see that Mr. Withers gets this?" She smiled in return, charmed at his accent. Whistling, he walked out into the dusk where Cody waited in his truck. He hopped in, and they sped away.

It seemed to Rizzo that the news was so important that it should be given in person. He was at the end of the trail, happily, and was anticipating seeing the frustration on Withers' face when he told him so. At least for now, there was nothing he could do.

The secretary interrupted Withers' Wednesday-morning editorial meeting to announce Rizzo's arrival. He was ushered into the office without hesitation.

"Well? Tell me." Withers demanded, clearly disappointed that Rizzo did not have Gigi in a headlock, her lovely arms and legs wriggling to get free.

"The car is parked at the apartment, but she's not there. The boyfriend has been at the shelter but not the Vaughn girl. She hasn't been to class either, and she's only taking one this summer from what I can tell. The professor, that Dunbarton guy, wasn't there either."

Lester Bothwell, who was seated in one of the violet chairs reviewing a draft of the next excerpt from the codex with commentary for the Sunday edition, perked up at Rizzo's report. "You say Ashley isn't teaching his class?"

"The teacher? No, not today he isn't," Rizzo answered. "Some graduate assistant is lecturing. I waited outside the door and asked him. He said the prof was out of town until further notice, probably next week."

Withers stared at Bothwell, wondering at his sudden curiosity.

"Ash is a former student of mine," Bothwell said, responding to Withers' stare. "One of the finest textual critics in the country, I would say, though severely limited by the restrictions placed upon his scholarship by fundamentalism. He would have a keen interest in the codex."

Withers contorted his face in skepticism. "Are you saying this fundamentalist took my book?"

Bothwell seemed surprised, as if such a thought could not have entered his mind. "No, actually, but if it became available to him, he would certainly want to see it. From what you've told me about this young student, it is not beyond the realm of possibility that she could have been involved in the theft. And since they are both apparently missing . . . "

"They must be together," Withers concluded. He spoke the words with a slow, sinister inflection.

He addressed Rizzo with authority. "You have to find them."

Bothwell squirmed in his seat, regretting immediately that he had made the suggestion. "I'm sure you would be better served to leave this matter to the police; after all, the codex has been returned, and there's no harm done to it." Bothwell's voice betrayed a doubt that the codex was ever missing at all.

Withers, unaccustomed to advice and holding back the urge to smack Bothwell in the head, gathered his wits and said, "Miss Vaughn is in my employ. She is very dear to me. She was writing a story for today's edition on the convention center episode, but she seems to have disappeared without turning it in. I'm quite concerned about her, if you must know. It could be that she is being exploited by others who are jealous of my success—there are plenty of such men out there, as you might imagine. This person or persons have already made serious false allegations against me, which I shall be forced to defend. If Gigi is mixed up in this matter, it would be far better for her if I would find her first." He spoke in such a way to indicate the matter was not open for discussion and turned back to Rizzo. "You know what to do."

"Not exactly, boss. The trail is cold."

"She's from California; you should go there."

Rizzo shook his head. "If she's laying low, she wouldn't go home."

Withers huffed. "Then find this professor." His ire was rising. "If he is involved . . . "

"Doubtful," quipped Bothwell. All eyes looked at him. "Well, I know him, you see. He is not so devious as to perpetrate this little caper. He's a professor, not a thief!"

"Then he shouldn't mind being asked a few questions," Withers declared.

Bothwell fidgeted in his chair. "He is innocent, I tell you. He comes from a fine lowcountry family, very old and well respected."

"Then why are you so uncomfortable with our making inquiries of him?" said Withers.

"I'm not, of course," Bothwell said, his face reddening.

"Good!" Withers replied. "Now, where exactly is this 'lowcountry?'"

The call Cody was expecting came Friday morning. He made the prescribed arrangements and rushed from the Kitchen to the seminary. A secretary was downloading the e-mail when he arrived, having been notified by phone that the transmission was coming. Ashley Dunbarton's graduate assistant leaned over her shoulder, reading the text of the professor's work.

"Unbelievable," he kept muttering, his face reflecting the glare of the screen.

"I've got to get that downtown this afternoon," Cody said. "Can you print me a copy?"

"Hang on, cowboy," the instructor said. "This is the real deal here. We've got to get Dr. Doerr to have a look at this, maybe the whole New Testament faculty."

"Forget it," Cody barked. "Print it, save it to disk, and delete it from the inbox and server. I'm taking the disk and the hard copy with me."

"You can't be serious!"

Cody walked up to him in anger. Cody was a good four inches taller and far superior in strength. "Why don't you go parse some Greek verbs or something?" he scolded. "Dr. Dunbarton told me no one—and I assume that must include you—is to have access to this document but me. He doesn't want any possibility, no matter how remote, that someone might mess with it without his authorization."

"This is stupid," the instructor said. "We're talking about Q here. Do you even know what Q is?"

Cody balled his fist and threatened him with it. "Do you know what this is?"

The secretary had already printed the e-mail and handed it to Cody with the disk. "OK," she said, clicking the mouse. "All gone."

Cody winked at her and ran to the office door, then turned abruptly and said, "Call Anna K. Soesbee at the *Stockyard Dispatch.* Tell her I'm on the way."

Anna K was waiting in the lobby when Cody burst in the front doors. "Here ya go," he drawled. She looked up at him admiringly, wishing it were she instead of Gigi he adored. She carefully accepted the paper and disk.

"Have you ever been to London?" she asked.

"Nope. But you'll love it. Ravenswood's supposed to have an enormous collection of old stuff."

She laughed. "Monographs, journals, personal letters, deeds, rare books, lectures . . ." She was counting her fingers, trying to remember everything Ravenswood had described.

"Yeah. And nobody sharp enough to organize it all—until you." He touched her nose playfully with his forefinger. Her lashes fluttered behind the glasses, and she nearly blushed.

"I suppose it really will be pretty cool," she said. "Not that I have a choice."

They stood awkwardly for a moment, not sure how to continue the conversation.

"Is everything ready?" Cody asked.

Anna K nodded. "The workstation will be unoccupied during the dinner hour. All I have to do is find Bothwell's article and replace it with this one. The operator will just load the text like always. Nobody on the line will suspect anything. They've never questioned anything I've ever sent down."

"Wouldn't you love to see Withers' face when he picks up the paper and sees this on Sunday morning?"

Q

Anna K's eyes widened. "No way! Too scary!"

"He'll be even more displeased when he finds your home phone disconnected and your office cleaned out," Cody joked.

"He'll be furious," she said, "but there'll be nothing he can do about it."

"Nothing left for us to do either," he said. "We've done all we can. I guess we'll just have to leave the rest to God."

She smiled a sincere, gentle smile. "E-mail me," she said, hoping for a parting hug or at least another pop on the nose, but Cody just returned the smile and backed away, hands in his pockets. She watched him turn and vanish through the doors, leaving her in the center of the lobby, misty-eyed but determined to fulfill her responsibility perfectly. In six months she would be back in Texas, and the evil Daniel Withers exposed and incarcerated. God's good name would be vindicated, and all would be well with the world.

Rizzo wiped the perspiration from the back of his neck with a damp hanky. His muscles and joints ached, especially his knees, from so much time sitting in the cramped car. For all of Withers' wealth, he was cheap when it came to expenses, and the economy rental was hardly suitable for twenty-four-hour stakeouts, though he did find it advantageous in traversing old Charleston's narrow and congested streets.

It was well before noon but already hot on this Saturday morning. Rizzo was parked in a small lot near the Lodge Alley Inn, where he had been since the previous day. Occasionally he had made forays along East Bay Street to stretch his tired legs and grab some food. He feared that he might have missed Gigi if she had ventured from the hotel, but his instincts told him she was still inside.

He had managed to find the Dunbarton residence easily on Thursday, and identified Mildred early on as she came and went in her Cadillac. She didn't seem to notice him there as she drove past, but several neighbors who were walking dogs and biking along the historic street gave him the strong impression by their haughty looks that he didn't belong there. He half expected the local police to shoo him away. Even so, he stayed through the night, watching from as close as he dared to get for any sign of Gigi Vaughn.

Around midnight he was alerted by the slow advance of high beams, and he slunk down in his seat as the car passed, another rental, though bigger than his own. He watched the driver park along the street in front of the house, and through his night goggles he watched the professor go inside. Frustrated, he determined to stay until morning.

He awakened early with the breaking day. Not long afterwards, the professor came bounding out the front door and sped away. Rizzo followed behind, staying far enough away to escape Dunbarton's notice, weaving in and out, since the early traffic was light. They arrived at the Seventh Baptist Church, a traditional building of red brick with white columns spanning a broad porch. Rizzo watched Dunbarton press an intercom button located at a side entrance to an adjacent building and wait for a moment before stepping inside. Within the next thirty minutes, several other men rolled in, following the same procedure.

Almost at noon, a group of men emerged from the building with Dunbarton in the middle of the pack. They were engaged in animated discussion, and Rizzo heard loud laughter as they made their way toward King Street on foot, presumably for lunch. There was

Q

no sign of Gigi, and Rizzo started the car and wheeled it back down the street in irritation. Seeing a Chinese take-out stand, he parked illegally and hurried inside to place an order. In ten minutes he was back at the church, pressing the intercom.

"I have a lunch delivery," he said.

There was a hesitant silence, but after a few seconds the intercom box vibrated with a loud buzz. Rizzo yanked the door open and entered a long hallway. Following the signs to the office, he approached a young secretary behind a high counter.

"Lunch delivery for Gigi Vaughn," he said.

The girl looked surprised. "A few of the guys are back in the conference room, but I haven't seen Gigi." She pressed a button on her phone, and a buzz could be heard in the deep recesses of the office. "Eva, is Gigi here?"

"No," the voice answered. "She hasn't been here today. I don't think she's coming in."

"She said she would be here, according to the message I got," said Rizzo.

"It's a lunch delivery she called in—Chinese," the secretary said.

"Oh, well, she'll probably be here any time then," said the speakerphone. "Do you want us to call the Lodge Alley to see if she's left there yet?"

Rizzo held back a sly smile. "That's OK. I'll just leave it. I've got a few more deliveries to make, so I'll swing back by in an hour or so with the tab." He grinned at the secretary and leaned over to thank the faceless voice.

"You're quite welcome," chirped the speakerphone. But Rizzo was already halfway down the hall, turning back to wave in hasty acknowledgment.

From the car he dialed information for the number of the Lodge Alley Inn and called for Gigi. The hotel operator broke in after several rings. "I'm sorry, but there seems to be no answer," she said. Obviously.

Rizzo circled the area several times before he saw the place, nestled in as it was—no, more like crammed in—like everything else in this unusual city. It teemed with tourists, a pedestrian jungle now invaded by businessmen in khaki suits and bow ties, hustling about during the lunch hour. As he maneuvered through the one-way streets like an ancient seafarer ever mindful of fixed north, he cursed to himself repeatedly, nearly running over oblivious sightseers several times. At one point he found himself directly behind a horse-drawn carriage, and his pounding on the horn only drew the ire of the passengers. Finally, bathed in nervous sweat and hopelessly annoyed, he happened to spy his destination and luckily managed to wriggle the little car into a space not far from the entrance.

He called again. No answer. Good.

Rizzo tried to relax. He had made only a few moves, but they had been profitable. The insufferable waiting had been worth it. He was close.

A group of college students strolled past his car. They were vibrant and attractive, obnoxious and free. They moved in short bursts, pushing each other playfully, grabbing and pinching, laughing together in confused courtship. He found himself smiling. Innocence.

He closed his eyes as their adolescent dialogue disappeared into a concert of traffic and hoofbeats and shrill voices. A jet roared high above. He felt the sun caress his face.

Q

Three days ago, Daniel Withers had put him on a plane, gripping his arm just before boarding. *You understand that the plan has changed.* Rizzo's eyes twitched underneath his closed lids as he recalled Withers' words. *I don't expect I'll ever see her again.*

Something made him jump. Had he been drifting off to sleep? No, he dreaded sleep. He squinted painfully against the light. The city was ablaze with life. Only he defiled it, a spot of darkness in an otherwise vivid landscape. This was crazy. What was he doing here?

Hours passed as Rizzo reflected on what had led him to this moment. A promising career thrown away, a grim dependency that cost him his family, a self-loathing that denied him the chance to crawl back—these aspects of his life flipped past like scenes in a slide show in his mind, complete with narration. But there was no plot to this story, no guiding principle. There was only the long list of poor choices made in ignorance, without thought, a man's life drifting like a boat without an anchor. And now, on this crowded peninsula, he was left alone with a man he didn't seem to know.

Anger arose and receded like the nearby tide as evening fell. He watched, waited for his prey to come home. He resolved to follow through. This is who he was, after all the years of misfortune. This is where he belonged. He would do his job.

Night arrived, humid but pleasant. Rizzo stood, leaning against the car in complete darkness, save for the hazy fuzz of light from the nearest streetlamp and the orange glow of his cigarette. He flicked an ember, puffed, and tossed the remainder of it to the pavement, crushing it with his shoe.

And then she came, walking arm in arm with a man he didn't recognize, instantly appearing like a specter.

In a the space of a heartbeat, if Rizzo allowed himself to have one, she had gone inside. He could sleep now, knowing he could awaken with the sun, for the last leg of the journey.

When Saturday finally came, he was ready. Sore but relieved that this sad episode would soon be over, he wiped his neck and waited for the chase to begin.

The man came out first and fiddled with a large camera that hung from his neck on a colorful strap. Rizzo watched as Gigi appeared next, wearing an orange top and white shorts, almost too perfect for a target. She should not be difficult to find, even in a crowd.

They walked around the building to a car. Rizzo spit out his cigarette and started the engine. In this labyrinth of a city, he would need to follow closer than usual to keep from losing them, or it would be another long night waiting for a new opportunity.

He followed them west across town to the city marina. It was nearing nine o'clock, and Rizzo puzzled at their choice of destinations. Then it struck him; they were getting ready to board a tour boat to Fort Sumter. The boat could be seen anchored at the entrance to the harbor. This was very bad, since he didn't see any way of getting to Gigi on the boat, which was filling up rapidly with people and would probably be at full capacity for the tour. There appeared to be two levels, an enclosed area below and an open one above, and he toyed with the idea of going along for the ride in some corner of the vessel, above or below where Gigi and her companion sat. Then, he could find a chance to catch them in some isolated nook of the Fort and finish the job. But it was too risky; he would have to dispose of the bodies somewhere out there, for if not, they would surely be discovered before the tour boat returned to the marina, and everyone on it would be a suspect. It was a long shot, at best. He decided to wait.

Q

Rizzo was immediately pleased with his decision. With Gigi's whereabouts solidly fixed for the next few hours, he was free to roam the city, sit down for a real breakfast, read the paper, and basically act like a normal person would who was visiting the seacoast town. He relished the respite from his mission, until he opened the paper and read news of a string of violent crimes, which drastically altered his sunny mood. He left the newspaper on the table beside his half-eaten salmon croquettes and headed back to the marina.

The white speck of the boat grew larger as it slowly approached the dock. Gigi was one of the first to get off. She and her companion—older than she by far—had unfolded a map and were discussing it as they walked down the ramp. They made directly for their car, and Rizzo was forced to follow.

They crossed the short bridge that spanned the Ashley River and turned left onto a long access road, which emerged at a restaurant, which looked much more like a fortress than the real thing lying in ruins at Fort Sumter. Again, it would be easy to track them. The restaurant was accessed by a high, broad stairwell, and there was only one exit to the parking lot. Rizzo waited patiently, walking for a few minutes at an adjacent marina, admiring the small boats. Had he known about these, he might have concocted a scheme to steal one and sneak out to Fort Sumter to do the deed, but he shook his head at the thought of it.

In a little over an hour, he was trailing the car back over the river and across the peninsula on Calhoun Street, passing several hospitals, a Catholic school, and what appeared to be a college campus. A large town square presented itself on the left, and they stopped at a traffic light across from an imposing yellow church with a high spire before turning south on Meeting Street. Rizzo was directly behind them; in this congestion, he did not fear being noticed. They could be going back to the hotel, and if so, he would have to make his move there. It wasn't ideal, but it would have to do. He couldn't wait another day, since there would be church and big crowds and it just didn't feel right to kill someone on a Sunday.

Rizzo became aware that his knuckles were white as he gripped the wheel tightly with both hands. His heart was pounding. He really didn't want to do this. She was a nice girl and cute as a button. Smart, too, it seemed. She could make things difficult for him. He wondered if he had the courage to do it after all. But he knew that if he didn't, he could not return to Fort Worth. It had been three days already, and for all he knew, Withers' thugs were already after him.

They came at last to a long pink building that looked like some kind of ancient stable, set at the center of two narrow one-way streets, dotted with shops of all varieties. The area was strewn with tourists on foot, cars struggling to break into the open, and several of those awful carriages meandering slowly about as if no one else had any right to the space. Rizzo soon lost them in the maze and was forced to drive in a loop north and south along Market Street until he glimpsed them. Now out of their vehicle, they entered a covered walkway that looked like a flea market of sorts, packed with tourists feasting on overpriced trinkets. He sped south toward East Bay, stuck the little car along the curb inside a full lot that belonged to a specialty foods store, and sprinted on stiff knees back to the market.

It was a strange sight, indeed; homeless men lay sprawled on empty tables at the back of the market, while just a hundred feet north, the edges of a loud congregation bartered and traded for T-shirts and baubles. Rizzo moved quickly into the masses; in seconds he spotted a blur of orange and advanced toward his prey.

Q

Gigi had been admiring the work of three basket ladies, but they could not convince her to buy. She shuffled away, stopping at a table piled high with beach towels, visors, kites, and mountains of decorative shells. Her companion must have been nearby but out of sight just now. Rizzo scanned the scene until he saw him, some three tables away. He reached down in his pocket and pulled out the knife.

The way was wide open to the south, and Rizzo's pulse quickened as he saw the opportunity unfold. A quick strike, a dash to the car, and he would be gone.

He watched her carefully, moving closer. He did not want to waste too much time. He tried to put the person out of his mind and focus on the task at hand. He stood opposite from her now, just a few feet away on the other side of the table, waiting to see if she moved to the right or left. Left would be better. If she went that way, he could come up behind her through a group of people, then rush straight to the car without anyone even glimpsing his face. He pushed a tiny button on the knife and released the blade, holding it against his leg, unseen below the surface of the table.

Gigi took the corners of a towel in her fingers and lifted her hands to let the folds fall out. Emblazoned on the fuzzy cloth was a facade of pastel houses and the inscription "Rainbow Row." The bright colors drew Rizzo's attention, if only for a second. When he turned his eyes back to Gigi, he saw that she was staring at him.

They both froze, watching each other intently. She didn't seem scared, but she was reading the intensity on his face. She knew why he was there and what he had been sent to do.

She turned her head to look behind her. She was trying to locate her companion, who was still where Rizzo had seen him a moment before. Perhaps she was thinking of running toward him for safety, into the crowd. As far as Rizzo was concerned, that was the worst-case scenario. If he got mired in the sea of people, he might never get out. He decided to force the issue.

Rizzo slid to his left and made every indication that he was coming around the table to get her. Instinctively she moved left also; had she possessed the presence of mind to keep moving with the table between them, she could have come back around to the crowded side. Instead, she came to the end of the table and broke into a run. Rizzo skirted the table and followed, hobbling. It was going according to plan, but she was faster and could easily evade him. He would have to try; this would be his only chance.

A throng of homeless men were shuffling about amid the empty tables at the south end of the market. They saw Gigi rushing toward them but didn't move, trying to make sense of the picture.

"Help!" she yelled at them, but this only frightened them more. Two of them stepped back to get out of her way, but one man, a balding black gentleman in a ragged tweed coat and baggy trousers with a brown bag in one hand, did not move. Gigi plowed right into him; the bottle crashed onto the concrete, and they tumbled together off the curb and into the street.

A dappled horse was pulling a carriage up the street at a leisurely pace. The guide was standing up, facing his audience, unaware of what was happening behind him. Gigi and the black man staggered out in front of the horse, who had stopped while the guide concluded his remarks. She regained her balance and dashed across the street, catching a glimpse of a champagne Mercedes coming up fast behind the stopped carriage. She looked back to mark the location of her assailant but saw something else; the drunk was staggering forward in front of the horse, still following the momentum from his collision with Gigi, moving directly into the path of the speeding car.

Q

"Go back! Get out of the way!"

The man did not respond, oblivious both to the warning and to the danger.

Suddenly, Gigi charged at him, screaming. He had been looking around in the street, perhaps for his lost bottle. He was standing now just at the edge of the carriage. The tourists saw what was coming, and they cried out in alarm. The guide turned around and saw the black man reaching for the corner of the carriage for balance. The Mercedes was coming fast. Rizzo finally arrived panting at the curb and stopped, shocked at what he was seeing. She had easily eluded him; why had she come back? Was she risking her own life to save this worthless bum?

Gigi tackled the man and dropped him hard on the pavement. A relieved cheer went up from the carriage as the car whizzed past. The horse snorted and stamped at the sudden commotion at his feet.

Rizzo crouched over the fallen girl. She was breathing hard; tears had streaked her face. Sobs burst forth between gasps for air. She raised herself to her knees and saw Rizzo there. He studied her face, as he had before. There was something special about this girl, something he didn't understand.

He helped her lift the stunned man to his feet. People were spilling out of the carriage to surround them. A crowd from the other end of the market had slowly wandered down. Emerging from it was the man with the camera, rushing to Gigi's side.

Rizzo backed away, losing himself in the masses, moving against the flow of humanity, all the way down toward Meeting Street. He wandered for a time through the constricted streets, a stranger in this city of cemeteries and steeples, each reminding him in their own way of the high calling of Heaven.

367

Part 3

A Certain Scribe

And yet I, a shape of clay
    Kneaded in water,
A ground of shame
    And a source of pollution,
A melting-pot of wickedness
    And an ediface of sin,
A straying and perverted spirit
    Of no understanding,
    Fearful of righteous judgments,
What can I say that is not foreknown,
    And what can I utter that is not foretold?

—From the *Hymns Scroll*, Hymn 6

One Year Later

GIGI WANDERED IN A CIRCULAR PATTERN AROUND THE OFFICE, staring at the walls. They were attractive enough by themselves, the bold floral-patterned wallpaper above the chair rail setting off the deep red below, exuding both warmth and energy, just as she had intended. She finally chose a spot and hung the Master of Divinity diploma proudly in the center. A second wall was selected, and upon it she placed a large photograph taken by her father, matted and framed, of the first page of Q. Its splendid parchment hue matched that of the seminary degree on the opposite wall.

The boxes that were stacked around the office contained mostly books, but there were some personal effects from her apartment in Fort Worth that she had left out of their proper boxes during the process of moving. She had to open every box, pull out what didn't belong in the office, and set it aside for relocation to her new apartment.

She took a pair of scissors and carved a neat cut down the center of the wide packing tape that sealed the first box. She opened the flaps and pulled out her Dodgers cap and flung it onto one of the shelves that filled the wall behind her desk. Rooting around, she saw that most of the contents belonged in the office: books, seminary notebooks and files, computer accessories, etc. But before moving on to the next box, she spied the edge of a thin paperback book and yanked it out from below Grantham's two-volume *Systematic Theology*. It was Daniel Withers' complimentary first edition of Q, with an introduction by Lester B. Bothwell. There were no words on the cover, just a large Q on a black background. The first page gave the title in Hebraic script: *The Withers Codex: The True Story of Jesus.* The frontispiece carried a nauseating full-color photograph of Daniel Withers.

Gigi sat down behind the desk and flipped through the little book. So much had happened since this first edition appeared on the desks of ministers nationwide almost a year ago. It did not have the impact Withers had hoped for, of course, since the good guys intervened and supplanted the fourth excerpt with their own views of the manuscript, penned by Ashley Dunbarton. That was a glorious Sunday, when the Associated Press ran the story from the *Dispatch* as it had done the previous three weeks but with a decidedly different twist, thanks to the clever undercover trickery employed by Anna K. Soesbee. The nation was finally treated to another more conservative view, which A.D. had since turned into a sure-bet best-seller: *Not Ashamed of the (Secret) Gospel: The Story of Q,* which was due for publication in thirty days. Gigi herself had authored and submitted a lengthy section detailing the events of those chaotic three weeks.

The Society of Saint Matthew had, of course, after a short legal battle, proven that the codex had been illegally sold to Withers by Ellis Cole after his father's murder (which he himself had facilitated to get his hands on a large inheritance), and retained full rights to the work. The name "Withers Codex" was immediately abandoned, and the complete text of the manuscript was made available to the public in various forms. Research showed a declining interest in the book itself, but just the opposite was found to be true of printed articles and televised features with Q as the subject. Most Americans, it seemed, were so accustomed to having things explained to them in an entertaining and user-friendly way that they had long since given up the harder work of struggling with sometimes incoherent primary sources such as Q. They were willing to trust the opinion of anyone who had certain credentials (or the credibility of a byline or a television face) rather than coming to their own independent conclusions. No one knew this better than Daniel Withers, who attempted to destroy Christianity by spinning Q into something it really wasn't, and he nearly succeeded. He began by planting seeds in the minds of people before they had an opportunity to think the matter through, and he provided an excuse for millions who find discipleship distasteful. There's no need to worry about Christ's exclusive claims and exacting demands if he himself turns out to be a man-made Messiah. Withers had the resources to spread this very message, an undertaking born in part out of his own desire to be his own master, subject to no one, not even God.

Gigi checked her watch and hopped out of the chair. Carter had told her he would meet her at the meeting, and she needed to get going to be on time. The secretaries stopped chattering as Gigi appeared in the hall; they didn't know yet if they could trust her as one of the girls. She gave a friendly greeting and heard their whispers resume as she turned the corner and headed outside.

A series of portraits graced the wall just in front of the door. Guests entering from Sunday school often paused to review the names of the dignified men, some pictured in clerical robes and others clutching a Bible or standing behind the pulpit. Members often resurrected the ghost of one of these pastors past to emphasize a point or a criticism. They were held in high regard, respected more now that they were dead since only their legacies—rather than their human frailties—were in view.

This is what ultimately undermined the cause of Daniel Withers. His credibility dashed by the scandal and subsequent imprisonment, he no longer had the benefit of the doubt in the public eye. Ironically, it had been this very problem that had rendered the Church vulnerable to his assault; with true ministry swaddled inside the comfortable cloak of religious habits and culture, the Church was perceived as irrelevant to many and had no weapons to fight with. Driving through Charleston to the meeting, Gigi saw the sharp contrast between rich and poor, white and black—a clash of cultures that coexisted together on this peninsula yet rarely came together, except in disagreement. Segregated churches of both races, spending a large percentage of their receipts on their own members, were making relatively little headway in bringing the Gospel to the uninitiated. If people stopped listening to Withers because of what he did, they have also stopped listening to the Church because of what it fails to do.

Gigi arrived perfectly on time at the building where the Holy City Ministers' Alliance held its regular meeting, but she found that everyone was already there. It was an unusually large crowd, and several pastors had invited members from their churches to hear Gigi speak. Without opportunity to greet anyone, Gigi walked up to the podium where Carter was getting ready to start.

"Ready?" he asked.

"I guess."

He stood and called the group to attention. After an invocation, he enthusiastically announced his guest.

"I am proud to introduce our speaker this morning, not just as the president of this body but as a fellow worker with her in Christ. Miss Gigi Vaughn, a graduate of Southwestern Seminary, has very recently accepted the call of Seventh Baptist Church here

Q

in our city as Pastor of Community Outreach, a new position established to help our church, and all our churches, to become more effective in meeting the needs of the total person through both social and spiritual ministries. I'm sure you'll know Gigi from her association with the much-discussed codex known simply as Q, and this is the subject we've asked her to address today. Please welcome Miss Gigi Vaughn."

Applause rang out in the room and quickly subsided. Gigi blushed at the pleasant reception and fiddled nervously with her glittering engagement ring. "I've been speaking on this subject for several months now in various places, and I'm getting a lot of credit for another's work," she said in response. "Dr. Ashley Dunbarton, who, as most all of you know, is a native of this city and grew up at Seventh, has been lecturing in mainly academic circles on what we've come to call the 'Dunbarton Hypothesis.' Everything I'm about to tell you is presented in complete form in his upcoming book, which I hope you'll go out and buy, because I've already pledged my portion of the royalties to some programs in our community outreach budget." There was eager laughter; they wanted to like Gigi. They were proud of their native son and of their churches for a renewed commitment. Charleston was famous for weathering storms, and this one, too, had passed.

"As you probably know, there is very little evidence that Christianity ever came to Qumran, that region near the Dead Sea where the famous scrolls were found. The early research on Q showed parallels between it and at least one of the documents found there, the Thanksgiving Hymns, which are part of what we have called the *Hymns Scroll.* We believe that the writer of Q was also involved in producing these. Aside from the technical similarities, we find the recurring theme of rejection and hope in both texts. Our writer was likely a very passionate man—devoted to his Lord and to a pure Israel, as were all the residents of the community.

"The critical question is why this is the only mention of Jesus in any of the Dead Sea Scrolls. To answer this question, we would need to make assumptions about the scribe himself and how he viewed Jesus. There are some interesting signs in his writings which point the way."

Gigi cleared her throat and checked the faces in the crowd for a snap estimate of how she was doing. So far, so good.

"Clear references abound in the notes that suggest that the scribe was a disciple of John the Baptist. We know, of course, that John's influence was extremely widespread; we even find people in the Book of Acts who describe themselves as followers of John. We should not expect that they all just switched to Jesus. This particular individual was attached to John and apparently shared John's confusion over the role that Jesus was assuming. Many scholars believe that John himself had roots in the Qumran community, and the discovery of Q only strengthens that connection.

"There is also evidence that Jesus held a powerful appeal for this person, who apparently followed him around, writing down his sayings. He could have been a Jewish leader, quite likely a scribe, but he displays a favorable attitude toward Jesus much of the time, an acknowledgment of this unusual Rabbi's spellbinding authority as a prophetic teacher who reinterpreted the Jewish tradition. Again, we see a connection: the Qumran community rejected the corruption of the Jewish religious system, which John challenged and Jesus exposed. It is not unlikely, then, that here we have a scribe who was something of a secret follower of Jesus, wondering all the while if he might be the true Messiah, waiting to see what would happen."

Q

"Not a disciple but a secret follower," someone interjected from the back of the room.

Gigi smiled. "The terms are somewhat incompatible, I agree," she said. "We think of a disciple as a *public* follower, even today. Everyone should see you living out your faith. But this guy was different; he was out there, in front of everyone, asking questions of Jesus, wanting, I think, to believe. But Q never goes that far; it only describes Jesus as 'the greatest of all teachers' or uses other flattering terms. I think the scribe believed in Jesus to the extent that he could, but he never saw the full picture. And I'll explain that in a minute."

She paused for a sip of water. She was really enjoying this.

"One more point should be made about the nature of the scribe's relationship to Jesus, and that is, he would not have been the only one who struggled with belief among the religious leadership," she added. "You'll remember that even very late in Jesus' ministry, Joseph of Arimathea publicly disagreed with the prevailing opinion. He was in the minority, to be sure, but there probably were others, perhaps our scribe included.

"Now, Dr. Dunbarton has posited that it would have been unheard of for a scribe to run off and join the group at Qumran. The reason he went may have been the result of ostracism from the other teachers of the Law because of his interest in Jesus or perhaps outright persecution. Or maybe he had listened to Jesus long enough that he couldn't in good conscience stay in the 'club,' and he got disgusted and went back to where John started. This is plausible, since John was preaching in the wilderness of Perea, not terribly far from the Dead Sea, and the idea of such a lifestyle may have attracted him. Something made him pull up stakes and go; we may never fully know why. It has been suggested that he actually applied for discipleship under Jesus and was refused; if this is the case, he may well have been a man without a true community anywhere, except at Qumran, where all were accepted who submitted to the rules. Any way you look at it, our scribe is a tragic figure indeed."

There was some murmuring at this, though not the negative kind. They were excited and interested in what she was saying. Thus encouraged, Gigi continued to the heart of her remarks.

"Liberal scholars who have reconstructed Q in the past have pointed out that there are no resurrection accounts, and they were proven correct when this manuscript surfaced. I will say that it is by no means complete; several shared pericopes between Matthew and Luke that should be there are missing, and there are some new things we don't have in our four Gospels. Having given the liberals their due, we cannot accept their explanation that the resurrection passages aren't present in Q because it never happened. Mark, remember, was used as a source document, and it does have the passion narrative. We have always affirmed that these are eyewitness accounts, and we believe the reason our scribe failed to document it is simply that he was long gone when it occurred. Qumran was relatively isolated, and it took a lot of time for the Gospel to catch fire. Most of the activity was in Jerusalem, then Antioch, and then out to other places with Paul. But the Romans were snuffing out Qumran and Masada about the time Mark put pen to paper, and John wasn't written for another thirty years. So we can assume the scribe, whether he knew about the Cross or not, never knew that Jesus had risen again.

"This leaves us with one more problem: if Q was written at Qumran, isolated as it was, how did Matthew and Luke get their hands on it? Well, our answer is simply that the scribe had been making notes all along and that somehow these were made available to the disciples and early followers. Dr. Dunbarton believes

Q

that Q represents the scribe's memoirs, if you will, of his impressions of this one peculiar rabbi whom no one else acknowledged in the community but who had once so captivated his own mind and spirit. He must have believed that these sayings had value, even though the man who uttered them had been disgraced and counted as a rebel. His comments are honest; he was dealing with his own strained emotions as he wrote it all down. These episodes shaped his life and his destiny—one man's search for a Messiah he thought might purify Israel. It may have turned out to be a failed experiment in his mind, but he wanted others to know about it after he was gone. He was clearly ahead of his time, and I believe God's hand was upon him."

Gigi put her hands behind her back to indicate her remarks were concluded, and she waited for questions.

"How can you say that, really? This book is far less than our Gospels. Do you consider this work inspired?" The man was holding out his hands in a gesture of begging.

"No, I don't see it as inspired," she answered. "Not in the technical way we define inspiration. There is too much personal opinion expressed. Even so, this gives tremendous credibility, in my mind, to the Gospels. Here is a source, which predates anything we have, with much of the same content. It validates the truth of the Scripture, because the sayings are there, along with a person's honest struggle in understanding them. Matthew and Luke obviously didn't just make this stuff up."

There was a wave of laughter as the man sat down, satisfied.

"I have a question," said Carter. "I understand this group of collectors owned Q for decades and didn't tell anyone. Now that we've seen it, that seems kind of strange. What's your opinion on this?"

"That's a good question, Pastor, and I can only speculate as to what was in their minds. Back then, there were few serious challenges to traditional Christianity, and no one really questioned the accepted tenets, or at least, they didn't do so too loudly. The Society of Saint Matthew was formed to find more documentation that would explain Q better, perhaps even locate the missing parts. They wanted to present it with an explanation to prevent precisely what eventually happened—that someone might come along and use it to make implications damaging to the faith."

"Didn't they trust God with it?" he followed up.

"Yes, they did. Certainly. It's just that they didn't trust men."

Rusty Rowe stood up along the side of the room. "All this is fascinating to us, you know, being ministers and all; we like theological riddles and could debate them all day long. What I'm wondering is how this whole experience has changed you personally." He seemed to have more to add but seeing her reaction, left it at this and sat down.

Gigi didn't answer at first. She fidgeted, not uncomfortable with the question but challenged to articulate an answer. "Naturally," she began deliberately, "I have given this a lot of thought, and I'm still trying to figure it out." She took a deep breath and exhaled slowly. "I know that none of this happened by chance—I mean, I found a Christian thief—his words, not mine—in an alley and the next thing I know, I'm trying to steal the lost book of the Bible, or so we called it then. I just happened to be studying textual criticism at the time—with a teacher who happened to be part of this Society. He earnestly tried to keep me out of it, worried about my safety. Then, I stopped to help a man on the side of the road, and as a result discovered where Daniel Withers was hiding Q, though it turned out to be a good guess. So there had to be a reason I was involved in this, and I knew it.

"This adventure came at a time in my life when I was questioning everything. I had a bad attitude about the Church and was cynical toward the chauvinism I was encountering. I thought this lost book might have some answers to put my mind at rest. I was uncomfortable with myself and the way things were."

She walked in front of the podium, realizing that while she was speaking, the thoughts were coming in an organized fashion for the first time. It was making sense as she articulated it.

"And that's just it, I think, that we are all kind of searching for this one answer, and we are trying so many things that don't work. The answer, of course, is our relationship with God, and we've given that away for other less valuable things. Some pastors wouldn't even go to church if they couldn't preach! We trade the wonder of intimacy with God for a prominent pulpit, control, popularity, attention—whatever you want to call it. Our members settle for the security of a name on a roll, or being known by the big-shot preacher, or they find self-assurance in some vain commitment to this cause or that. For me, I wanted to be taken seriously. It has to do with my mother, and that's another story. I wanted to be heard.

"The reason for all this, assuming God is behind it, isn't that Q would say, 'Hey, women preachers are OK.' The reason is to show us that we already have what we need. You don't read the Bible to know God; you get to know God by following him, actually *doing* the things Jesus did. We were shaken by this crisis because it threatened to undermine what we believe to be the bedrock of our faith—the Bible. But it isn't the Bible—its Jesus himself. It also exposed how shallow we really are, and we nearly walked into a knockout blow. The Church in China is illegal, but it is still among the fastest growing in the world. Unchurched Americans believed Withers, frankly, because we are so unbelievable. People need to see us acting like Jesus, that's where the joy and peace come in, and then the harvest comes. As for me, I figured if I could just do that, I *would* be heard, loud and clear."

She looked out at them sitting quietly, processing her words. Some of them smiled. She realized they were thinking her own thoughts.

"And here you are, preaching to a room full of men, *clergy*men, no less," observed Carter.

"Yeah. Ironic, isn't it?" Gigi admitted, giggling. The room laughed with her.

"And how about this poor scribe?" said Rusty. "Nobody respects him or seems to want him. Now, two thousand years after he's dead, his voice is being heard, too, and it's having an impact even he never could have dreamed of. It's amazing when you think about it."

Gigi tilted her head, her thick black hair falling across her forehead. She had no words for this statement. She looked down at the floor, humbled, as they all were. It was an uncomfortable moment, the realization that all we are so sure of is often proved to be foolishness, that only God can take our vain efforts and make them useful, and then only in his time.

About the Author

Paul A. Nigro graduated from Clemson with an English degree in hand and a writing career in mind. Instead, he nearly became a professional grad student and served ten years as a pastor before retiring at age thirty-five to explore life on the other side of the pulpit.

He is currently president of Paddock Pool Equipment Company in Rock Hill, South Carolina, and continues to speak and minister in local churches. When he is not playing with imaginary people, he spends time with the real people who matter most: his wife, Cindy, and their two children, Julia and Vinny. This is his first novel.

For further information, see *www.paulnigro.com*

Additional copies of this book and other book
titles by RiverOak Publishing are available
from your local bookstore.

If you have enjoyed this book, or if it has impacted your life,
we would like to hear from you.

Please contact us at:
RiverOak Publishing
Department E
P.O. Box 55388
Tulsa, OK 74155

Visit our website at:
www.riveroakpublishing.com